"Vivid worldbuilding of a fascinating alternate Earth, peppered with touches of whimsy. This is a promising debut!"

Emmie Mears, author of the Ayala Storme series

"Paige Orwin delivers in this wild debut about Time and War teaming up to battle the evils of eternal peace. By the time you're done you won't fear the reaper; you'll want to wrap his lonely, cross-stitch obsessed self up in a hug and never let go."

Alis Franklin, author of Liesmith

PAIGE ORWIN

THE INTERMINABLES

ANGRY
ROBOT

ANGRY ROBOT
An imprint of Watkins Media Ltd

Lace Market House,
54-56 High Pavement,
Nottingham,
NG1 1HW
UK

www.angryrobotbooks.com
twitter.com/angryrobotbooks
It knows

An Angry Robot paperback original 2016

Cover by Will Staehle
Set in Meridien and Sperling by Epub Services

Distributed in the United States by Penguin Random House, Inc.,
New York.

ISBN 978 0 85766 591 1
Ebook ISBN 978 0 85766 592 8

Printed in the United States of America

9 8 7 6 5 4 3 2 1

To Papa Charlie, who told the best "windies" of all

CHAPTER ONE

A spectral apparition shot overhead on rotten vulture's wings.

Edmund Templeton, perched atop a rusted orange gantry crane some eight or nine stories above sea level, folded up the map he'd been inspecting and tucked it into his black double-breasted suit jacket. Good. The mercenaries must be further inland. If he were them, he would have kept his distance, too.

He glanced over his shoulder at the faint, fog-softened outlines of crumbling towers that rose across the brackish waters of the sound. It was a skyline that should have been familiar – it was New York City, after all, or had been – but the Wizard War had changed that. Now the only constant was the dark spire that loomed over its lesser and ever-changing brethren, auroras crackling from its peak.

It was worse than Boston. He hated being this close.

He climbed back down to the crane's cabin, holding onto his top hat. The evening wind tore at his opera cape, but he'd just replaced the buttons: it would hold.

His first official assignment since 2013, and it had to take him within thirty miles of New York. He'd lost friends in New York. He'd lost Grace in New York.

He was the Hour Thief, the oldest and one of the most powerful agents of the wizard's cabal that now tried its hardest to be a government, and he had been put out of commission for almost eight years by New York.

He shook his head, admonishing himself. Not now.

Focus on those mercenaries. Their mysterious employer. The artifact smuggling that the Twelfth Hour had so far failed to keep in check.

Focus on 2020.

The apparition wheeled back into sight. It circled once, streaming contrails of barbed wire, and then alighted on the gantry above him with a booming rush that sounded like distant artillery.

"I'm in the cabin," Edmund called, unfolding the map again. Less wind down here. He retrieved a thin marker and noted changes to the coastline. There had been a small enclave of survivors here, last he knew, but they seemed to have left in a real hurry some time ago.

And about those gouges on the beach...

A ghost swung down onto the cabin catwalk.

It was a man, bespectacled and broad-shouldered, wearing an army uniform tunic, field cap, and leg wrappings of a style not sported since 1916. Austro-Hungarian. The First World War. A medic's cross banded one arm. He might have resembled a hawkish clerk, with broad cheekbones and a hooked nose, if the burn scarring that twisted the left side of his face into a ruined mockery of a grin hadn't countered that impression. Barbed wire coiled at his feet.

Istvan Czernin. Best surgeon in the world, and one of the most dangerous entities the Twelfth Hour had ever captured. He was *des Teufels Arzt*, the Devil's Doctor, the legendary apparition who had haunted battlefields across Europe and Asia for decades, leaving a trail of blurred photographs, tight-lipped veterans, unofficial unit insignia, and mysterious gashes in the wreckage of tanks and aircraft.

He'd tried to kill Edmund once, a long time ago. Edmund liked him better as a friend.

"I found the convoy," the ghost began in a cadenced Hungarian accent more than reminiscent of Dracula. "Four tanks, just as Miss Justice said, and they're having a terrible time trying to conceal their exhaust."

Edmund marked "krakens" off the shore. "I believe you."

"It's the coal, you know. I don't know what they do to refine it." The ghost peered over his shoulder. "Is that a map?"

"Someone has to do it."

"But the satellites–"

"–aren't wizards, don't know what to look for, and I don't trust their accuracy. Besides, I thought you liked my maps." He brandished it. "Which road?"

Istvan hesitated. "I liked you making use of your naval cartography," he said.

"Gee, thanks. Which road?"

"The bridge," Istvan said, reluctantly. He pointed at the stretch marked across the sound. "They've taken the bridge."

Edmund took a deep breath. This kept getting better. "The bridge."

He looked back towards the shore, where the latticed bracing of a steel cantilever bridge jutted into the water and stretched impossibly for miles, with no evident endpoint save the distant downtown skyline. Below it bobbed a tangle of floating piers, shipping containers cut apart and bolted to them, and a mess of abandoned rafts and canoes, and likely worse things.

"They are carrying Bernault devices," Istvan pointed out, "Twenty of them. Edmund, the bridge is the shortest route. With a cargo that dangerous–"

Edmund put the map away. "I know."

Twenty Bernault devices. Palm-sized spheres that were perfectly safe until jostled too hard, at which point they jostled back in a wildly uncertain radius of radiant destruction. The things had a habit of materializing in the middle of former city centers, where the worst of the fracturing held rein, and if there was a pattern to when and where, no one had found it.

One of the many, many new problems that had come along with the Wizard War.

On August 31, 2012, Mexico City dropped off the map. Torn apart. Sunk beneath a lake that had been drained long ago. Survivors insisted that there had been a monster made of stone, that it had come from below.

The news flashed around the globe. Governments expressed their concern, pledged to send aid, and promised that the matter would soon be resolved. Everyone else worried about the unknown: conspiracy, aliens, ancient curses, cosmic alignments, mass transcendence, the wrath of God.

Seven days later, she struck.

No announcement. No name. No one knew her name. Even the Persians had called her by title. The Arab mystics who defeated her in the Dark Ages had merely appended one of their own.

Shokat Anoushak al-Khalid. Glory Everlasting, the Immortal.

She targeted cities. Only cities. All cities.

2012 was a year of magic revealed after millennia of secrecy. A year that saw every major population center in the world ripped out of normal existence, drowned in the impossible, walled off by impassable spellscars hundreds of miles deep. A year of armies, of mockeries of machines with scything mandibles, twisted beasts of vine and earth and fire, skyscrapers shredded by steel claws and drawn upwards, tornado-like, new spires accreting on new skylines emerging with a roar from solid stone.

Fifteen hundred years of preparation. Long enough that even most wizards had never heard of her. Long enough to utterly divorce her from anything human.

The Wizard War lasted only eleven months.

Sometimes, most often at night, Edmund wondered if she were truly dead.

"Big East" now ran from Boston to Washington DC, a gaping wound in reality populated by structures and inhabitants torn from a thousand elsewheres and elsewhens, a crumbling patchwork of survivors' enclaves and petty fiefdoms surrounded by broad swathes of anarchy and ruin. It wasn't the only fracture – Greater Great Lakes and Fracture Atlanta were the nearest two others – but it was the only one clear of monsters. It counted among its many battlefields the former city of Providence, where Shokat Anoushak fell.

No one went to Providence.

Edmund had never thought of leaving. Not once. Home was here, and the Twelfth Hour was here, and the survivors who poured into the remote areas of the continent wanted nothing to do with wizards. She had been one, after all, however far removed from the knowledge and practice of her modern-day descendants.

He could still wish for an assignment further inland.

"You know, I could see to the mercenaries," offered Istvan. He plucked at his bandolier, turning his head to hide the worst of the scarring as he did. "I'm sure that's why I was permitted to come along; you don't have to go out there."

Edmund shook his head. "I'll be fine."

"You're certain?"

"I'm certain. I appreciate the offer, but I'm the Hour Thief, remember? I have a reputation to consider."

He tried a smile. It fit into place like a well-used shoe.

Istvan regarded him a moment. He was impossible to fool – Edmund knew that – but they both had a job to do and Edmund was stubborn.

Finally, the ghost sighed and looked away. "They're some miles out, still," he said. "I'll show you to them. Do mind the wind, won't you?"

Edmund nodded. "I'll be fine."

He ran through his habitual checks. Shoes tied. Tie straightened. Cape properly fastened, buttoned to his suit jacket so it would tear off rather than choke him if something caught it. His Twelfth Hour pin, two crescent moons together forming a clock face marking midnight, shone at his lapel: as close to a police badge as it came in Big East.

Istvan had never understood why he added the cape to his ensemble, much less the aviator goggles or the fingerless gloves, but at least the other man could appreciate the conceit for what it was: an effort to disguise the truth as something more palatable. Mystery men were heroes, no matter their methods.

Magic didn't care for morality. Magic demanded, and if disrespected it would simply take. Magic, and the ancient immortal wielding it, had destroyed civilization as most knew it in a single night and day.

Edmund had been thirty-five for seventy years.

He retrieved his pocket watch. It was brass, attached to

one of his buttons with a sturdy chain, with an embossed hourglass on the front that was starting to wear off again. "Right," he said. He flipped open the watch. "Lead the way."

Istvan vaulted over the catwalk railing.

Edmund eyed the bridge. The roadway seemed clear, but with mercenaries around, he wasn't about to trust a visual inspection. He waited for the sight of vulture's wings hovering near one of the upper spars.

Then he convinced himself that he was the center of all universes, just as he simultaneously convinced himself that the center was in fact the bridge spar, which would have been a useless mental exercise if he hadn't made sure some time ago to catch the attention of someone or something (opinions differed) that cared about these things and didn't like such a disjointed affair as two centers at once. An offering of cartographical calculations, based on a cosmological model proven comprehensively wrong long ago, and–

Edmund snapped his pocket watch shut.

He stood on the spar. The wind tried to yank him into the sea. He grabbed at his hat before it left his head, hastily eyed the next spot along the bridge, and repeated the same mental gymnastics as before, focusing on the smooth metal between his fingers. The flick of the wrist. The snap of hinges.

Again. And again.

That old model was wrong, sure, but compelling – an idea that worked wonders in its own blinkered context, and there was a power in ideas, if you knew how to ask them. If you didn't mind how sharply-honed they were. If you had the discipline to sincerely believe multiple worrisome and contradictory notions and the stubbornness to not get nihilistic about it.

It helped to have a guarantee from another power that he wouldn't spatter himself across the heavenly spheres if he slipped up. Teleportation was tricky like that.

Edmund covered what had to have been three miles of bridge in less than thirty seconds.

The structure seemed to be getting larger: broader, or more reinforced. Some parts of it were covered, clad in vast sheets of iron.

A skeletal hand grabbed his boot.

"Down here," hissed Istvan. Tattered feathers tumbled into the murk below and vanished. The sun was too low, now; the fog getting thicker.

Edmund caught his breath. Great.

He peered over the edge, searching for hand-holds amid the metal latticework, and discovered that Istvan had led him to a ladder. He tucked his pocket watch away and swung himself down.

This section was covered, out of the wind, and he gave thanks for small favors.

He climbed.

The ladder stretched away below him. Iron cladding rose up around him. Red bulbs guttered along rusted beams. The bridge creaked with the wind, more claustrophobic by the minute, saturated with the smells of paint and grease.

He focused on breathing.

It felt like thirty stories to the bottom. It might have been five.

The ladder reverberated with the sound of engines. Headlights flashed below them.

"All right?" asked Istvan from somewhere further down.

Edmund paused where he was, holding tightly to the rungs. "I'm fine. How far away are they?"

Istvan dropped to the roadway. He turned towards the headlights, shaded his eyes, then called back up, "Not far."

A burst of machine-gun fire ripped through his chest.

"I think they've seen us," he added.

Edmund straightened his hat, only half-deafened. He fingered his pocket watch. Took a breath. Smiled. "Wholly possible," he said.

Then the Hour Thief let go of the ladder.

Another burst, fired from a weapon he couldn't see. He twisted out of the way – he couldn't see the bullets, either, but that didn't matter – and snapped his pocket watch.

He reappeared next to Istvan.

Plenty of time. Bullets were fast, but they couldn't cheat causality, couldn't fit an extra moment between moments, couldn't rely on the protection of something best left unsaid. Focus, and he could outspeed anything he was aware of, no matter how implausible. Even if something did hit him, it wouldn't kill him.

Nothing could kill him. Nothing but running out of time.

That was the agreement.

"Thank you for the warning shot," he called above the dull roar of engines, "but I prefer to negotiate. Give me some time and I'm sure we can work something out."

No return fire.

Edmund waited. They had to know who he was. Just about everyone in Big East did.

Or used to, anyway.

"The Herald recognizes your right to parlay," boomed a voice from past the headlights, distorted by some kind of electronic filter. The accent suggested a native language somewhere between Russian and Japanese: nothing

Edmund knew, which these days was no surprise. "Keep well-leashed the unquiet spirit you command and make good account of yourself."Acknowledgment. Agreement. Implicit acceptance of the bargain. What they'd said about Istvan wasn't strictly true, but that part didn't matter.

Edmund nodded, relieved. "Thank you," he said. He dropped his watch into a pocket, stolen moments secured and added to his collection. He hadn't chosen "Hour Thief" as his moniker for no reason. "I'm glad you see the value in learning the whole score."

A hatch clanked open.

Istvan neatened his bandolier and the ornamental buttons beneath it, brushing away the last of the bullet holes like they were stains. "Machine-guns," he sighed.

Edmund squinted at the headlights, trying to make out the machines attached to them. They seemed to have filigree along their sides. Spikes. "Don't take it too personally."

"Have they no sense of history?"

"Less than a full dollar."

Istvan winced. "Must you?"

Edmund realized he was grinning. Gratified at this turn of events. Harboring some genuine hope that his first run in a long time might turn out OK. "Sorry."

"You're not sorry."

"You're right."A man clad in a cross between archaic plate armor and nineteenth-century military finery stepped into view, sharply back-lit: the shadow of a long coat, loose pants tucked into armored boots, an exposed breastplate that glittered gold. A scarlet cape fluttered from spiked shoulders. An elaborate crest crowned his helmet, fully enclosed, embossed cheek guards sweeping upwards to meet a visor that flickered with internal lights. A saber hung at his side.

A sharp inhale to Edmund's left. Istvan. The ghost didn't breathe anymore, really, but habit was hard to break. The barbed wire at his feet looped bright and bloodied: a sign of eagerness he couldn't hide and that Edmund wished he didn't recognize.

This was going to be something, all right.

The man before them was a mercenary of Triskelion. A member of a stranded army from an alternate history, rarely seen but widely feared. Edmund knew that Istvan had never fought onc before.

With luck, today wouldn't be his first chance.

The mercenary thumped a fist on the emblazoned eagle of his breastplate. "I am the Armsmaster," he boomed in his distorted timbre. "What is it at this late hour that you seek?" Edmund smiled. "We received word that you're carrying twenty Bernault devices for one of your clients," he said, keeping his voice carefully even. "Someone called 'the Cameraman,' I believe?"

The mercenary stared down at him. "We do not give up names, Hour Thief."

"I understand."

An ominous clanking came from beyond the lights. Edmund tried to estimate how many men it would take to handle four tanks. Five to a machine? Four?

Fewer, if they were automated?

He kept talking. "I'm sure you're aware of the Twelfth Hour's stance on the sale and export of artifacts from deep fracture zones, particularly Bernault devices, so I won't remind you." He tapped his lapel pin. "I'd like to come to a mutual arrangement, if at all possible. This doesn't have to become a problem."

Flashes of red. Dark outlines moving through the shadows.

Istvan touched his shoulder, a chill that instantly numbed. "Edmund…"

The world lit up like the sun.

Edmund threw himself sideways, expecting a hail of gunfire any second. He spent a moment to blink away blindness. Couldn't outrun light. Spots danced before his vision.

A popping burst around him. He spun around –

– and then the area flooded with mist.

He sucked in a lungful of it before he could stop himself. Sputtered. Coughed. Waved an arm in a futile attempt to clear the miasma, trying not to breathe, a familiar and unwanted panic rising in his throat.

Gas. Tear gas.

The light slanted in a swirling haze, shafts and strange shapes. The roadway rang with running feet. The seals of his goggles held, but his lungs burned. Not enough air. Not enough air, and outside there was nothing but water. Water and krakens.

Drowning. Not again.

He staggered away, face buried in a sleeve.

A jagged shape rushed at him. It held a saber in one hand.

Edmund fumbled for his pocket watch.

"Come now," said a voice like Dracula, "you aren't finished with me, yet!"

Steel met steel. A trench knife; skeletal fingers; a bloodied sleeve. A death's-head, grinning, incongruously wearing an antique field cap and glasses. Vague figures stumbled through a stinking haze of bitter mustard and chlorine.

"You know," said Istvan, mud-spattered and bullet-riddled, "I was once told that a man wielding a knife would always lose out to a man wielding a sword."

The mercenary hesitated.

Vulture's wings flared in the mists, vast and rotten, tattered feathers tangled with trailing loops of barbed wire. Istvan shrugged a rustling shrug. "I suppose that only holds if both combatants are men, hm?"

The mercenary bolted.

Edmund scooted away, shaking, as Istvan laughed. Outstretched feathers passed through him. Poison swirled around blood-smeared bone.

He was used to it – used to the sudden cessation of flesh, the smell, the cold, the phantom blast marks and bullet holes that appeared on every nearby surface – but he would never be comfortable with it. Never.

Istvan was the ghost of an event as much as the ghost of a man. A soul torn to pieces and reconstituted by disaster. A member of a class so vanishingly rare that Edmund had heard of only three others: one tied to the Black Death, one to the Shaanxi earthquake of 1556, and the last to the atomic bombing of Japan.

A sundered spirit.

Istvan was tied to the First World War. He was by far the most active, the most combative, and the most far-ranging of his kind, and Edmund was the only survivor of an earlier attempt to capture him in 1941. In a very real way, he was violence.

He couldn't help himself.

"Istvan," Edmund tried to say, but his throat wouldn't work.

He couldn't breathe.

The horror that was now his closest friend leapt into an oppressive hover that scattered mud and wire all over the roadway. "I'll deal with this," he called, "Don't you worry, Edmund!"

He shot away. The memory of artillery boomed and

flashed in his passage.

Something else responded, blowing a hole in one side of the bridge.

The roadway shook.

"Go on," Istvan shouted, still laughing, "God is on your side, isn't he? Doesn't he play national favorites?"

Wind screamed through the gap. Spray. Saltwater.

Edmund fled.

Istvan chased flashes of men through smoke and fire. Stray bullets zinged from the bridge supports. Grenades burst around him: flashes, more gas, a few that exploded with a sharp snap and roar. The mercenaries shouted in a language he didn't know. The wind tore at his wings. The memory of pain – Edmund's pain, chemical fire clawing at the wizard's innards – tingled in his awareness like the afterglow of a fine wine, spiced with a more present, broader terror.

So familiar. So delightful. A meager trickle compared to the old days, but more than enough to make it all worth it. He couldn't kill anyone – not chained as he was, not without direct order – but the chase...

Oh, the chase!

Triskelion mercenaries. Members of the only real army for a thousand miles. Fierce enough to occupy the spellscars, dangerous even in small numbers, coordinated and disciplined and so very splendid.

He'd hoped this would happen. He hadn't said anything – but he'd hoped.

It would have been perfect if the mercenaries didn't keep vanishing.

A shell exploded on one of the overhead spars. Istvan swooped through a jagged hole in the bridge cladding and then back around and up through another blown in the roadway. Torn bolts and lengths of shrapnel pattered through him like ghastly hail.

One of the men ducked the wrong way.

Istvan pounced on him.

The mercenary slapped at his right gauntlet. The air contorted about him, gas coiling into mathematical patterns with a clanging, ripping sound, like a bullet through iron – and then he disappeared.

Gone. Teleported.

"That's cheating," Istvan shouted. Edmund cheated, as well, but he was Edmund; he was permitted. No one else Istvan had ever encountered could disappear like that.

Three more men vanished from his awareness. Istvan whirled about.

One of the tanks sat there, squat and square and belching smoke from gilded stacks. Spikes jutted from its sides. Scorch marks marred its barrel. It was the only tank that had fired so far.

The tanks couldn't teleport, probably.

Istvan darted for it. The Bernault devices were in there, if they were anywhere, and what else had he come for if not to help secure them? How they hadn't burst already he had no idea – the things were terrifically temperamental – but that didn't matter.

Edmund would move them, of course. Later. Once Istvan cleared the way for him, and he had recovered.

Poor, dear Edmund.

The hatch of the tank was open. Istvan swung inside –

– and discovered a tangle of wires attached to at least a dozen ominous bundles stuck to the interior walls.

"Oh," he said, "That's clever."

Fire.

Once, in life, he'd survived a near-miss by British

artillery. The Boer War. That was where he'd ruined part of his face, his left arm, most of his left side, scorched and partially paralyzed... and that was what had landed him, for the next few years, in a prisoner-of-war camp in Ceylon.

Now, of course, explosions mattered less. He couldn't recall how many times he'd been struck since the Great War, but it was a great many.

It still hurt.

Istvan found himself floating dazedly just outside the bridge. Smoke billowed from the rents in its armored sides. Sunset cast orange blazes across the sky. No hint of the mercenaries – that wonderful well-masked terror – or anything else living.

He traced two fingers across where his dueling scars had been, scorched phalanges against bare bone. A cursory wingbeat revealed that more of his feathers than usual were still missing.

Well-played.

Oh, they would have to do that again.

Istvan wheeled about and made for shore as pieces of tank and pieces of roadway fell, burning, into the sea.

He found Edmund back at the gantry crane. Hat off. Goggles off. Sitting down, back to the cabin, staring less at and more in the general direction of the bridge. The terrors still lingered but he wasn't breathing too hard, which was a good sign.

Istvan had been forty-four on his last day of life and looked older, scarred and weather-beaten. Edmund, on the other hand, boasted an elegance almost feline in quality, dark-haired and dark-eyed, his narrow face framed by a trim goatee and sideburns. He looked every bit the thirty-five he insisted he still was... save for the near-permanent weariness of his expression, and the gathered shadows under his eyes.

He smelled powerfully of tear gas.

Istvan alighted beside him, folding wings that evaporated into wisps of wire and chlorine. "Edmund," he said, breathlessly, "it's quite all right now."

The reply was flat. "They're all gone, aren't they?"

"They are. Teleported, of all things. I didn't know they could do that – I think this is only the third time in a hundred years I've encountered an enemy who can do that. It's so rare." He sighed, savoring what he knew he oughtn't. "Don't they say you always remember your first?"

"Something like that."

"You know, I don't think they had the Bernault devices," Istvan continued, dropping down companionably beside him, "The entire bridge would have burst, if they had. Did you know that they wired one of their tanks? I think they were expecting us."

Edmund stared down at the barbed wire twining around one of his shins. "Great."

"Where do you suppose they learned to teleport?"

"Why don't you ask one of them?"

Istvan paused. "Edmund, they've all gone."

Edmund sighed. Then he sneezed.

Istvan patted his shoulder. Tear gas was nothing, really. It didn't destroy vision or burn flesh or drown victims in their own bodily fluids or anything of that nature, after all. The poor man would be perfectly fine.

"What did it look like?" Edmund asked once he'd stopped coughing.

"What, the teleport?"

"Yes."

Istvan considered. "Lines in the smoke," he said. "And

a sort of clanging. A rush, like a train. Do you know it?"

The wizard shook his head. "You're sure the devices aren't there?"

"If they were, they would have burst by now." Istvan glanced at the horizon, which hadn't gone up in a blue-white conflagration, and then shrugged. "I truly don't think they had the devices with them in the first place."

"Go make sure."

Istvan nodded. He swung himself up onto the catwalk rail. "Edmund?"

"Yes?"

"The Magister isn't going to be happy about this, is she?"

Edmund retrieved his pocket watch. "Not at all."

CHAPTER TWO

"You lost them."

Edmund turned his hat in his hands, aviator goggles dangling from his elbow. The Magister's office was a foreboding den of dark wood and stained glass, heaped all about with collections of dusty brass instruments, Chinese lanterns, and severed bird's wings, its single window looking out over choppy waves. "That doesn't mean we can't find them again," he said.

"They were ready for us," Istvan added, standing beside him at rigid military attention, "They were expecting us."

A pen tapped on coffee-stained oak, an ancient desk scarred by generations of smoldering cigarette butts and more lethal things. The woman behind it was small, brown-skinned, clad in a grey business suit two sizes too big for her gaunt frame. More pens strained to keep her hair wound in a tight bun. Pockmarks across her cheeks spoke of a past battle with illness, while a missing ring finger spoke of battle of a different sort. She was in her mid-thirties, as far as anyone knew, but had the sort of face that time dared not touch for fear of laceration.

Magister Mercedes Hahn. Self-appointed overseer of

everything magical and strange in Big East. Edmund's successor, and a far better Magister than he had ever been.

The woman who had killed Shokat Anoushak.

She had just showed up one day, announced that the Wizard War would be over within the week, and it was. One stroke. Providence leveled in a titanic blast. No one knew how. Anyone who might have asked was no longer on roster.

Her election to office had been immediate and unanimous.

"Mr Templeton," she said, "I permitted your friend to accompany you on this assignment in hopes that you had recovered both your health and your senses. Is this not the case?"

Edmund reached for his pocket watch, clasping it in a gloved hand. "I'm fine."

"Tell me why I shouldn't restrict Doctor Czernin back to infirmary duty alone and insist, for the last time, that you take a position in administration."

"You know I can't do that."

"You've done it before."

The skull of Magister Jackson stared at him from one of the bookshelves. He tried not to look at it. "Mercedes, with all due respect, a year in your chair was enough."

Her lips thinned. "Not every year is 2012, Mr Templeton."

"Magister," said Istvan, "we will find the Bernault devices, I promise you. I'll talk to Miss Justice to see if her satellites have found anything else, and I can fly a search pattern besides. Once Edmund recovers, we–"

Edmund tightened his grip on the watch. "Istvan, I'm fine."

"No, you aren't." The ghost stared straight ahead.

"After an attack like that, you need to rest, and we both know you won't be able to focus on anything tomorrow."

Mercedes twirled the pen through her remaining three fingers. "Doctor Czernin, none of that would be necessary if you hadn't decided to give in to your baser impulses rather than use your considerable medical talent to incapacitate a captive for questioning."

Istvan wilted. He rubbed at his wrists. "Magister, I–"

"Quiet."

He cut off with a pained wheeze.

Edmund winced, though this wasn't the first time and it wouldn't be the last. Istvan had been chained now for almost thirty years; twenty of those spent locked away in the Demon's Chamber, the Twelfth Hour's most secure prison. Edmund had gone to visit him, sometimes. Edmund had helped put him there.

He hadn't expected to feel bad about it, but that was a hard feeling to avoid when a man seemed earnestly happy to see you again, invited to you to coffee, and then was marched away to be magically shackled, hand and foot, bound so tightly that he could barely move before he was abandoned, alone.

The Twelfth Hour had only agreed to release him so he could help with the overflow of wounded during the Wizard War. Later, so he could fight.

Edmund was responsible for that, too.

He'd held those chains, once. Only the Magister could give Istvan orders.

"Mercedes," Edmund began in the new silence, "Those men were Triskelion mercenaries. Those don't come cheap, and they were hired by someone with enough resources to provide a working method of teleportation, magical or otherwise. That might even have been their payment. Bernault devices or not, our 'Cameraman' just got a lot more dangerous."

She gazed at him a moment. The pen tapped on the desk.

"I'm going to need Istvan's help," Edmund said.

The ghost cast him a grateful look.

"Remember, Mr Templeton," Mercedes replied, "without you our field of operations has been limited. The number of people trying to use what they don't understand has grown, along with the notion that we shouldn't be 'hoarding' the dangers that we do. Even now there are forces who would seek to have us removed altogether. Regardless of whether you intended it or not, the Hour Thief has become representative of all wizards and I expect you to comport yourself as such."

Edmund flashed a tired smile. "I do my best." She set the pen down. "That said, I want those twenty devices found. I want whoever is behind this caught, and I want it made very clear to any other potential buyers that we do not take artifact smuggling lightly. I don't care what you have to do, but do it soon."

Edmund glanced at the room's picture window. Outside rolled the waves of the Atlantic, though the office was underground. They seemed choppier than usual. "I understand."

Istvan nodded, still unable to speak.

"Good." She leaned back in a puff of ancient incense. "Mr Templeton, go home. Doctor Czernin, you may speak. You have ten minutes and then I expect you back on duty until midnight."

"Yes, Magister," said Istvan. His voice was raw.

"You are both dismissed." She reached in a pocket for her phone, tapping a quick tattoo on the screen. "See to it that this incident is added to the wall."

Istvan started out before Edmund did, turning stiffly

on his heel like the military man he had become. Edmund scrubbed at his aching eyes and followed, instinctively avoiding ghostly barbed wire. It really could have gone better. He'd taken some time to get over the worst of it but he could still taste a heavy bitterness in the back of his throat. Being gassed was like drowning. He'd drowned once.

The door shut and latched behind him with seven ratcheting clicks. Mercedes' office – and the office of all eight of her predecessors – sat at the end of a long hall, leading back towards the library and opposite the vaults, lit by wrought-iron lanterns. Photographs of Twelfth Hour Magisters and membership hung in alcoves spaced every few feet or so, one for every five years of the cabal's existence.

The first held seven pictures and was dated 1895.

"I'm sorry for leaving you to choke," said Istvan as they strolled past the nook for 1925, which held thirty pictures. His accent, a soft, cadenced Hungarian he normally quashed as best he could, had thickened into full Dracula-esque force, a sure sign he wasn't paying attention. "I oughtn't discount the effects tear gas can have on a man, I really oughtn't. I know how painful it can be."

Edmund swallowed. It didn't seem to help much. "Don't worry about it."

"I simply haven't... You know I fought duels once, and..." The ghost scraped a hand across the scarred half of his face, tracing a pair of raised ridges across cheek and jaw. "If I had been in my right bloody mind at all, Edmund, I would have kept at least one from getting away."

"Can you do anything about it now?"

"No, but–"

"Then don't worry about it." He pulled his gloves off. They passed 1940 and a framed black-and-white picture of him at twenty-one, sporting a wispy beard and a fedora. There had been about fifty members that year.

He was hatless in 1945, and haunted.

"And if someplace is blown to bits because I didn't act?" demanded Istvan.

Edmund jammed his gloves in a pocket. "I don't know."

"All twenty in one place would be bad enough, but what if they were to be split up? Twenty explosions like that, all over the city..." He snarled to himself. "Oh, I should have paralyzed the bastard, not tried to fence with him."

In 1950, Edmund wore a top hat and opera cape. In 1955, he wore the same thing but in color. In 1960, he wore the same thing again and still in color. And again in 1965. 1970 was the Year of the Ill-Advised Mustache, but he was back to normal by 1975, and after that there was no change at all save for the ever-increasing weariness of his expression – the smile more fixed, the eyes more ancient – and the ever-growing sea of new faces surrounding him. By 2010, the Twelfth Hour was nearly two hundred strong.

Only sixty survived to 2015.

Edmund glanced over the candles arranged in the alcove, to make sure they were all still burning. They were.

Much of the Twelfth Hour's present wizarding membership came from the wreckage of other cabals. The teaching of magic, dangerous at the best of times, had all but halted. The majority of those on roster now weren't wizards at all.

Istvan paused beside him. "I always hated that picture."

"Your cheekbones are fine."

"No, they're hideously Mongolian, but that isn't the worst." He sighed a long sigh. "You're all in color and I'm still in black-and-white."

Edmund shrugged. "I'm still in just black."

"That's by choice. That's different." He plucked at the decorative piping on his sleeve. "You've no idea how splendid all this looked in the old days, Edmund. How it shone. How terribly attractive it was to fair maidens and snipers."

Edmund rolled his eyes as bullet holes flickered across the specter's chest. "I think I've done well enough the way I am."

Istvan chuckled. "I never said you haven't."

Edmund reached for his pocket watch again. *Go home. Rest up. Take care of yourself, or you won't be able to help anyone else. We both know that you won't be able to focus tomorrow.* He wished that none of that was right. "Istvan?"

"Hm?"

"I'm going to head home. I don't want to inflict this smell on anyone else."

He flipped the watch open.

Istvan touched his sleeve. "Ah... before you go, I was wondering if you might be open to chess later. With all that's happened, and the visit to the memorial tomorrow, well..." He glanced at the candles. "I thought you might like some company."

Edmund took a breath. Right. That. There was that, wasn't there. He'd been trying not to remember that. "I'm open to chess."

"Oh, good. I've been meaning to test that new rule for the knights, you know."

"That's cheating, you know."

Istvan cast him a lopsided grin. "You cheat, you know."

"I do." Edmund tipped his hat. "Just not at chess. Evening, Istvan."

He snapped the watch shut.

The wizard vanished in a golden haze.

Istvan fiddled with his wedding ring, twisting it around and around his finger. There had been something more in Edmund's movement, the coiled reluctance of it, the tightly-wound grief and dread and anger: a raw and oaken sweetness edged with citrine spice, hazing about him like the lingering smell of tear gas.

He hid it well, but Istvan always knew.

Tomorrow was the seventh anniversary of the end of the Wizard War. Edmund had seen it through – as Magister Templeton, elected unwillingly after the disappearance of Magister Geronimo – but it had taken its toll on him.

He'd been the only one to know anything about Shokat Anoushak. He'd obsessed over her, before the war. She was only example of a truly long-lived immortal anywhere on record, and during the years he came to visit Istvan in the Demon's Chamber he would almost always bring sheaves of dusty documents with him, translating old stories from faded Arabic and trying to make a map of historical sightings.

Of course the wizards had chosen him as Magister when she came back.

And then there was the matter of Grace...

Oh, Edmund had been dreading the memorial visit all week. Best to provide something other than gin to keep him occupied the night before.

Ten minutes before a return to duty.

Istvan started for the wall.

The headquarters of the Twelfth Hour glittered. From scarlet carpet to stacked wall sconces to sunburst railings, it was a study in the worst excesses of Art Deco, an aggressively sterile structure of gold, chrome, marble, and mahogany paneling that seemed to have obliterated all of its curves in favor of yet more triangles. Blocky columns bore repeating images of stylized books and staves. Interlocking patterns spread across the ceiling, almost Moorish, lit by sunken yellow glass panels instead of proper chandeliers. The central library was three stories high, all of them dreadful.

It had once been a gentleman's club of sorts, named for its hours of operation and its dedication to combating magical disaster. What arrives at the end of the eleventh hour? None other than the Twelfth.

As for the additions that had appeared with the Wizard War, well... Hindu temple architecture was sturdy, at least.

Istvan strode past scattered tables and took the stairs rather than make a scene, enduring questioning glances from surviving wizards, allied citizenry of New Haven, and stranger things: an animated floor lamp, a giant lizard in a purple parka that stumped along on a cane, a posse of armored policemen from a possible future. A flock of ravens hopped from shelf to shelf after him, cackling to each other.

They had all known that the Hour Thief was finally returning to real field duty after fourteen months missing and then years of sticking to nothing more than librarian work and his usual mysterious excursions by night. He was former Magister, after all. The Twelfth Hour's calling card. The "wizard-general," dashing and unkillable.

It was nice that he kept the library so neat and clear of casualties, but that wasn't why he was famous.

Where was he now? Had something happened?

Istvan found himself grateful that he had his own brand of fame, and no one present dared approach to ask.

He climbed to the highest story, closest to the above-ground entrance, and found the map wall where the shelves ended. The map itself was fabric stretched over a frame, studded with colored pins that marked recent mission sites, artifact sightings, and known movements by enclaves the Twelfth Hour had an interest in watching. A table before it held the pin box, a notebook, a tray of pens, hot water, and what passed for tea.

A tall, heavyset black woman stood before it, filling a chipped coffee mug. Greying hair spilled down her back, braided into dozens of strands.

"Miss Justice," called Istvan.

She glanced up. She spotted him, and raised the mug to him. She wore a glittering green shirt and glittering green earrings and didn't look at all like she had lived through the ruin of civilization. She also wore pants, but women did that now.

Janet Justice. The Twelfth Hour's primary information and surveillance specialist. She wasn't a wizard, but what she did was as close to magic as modern civilization had ever produced.

"*Guten Tag, Herr Chirurg Czernin*," she said in schooled German.

Istvan took his hat off, folded it, and tucked it beneath his bandolier. "*Grüß Gott, Fräulein Justice*," he responded in the same tongue. <I was planning to speak with you tomorrow.>

She stirred her tea. She was one of the few non-medical people on task often enough late at night to encounter Istvan regularly, and over the years had

proven both fearless enough and good-natured enough
to humor a ghost asking about computers in return for
an opportunity to practice her second language. <I'm
here now. How did Operation Hour Thief go?>

<That was what I wanted to talk about.> He hunted
through the pin box and chose a red one. <Ah... does
tear gas corrode electronics?>

She raised an eyebrow. <Tear gas?>

<Edmund was carrying his telephone. Will it be
damaged?>

<If he brings it in, I'll have a look at it.>

Istvan nodded, regarding the map. It covered a rough
approximation of the northeastern United States, divided
into fracture zones, spellscars, and what remained of the
nation before. <Thank you.>

Big East followed the new coastline, a half-flooded
urban wasteland home to, among other things, the Black
Building, the Magnolia Group's crashed spaceship, the
Wizard War memorial, and dozens of tiny survivors'
enclaves, scavenger camps, and odder things that
came and went. The Twelfth Hour claimed former
Yale University, much of New Haven, and the nearby
Generator District as its own, though its ambitious patrol
territory covered most of Big East. The crater that marked
Providence loomed in the north, forbidden ground
dominated by the fortress-state of Barrio Libertad.

Beyond Big East stretched the spellscars, a vast band
of twisted wilderness and deadly magics, and past that
lay what passed for "normal" regions, administered by
government remnants and flooded with refugees.

The pattern was the same for the Greater Great Lakes
fracture, Chicago through Toronto: impossible cityscape
ringed with impassable horror, its original population
fled, transformed, trapped, or dead.

It was the same the planet over, as far as anyone knew.

<Is he OK?> asked Miss Justice.

<He will be,> Istvan replied. <He only needs to rest.>

He pushed the pin into an area thirty miles outside former New York City, where he and Edmund had lost the mercenaries. Triskelion itself lay in the spellscarred Appalachian mountains of former Pennsylvania, further west, sandwiched between Big East and the Greater Great Lakes.

What were they after? One warlord or another had been trading Bernault devices from both fracture regions for years, as far as anyone knew, but not once had a Bernault-powered weapon been deployed against anyone. It was as though whoever was behind it collected the devices merely for the sake of collecting them. Or stockpiling them.

For what? Against what? How many did the Cameraman have now?

Was he planning to sink all of Big East into the sea?

Istvan shook his head. <The mercenaries knew we were coming,> he said. <The convoy was a decoy. They've learned to teleport somehow, and I've no idea where they went.>

Miss Justice grimaced. <I'm sorry it didn't work out.>

<If I could ask a favor?>

She set her cup down. <Sure.>

<Keep monitoring the area around New York. Look for anything moving, any potential signs of camouflage.> He didn't know how, exactly, she stayed in contact with the satellites or how they stayed in orbit, but they were so high up that the Wizard War hadn't touched them and they had proven, overall, surprisingly useful.

<The mercenaries left their tanks,> he continued, <Why would they leave their tanks, if they could take

them along, and why bother with a decoy at all if they could teleport the devices? I think the real convoy is still on its way.>

She nodded. <I'll keep an eye out.>

<Thank you.>

Istvan scribbled the date and a note on the day's events in the notebook. *June 28, 2020: Failed interception of Triskelion mercenary Bernault convoy, x20; Mr Templeton, Dr Czernin. Decoy. Red NYC, 30 m.*

<You know,> said Miss Justice, leaning against a nearby bookshelf, <Mr Templeton just asked a favor recently, too. If I didn't know better, I'd think I was popular with the older set.>

Istvan chuckled. <Don't let him hear you say–>

He winced. He rubbed at wrists that burned in their shackles, the chains he couldn't see enforcing orders he couldn't break.

Ten minutes, and then I expect you back on duty until midnight.

He put the notebook back with a grimace. <I'm afraid I'm needed. Now.>

Miss Justice frowned, but took it in stride. She'd seen it happen before. <OK, then. You're still welcome to drop by whenever you're free.>

Istvan nodded his thanks, retrieved his field cap, and bolted for the infirmary.

CHAPTER THREE

Edmund's front door was locked. It was always locked. His primary point of entry was inside and had been since he'd moved in fifty years ago. Aside from the sudden conversion from apartment block to free-standing structure, unreliable utilities, the usual difficulty in procuring anything not used or broken, and the occasional giant tentacle washed up on the beach, not much had changed since before the Wizard War.

The house still boasted only a single floor. It still had all of its original furniture. It was still comfortable for two people, yet more suited to one. Despite multiple recommendations over the years, he had never arranged to replace the wallpaper. Fading shafts of twilight slanted in through the blinds. He hung his hat and cape on their well-worn peg by the door, tossed his goggles on the table, and laid out new bowls of food and water for his cat. He put the map he'd drawn in a folder with others like it and put the folder away. Then he heated some of the water he'd drawn from the river that morning, lugged it to the backyard, dumped it in a strategically-placed plastic tank, and drew the curtains.

Shower. He desperately needed a shower.

Once he felt more like a human being again, he threw on a plain white bathrobe, poured himself a glass of gin he assured himself he deserved, and retrieved his ledger from the desk in his bedroom. The mercenaries had at least graciously given him what time he'd requested, and he noted it down in its proper column to form a running total.

Some Time. A Few Moments. Enough Time. Time to Spare. Time to Think About It. All the Time I Need.

Each phrase formed a distinct semantic unit, together with many other permutations less common and even more unforgivable. Each was worth a somewhat flexible but unmistakable span of moments, hoarded and spent like anyone else might spend coin.

The ledger held thousands of notations. Other ledgers, filled and emptied in turn, occupied the desk's upper shelf.

Years of time. None of it acquired honestly.

Oh, he asked for it, sure. And it had to be freely given. But no one who agreed to it knew what he was doing, or noticed that he was doing anything at all.

He was, for all intents and purposes, a conman who dealt in stolen moments. The hours that slipped away when no one was watching. Lives, plain and simple. He'd been thirty-five for seventy years, and he could say that only because none of the time he'd lived since 1954 was originally his.

As long as he had marks in that ledger, he could dodge bullets, survive drowning, appear just at the right moment, give others all the time they needed, live forever. If he ran out... well, that was time he wouldn't get back.

He didn't plan to run out.

He hadn't spent any that day beyond the usual. He marked it off.

The ledger went back into its drawer. The tome that bound together long-ago events, good intent, and terrible power requested foolishly was elsewhere, well-hidden among other books that seemed much more interesting.

He poured himself another glass of gin on the way out.

The hallway outside his room, like the rest of the house, was bare of photographs. The kitchen still looked like it had in the Seventies, dark and mood-lit, with spare wooden cabinets painted avocado green, flowered tile, and a chrome gas stove with a jury-rigged tank he kept carefully rationed. A small table took the place of a kitchen island, three chairs drawn up beneath it. The lone windowsill was empty: no herb garden, no flowers, no decorative bamboo. All suggestions at one time or another. The sill stayed empty.

No photographs in the den, either.

What he did have was books. Hundreds of them, written in or about almost fifty different languages, packed floor to ceiling. A filing cabinet full of copied Innumerable Citadel records sat in the corner. A half-dozen boxes of others sat nearby, yet awaiting translation. A few slim folders held collections of wards, magical inscriptions vetted by centuries of use that were mostly safe to copy.

Copying was always safer. Innovation in magic was best done in tiny increments, based on what was already well-established. The task of inventing wholly new rituals – wholly new ways of breaking reality – fell exclusively to people so driven and so desperate that they accidentally tapped into forces more than themselves, caught the attention of *something*... and survived long enough to pass down the experience.

Spellbooks – real, original spellbooks – weren't books

so much as collections of notes and mad ramblings, the rituals they detailed encoded in esoteric ciphers and lost within tracts of poetry, political commentary, and other nonsense, doodles adorning the margins. Even the Twelfth Hour had a limited number of those. Those were dangerous. Those stayed in the vault. Edmund knew; he had cataloged them.

Stolen one, once.

He retrieved a Sherlock Holmes novel, put a jazz record on (his old upright radio could only catch one station at nine in the morning), put his glass on the coffee table, and collapsed on the couch. An enormous black cat jumped up beside him.

He scrubbed a hand across his face. "Evening, Beldam. I hope your day went better than mine."

She wrinkled her nose at him.

He sighed. He could still taste the bitterness of tear gas in the back of his throat, he swore, even after two drinks. Three drinks?

He ran over the last few minutes in his mind: two drinks.

"Sorry about the smell," he muttered.

Beldam headbutted his side. He scratched her ears.

She lived here, and Istvan was the only one who visited. As far as anyone else knew, Edmund Templeton was the reclusive bachelor at the end of the block who kept strange hours, suffered strange fits, and never entertained. He would help with harvest and he wouldn't shirk latrine duties, and he'd offered an opinion when they tilled the green, but not much else. He never took any shares from the commons. Cordial, but distant. His house was haunted.

If the residents of New Haven suspected any connection to Magister Templeton, they kept quiet. Istvan's erratic presence had proven a remarkably effective deterrent.

Edmund was left alone with his cat and his thoughts.

He should have known the day wouldn't work out. Should have expected it. Just like the mercenaries seemed to have expected him.

Today hadn't been Istvan's fault. It was Edmund's, for not being able to handle it. For doing nothing. For panicking. For running. For giving in to something his own mind manufactured, something that wasn't even real.

Edmund reached for his glass and finished it off.

Istvan had gotten carried away, sure. Istvan could have tried harder, sure.

But it had been Edmund's job to get to the Bernault devices. Edmund's job to find and secure them. Edmund's job to make sure they were hitting the right place at the right time. Edmund's job to not panic when things went wrong.

He had planned that operation, not Istvan.

He considered a third drink, and then reminded himself that Istvan would be arriving that night for chess.

Let it go.

Water under the bridge, the whole smoking wreckage of it. What was done was done. It was all something to deal with later.

Tomorrow. After the memorial visit.

Seventh anniversary of the end of the Wizard War. All those people, watching the Hour Thief – watching him – make that trek up the stairway, probably in the rain, carrying that lily to...

Edmund reconsidered that third drink.

Grace wouldn't have liked it. She had been an engineer, a pragmatist, a firm believer in "real problem-solving", and the very notion that every problem could actually be solved. She hadn't believed in magic until magic happened, and when it did, she immediately decided it was some unknown branch of science.

There was no forbidden knowledge. There was no question that shouldn't be asked. There was no damnation.

In Grace's eyes, everyone could be saved.

Don't you dare give up, Eddie.

Punch it in the eye.

But Grace wasn't here. Explosions of that size didn't leave much to bury.

No. No, if he had another one, he'd have more than just another one, and Istvan would never let him hear the end of it. Istvan was coming for chess after midnight. New rule for the knights, he'd said.

Beldam headbutted him again.

"Sorry," said Edmund.

He put his glass down, opened his book, and scratched her ears.

Istvan hurtled through the wall, chains burning.

Double doors slammed shut, the converted meeting hall that served as the Twelfth Hour's infirmary echoing with a yelp, a crash, and hastily receding footsteps. A number of lingering earthquake patients sat up, startled. The ordinary staff took no notice.

A nearby nurse sighed, kneeling down to pick up an overturned gurney. "Was that really necessary, Doctor?" he asked.

Istvan folded wings that dissipated into wisps of gas and wire, the memory of artillery dulled back to silence. The pain at his wrists and neck faded: he was present, now, and on duty. "I was in a hurry."

"You could have used the door in a hurry."

"Was that another applicant?"

"Yes."

"Oh." Istvan ran a hand across the reformed flesh of his face. "Well. If he truly thinks he's up to the task, Roberts, he'll be back. Now," he continued, sifting through the infirmary's usual dulled yet pleasant ambiance of misery and pain, "are you certain this was all the patients we had? No one at all nearly died today?"

Roberts patted the gurney, retrieved his clipboard, and looked it over. Istvan wasn't a small man, but Roberts was a head taller and broader twice over, young and round and descended from the native inhabitants of some tropical island or other. More importantly he had a good head on his shoulders and a remarkably steady disposition, which was why he'd made the cut several years ago. "Not that I can see. It's been a good day so far."

"Rather bland, yes."

Istvan looked over the rows of pallets. The infirmary was a makeshift one; dividers built of cloth, machinery cluttering every alcove that would fit it, a hum of activity bustling below more grand pillars, sweeping arches, and gilded paneling than the Vienna Court Opera. The wizards had discussed grand plans here, once; now the order of the day was making sure those remaining lived to see any plan to fruition. Much cleaner than the muddy field hospitals to which he had grown accustomed, it was an altogether agreeable facility that would have been ideal had it only been just that tiny bit more disagreeable.

Every so often he found himself missing the trenches, the tunnels, the splintered timber, the occasional excursions to enemy lines that he could never remember as anything more than a euphoric blur of brilliant sensation; massacres permissible and even laudable because that was how war worked.

Istvan rubbed at his wrists, where the chains weren't visible. He'd hoped for more cases, more suffering. Something to take the edge off what had happened with the mercenaries and Edmund. "When do you suppose we'll have another shock?"

Roberts flipped some of the pages on his clipboard over. "Dunno. They're wondering now if some of the city-monsters aren't quite dead, or if the earthquakes might be some kind of gradual settling."

"Oh, it's always a gradual thing," Istvan sighed. "It starts small and then you find yourself invading Italy."

"Yes, Doctor. Did you sign off on Martha back there?"

Istvan glanced at the clipboard. "She should have full control of all six limbs in another few weeks. I told her to be patient."

"Right."

"I'm not a wizard, you know – eight years isn't enough time to become an expert on the fallout. Not for me, not for anyone. I did the very best I could and she's lucky to be alive at all."

Roberts held up his hands. "I wasn't saying anything."

Istvan crossed his arms across his bandolier, gazing over his spectacles at the far corner. They kept all the worst cases there, people with afflictions he'd never seen before the Wizard War, never known were possible. They likely hadn't been before Shokat Anoushak appeared with her beasts and her spellscars and her ancient brand of madness, ripping apart the possible and rampaging across the results of her handiwork until that last terrible convergence at Providence.

"I suppose I ought to have another look," Istvan admitted. Was it petty of him, to wish that a hundred and forty years of medical experience counted for more? "Perhaps I…"

He paused. Over the background pain and worry of the infirmary, and the minor annoyances typical of any human gathering, something else was approaching. An ache, dulled and clouded. Fear, sharp and urgent, but not overpowering; a complex medley of motivation and restraint. There was a smoothness to it, a confidence he recognized.

"Roberts…" he began.

The nurse set his clipboard aside. "On it."

Istvan was already at the doors when the team rushed through. The man on the gurney was young, clad in jeans and a thin jacket. Pale, brown-haired, clean-shaven. Barely breathing. The front of his jacket was torn into bloody ribbons. His skin was blistered with frostbite.

It was June, and the man had frostbite.

Istvan cursed. That was the one mundane thing he couldn't treat in confidence. "Severe hypothermia and frostbite, wounds to his chest, very weak vitals," rattled off one of the medics as Istvan confirmed those details for himself. "Recommend–"

The man's heart stopped. Istvan forcibly restarted it, reaching through bone and muscle to the organ itself. "Go on, then," he snarled. "I can keep him bloody stabilized but I'm not helping the cold!"

All present scattered before he finished the sentence. Roberts and three others were already setting up the nearest machine in a flurry. Istvan could keep nearly anyone alive through nearly anything that didn't kill a man instantly, but cold… oh, his own presence only worsened it, chilling flesh and spirit alike until it wore down to attrition. The human body could only be revived so many times.

"I bloody hate frostbite," he said to no one in particular. He traced his fingers through the wounds. "Someone get this jacket off – the man's been clawed and the wounds are contaminated."

Roberts and his team began hooking up all manner of diagnostic devices and life-sustaining apparatus, moments before others arrived with warming blankets and precious doses of the appropriate drugs. They had all been so relieved to get the electricity working, five years ago.

Istvan remembered trying to save lives with the medical equivalent of a rubber band and a toothbrush. He'd operated before penicillin. Before blood types. When the vaccination of diphtheria was the news of the day, along with the exciting idea of using Röntgen rays to see inside the body. Surgeons had operated without washing their hands a mere generation before.

The blood was still congealed.

"Did you pull him off a bloody mountain?" Istvan demanded.

One of the medics shook her head. "We responded to a call. Some sort of animal, they said."

"Yes, I can see that, but the cold?"

"We don't know." She shrugged helplessly. "We thought it might be something escaped from the spellscars, or a Conduit, or something."

Well, now. The spellscars suggested a monster that had gotten past the patrols, while a Conduit... oh, that was another matter entirely. That was someone coursing with strange power, burning up with it, at the mercy of some outside source of one kind or another. Ordinary people, most of them, irrevocably transformed during the Wizard War. They were fantastically rare.

Grace had been one. Unnaturally fast, unnaturally strong, wreathed in lightning. Istvan had set one of her arms after she broke her own bones punching through concrete. She had never agreed to let him study her, mostly because she hated him, and Edmund, during their not-infrequent quarrels, had never been able to convince her otherwise.

Edmund had once suggested that Istvan was a sort of Conduit as well, linked as he was to the Great War. Istvan had disagreed: Conduits, unlike him, were alive... though for how long was anyone's guess.

He busied himself with circulation, nudging chilled fluids along their proper course. The claw marks weren't deep, at least, though their recipient would have some impressive scars to show off later. "I suppose we'll have to ask him."

She blinked. "Now?"

He chuckled. "No, of course not. He'll stay under until we're sure he won't have a stroke or a coronary." He patted the man's hand, fingers smeared with the memory of blood. The pain of frozen tissue reviving was more than familiar, at turns sharp and mellow, a languorous blossoming as frustrating as it was exquisite. He sighed in appreciation. Perhaps it would be a tolerable evening after all. "Roberts, you recall how many men I lost in the mountains?"

The nurse didn't glance up. "You've mentioned it a time or two."

"Spread across three regiments, guns setting off avalanches, ridges full of bloody Italians... I don't know if anyone here has ever fought in the cold, but it dampens the pain terribly. Give me summer in the valleys, heat exhaustion, holding a river that isn't frozen. None of this natural anesthetic business."

Roberts rolled his eyes.

"After all, what good is war if you can't appreciate the full measure of a bullet tearing through your ribs, hmm?" Again, he chuckled. One of the monitors sounded, a long, low, solid tone, and he reached over to revive the man a second time. Something was clotted... ah, there it was. The medication ought to help with that, once it took effect. "Gently, now, we don't want to thaw him out so quickly he shatters."

"Working on it, Doctor."

Istvan nodded, checking the man's brain for additional clots. Oh, his people really were quite skilled, all of them. More than capable. "Someone start a... ah, you already have. Room temperature, normal saline? Good. I'd like a bit of plasma warmed, just in case. I'm not seeing any other thromboses and I do believe his heart has finally decided to cooperate."

"They aren't dead until they're warm and dead," quipped one of the nurses.

Istvan pressed a hand to his chest. "Why, Mrs Torres, where ever does that leave me?"

"Beyond the scope of medical science, Doctor. Nothing we can do for you."

He laughed. There wasn't.

There really wasn't.

CHAPTER FOUR

"A beast that claws and freezes its victims to death? I'd say it was one of Shokat Anoushak's creatures, but I hadn't heard of any perimeter breaches and I don't recall ever meeting one like this." Istvan turned a captured black pawn between his fingers. It was past midnight and that awful jazz wailed from the living room again, but he felt quite chipper after the surgery and anyhow, it was Edmund's house; a bit of saxophone could be forgiven. "Why didn't it attack anyone earlier? Have you ever heard of a beast like that?"

Edmund propped his goateed chin on a fist, regarding the chessboard with narrowed eyes. He wore a clean shirt and suspenders and smelled much better. "Can't say that I have." "Really? I thought you'd seen everything."

"Are you moving or not?"

"That depends. Have you fortified those three squares?"

"Last I remember, yes."

Istvan grinned. "That is a terrible shame." He pushed a piece forward.

Edmund frowned. "Is that the cannon from the Monopoly set?"

"It most certainly is, and as my armored cavalry has your infantry formation quite flanked–"

"Hold up, I thought we agreed that in this match the knights would move like proper knights. In Ls. You can't do that."

Istvan waved a hand. "No, we agreed that knights would move like proper knights. These aren't knights, Edmund, and they haven't been for the last two minutes." He plucked a cornered black rook off the board, followed by the pawn behind it and the bishop behind that.

They sat at the kitchen table, Edmund's chair facing the front door and Istvan's opposite, surrounded by flowered tile, flowered wallpaper, and avocado-green cabinets. Edmund's hoard of tin cans, glass jars, sugar packets, dental floss, and other items deemed useful or reuseable occupied every shelf not playing host to something else, arranged in neat rows. Newly-canned tomatoes sat atop the refrigerator. The pair of bowls for Beldam, the cat, lay near the entryway to the den. Beldam herself hated Istvan on principle and had fled down the hall when he arrived. The house itself was bare of photographs and packed with books, and Edmund refused to get rid of the horseshoe nailed sideways above the door.

"That was a hill," Edmund objected.

"Which was?"

"The middle square. You can't fire a conventional cannon like that through a hill."

"Hm." Istvan traced a finger across his scarring, considering. They were his rules, though they seemed to have developed on their own in the years before the Wizard War and had grown more and more elaborate once he had finally been permitted to leave Twelfth Hour premises. "Not yet and not at that angle, no." He put the bishop back. "I'll deal with you later."

Edmund skated his lone surviving rook past Istvan's knights and balanced a penny atop it. He seemed better – cleaner, certainly – but preoccupied, wounded and tired and wonderfully apprehensive, and perhaps a bit resentful, if the sharper edge of the medley were any indication. He had led armies once, seven years ago tomorrow, and still hadn't quite recovered. "Istvan," he asked, "just how bloody was your shift in the infirmary today?"

Istvan blinked. "Oh... not terrifically. Why?"

"You're awfully cheerful, is all."

"Am I?"

Edmund shrugged and stacked two more pennies on the rook. Quick, precise motions, those of a man who had spent a lot of time turning pages.

Istvan looked away, fiddling with his wedding ring. "Perhaps my tolerance is lower than I thought," he suggested. "You know it's only gotten worse since things have started getting better."

"That would explain what happened at the mercenary convoy, wouldn't it?"

Istvan flinched. "Edmund, I'm sorry."

The wizard rubbed a hand across his face. "Your move."

"Edmund, I promise that we'll find the devices. They can't be far, not through that terrain and not with the need to remain hidden. In fact, I spoke to Janet Justice earlier: she will be watching from the satellites for anything odd, and after we've finished this game, I'll–"

"Your move."

Istvan reached for his queen.

The next several turns passed in relative silence, save for another brief dispute over Istvan's entirely legal straight-galloping armored cavalry. It was ridiculous, perhaps, but chess was, at its heart, a war game. Istvan had simply updated it and made it just as unpredictable and unfair as war actually was.

It was better than the alternative.

"Edmund, bishop or not, he's far too visible and I've a clear shot this time." Istvan removed the offending piece and added it to his collection of black foemen, improvised artillery, and plastic battleships. "Oh, and my zeppelin is still bombing your king."

Edmund sat back in his chair. "That's fine, because I just added defenses."

"Ah, incendiary rounds. What range?"

"What?"

Istvan rattled off a diatribe on raised flight ceilings as compensation for opposing ground-based emplacements and the much-inferior endurance of heavier-than-air craft. It was information more memory than knowledge, remembrances of engineering meetings and flight crews, of turning out on lawns and balconies to watch as great behemoths burst flaming in the sky like fireworks.

During the war itself, men had asked him how the Emperor was doing, where the enemy was, what the other regiments thought of their progress – and he knew, because he always knew, experiences that weren't his surging through him at all hours in a confusing flood of disjointed images, countless experiences seen through other eyes.

The Great War. The fate of millions – the means, the hopes, the ends – all poured into what was left of him, a Hungarian surgeon from Vienna who hadn't wanted any of it. What had seemed almost a strange omnipotence had ceased, suddenly and forever, at war's end. Now it was only history.

They'd just finished haggling a range compromise

when Edmund cast a glance at the clean glass sitting next to the kitchen sink and sighed. "Istvan, what if they use gas again?"

Istvan paused mid-move. "You know what to expect now. You'll manage."

"No, I won't."

"Edmund, I've known you for thirty years and I know you can manage."

"Twenty-eight."

"Edmund."

"Twenty-eight and some, if you must count the Ukraine."

Istvan reached for him. "Edmund, please don't give up over this."

Edmund jerked away, terrors roaring to the fore. "I'm not giving up!" he shouted. "I never said I was giving up. I can't, Istvan. You know I can't. Not now, not ever." He pushed his chair back. He was shaking. "Not tomorrow."

"Edmund–"

"It's been seven years, Istvan, and seven is a bad, bad number. I don't like seven. July is coming up, and that's another seven, and only seven days after that there's the seventh, and…" He ducked past the zeppelin hanging from its string and started for the hat and cape hung on their hook near the door. "I'm going to Charlie's."

Istvan stood, cursing his choice of words. The pub. The anniversary. The memorial visit. Oh, he shouldn't have said anything. "I'll come with you."

"Don't."

A blink – and Edmund was the Hour Thief, his jacket donned and his hat straightened and his pocket watch in his hand, motion between moments, fueled by the time that he stole on his nightly patrols using methods he never talked about. A ritual, he'd said, performed long ago. A good idea at the time. Immortality... and a debt he could never repay.

"Don't," he repeated. He flipped his watch open. "I'll be at the memorial in the morning."

A snap. He vanished.

Istvan sat back down. Barbed wire knotted itself around the table legs. The zeppelin spun overhead, ponderous and ineffectual, its mission suddenly absurd.

Bloody Grace. This was her fault.

Far be it for Istvan to speak ill of the dead, but Edmund would have never suffered so, those fourteen long months in the watery dark, if not for Grace Wu.

No one bothered him at Charlie's. Everyone knew who he was – the woodcut outside even had his image on it, signed, beneath the proclamation "So Vintage We're the Real Deal" – but Edmund had a booth of his own and everyone knew to leave him be. The deal was simple: he kept an eye on the place and allowed the use of his face, and, in return, gin was always on the house.

In return, he had a place where he could forget.

He sat in his booth, in a corner facing the door and opposite the piano. Other patrons drank and talked and sulked a safe distance away, surrounded by dark wooden panels and pressed tin, lit by hurricane lamps, the air smelling powerfully of tobacco. The bar stools had swept legs, designed to accommodate the brass rail footrest running along the bottom of the counter. Smoke-fogged chandeliers hung from the ceiling. The cash register was mechanical, and never used. Barter was the order of the day now.

Outside loitered men in suits and hats, lighting cigarettes beneath the street lamps. Cars rolled past with bulky lines and rounded headlights, designs that

Edmund hadn't seen outside a showroom in sixty years. At Charlie's, it wasn't summer. It was spring. April, in fact.

April 11, 1939.

No one could reach the people in the windows. Step out the door, and you were back in Big East, back in the rain you couldn't hear falling from inside.

Edmund didn't think about it too hard. All that mattered was that the stock in the back rooms reappeared every day. The same bottles, over and over, without fail. Nowhere else could match Charlie's for sheer consistency and utter lack of shortage.

He sat with gin in hand and booth solidly under him and listened to disjointed words smear themselves across a strange haze of arms and teeth. Already he wasn't quite sure how much of the day's stock he had put away himself.

A good start.

Seventh anniversary. Seventh month after that. Seventh day. Had to be careful at times like this, when it all converged. Had to watch the sky.

Couldn't have another Hour Thief. One was enough. No more of that.

A shadow approached his table. It slid up and over the cracked wood, snuffing out reflections of the lamps that shone in empty glasses. When it went up the wall, it took the shape of a battered cowboy hat.

"Someone left this for you," said an old man's voice.

A white box appeared on the table, pushed over to him by gnarled fingers.

"A gal," the voice clarified. "Pretty, too. God help you."

The shadow receded.

"Thanks, pal," said Edmund. "You're a real friend."

He stared at the box. It was paper. It was about the size of a pie tin. Pinned to it was a smaller piece of paper, with writing on it. A note. Beautiful cursive.

"Huh," he said.

Mr Templeton, it read, *I hope this note finds you in good health. I regret the recent loss of twenty Bernault devices as greatly as you do, and I would like to offer information on their whereabouts. Tomorrow, at noon, look for me. I know your booth. Come alone.*

In hope and confidence, Lucy.

"Huh," he said.

He got the box open. Pie. Apple pie, with the most perfect, straightest lines on top he'd ever seen.

He liked apple.

How had she known?

Clouds dimmed the night. The lights of New Haven, scattered like pearls, followed erratic paths to the coast, strung from the mountainous shadow of the Twelfth Hour. Fear of wizards had weakened, and fear of deprivation had grown: those that counted themselves under Magister Hahn's protection had swelled closer and closer to its walls as the years passed. Yale's crumbling Gothic towers hunched over irrigation ditches and plowed greens, wrought-iron gargoyles perched on its rooftops.

Istvan lingered by Edmund's chimney a moment longer, holding onto the rough siding. Harbor waves crashed over the old docks, slowly rusting away drowned storage tanks and smokestacks. There were highways sunk under the sea now, too, storefronts and homes and churches. Auroras rose from distant Manhattan, spitting and crackling, the outline of the Black Building's twisted spire silhouetted three miles high in their embrace.

Edmund wasn't coming back.

Istvan turned and leapt. Tattered primaries clinging tenuously to bloodied bone flared, caught. One wingbeat. Two. He rose in a broadening circle. Beyond New Haven's boundaries, the Generator district glowed like a beacon, pillars of steam billowing from curved towers. A storm rolled over it, dark and sullen. He couldn't see Charlie's from here, though that was where it lay, hemmed in between lengths of pipe and wire.

He tilted, streaming contrails of rusted wire – a maneuver more aircraft than bird – and spun into a straight vertical climb. Stray droplets scattered as he broke the cloud deck, flecks of muddied scarlet that dissipated into nothing.

The moon was waxing. The stars, at least, hadn't changed.

Edmund wasn't coming back.

Istvan swept his wings back and shot northward. The clouds below reminded him of coal-burning armadas, and in the moments after his passage they roiled with the remembrance of poison. Flying machines had first appeared in his war, and only grown faster since. Flight was his, just the same as massacre, mud, and grinding inevitability. Flight was the one undeniable positive of what he was. It had taken him months of tumbling off cliffs in the Italian Alps to convince himself he could do it.

Let Edmund not come back. Let him go to Charlie's and drink. He was the Hour Thief; he could do that. No one could stop him from doing that.

Let him go.

Istvan dove. Clouds whirled past and through him. Rain sleeted by like bullets. Lightning flashed with a crack and roar. He shot through a flock of geese that squawked and scattered, readjusted his course, and broke the lowermost cloud layer like a falling shell.

Below him whirled Big East, collective desperation clad in concrete. Horizon to horizon, it sprawled, blockaded by spellscars: a city of sputtering light, shanties and skyscrapers, crashed spacecraft and solid fog, highways that crawled like snakes, chimerical beasts and stubborn people that had somehow survived it all, scraping by side by side. Rubble stretched in great scars across the old paths of engagement – some deep and furrowed, rock ripped away by enormous claws.

Somewhere down there rolled a convoy of mercenaries with twenty Bernault devices, provided they hadn't split forces to throw off pursuit. That wasn't what Istvan had crossed a hundred miles to find.

Not yet.

Before him, where the city ended, lay the last battlefield of the Wizard War.

Buildings scoured to their foundations. Bridges collapsed. Ships and the skeletons of gargantuan horrors rusting half-sunk in murky water, all of it shimmering with unnatural heat. A new dam closed off the harbor: the rim of a crater that enclosed acre after acre of glass and dust. A circular bastion armed with immense turreted guns glowered in the center, shining pinprick spotlights across fields of crude shelters, faint scratchings of agriculture, and the remnants of yet more monsters. Its walls were higher than the original skyline, and had indeed replaced it.

Providence.

What was left of Providence.

No passage. No permissions. Barrio Libertad ruled there now, an implacable fortress-state that offered only garbled snippets of travelers' warnings in halting Spanish and vague rumors of either concentration camps or some sort of paradise lurking just beyond or just within its walls. No wizard that had gone there had ever returned. Magister Hahn had blacklisted it the moment she was elected.

Istvan hadn't been able to return to his own battlefields for over thirty years. He didn't even know if they still existed.

His chains caught at wrists and neck. Too close to the border. He rolled away before discomfort became pain, banking southwards into the start of a half-hearted search pattern.

Oh, it wasn't right. Such an important place, and not even a proper dedication. Nothing offered, nothing taken, nothing solid to bury.

Barrio Libertad could have at least allowed the collection of some dust.

CHAPTER FIVE

The next morning, Edmund found a pie box in his fridge. The pie inside was half-eaten. It had a note attached to it, written by someone named Lucy who claimed to know where the Bernault devices would be.

At noon, look for me. I know your booth.

Edmund stared at the note for a long while. He felt like he'd read it before. He couldn't remember eating the pie.

It had been at Charlie's, hadn't it?

He never had visitors. Certainly not female visitors. Not since...

Edmund closed his eyes, wishing his head would stop buzzing. Then he put the note on the table, put the pie back in the fridge, and went to go get dressed.

He'd have to spend some time. No way around it. Couldn't be seen in public with a hangover, especially not on a day like this.

A Good While did it: hours of recovery slipped stealthily into the gap between nine and nine-thirty. Real hours, experienced like any others. Stolen hours, put to the kind of use he'd never considered when he first started. It wasn't right, was it, using part of someone else's life just to feel better after a night out?

At least it didn't make the process of recovery any less miserable.

Once he could think again, he made and finished breakfast, washed the dishes, left Beldam more food and water, tucked the note from "Lucy" in his pocket, and opened his door.

The remaining inhabited homes of New Haven wound along cobbled streets to the seashore, power lines strung in zig-zags from roof to roof. Boats bobbed in the harbor. A pagoda perched on the bluffs above, painted scarlet.

It wasn't raining. Not here.

Edmund nodded and closed the door again. Then, a moment of concentration, the snap of metal on metal – and he was on the bluffs, looking down at the rolling waves of the Atlantic. The pagoda reared against the rising sun. Wiring strung from below ran up and through one of its windows.

Lilies grew around it, escapees from flower beds. Edmund picked one. He tipped his hat at the nearest window.

Then...

He took a breath. Had to do it.

A snap–

It was raining. It wasn't even a real, earnest rain: it was a misted drizzle, grey water dribbling sullenly from grey skies, pooling in grey puddles that reflected the few mourners who had come to pay their respects. Some held umbrellas to ward off the weather; the rest simply endured it. Most of them were human. They wandered across the rubble, small crowds that huddled and spoke in hushed whispers, glancing at him, pointing, and then doing their best to pretend that he wasn't there.

He knew that a lot of people blamed wizards in general for everything. He also knew that very few of them would be willing to make a point of it to his face. Not to the wizard-general. Not to the Hour Thief.

He was one of the "good ones" ... but still not one to approach off-hand.

Istvan leaned against the memorial inscription, waiting for him. "You are directly on time," he said. The barbed wire around his feet looped loose and bright: he was in a better mood again, like any ghost surrounded by grave markers.

"A wizard is never late, nor is he early," Edmund automatically replied. He stepped to the inscription, adjusted his hat, and touched it.

In Commemoration, it said. *June 29, 2013*.

That was all. The end of the Wizard War. Nothing about Shokat Anoushak. Nothing about her sudden defeat at the hands of Magister Hahn. Nothing about transformed beasts or torn skies or streets coming to life to choke those who walked on them.

The memorial itself was enough.

Edmund lifted his fingers from the letters. Pressed in steel, they were a scratched footnote on a talon forty feet high. It arced over his head, serrated in scalloped and smoky glass. It joined a toe, a foot, a stout foreleg, a torso that had crushed twelve blocks when it fell, a skull that lay blown apart by far too great a sacrifice over the rerouted Hudson Canal. Craters peppered concrete-scaled hide, sections of exposed ribcage braced like the frame of a ship and dripping with elevator cables, electrical wire, and utility lines. Its rearmost sets of limbs and most of its tail weren't visible, sunk into bedrock. A crest of steel bridge towers and sleek white windmills jutted skyward from its broad back. If cities could be raised again after death, this was it.

The names of the lost covered its surfaces like so much graffiti.

No state or government had decided that this should be the place for a memorial. It had just happened, in aggregate, one name added after another until there was nowhere else logical to put them. No one was even sure who had carved the inscription.

"Let's go find Grace," Edmund said.

Istvan nodded. He swung into his usual place on Edmund's left, setting a hand on his shoulder. "I am sorry for last night," he said quietly. "I didn't mean to set you off like that."

Edmund drew his cape closer. "Don't worry about it."

"I'm glad that you came."

"I made a promise, Istvan. Wouldn't miss it."

Flattened rubble crunched beneath his shoes. A surviving bridge lay over the canal, a delicate covered thing of latticed wood with shrapnel holes punched through its roof. The water below it ran mostly clear. A broken trail to the east still hadn't been rebuilt. Above it all towered the beast, rough sides quiet, windmills turning lazily in the winds.

A slow procession wound its way up a set of salvaged fire escapes. Edmund and Istvan joined it, climbing, people retreating from them before and behind.

Edmund concentrated on the railings. On not slipping. The Hour Thief was the only wizard more celebrated than feared... but he was still a wizard. Still so rarely seen in the public eye that no one quite knew what to do with him.

"It's mostly me," muttered Istvan.

Edmund shrugged. Istvan was the one who had

pushed him into this, years ago, insisting that it would help. Istvan was the one who had noticed, after some months, that someone had chiseled "The Hour Thief" next to Grace's name, and insisted on seeing the mistake corrected. The whole fiasco had only reinforced the popular notion that he and Istvan were somehow connected, that the Hour Thief's powers included the summoning and control of vicious spirits, that a dread pact between himself and Death was responsible for his supernatural speed and near-invincibility.

Not true, but not too far from it.

Edmund checked his pocket watch. It was a quarter to eleven.

Tomorrow, at noon...

Istvan peered over his shoulder. "Are you quite all right?"

Edmund put the watch away. "Fine." He stepped off onto the beast's neck, its "flesh" not giving way in the slightest. "I'm just fine."

Istvan looked at him oddly, but didn't say anything more.

Edmund adjusted his hat again and pressed on. He had his lily, everyone was still casting surreptitious glances at him, and it was better to get this over with. He'd made a promise.

The ruin of the beast's skull could have cupped a Little League game. The eerie whistling it made was just a trick of acoustics, the wind again. He swung down over exposed vertebrae, stone and iron, a mockery of anything living, and traced the ridge of its shattered eye socket.

There. Chiseled.

Grace Wu.

Come on, she'd said, *live a little. Indulge a girl before she dies a heroic death battling the forces of evil. Preferably punching a dragon. If there's magic now, are there dragons, Eddie?*

I can't say that I've ever met one, he'd said.

She'd flashed that cocksure smile. Punched his shoulder, twice, gently, because if she wanted she could crack concrete. Bend steel. *Well,* she'd said, *if you ever do, you have my number.*

He hadn't meant to fall in love with her. He'd known it wouldn't work out. He'd told her so. She was a Conduit, channeling power no wizard could hope to control through her very bones: neither one of them even knew how long she would live.

But Grace... Grace had been sharp in all the right ways and curved in all the right places, beautiful, brilliant, and brave. More than he was. More than anyone. Unforgettable.

That was the problem. That was what always happened if he didn't take the coward's way out.

He knelt, and set the lily down. Its petals drooped against yet more names: a sad, small, pathetic sort of offering, all told. Hollow.

She probably would have asked him what the hell he was doing. Why he'd vanished for so long. Why he would agree to come here, but go nowhere else except at night. Patrol and Charlie's. Guilt and oblivion.

Eddie, if you're going to do what you do, if there's really no way out of it – which I think is bullshit – you had better put that time to good use.

They'd gotten into more than one fight, near the end. He was trapped, and he had no interest in becoming a widower who-knew-how-many-times-over, and he'd told himself that this dalliance would be brief, and then...

So much he hadn't been able to say.

He still loved her.

"I'm trying," he said. "I promise I'm trying."

He patted his pocket, where the note was. Meeting at noon. If this Lucy woman was real, and sincere, and did know what she claimed to know, he could be back on the trail that day. A start. A fine new start.

A good use of time.

Istvan knelt beside him. "Are you certain you're all right?"

Edmund stared down at the lily a moment longer, then straightened. "I have someone to meet," he said.

Istvan started. "What?"

"At Charlie's. Noon. Her name's Lucy."

"What?"

Edmund held up his hands. "I don't know her and I've never seen her, but she makes a mean pie and left a note claiming to know something about the Bernault devices we lost."

The ghost looked aghast. "What?"

"I'm sorry. It said noon. Maybe we can come back later and–"

"Edmund, some woman you've never seen gave you a pie last night and you ate it?"

"Istvan, a pie isn't going to kill me."

The ghost stared at him. Then he advanced, loops of barbed wire following in rusted tangles. "What on Earth were you thinking?"

"Istvan–"

"A note? How could she have known anything about the devices? Why leave a pie? This is ridiculous! You're not really going to meet her, are you?"

Edmund tried to push the other man away, shivering at the proximity. "I'm not. The Hour Thief is."

The shadows of feathers flared. "That's hardly–"

"If she has information, I want to hear it. If it's a trap, it's a trap. I've been through worse."

Istvan snorted. "Oh, of course you have." He turned away, throwing his hands up. "You know, Edmund, I wouldn't dream of telling you what to do."

"No, you just go ahead and tell me," Edmund agreed. He checked his watch again. It was almost eleven. "Istvan, can I at least trust you to stay clear? She said to come alone, and I don't want to start this off on the wrong foot."

"Edmund–"

"Can I trust you?"

The ghost crossed his arms. He glanced at Grace's name, with the scratched-out mistake beside it, and then back to Edmund. He'd never liked her, and the feeling had been mutual, but he was what he was, and all of his favorite holidays involved the remembrance of one war or another. He seemed almost as disappointed as he was angry.

"So we're finished here, then?" he asked.

Edmund nodded. He'd come, he'd climbed, he'd commemorated. Grace wouldn't have wanted him to wallow in misery when there was a new lead to follow. "I think so," he said.

Istvan looked away again, sullenly. "This is all a bit sudden, isn't it?"

"I don't know what you're talking about."

The ghost sighed.

Edmund turned his pocket watch between his fingers, not looking back at the skull wall. Seven years of mourning. That was enough, wasn't it? That was enough for anyone.

Even Grace.

"I'll tell you how it goes," he said. "I'm sure it will be fine."

Istvan muttered something to the contrary in Hungarian. Edmund pretended he hadn't heard.

CHAPTER SIX

Edmund sat by himself in his usual corner at Charlie's. It wasn't quite noon, but he'd made sure to arrive early, clad in his full regalia. He'd taken the time to wash it again, just in case the gas smell lingered.

Unlike Istvan, he preferred to make a more pleasant first impression.

It was a quiet lunchtime. Pairs and loners straggled through the doors. A party of workmen took up most of the center tables, dirt-spattered and soaked through. A couple of women in what looked like East Command fatigues sat at the bar. Edmund wondered how they'd gotten through the spellscars, and what they were looking for this time. Most of the people left in Big East were there because they couldn't leave, they wanted something, or they were too stubborn for their own good. Anyone from outside – sent by the federal government, no less, or what was left of it – had to be wanting something.

The coat rack near the door dripped puddles on the floorboards. The same people as always strolled along in the windows outside, their streets whole and dry. Rain drummed on the roof.

Edmund checked his pocket watch. Noon, on the dot.

A woman stepped through the door. Raindrops rolled off her umbrella as she folded it. She was tall, fair-skinned, and dark-haired, and wearing a style of dress beneath her artfully unzipped coat that matched the era outside. Yellow. Plaid. It looked good on her; brought out her smile. She looked at his booth – directly at him – and started over, weaving between tables like she'd been there a hundred times before. Like she belonged there.

Lucy.

He stood, adopting a well-practiced smile of his own as she approached. His hat was already off, set on the seat near the wall, and booths didn't have chairs to pull out. "Good morning."

"And to you," she replied. She spoke with the lightest hint of a southern drawl, her words rich and measured. When he moved to help her with her coat and umbrella, she let him, like she'd been expecting it. "I'm glad you chose to meet me here. To meet me at all."

"My pleasure." He waited for her to slide into the seat opposite, then sat down again himself. "Would you like anything to drink?"

She shook her head. Her hair just brushed her shoulders. "Thank you," she said, "but not now."

"I'll take that rain check."

She smiled. "It's true, then, what they say."

He raised his eyebrows, a gesture only partly visible behind the mask. "Oh? What might that be?"

"That you are as charming as you are dangerous, of course." She leaned forward, crossing her arms on the table. "A real Man in Black. Like the ones in the movies. Do you fence, too?"

He leaned forward as well. "Would you like me to?"

"Not here." Her eyes were hazel. She glanced across

the pub – no one watching, or at least not openly watching – and then dropped her voice to a hushed contralto. "Can we be frank, Mr Templeton? I don't have much time to talk."

"Please, call me Edmund. All I know is your first name; the least I can do is return the favor."

"Edmund, then. I know where those Bernault devices are, and where the mercenaries are taking them. They're being transferred. Tomorrow."

He pulled his cape closer. There was a chill draft coming in from somewhere. "All twenty?"

"Yes."

"Where?"

Lucy reached below the table and withdrew a piece of paper, pushing it over to him. He unfolded it. *North City, Oxus Station, 3:15 pm*. The words were penned in the same hand, elegant in its simplicity.

He shook his head admiringly. "Where did you learn to write like this? No one writes like this anymore."

She shrugged. "Practice. I always thought it was important to make a good impression."

"You've certainly done that." He folded the note again and tucked it into his lapel pocket. He wasn't familiar with Oxus Station but it would be easy enough to find it. He had time.

Lucy drew back. Hesitated. She appraised him, eyes lingering on the Twelfth Hour pin, his smile, his sideburns. He knew the drill; he waited. Finally, she picked herself up. "I'm sorry, but... I should go."

He stepped out of the booth and straightened his cape in an eyeblink, offering her a hand out. "Thank you for your help."

She jumped at his sudden change in position, then smiled. Her dress really did accentuate the expression perfectly. "Of course." She took his hand.

He helped her up. "Where are you from?"

"I can't say." She glanced at the door. "It was dangerous to even come here."

He nodded. He could be a dangerous person to associate with, at times. "I understand."

She shrugged her coat back on, again acting as though his assistance were perfectly normal, and took up her still-damp umbrella. "I wish you the best of luck. I'll try to keep in touch."

"I'd like that."

"I would, too." She turned to go, but again, she hesitated. Looked him over. Mouthed something under her breath.

Edmund.

Like she was testing the name for herself. Like she couldn't quite believe it.

Then she started for the door, weaving from table to table, and again it struck him just how much in place she seemed. Charlie's was from another time, an era only he, Istvan, and very few others could remember. It had more in common with the people outside its windows than the people who frequented it. Patrons who liked it because it was old. Because it was exotic.

He watched the door swing shut behind her, the clouded sunlight from present-day 2020 flooding through with the whisper of rain. Just a moment – droplets rolling from an opened umbrella, the polished heel of her shoe – and then the latch caught and plunged the building wholly back to 1939. That dress. That walk. That smile.

She was timeless. She was like him.

He reached for his hat, and found it after a few tries.

Well, not exactly like him. He was the Hour Thief.

He lived on stolen time. Fled from an ever-increasing karmic debt he would never be able to repay and could never regret. Not now. Not ever. What he did was the blackest of magics, despite the best of intentions, and there was only one final destination he could look forward to meeting. One very convincing reason to keep doing exactly as he was doing.

Really all of forever was a hell of a long time, but he'd left himself no choice.

He patted Lucy's new note. It seemed he had a date tomorrow at 3:15 with twenty Bernault devices. Yellow-dress Lucy. He smiled to himself. Just because he was damned didn't mean he had to be dour.

The draft had intensified, somehow. It was coming from his right. The north. He looked over the bar but there didn't seem to be any holes. Something smelled odd, too, he realized; had the tear gas not come completely out after all?

Barbed wire coiled around the table leg.

"You," said Istvan, "are acting like a complete nitwit."

"'Would you like me to?'" Istvan repeated as they rounded the corner of Charlie's, the woodcut with Edmund's masked face on it swinging above their heads. Steam billowed from pipes that cut off at the building's edge, as though it had dropped itself in with razors and never left. "Edmund, you don't know a thing about fencing."

Edmund tipped his hat at a passing gaggle of well-dressed geese, droplets rolling from his goggles. "I never said I did."

"And you've given her your name after one meeting."

"She already knew it." He slipped his hands in his pockets and then added, with a sly smile, "I appreciate a lady who does her legwork, Istvan, and hers weren't half bad."

Istvan turned his scarring from a curious work crew perched on scaffolding the next block over, paused in the midst of patching holes in one of the hundreds of steam pipes. A tower rose behind them, white and curved and spouting great puffy clouds.

He didn't like this. Edmund had been a charmer as long as he'd known him – he had the looks for it – but after the death of Grace it had become perfunctory, another habit to add to a long list. No heart in it. The man certainly hadn't seen anyone since.

This time... oh, Istvan wished he could know for certain this time. His senses were keyed to violence and pain, not joy, love, and Christmas. Happiness and flat dispassion might as well have been the same. Lucy had come off as one or the other, blank as anything. And Edmund, well...

Istvan turned his wedding ring around and around a dead finger. "You realize she will now tell everyone that you can fence."

"It's a risk I'm willing to take," Edmund replied. He stopped at the edge of the sidewalk, pulled out his pocket watch, and vanished, reappearing in the same instant at the opposite side of the muddy street, beneath one of the larger pipes and an awning strung over it. Water streamed from its edge like a curtain.

Istvan slogged through the mud rather than startle everyone into running for cover. He hated rain. Ghost he might be, and it didn't hurt when it fell through him, precisely, but water didn't belong in one's lungs and it certainly wasn't supposed to slosh about one's ribs or spine or skull. Tangles of electrical wire hummed and hissed and spat above him: at least five people had been electrified by accident in the Generator District over the past month alone.

The work crew waved over a figure clad in an armored harness of garish reds and yellows, who leaned against a ladder and gazed at him through pilot's goggles. Istvan looked away. Had everyone come to watch?

Edmund picked up a tin can someone had discarded, looked it over, and shook water off it. "Now, we're not getting any drier. Preferences?"

Istvan shrugged.

Another flash of that watch–

The Twelfth Hour's roof post-Wizard War was a strange hybrid of stern Roman angles, modern glass, and exotic decadence, ringed about with elaborate carvings of stone nymphs entwined in sinful poses. Twenty stories high; miles away from where they had been. Sunlight glistened across pools and puddles, the storm just passed and rolling across the sky towards the west.

Edmund propped his elbows on a balcony wall. "Didn't I ask you to stay clear?"

"You did."

"Istvan, *alone* is a very simple word. It means 'with no one else around.' Not 'with no one else *visible* around.'"

"I'm well familiar with the word, Edmund, and I'm not about to apologize." Istvan drew up beside him and crossed his own arms on the stone. It was rough and pitted, even through the fabric of his uniform, and he knew that was because there was no fabric really there. No flesh to muddle relic sensation.

From here, the prow of the Magnolia Group's buried space vessel was just visible, a triangular slab of armor studded with spotlights and stenciled with what looked like primitive petroglyphs. They had helped the Twelfth Hour weather that first winter, trading produce from their hydroponic gardens in exchange for protection.

"I asked if I could trust you," Edmund muttered, setting the tin can on the wall.

Istvan sighed. "Edmund, please. Why would she ask you to come alone if she meant perfectly well?"

"To minimize her risk. Information like this is dangerous. It was a more than reasonable request."

"I don't like it."

"Noted." He was annoyed – had been annoyed since Istvan's appearance, a fine layer of citrine spice dusted across his usual mellowed resignation, itself a patina over fears old, dark, and oaken – but of course was trying not to show it. He turned around, leaning on the wall as he retrieved the note from his lapel pocket.

Istvan beat a fist on the stone. Soundless. How to explain it. How to put it in words. "Edmund, didn't she seem... strange to you?"

"She did leave that pie."

"That isn't what I meant. She was blank, Edmund. Wholly blank. Bland. Tasteless."

"Talk like that is why you never get a date."

Istvan turned around. "Edmund, I am bloody serious!"

The wizard sighed. He tucked the note back in his pocket. "Can we hold the debate until after we know whether or not Lucy's information checks out? Please?"

"What, until tomorrow? That's like waiting to see whether or not the tiger will eat you after you've been locked in its cage."

"Istvan, I'm the Hour Thief. I can teleport."

"That hardly–"

Edmund changed.

It was the small things: a shift of his stance, a straightening of his shoulders, the flash of that faint, pleasant smile. An act. That was all.

And yet he was suddenly more than himself. Immovable. Unkillable. A man who could strike in an eyeblink; who could stand, in waiting, forever. Every detail carried a deceptive weight, from the silver and dark enamel of his Twelfth Hour pin to the groomed sideburns that framed his lean, masked face. His eyes were visible but only just, a plain hazel behind tinted lenses. Thirty-five and never counting. He'd led armies, once, and still hadn't quite recovered.

A real Man in Black, the woman had called him. She had no idea.

Istvan turned back to the wall. The city. The pools of rain. The stone around him flickered with bullet holes, barbed wire tangling around his feet. Edmund was doing it again. That... *thing* he did. Istvan wished he knew whether or not it was conscious, and knew he could never ask. "You intend to go forward with this," he said.

"I see no reason not to," said Edmund, who was now only Edmund again.

There wasn't. Not when reduced to the facts. The Bernault devices had to be found one way or another, trap or not, and the ever-pragmatic Twelfth Hour had sent Edmund on suicide missions several dozen times over his long career. An acceptable risk.

As for Lucy... well, blankness could mean either impartiality or happiness, after all. She had done the job she wanted to do. Met the man she wanted to meet. The results were only to be expected. Edmund had that effect, when he wanted. He always had. Even after Grace Wu, when his heart wasn't in it.

"You're right," Istvan admitted, begrudgingly.

Edmund shrugged. "You don't have to come along."

"I bloody well will come along."

"I appreciate the help."

"You ought." Istvan turned back to the sprawl of Big East, the stone that scraped through his sleeves. A whole metropolis consumed in its worries, and he was so desensitized to it that it did no good at all.

Edmund picked up the tin can again. "Listen, Istvan, I've dealt with this kind of thing before, and like her or not, Lucy seemed genuine. Not everyone is a buffet of suffering. Tomorrow will go over just fine."

Istvan flicked a chip of stone off the wall and watched it tumble end over end to the root-cracked street twenty stories below. That's what they always said. Then someone cracked your codes, spotted your scouts, had artillery positioned where you weren't expecting, and invented armored cavalry.

"I've infirmary duty," he said. "You know where to find me once you've decided to embark on this nonsense."

Edmund nodded. "I was thinking we should arrive at Oxus early. Check the place over. Avoid any surprises."

Istvan grimaced. "Edmund, you know I—"

"Hate stakeouts, I know."

"And what will you be doing the rest of today, then?"

"I'm going to go home, draw some water, look for more canning jars, and then go on patrol." The wizard shrugged, not quite looking at him. "I'm sorry we didn't hang around the memorial, I really am, but I couldn't let this go. You saw her, Istvan. Who knows what else she might know? This could be the start of a good thing."

Istvan regarded him a moment. Smitten, he was, completely smitten, after a single meeting with a woman he knew nothing about.

Normally, at the memorial, they would have wandered a bit, contemplated, watched others go about their own remembrances, that sort of thing. They never talked about the battles themselves, of course – Edmund didn't want to remember and Istvan didn't remember terribly much – but simply being there for the day was enough.

Bloody Lucy. Bloody pie. What if it had been poisoned?

He swung himself up onto the wall. Edmund ducked the sudden snap of wings. Istvan wasn't sorry. "Tomorrow, then," he said, fleshless, the words swirling through poison. "You'd best tell the Magister, so I'm not dragged back to duty when you need me most." Edmund nodded. He'd taken a step backwards.

Istvan nodded, turned, and fell. A step into nothing, the Twelfth Hour's colonnade tilting dizzyingly around his head, the cracked streets and summer-green trees rushing up from below, wind whistling through the bullet holes in his uniform…

Edmund's presence flickered out. Gone. Vanished.

Istvan hadn't been able to detect Lucy's existence in the first place.

He pulled up just before he hit the pavement, spun over the green and its laborers, and shot off over the Atlantic at a velocity that would have torn him apart and shattered every window in a thousand-foot radius had he possessed any mass at all. New Haven fell away behind him, leaving only water. A lighthouse perched on a lonely rock. A container ship, part of its stern crushed.

The waves blurred together. Some memorial. Some anniversary.

Stakeout tomorrow. He hated stakeouts.

A tug at his ribcage. Istvan turned back.

CHAPTER SEVEN

"Oh, I bloody hate stakeouts."

"You've made that very clear. Six times."

"We've been here for hours."

"That's the idea."

Istvan leaned back against the cold metal of a roof beam, one leg swinging off the side. Oxus Station bustled below, as it had since that morning, forever ago. It was a great iron skeleton of a building, arched over the parallel lines of a river and one of the only unbroken stretches of train tracks left in Big East. Outside lay a displaced neighborhood of dusty alleys, sky-blue doors, and steel minarets. The ocean hadn't reached so far inland before, but the river led to it now, and postwar commerce, ever-inventive, had taken quick advantage.

A marketplace had sprung up in place of passenger annexes. Hopeful scavengers crouched over blankets spread with matches, batteries, knives, produce of uncertain quality, cans of propane, soap, underwear, and trinkets that were most assuredly magical or would protect someone from it. Chickens scratched in makeshift pens. A woman led a cow before a shouting crowd. Groups of armed guards stood at the entrances: Edmund had explained the situation, and they had reluctantly agreed to help keep watch. He was, after all, the Hour Thief, and it wasn't wise to refuse a wizard's request... especially when he had his "chained spirit" with him.

Hours and hours. The Triskelion mercenaries were due to arrive soon, yes – if they arrived at all – but Istvan had finished three rather complex embroidered floral embellishments in a single sitting and while the work did keep his hands busy, there was no danger to it. No excitement. He couldn't even jab himself with the needle.

A flotilla of fishing boats had come through in the early morning, and a barge carrying coal later on, but neither they nor the one train that had rattled past had carried mercenaries or incriminating crates. "Edmund," Istvan sighed, "this Lucy woman never even told you how she learned of this rendezvous in the first place."

Edmund crouched further along the same beam, watching the rush and clamor of a train being unloaded. He didn't turn his head. "Istvan, we've been over this."

"Don't you think it's too convenient? No one simply knows things about two dozen superweapons loaded on trains."

"After last time, I'm willing to risk a little convenience."

"But what if she's working with the mercenaries? Or with this 'Cameraman' the collector's gang were going on about? One meeting isn't enough to gauge motive."

"We've been over this," came the stubborn reply.

Istvan picked up his embroidery again and stitched in what might have been either a seed or a grenade. He wasn't sure. It didn't matter. Edmund still didn't seem nearly as depressed as usual for this time of year, which wasn't right, but... but how on Earth was Istvan supposed to point that out? *You know, Edmund, you seem happy. Is something the matter?*

Something chimed, muffled and tinny.

Istvan paused. "Edmund, was that...?"

Edmund cursed below his breath and fished the device responsible out of his other jacket pocket. It was roughly the same size and shape as a pack of cards and combined the services of a clock, a calculator, a telephone, a radio, a camera, a film projector, a phonograph, a library, a dedicated staff of field researchers, an electric facsimile of the Delphic oracle, and a flashlight, but it was easier to call it a telephone. "Hello," he said, still watching the station, "you've reached Edmund Templeton." A pause. "Yes, Janet, I am aware that this is my personal number. What's the word?"

"Miss Justice?" Istvan asked.

Edmund waved a hand at him. "You don't say," he said. "Thanks for keeping an eye out."

Istvan frowned. Had Edmund asked her to watch for the mercenaries, as well? Could she corroborate their position through the station latticework?

"Yes," Edmund said. He switched the phone to his other ear. "Yes, that would be wise."

Istvan shook his head and let his attention drift. The crowds below tasted of annoyance and discomfort, and not a little nervousness, but that was only to be expected for travelers so far from home and in so harsh a country. The spellscars weren't far off. Nervousness alone did not a weapons-smuggling mercenary make.

Oh, what was keeping them?

"Don't worry," said Edmund, "I have time. Whatever works best for you."

A lorry appeared. It was a long, covered, military-type vehicle, belching black fumes, pulling in as close to the train as the crowds would allow it. Plenty of cargo space.

The driver wasn't shutting off the engine.

Nervousness and fear, tempered by professional calm...

Istvan set his embroidery aside. "Edmund..."

The wizard followed his gaze. "Sorry to cut you off, but something's come up. I'll call you back." He hung up, however that was done, and replaced the telephone with his pocket watch, crouching low on the beam. "Right," he said. He adjusted his goggles.

"Just as planned?"

"I hope so." Edmund touched the silver pin on his lapel. "Be careful. There are a lot of people down there, and some of them probably won't hear me."

Istvan fought a grin. It was his job to draw fire away from the crowds, to encourage an evacuation, to capture a mercenary if possible. Oh, the screaming, the running, the uncoordinated panic... he shouldn't have been anticipating it so, but he was. Gunfire in the market-place: as good a reason to flee as any!

Of course, if a Bernault device or twenty went off, no amount of running would save anyone.

A trio of familiar figures stepped off the train. Triskelion mercenaries. Caped, spiked, armored in gold and crimson. One man carried a sabre. The others, rifles. All peered about the station with an air of suspicious professionalism, lights flicking behind dark visors. A crate rolled behind them, pulled on broad and silent wheels.

Istvan twirled his trench knife between his fingers, a motion unnaturally fluid for such a heavy blade. It was solid, unlike the rest of him, and if anything perhaps somewhat more than real: a relic just as bright and deadly as it had always been, fished from bloody snow long ago. It wasn't designed for throwing, but he could hit a man in the eye at twenty paces with it.

Ambush. He loved a good ambush.

His wrists tingled: a reminder of chains, and a warning. No unsanctioned killing. Not anymore.

He looked to Edmund.

The wizard drew a deep breath, fears rippling like red wine. "OK," he said. He smiled that faint, transformative smile. "It's our time."

Istvan winced.

The Hour Thief was already gone.

Edmund appeared atop the truck. "I don't suppose you have time to spare for me?"

The mercenaries whirled, bringing up sabers and reaching for grenades and readying strange rifles. On the attack. Implied affirmative. If they had time to kill him, they had time to spare for him, and that truth guided more than bullets his way.

"Thank you," he said.

They fired at him. He ducked – just in time – and teleported again, reappearing behind the nearest man, sweeping his legs out from under him, and knocking the rifle out of the hands of his companion before either of them rediscovered where the Hour Thief had gone. The other rifle thundered. Sparks. Smoke. More than enough, but far too late: Edmund had all the time in the world, several moments of it stolen from the rifle's owner, and it simply wasn't his time to die.

A thrown gas grenade spun towards him. He caught it and hurled it into the back of the truck. Once was enough: they weren't catching him out with that trick again.

The toppled mercenary hit the floor with a rolling clatter.

A yell went up: marketgoers, scavengers, passengers, station-workers, entire families diving behind anything that looked solid, news rippling across the crowd with the crack of the gunshots. No more than a few moments, for them. Grace had argued that his magic might have something in common with special relativity, but like anything magical it was best not to think about the particulars. The Hour Thief simply had time. More time than anyone else.

That didn't mean he couldn't share it. He had more than enough in reserve, still, and could afford to give a little to a few hundred bystanders without worry. Just enough time doled out to, say, dodge a stray gunshot.

Edmund teleported atop the train, cupping his hands around his mouth. "Everyone unarmed take time to get away from this fight!"

Heads turned. Some of the scavengers tried to pick up their wares.

A skeletal apparition dropped from above. It unfurled an eighteen-foot wingspan.

"Run while you have a chance," Istvan shouted, which was a particularly unfortunate thing to say with his accent.

Edmund hoped no one would get trampled.

He dodged another volley of gunfire and teleported next to the crate, spending a moment to examine it. A hundred pounds, maybe. Not small enough for one man to pick up comfortably but light enough for two to manage. It looked like wood, but there were no nails, no gaps, and no seams visible aside from what delineated a lid. The cart carrying it rode on thick shock-absorbent springs.

A sabre slashed at where he'd just been.

No more use of the rifles. That was good.

"That's the spirit," he said.

The mercenary backpedaled.

A rush of cold and wire and tattered feathers hurtled over Edmund's shoulder like a missile. Istvan was forbidden to kill without order, but he had a way of cutting through idiot bravado that he hadn't learned in his surgical training.

"That's the spirit," Edmund chuckled to himself, sheltering behind the crate. He rubbed a thumb across the open face of his pocket watch, crouching as low as he could. Just a moment longer to adjust for the odd cargo–

He snapped his watch.

A flock of paper cranes startled into flight. Wind tugged at his cape. He squinted against the afternoon sun. He was on the station roof, in a flattened area he'd scouted beforehand. The crate was there, too, safely beside him. Cart and all. He propped a brick beneath one of the wheels. So far, so good.

Another snap–

Fire poured into his lungs. He coughed, tried to draw a fresh breath, and choked on it, panic rising in his throat. Couldn't breathe. Couldn't breathe. Grenade. Tear gas. They'd gotten one off after all.

He fled into clearer air, almost tripping over his cape, reminding himself that the floor couldn't be tilting beneath him because Oxus Station was on solid ground. Only a gas grenade. Only a gas grenade. No water anywhere. He was the Hour Thief. He didn't have time for this. "Istvan!"

The clash of metal on metal rang through the mists. A distant booming thudded in his chest. Artillery, or at least the memory of it. The region where the crate had been, from the truck to the train, was a haze of white and sickly yellow-green. "Edmund!" laughed Istvan. It was a laugh Edmund recognized, with a shrill, off-kilter edge to it. Not a good sign, if this went on much longer. "They've got another bloody box, wouldn't you know it?"

Edmund wiped at his nose. "What?"

The engine beside him roared. The truck lurched forward. He twisted out of the way... and then heard the crash. Like wood splintering. Glass striking concrete. The bitter taste of tear gas in his throat and on his tongue went cold.

Glowing globes of blue flared within the fog.

Oh, hell.

Edmund gasped in a breath and dove for them. Four of them. Rolling in separate directions. Golden armor brushed past him, spiked shoulders just missing his face. His hat fell off. Heavy boots clomped past. Barked orders in the mists, muffled and foreign. A visor that glittered red. Wings rustled around him, a dry scraping of bone on bone, a call he couldn't make out. The gas stung his nostrils, burned his skin....

...and then he had all four Bernault devices in hand, wrapped in his cape, glowing. No sound. Ice to the touch. Brighter... and brighter...

Anywhere better than here.

He teleported straight up.

Ice crackled across his goggles. Air rushed out of his lungs. He dropped more than threw the devices, triggering the return teleport more out of instinct than conscious thought.

Concrete hit him in the back. Then the detonation of four smuggled superweapons hit the concrete.

He opened his eyes and uncovered his face only after the glass stopped falling.

A skeleton in an ancient uniform was leaning over

him, translucent, vulture's wings folded like old letters. "Well," it cackled, "that was exciting, wasn't it?"

Edmund covered the yelp with a cough. Istvan. Just Istvan.

The ghost reached for him, steadying a bloody hand on his shoulder, and the hammering of his heart slowed to something manageable. Pain and terror, drawn off and drained – as Istvan claimed – like wine.

"Right," Edmund croaked. The roof looked to be in one piece. That was good. The glass crunched as he sat up. "What happened?"

Istvan let him go with a chuckle. "Oh, it was a dreadful shock, but no major casualties." He waved at the few visible spectators just emerging from behind benches and pillars, then hooked a thumb in his belt. "Where did you send those devices, anyhow? Outer space?"

"Maybe."

"Oh, and the mercenaries are gone, of course. I do wish we could follow that teleport of theirs."

"Would be nice."

"You know," Istvan continued, twirling his knife in that way he did when he was feeling just a bit too cheerful, "it was odd. I couldn't reach through their armor. I tried, believe me, but it was solid as anything. Do you suppose the Cameraman is responsible for that, too?"Edmund coughed again. He covered his mouth and realized that his nose was bleeding. A fair price to pay. "Maybe. The crate?"

"The crate?"

"The one on the roof? With... I don't know, sixteen Bernault devices in it?"

Istvan tilted his head, somehow managing to look embarrassed without flesh. "Oh," he said. "I hadn't checked." He leapt into the air, tattered wings scattering dead feathers, circled once – and arrowed straight through solid iron.

Edmund looked for his hat, trying to will his hands to stop shaking. The station was a shambles, broken glass littering every surface, but still whole. Chickens squalled in their cages. The low murmur of voices babbled from sheltering booths and columns. OK. Everyone was OK. He wasn't the only one left and nothing was sinking. The truck was still running. Someone, thought Edmund, should probably shut it off. Clouds of tear gas still hung nearby, rolling back towards him after Istvan's departure. He edged away.

Not like the *Morrison*. Not like... not like any of that.

He shook out his goggles, just in case.

No, it's the Hour Thief, people were saying. *What happened? Did you see the ghost? The ghost was here, too. Man, he's just like the woodcut at Charlie's, isn't he?*

He smiled at that last one, faintly. The woman responsible flushed and looked away, nudging at a piece of glass with her foot. The one next to her continued to stare, as though trying to determine if he were real or not. They both wore the pressed white jumpsuits of the Magnolia Group. Blonde. Identical. Probably helping maintain the trains, if they were this far north.

He found his hat, and put it on. His hands were still trembling. He reminded himself that the shakes weren't the Hour Thief's problem: he hadn't been invented yet when the *Morrison* sank. He had come later. The Fifties. Once he was needed.

Just keep breathing, and the Hour Thief could take care of it. That's what he was there for.

An older couple came up to him, asking if he was all right.

Don't worry, the Hour Thief said, *I'm rarely wrong. We'll be out of here shortly. My thanks for your concern.*

What happened?

Some very dangerous men made some very poor choices.

"Twenty devices," reported an accented voice from above. Istvan dropped beside him, wings fluttering and folding, feathers trailing wire and poison. The gathering ring of spectators scattered, suddenly busy inspecting cuts and picking up dropped possessions. "I couldn't figure out how to open the box, of course. Someone else will have to do that."

Edmund shrugged, nodding politely to the couple as they retreated. "Better if it stays locked. You're sure there's twenty?"

"Positive."

Well, Lucy had been mostly right. Maybe those stray four had been intended for someone else. Two buyers? Was there a competitor to the Cameraman? Were the mercenaries skimming off the top?

"I checked over the rest of the station and it seems sound," Istvan continued, "Iron. Flexible. It probably handles the earthquakes the same way, great bloody skeleton of a structure." He grinned, a lopsided veneer of an expression over the flicker of bone. "Shame we couldn't test it on the one in Paris."

"Mm," Edmund agreed, trying not to feel ill at the reminder. Four Bernault devices. If even one had gone off at ground level...

He swallowed, tasting gas in his throat. They were fine. They were all fine.

Istvan peered at him, still flickering, still struggling to repress that strange grin. "Why don't you check the box for yourself? I'll explain what we're on about and make the rounds for wounded while you stay up there a bit, hm? It's still sunny out, you know. Does a man good."

Edmund shook his head. His palms were clammy, but he was wearing gloves. No one would know. "I'll talk. You do what you have to do."

"You're certain?"

"No, but I'm less dead."

Istvan burst out laughing. "A fair point!" He wiped a spectral tear from his eye, and then hooked a conspiratorial and too-celebratory arm around Edmund's shoulders. The fighting had definitely gotten to him. "Very well, you inform the masses that I'm here to help and then I shall help them. Oh, I knew there was a reason I kept you."

Edmund let out an easier breath. "Likewise."

CHAPTER EIGHT

The door was circular, half again as tall as he was, made of equal parts wood, steel, and ancient bone. Its lines were arrayed like a cross between a ship's wheel and a dreamcatcher. Carved sigils marked every spoke and intersection. It sat in one of the original halls, a space long and narrow, filled with warm lamplight and low conversation.

The Magister stood framed before it, the sleeves of her too-large jacket rumpled over crossed arms. The Twelfth Hour's double crescent and clock glittered at her neck, a symbol repeated no fewer than twelve times on the door. "Next time," she said, "try to dispense with the dramatic."

"I do try," Edmund replied. He pulled the recovered crate on its shock-dampening cart to a careful halt, trying to ignore the offended expressions of passersby. Gassed twice in one week. "I always try."

"Remarks the man in the cape," Istvan chuckled beside him. "Oh, Edmund, you're far more prone to the dramatic than you ever admit, even to your own bloody self."

Edmund sighed. The ghost had returned to his usual

appearance, though faint bloodstains still flickered across his sleeves, and he probably wouldn't be fully sober for another few hours. He had earlier announced the lack of fatal casualties with a wistful relief bordering on disappointment and hadn't stopped talking for more than a minute at a stretch since. "If it's all the same, I'd like to get these devices locked away before we discuss my fashion sense. It wasn't a flawless operation, I'll grant, but we did our best."

"A rallying cry for our age," Mercedes said dryly. "Sometimes, Mr Templeton, I wonder how you've lasted this long."

He shrugged. "Cowardice."

"I'm sure."

She turned. She wasn't a tall woman and had to reach up a bit to set her palm in a central depression, all but her missing ring finger splayed. The door shuddered. Then it rolled back into the wall, despite the total absence of anywhere for it to go, and halted in place with a stony crash. The hallway was too small for so many echoes.

Beyond lay total darkness.

Edmund reached for the cart's handle as Istvan started chattering again. No use offering an "after you" to Mercedes; he had very few rights where the high-security vault was concerned. Part of being on indefinite probation. Part of his penance for stealing a book from it, long ago.

He stepped over the threshold.

A moment of nausea. Vertigo. Of being stretched, or perhaps twisted, a sensation of watching eyes and cold water. He couldn't see or feel it but he held tight to the cart handle he knew he gripped – and then he was through, the world beyond resolving itself like a room that had just stopped spinning. A cave, hollowed out of what appeared to be porous rock, like sandstone or pumice.

It wasn't.

That the vault had been a prison once was just one of the many facts about it Edmund preferred to not dwell upon; that the walls were bone, hollowed out of a creature something like a toothed whale (if whales grew to the size of continents), was another. No one knew if it was alive, dead, or somewhere in the fuzzy in-between. The details of what exactly had been imprisoned were likewise uncertain. What was important was that it was a dimension all of its own, useful for locking away anything that needed locking away. Magister Jackson had won it in a game of cards in '34.

Istvan appeared beside him, swimming into view like a heat mirage. Mercedes followed.

The door, showing only the same pitch blackness as before, rolled shut behind them.

Edmund drew his cape closer. He'd worked with the place for decades, but that didn't make it any better.

Istvan patted a bone spur. "Oh, you strange, enormous horror. I can never tell if you're in pain or not." He sank a hand through the surface, drew it out again flayed, and then chuckled to himself. "Edmund, have I ever told you how it–"

"You have."

"Oh. You know, I could have sworn I–"

"Trust me, you have."

Mercedes gestured further into the vault's gaping interior. "Lead on, gentlemen. Unfortunately Thinkable Matters ought to do for now."

Edmund nodded. Istvan would have been stronger than him in life but a ghost couldn't pull a cart and Mercedes was the Magister, a woman, and only there to keep an eye on Jackson's "damn fool Templeton," so that naturally left him to do the heavy lifting. The wheels rolled across the pitted floor with a sullen crackling, like the vault resented their presence. Istvan fell into step beside him. Mercedes, shod in the sensible sort of shoes worn by all wizards who survived any length of time, padded watchfully behind.

"I am curious," she said. "Coincidence doesn't usually work in your favor, Mr Templeton."

"It wasn't a case of right place, right time," he agreed, levering the cart over a shallow rise. "We had help."

"Did you."

Istvan threw up a hand. "Some bloody woman who bribed him with a pie. She left a note at the pub, they met, they got on, she gave him another note, and so on. Absolutely appalling. You should have heard what he said to her!"

Edmund cut in before he could say anything more. "She calls herself Lucy. I'm not sure where she got the information, but I can't argue with the results. And," he added, "it was good pie."

"Your consummate negotiating skills at work, I'm sure," said Mercedes. "Have you—"

"Oh, you never knew him before all that nonsense with Grace Wu," Istvan interrupted. "It wasn't for show, then."

Edmund winced, feeling Mercedes' eyes boring into his back. "Istvan, please don't."

The ghost ignored him. "Women, all the time, hanging off him like limpets. This Lucy is only the latest of dozens, mark my words!" He laughed that strange laugh, a sound he couldn't duplicate in any other state. He scraped the blade of his knife along the wall. "I don't like her," he continued with sudden venom. "I don't like her at all. She's too happy and I don't like her accent and I don't like the way she—"

"Quiet," said Mercedes.

Istvan cut off with a pained wheeze.

"He can't help it," murmured Edmund.

Mercedes drew even with the cart, watching with sharp eyes as he levered it off a bone protrusion. "Have you made arrangements to identify her? I can't imagine the whereabouts of twenty Bernault devices to be common knowledge."

Edmund edged the errant wheel back on course. "I haven't just yet. I wanted to make sure that her information was good."

"It seems it is."

"So it seems, though I'd like to ask her about the four extra devices we found. If Triskelion's gone into the conquering business, I'd rather know before they start."

"When are you meeting with her next?"

"I'm not sure."

They walked, freed wheels crackling in the newfound silence. Bone curved before and behind them, hollowed out by chisels and eons of slow weathering, the wind rippling its surface smooth. On every shelf lay the forbidden. A wooden mask, its mouth forming slow, silent words. The powerful scent of flowers and camphor drifting from an empty painting. A dowel of dark stone, hovering inches above its identifying card: *Hovering Dowel, IC Sanctuary 4, March 11, 2016.*

Every five minutes thudded a distant stroke, unless someone began listening for it.

Edmund paused – he shouldn't have, but he did – at a length of white silk, yellowed with age. The Sanskrit painted upon it still trembled with remnant power. Blood speckled one silken corner.

"Do you have any guesses on the matter?" asked Mercedes.

He tugged at the cart, pulling away. An affair fifty years past and more. "I'm hesitant to assume anything until I know more about her."

"Then you assume this 'Lucy' will make another appearance."

He shrugged, somehow wishing the Magister hadn't made the name sound like an alias. Lucy had seemed genuine, she really had. She'd been something special. He was hard-pressed to figure out how, exactly, but that could wait until he saw her again.

He was sure that he'd see her again. She knew where to find him after all.

"Have you checked the cabal rosters?" Mercedes asked.

Edmund shook his head. "She didn't strike me as the wizarding type, but that is an idea. I'll do that."

The Magister raised an eyebrow. "I ask only out of concern for a venerable heirloom. We can't have a mystery woman making off with the fine china."

He smiled. "Thank you, but I'll be fine. I'm the thief here, remember?"

Istvan gave another wheeze, which could have meant anything but was probably sarcastic.

A half hour more and they finally reached the proper set of shelving, which looked much like the rest of the vault save for the sign drilled into dry bone, hand-lettered in spidery script: Unfortunately Thinkable Matters, home to all manner of small, easily concealed, user-friendly doomsdays. Some of them came from the old Innumerable Citadel enclaves, the great magical power of the Dark Ages, Arabic calligraphy pressed into steel, brass, and stone.

It was their records, painstakingly copied during Edmund's one and only trip to the Middle East, that detailed all that the ancient world had known about Shokat Anoushak. She had been the greatest wizard of her time – perhaps ever – and the only successful immortal ever mentioned in any occult history. For eleven recorded centuries she lurked, page after page, empire after empire: the Achaemenid Persians, the Parthians, the Greeks, the Romans, the founding of both Christianity and Islam. She rode with her own cadre of Scythian warriors, and then with the Huns. She burned cities. She created monsters of every stripe ever imagined by Man. It was the Rashidun Caliphate who cast her down during the conquest of Iran in 651 AD, erasing her from common memory.

The Innumerable Citadel, and through it the foundations of all modern Western magic, was built on her works. She'd been brilliant, a genius like no other… but utterly, irredeemably mad. Pitiless. Uncaring as a storm.

Immortality: an example in action.

Istvan had accused Edmund of staring into the abyss, studying her. "Your bloody dust obsession," he'd called it. He was probably right.

Edmund drew the cart up next to the nearest open space, between a set of marbles and what looked like a rug that breathed shallowly in its shackles. The shelf was too high to slide the crate onto it and he didn't dare try to lift it on his own. Not with twenty Bernault devices inside. Teleportation was likewise out: wherever the vault was, it didn't take kindly to reinterpretations of its strange geometry. He tapped bone, wishing it didn't feel so wet when it didn't look it. "Excuse me, if you don't mind…?"

The shelf rumbled downwards, a section the width of the crate sagging into a new configuration.

"Thank you." He didn't know what he was talking to, but when in doubt, be polite. Where magic was concerned, there was no such thing as a rude wizard. Not for long.

A few careful minutes, and he had the crate fitted in place. The shelf eased itself back upwards.

He dusted his hands. "All right."

Mercedes set a notecard in front of it, lettered in her own blocky script. *Bernault Devices x20, Oxus Station, June 30, 2020.*

The vault was smaller on the way out. They reached the door within ten minutes, and had it closed behind them not long after that.

"Mercedes…" Edmund began.

"Go home," she said, retrieving her phone from her pocket. "You look like you've been dragged through a demolition site and smell like you've been protesting the regime. Think of the ladies."

He snorted. "I try not to."

She turned to Istvan, who was pacing before the door in silent, translucent frustration. "As for you, feel free to burn off the last of that energy and then I expect to see you on duty until further notice."

The specter drew to a stiff halt and saluted, then glanced pleadingly at Edmund.

Edmund sighed. "Mercedes, he can't work if he can't talk."

"He's managed before," she replied, but she did nod at him before flicking a finger across the screen of her phone. "Speak."

Istvan winced. "Thank you." The words emerged raw. "Doctor Czernin, I am willing to tolerate a great deal, but regardless of mental state you will not interrupt me again. Do you understand?"

He rubbed at his throat, as though shackles were fastened there. "Yes, Magister."

Edmund shook his head. The chains had come to seem a bit harsh over the last two decades, and it would have been nice if such measures weren't necessary, but... well, Istvan was what he was.

Sundered spirit. As much event as man. He, like Edmund's teleportation, was Conceptual: the magic of ideas, of perfect forms, of Plato's geometry, drawing from a perilous plane of being "above" the real world where fire became Flame. It was the less dangerous of the two types recognized in the West, but that didn't mean it was safe.

Edmund had first met him in Ukraine, in 1941, as part of the ten-man "777 Brigade." All young. All out to save Europe from evil.

Only Edmund had survived.

Sixty years later, word came in that the Devil's Doctor had been sighted in the Persian Gulf... and Magister Geronimo wanted Edmund to help catch him. To bind him. To step into the Conceptual realm with five steely-nerved specialists, and face the memory of a world war distilled and magnified into the archetypal War to End All Wars, death in a thousand forms, a maelstrom screaming around the skeletal remnants of a man that still thought of himself as human.

The chains drove a divide between ideas. They distanced man and event, forcing a calm like the eye of a hurricane. The man could be controlled. The War couldn't. It was a blessing that conventional reality was too imperfect for it to spill over into anything other than Istvan's shocking capacity for violence.

Edmund reached for his pocket watch. "You have my number if you need me," he said.

Mercedes waved a hand at him.

"I'll see you when I see you, I suppose," rasped Istvan, his accent lapsed back into that Dracula-like cadence he tried so hard to avoid. He tossed a rueful salute. "Enjoy your shower."

Edmund nodded. "I'm sure I will."

A snap, and he was home. Beldam regarded him lazily from the couch, not startled at all by his sudden appearance.

"Don't wrinkle your nose at me," he told her. "It wasn't my fault."

She sneezed.

Edmund hung up hat, cape, and goggles. They went by the front door, like they always had, and as he turned toward the kitchen he paused. There had been something new outside the front window.

He opened the door.

A white box sat atop a salvaged stool in the yard. Pinned to it was a note.

Inside it, for the second time in three days, was a perfect apple pie.

CHAPTER NINE

The infirmary was a madhouse. That was just how Istvan liked it. He'd been working for hours with hardly a pause, through the night and into the morning, a pale dynamo whirling at the heart of a human machine that converted suffering into survival.

Six patients. Six cases of inexplicable frostbite. Twelve broken bones. Eighteen lacerations caused by animal claws. Four lines of puncture wounds caused by animal teeth. One crushed spine. Ten attendants propelled by little more than their sense of duty and near-toxic concentrations of caffeine. Bright lights, blue gloves, shouted orders echoing from pillar to ornate pillar. The meeting hall had once been the place to launch campaigns, but now it was the place that received their bloody harvest.

Habit and expectation remained in full force: his immaterial form was soaked to the elbows in crimson. The intoxicating atmosphere of pain and terror was almost enough to stifle his own worry; to drown it beneath a downpour of good cheer.

Almost.

Edmund was more than capable, he knew that. The

man was a survivor. He had lived through a half-century
and more of the most dangerous tasks the Twelfth Hour
could set for him, and on top of that he was the very
same enigma that had driven Istvan to distraction for
years. The impossible soldier. The only one that had ever
gotten away. Meeting alone with a strange woman – at
his insistence, as the second note requested – shouldn't
have been worrying. If anything, it should have been a
sign of improvement. After a relapse so hellacious the
man had all but locked himself in his house for fourteen
months and refused to permit anyone living nearby....
well, if he wanted to see someone, so be it.

Edmund was entitled to do as he liked. It was none of
Istvan's business.

Istvan stepped back from the woman with the crushed
spine. "Careful with her, Torres. I did what I could, but I
can't restore feeling in her legs until that bloody frostbite
is dealt with. Keep her under sedation as long as you can
– if she wakes up, she'll wish she were dead, and I don't
want to risk another attempt at resuscitation."

The nurse nodded once, expression behind her mask
an even mixture of drawn and determined. "Dead to the
world until further notice, Doctor."

Gurney and occupant wheeled away. Istvan watched
them go. While being a ghost had its benefits – an
immaterial touch that negated the need for invasive
surgery, no threat of bacterial contamination, the ability
to shift blood and bone about with a precision only
modified possession could grant – the fact remained
that he couldn't support anything so heavy as a human
being himself, much less move one. Wounded men had
to be treated where they fell. Where shells, all too often,
continued to fall.

He took a deep breath. Unnecessary in some ways,

vital in others. Edmund would be fine. He could take care of himself.

Roberts stepped to his side. "Doctor, our first case is awake."

"First today, or first at all?"

"The very first."

Istvan wiped his hands on a cloth that hadn't been there before, then tossed it aside. It vanished. Oh, he hated frostbite. "Show me."

At least the poor man had stopped hyperventilating.

"I know what you might have heard, but I'm really not the malevolent sort," Istvan repeated. He had reined in his more terrifying aspect, but that only helped so much. "Negative, oh, yes, but I've never felt any particular urge to, ah... murder *every* living thing in sight, as you seem to think. I'm as intelligent as yourself and I can very well make decisions as to who my next target may be, thank you."

The man swallowed. He was still shaking, but that would cease in time.

Istvan patted his hand. Drawing off fear was a procedure rather like sucking venom from a wound – if venom were in fact wine – and the simple weakening of that particular emotion could work wonders. "Now, then, what was your name?"

"R- Ross." The man took a deep breath, staring over Istvan's shoulder at where Roberts waited. Solid, ordinary, living Roberts, parked like a kindly brick wall. "Ross Fillmore."

"Do you know where you are?"

"Yes. This is... this is the Twelfth Hour." He pointed at Roberts. "That's what he told me. He said I was brought in days ago. That I almost died."

Istvan chuckled. "Oh, hardly. You were in good hands."

Mr Fillmore peered up at him. He had brown eyes, darker than Edmund's hazel; his pupils were darting pinpoints of disbelief. "You're really a doctor? The... the Devil's Doctor?"

"I'm really the one who stopped two heart attacks while we thawed you out and ensured you didn't lose any of your higher faculties, yes."

"Oh." The texture of the man's emotions had shifted; now it was as though he couldn't decide between continued fear or embarrassment, and was doing his best with a whorled blend of both that wasn't at all unpleasant. "Thanks. I guess." He scrubbed his hands across his face. "Sorry, I don't think my brain's working at a hundred percent right now. Kind of woozy."

"That's normal," Roberts pitched in.

Istvan nodded. It was a good thing the nurses had seen fit to assemble a curtained partition around the bed; the overdone opulence of the greater infirmary may have burned out Mr Fillmore's exhausted synapses. Plain cloth was far easier on the eyes than inlaid chrome. "Do you remember what happened to you?" he asked.

Mr Fillmore stared down at the sheets. His skin was still blistered, but healing nicely.

Istvan drew off as much pain as he could. "Do you remember anything?"

"I was walking," the man finally said. He frowned. "Going home, I think. Near Cheerful Gardens. I'm not a New Haven man; I help maintain the Generator district. Patch pipes, keep an eye on the water collectors, you know. I was... I was passing the gardens, and..." Panic surged; Istvan clasped his hand tighter. "Claws. Out of nowhere. It just… It was a… a bear, or something. Huge and cold and… I think I fell on ice, but…" He shook his head, rubbing shaking fingers across the gashes ripped into his chest. "I don't know. I don't know what it was."

"A bear?" repeated Istvan. He looked to Roberts.

The nurse shrugged broad shoulders. "I checked with the perimeter and they said something could have gotten through during that dysentery outbreak. We're a long way from the spellscars, but that didn't stop the monsters before."

Istvan looked back to Mr Fillmore. "Do you remember what the bear looked like? What color was it?"

The man swallowed. "White. All white. With… with blue on." He hesitated, as though fearing ridicule, then added, "I think it had stripes. Blue stripes."

Istvan nodded, slowly. "A striped bear. One that freezes flesh by mere proximity." He didn't remember ever fighting a beast like that, but then again the creatures had come in dizzying variety during the Wizard War and there was no telling what the spellscars might produce next. It was a wonder the perimeter guard hadn't missed more of them over the years. "Tell me, Mr Fillmore, why do you think it–"

The curtain whisked open behind him.

Istvan turned. "Roberts, what are you…"

"Doctor Czernin, I'd like to see you in my office," said Magister Hahn. She eyed Mr Fillmore. "As soon as you're finished here."

Istvan exchanged an uncertain glance with Roberts. "Yes, Magister."

The curtain swung shut.

"That was the wizard president," said Mr Fillmore.

"Yes," said Istvan. "Yes, it was."

•••

Lucy knew French, Edmund discovered. She had a passable accent, but more importantly she got all the tenses right and didn't misuse the subjunctive. He knew fourteen languages himself, a course of study part hobby and part necessity (he couldn't take time if the target didn't know what he was asking), but French was a good place to start.

She turned down his offer of a drink for a second time, sat at the same booth as before – his booth, of course, there was no other place he could possibly invite her – and showed off the contours of her dress quite nicely. It was yellow again. Not the same pattern, but yellow. She liked yellow.

Again, he asked where she was from.

Again, she deflected the question. She was good at that. Almost as good as he was.

"What an unusual *boutonniere*," she said, nodding at the purple flowers on his lapel.

"It's thyme."

She laughed.

"Your information was good," he told her, and he meant to bring up something about Istvan's concerns, but this didn't seem like the time. Nothing had happened to his house yet, right? "I can't thank you enough."

"You're welcome," she said.

"Would you happen to know anything else? There were twenty-four devices in that shipment, not twenty. Who's behind this? What's the target?"

She looked around, as though she feared she might be followed. As though she feared someone – perhaps invisible – might be listening. "I don't know if I can say."

"You can say."

"How do you know?" she asked. "How do you know if it's safe?"

"It's all right," he replied, and for the first time in a long time it felt like it really was. "You can trust me."

She smiled, then. Her teeth were perfect. "How," she asked, "can I trust a man who wears a mask?"

Istvan stood, at attention, while Magister Hahn turned a pen between her fingers and stared at him. Through him. Finally, she set her pen on her desk. "Doctor Czernin."

"Yes, Magister."

"Has Mr Templeton gone to meet Lucy again?"

He frowned. "Yes, this morning."

"As I thought." She stood, pushing away the high-backed chair of her office and stepping around the desk towards one of the bookshelves. She stopped at the skull. She didn't touch it, but she did regard it for some time.

Istvan stayed where he was.

"Doctor Czernin," the Magister began again, "I want you to keep an eye on him. Follow him, if you have to. If he leaves Twelfth Hour territory, you will accompany him. If at any point it seems as though he's acting contrary to our interests, you will do whatever you must to ensure that our people aren't hurt."

"Pardon?" Istvan wasn't sure what he'd been expecting, but it wasn't this. Usually he was the one on the chopping block. He peered over the corner of his glasses, not turning his head. "Magister, he wouldn't do that. I don't understand what–"

She turned. "Mr Templeton has been a member of this organization longer than anyone else in our history, and there is a reason for that, Doctor Czernin. He isn't on indefinite probation for nothing. Magister Jackson didn't give up his life for nothing. Mr Templeton is our seniormost wizard precisely because he knows one of the subtlest dark magics that has ever bubbled up from nightmare." She strode nearer to him, leaving the skull on its shelf. "Yet when Shokat Anoushak returned with her armies and her war, you will note that the Twelfth Hour followed him to near-extinction without protest."

Istvan's jaw tightened. "Magister, those losses haunt him more than anyone. More than you can imagine."

"That hardly matters."

He faced her. He wasn't a giant of a man, but she barely reached his collarbone. "You forget, Magister, I put him back together. I was there, all that year when he wouldn't see anyone else. When he was terrified he would lose everyone else. When he wouldn't leave the house, when I had to prod him to eat or sleep or exercise, to do anything at all that wasn't sitting and staring, when he couldn't stand the dark, jumped at every drop of water, when he was drowning, Magister, every bloody night!" He realized he was shouting. He clasped his hands behind his back again. "I know, if anyone knows, that Edmund would never – never – do anything contrary to you or your people, not unless something was terribly wrong and he were sorely pressed."

"Qualifiers don't make for a very convincing 'never,' Doctor."

He held out his hands, intending to make some point or other, then stopped. He knew Edmund worried. Worried about his influence, his longevity, his sanity, the state of his soul. The man didn't talk about it. He did his level best to never think about it.

Some of those nights he had woken sweat-soaked and shaking. Shouting. Not of his shipmates and not of the battles, but of the enemy they'd faced. The one Edmund had studied so obsessively. The immortal, like him, who had struck the first blow of the Wizard War...

and shattered the world. Millions upon millions dead. Not even coastlines running where they had been.

"He wouldn't," Istvan repeated.

The Magister nodded, not in assent but in confirmation. "Your friend may not be as famously lethal as you are, Doctor, but he is a dangerous man. I can't have him compromised further. Watch him."

Istvan looked away. He rubbed at his wrists. "Yes, Magister."

"You are not to tell him of this conversation."

"I will not."

"Good." She returned to her desk, drawing close a stack of papers with odd diagrams drawn upon them. She always seemed to have those about. "You are dismissed, Doctor."

Istvan took a half-step backwards, preparation to turn about. *Gone to see Lucy*, she had asked. She was so suspicious of the woman's motives as well? Enough to worry that she might turn the Hour Thief himself against them? That was… rather more extreme than Istvan's own misgivings, wasn't it?

If Magister Hahn knew anything more, she wasn't saying. Typical wizard. Not even the rest of the Twelfth Hour knew what she'd done to end the Wizard War at Providence, and it seemed like that was a detail that perhaps ought to be recorded for posterity, if nothing else.

"Magister?" he asked.

"Hm?"

"Shall I search for him?"

She took up her pen. "Do whatever you think is prudent, Doctor."

"You do what you have to do," he said. "You don't think about it."

Lucy crossed her hands one over the other, pale fingers interlaced on dark wood. "You could have died, Edmund. There's no way of knowing for sure how soon a Bernault device will ignite after it's dropped."

He shrugged. "I had time."

"What does that mean?"

"It's language, Lucy. If your time isn't up, nothing can kill you. Would you believe me if I said I drowned in '45?"

She laughed an uncertain laugh. "Should I?"

"Believing is better than knowing in my business, Lucy. Magic holds all kinds of truths. Even ultimate truths, the kind men spend their lives chasing. There are books out there that can tell you how the universe really works, why we're here, what's the purpose of it all." He raised an eyebrow. He'd taken his goggles off. He couldn't believe how easy it was to talk to her. Tell her even about the *Morrison*, about how he'd been trapped below decks, underwater, for hours after those Kamikaze attacks, the only man aboard unable to die. It wouldn't hurt, somehow, if she asked. He hadn't felt this good in years. Ages. "I'll tell you, Lucy – there's a reason so many wizards go mad. Belief is much, much safer than truth."

"Then I'll believe you," she said. She drew a nail across the surface of the table. "And I'll hope that you aren't one of the mad ones."

"I try not to be," he said.

"Is that a kind of Conceptual magic, living so long?"

He shook his head. "I said there were two kinds, remember? Conceptual magic has to do with what is, the essence of things. We're talking about the magic that comes from elsewhere. The other kind."

"And what do you call that?"

He smiled. "'The other kind.'"

"The kind I probably shouldn't have asked about, then?"

"Bingo."

She searched his face, probably looking for lines that weren't there. They always did. "It must be strange," she said. "Knowing all of these secrets but knowing that you can't really know them. Knowing there's answers and never asking. Deliberately staying in the dark. What kind of life is that?" A smile, small and maybe a bit sad. "I'm sorry, you must see it differently."

"Don't be sorry."

"After everything that's happened, I... I don't know. I'm still not sure what to make of all of this. Of magic. I know some people blame the cabals for the Wizard War, but you seem so... normal. Are all wizards like you?"

Edmund chuckled. He didn't chuckle often. "Not all of them."

She leaned closer. Her eyes had flecks of green in them, like marble. "Only most?"

"Some."

"Wizardry favors the witty and wise?"

"That's right, and I see you know your Indo-European roots."

They were inches apart now. "Some," she breathed. "What makes you different?"

"For one, I know when a place isn't suited for a lady of your caliber–" and then he stood beside her, holding out a hand as he had the day before, smiling as he continued, "–and what to do about it."

She didn't jump this time, he noted. She learned fast. He'd already known she had nerve – approaching the Hour Thief with dangerous information about weapons of mass destruction required a measure of that – but speedy adaptation was something he could appreciate in a woman. Legs didn't hurt, either. She had great legs.

She laughed instead. "Do you?"

He helped her up. "I do."

He offered her an elbow and she took it without hesitation, like she'd been expecting it, like it was normal and not an antique habit to be puzzled at. They strolled out of Charlie's together, arm in arm. If the bartender on duty thought anything of it, he didn't say a word.

Edmund reached for his pocket watch as they stepped outside. "Would you care for a short walk?" he asked.

"With you? Not at all."

Some stealthy sleight-of-hand, a pocket watch retrieved, a snap –

– and they were ten miles distant, on the bluffs next to a red pagoda, overlooking a fishing village on the coast of the Atlantic. Wild lilies nodded in the wind.

"Beautiful day," he sighed. He gazed deliberately out at the horizon, the Black Building spiraling up into wispy clouds. "Don't you think so?"

This time, she jumped. He grinned to himself.

He'd specialized in teleportation for three reasons, even though everyone had told him to stay away from the discipline: it was convenient, it synergized very well with a magic that operated between moments, and he knew he couldn't kill himself by accident.

But there were fringe benefits. Whisked away. Just like magic.

"I hope you don't mind seafood," he continued, "The lobster catch has been–"

She grabbed at his face. His tie. Pulled him down, and…

…and then he couldn't remember. It must have been something he didn't want to remember. That happened sometimes, not wanting to remember.

He took his bearings. He was on the bluffs. He was sitting on a rock near the lilies. His tie was crooked.

A gorgeous woman sat beside him.

"You shouldn't have," she said. "I haven't been invited to a picnic in ages."

He blinked, feeling vaguely confused but not unpleasantly so. Lucy. Right. Time sure flew when you were having fun. "Well, I'm glad I had the right idea, then. You said you liked seafood, right?"

"I'm sitting next to the Hour Thief," she said. "The food barely matters."

"Nevertheless." He straightened his tie. Then he stood, and offered her a hand up. "Take some time to walk down to the house with me, will you?"

"Of course," she said.

CHAPTER TEN

The frostbitten patients were still recovering. Mr Fillmore, stable. A warning to the staff – he wouldn't be available for a short time, he would be out of contact – and then Istvan departed the Twelfth Hour on silent wings. It was starting to rain again, which was odd for July, but the weather had never been the same since the Wizard War.

Oh, he hated rain.

He circled the Twelfth Hour once, rolled over, and shot into a climb. The sun above the cloud deck was high in the sky, a hard brilliance blazing in a deep blue-black, marking a time just after noon. Lunch.

Edmund had probably taken Lucy to lunch.

Istvan tilted into another roll, and dove. Westward, some fifteen degrees north, following the trail of power lines strung in snarled tangles on poles mostly upright. One of the Generator district's many plumes of steam sped towards him and he plunged through and past it, sweeping low over where he knew Charlie's lay.

No Edmund. If Lucy were there, she was undetectable, but surely no one could be that blank. That untroubled. Not all the time.

Istvan swung around, covering a half-mile and more

with each wingbeat. Generator was one of the better-off regions, and Big East's medley of misery and terror was correspondingly thinner, mixed with the tang of ozone... but even then, Edmund's distinctive richness didn't stand out.

That left only a small scattering of other possibilities. Edmund was remarkable in many ways, but innovation wasn't one of them.

Istvan soared back eastward. Skimming past the pagoda on the hill was enough.

Edmund had gone home.

He'd gone home, and while Istvan couldn't make out any sign of Lucy, Edmund had no doubt taken her with him. He barely knew the woman! How could he... he'd never moved so quickly before, he would never...

He had standards, the idiot!

Istvan buzzed a trio of scuttling finned creatures on the beach. They squealed high-pitched gargling noises and dove back into the water. It didn't really make him feel better.

The Magister had suspicions. Serious suspicions. He had to look into it.

They were probably only there for lunch. Edmund had standards.

Istvan returned to the house, alighted on the roof, and swung down out of view of any of the windows. He crept around to the front door. He concentrated on not being there, on the expectation that if anyone glanced his way it was because they were peering beyond him. He was immaterial; there was nothing to see.

He set a hand on the dark wood of the door – nothing to see here, no one come to eavesdrop – and then stepped cautiously through it. Beldam the cat lay on the couch, tail switching. She turned green eyes on him as he approached.

He held a finger to his lips.

She hissed, jumped off the couch, and shot into the kitchen. Stupid animal.

"Oh, she's lovely," said a woman's voice. "Is she yours?"

"She is," Edmund confirmed. "That's Beldam."

"Beldam," repeated the woman. "Come here, Beldam."

Cat claws scrabbled on tile.

Istvan crossed the living room as quietly as he could and peeked around the dividing wall into the kitchen.

A picnic basket, its cover thrown back, sat on the kitchen table, displaying a large paper box, a pair of boiled eggs, and a plastic bag containing half a wheel of cheese. Lucy sat in a chair next to it, stroking a grumpy-looking Beldam with slim fingers and cooing at her.

Edmund stood at the counter, pouring either tea or cider into glass jars. His hat was off. His goggles were off. His smile was softer and more relaxed than Istvan had seen in years. His affect was like polished wood, steady, solid, and smoothly rippled as it always was, but the usual worries were diluted.

Istvan frowned. No, not diluted. Smothered. As though they were wrapped in a thin film he couldn't detect. Lucy, as before, was blank. Empty. If he hadn't been facing her, listening to her, he wouldn't have known she was there at all.

Edmund capped off the jars and set them in the basket. "That should be it." He swept the cover over them and picked the whole collection up with a smile. "You were saying about this wonderland of yours?"

"Oh," said Lucy, "Yes, it's very peaceful. No panics. No emergencies. No Bernault devices. You've had your fill of explosions, I can tell."

"All in the buffet line of duty," said Edmund. He took Lucy's hand. "Though I wouldn't say no to a few hours' respite."

She stood, dropping Beldam. "Only a few hours?"

"That's up to you, doll. How many would you like?"

Beldam looked at Istvan like this was all his fault and stalked under the table.

Istvan grimaced. He should have been encouraged, he knew – Edmund, after so long, honestly happy in company – but he wasn't. He could have been amused, but he wasn't that, either. Instead he felt physically ill.

"Edmund," he said.

The other man's smile vanished.

Lucy leaned closer to him, stroking his hand. "You never mentioned company."

"Wasn't worth mentioning," Edmund replied. "I've been told I'm company enough by a number of very authoritative sources." He regarded Istvan with the disdainful squint reserved for overeager servants or particularly noisy groups of starlings. "Remember what I said about 'alone,' Istvan? Have some respect for the lady, will you?"

Istvan clasped his hands behind his back. Visible now, flickering hints of wire and bone. Trembling, in anticipation of pain or at the remembrance of his orders or at something else, he didn't know. "I don't think you ought to be doing this," he said.

"What?"

"Seeing her."

Lucy let out a little gasp of indignation. Or what sounded like indignation. There was no flavor, no texture, none of the acidity of repressed anger or the sweet florals of shock or any of the verdant dryness of dislike or dismay. Nothing. The woman was hollow, like deadwood.

Istvan rushed forward before she could interrupt. "Edmund, there's something wrong. I told you before, but–"

Edmund hitched the picnic basket into the crook of his elbow. "Istvan, are you planning to hate every woman I ever meet?"

"No!" Istvan realized he'd brought his hands forward and that they had become fleshless claws. He folded resurgent wings back into smoke. "No," he repeated, thinking how stupid it was for a nonexistent heart to hammer. "It isn't that at all. She's... Edmund, she's blank! Empty! There's nothing to her and this entire business has been wholly unnatural!"

"Says the dead man walking."

Istvan flinched. "Edmund–"

"No, you listen to me. Lucy is the one who gave us the information that led to those Bernault devices. Remember that? Remember how she risked her own safety to meet me, is still taking a risk now, and did all that work to find my house in the first place? Remember that box we locked up, all those weapons that won't be hurting anyone else?"

"Edmund, please–"

"She's never done anything but try to help, and this is how you repay her? How you repay us?"

Edmund stepped forward, radiating threat. The man's presence was larger than his frame, and Istvan had never understood how he could do that. He wasn't conceptual, not like Istvan, wasn't really the Man in Black, not here – but God, he could come close. The strange muting of his aspect was more pronounced now, a coating of lace and cobwebs, like he'd been propped in an attic. That was wrong. He was acting all wrong. The Magister was right to be so worried.

Istvan realized he'd stopped breathing and then remembered that he didn't.

Lucy draped an arm over Edmund's shoulder, a mannequin in motion. "Why don't we just go?" she misted into his ear. "We shouldn't have to listen to this."

"You're right," said Edmund, "we shouldn't."

He reached for his pocket watch.

The kitchen window shattered.

Istvan whirled.

A figure in scarlet rocketed towards Edmund –

– who suddenly wasn't there, and Lucy wasn't, either, and they were both on the other side of the table, which had been tipped over while Istvan wasn't watching.

"Lucy," called Edmund, "take a moment to–"

An armored fist slammed into the table. The wood cracked. Lucy toppled. Edmund wasn't there. He spun from the attacker's right, kicking her legs out from under her.

It was a her, Istvan could see now, shorter than he was and built with the arrogant strength of a boxer. She wore an outlandish cowl and goggled mask, circled by a band of dull copper. Strange jointed contraptions ran the length of both arms, sheathing shoulder to fist in gleaming yellow. Straps secured armor plating on her chest and back, marked with a jagged line: an insignia Istvan didn't recognize.

She was almost as fast as Edmund.

It had been perhaps two seconds.

The woman's back hit the floor. Beldam zipped past Istvan into the living room. Lucy struggled from the wreckage of the table, kicking off her heels, catching up her dress. Istvan was looking straight at her but it was like watching a phantom, a mirage, an empty space that dissolved into the bedlam around it. It wasn't right.

He realized he was staring, uselessly, and drew his knife.

The attacker rolled back to her feet. Sparks skittered across the floor.

Edmund still held the picnic basket. "Now, Miss, if you'll spare a few moments, I'm sure we can iron this out."

"No deal," the woman said.

She lunged. Edmund dodged. The basket wasn't so lucky.

It exploded in a flash of lightning. Arcs leapt for the metal of the stove, the refrigerator, the kitchen knives. Istvan covered his eyes. Something large soared through the air past him, followed by a crash. More glass falling.

Lucy ran. The figure in scarlet shot past, overtaking her in a flash and knocking her against one of the bookshelves with a sizzle. Unconscious.

Istvan gaped. "What on Earth are you—"

"Don't touch her," came the response. Behind those orange goggles, the woman's eyes slanted in distinctly Oriental fashion.

He could taste her revulsion, and her scorn.

"What?"

She prodded at his bandolier. "Don't touch the nice lady."

He stiffened. Odd costume. Odd abilities. A method of operation uncannily and depressingly familiar. That exasperating facade of brazen confidence, and misplaced dislike to boot... oh, Istvan wasn't in the mood for this at all. He only endured Edmund's tomfoolery because most of his "costume" was, at the very least, actual clothing.

He prodded her back, finger sinking through armor

to bone. "She could be badly hurt and I, Miss Scarlet, am a doctor." He stepped through her – a slithering rush of shock and wet – and knelt beside Lucy. "I don't understand the need of you people to bloody concuss everyone!"

The woman whirled around. "No, seriously, don't–"

He ignored her. He pressed a hand to Lucy's forehead.

Something thundered in his chest. Liquid rushed through his arteries, hot as molten iron. Half-remembered impulses fired across his nerves like lightning. Fingers shorter than his own clutched at nothing, rictus-tight. Pain shot through his head, the great-grandmother of all migraines, a sensation distressing and exhilarating all at once. He struggled to focus unfamiliar eyes.

"What?" His voice emerged a high-pitched yelp. Motion accompanied the sound, a wet buzzing, a constriction in his chest.

What was he... He hadn't meant to –

He flailed too-thin arms, wire tangling around flesh that wasn't his. A scarlet blur pinned him down with a leaden elbow, grabbing at one of his wrists. Lucy's wrists. Shackles blazed at the edge of his vision. Dust coated the back of his throat. Suffocating pale strands wrapped themselves about his brainstem. Calming, soothing.... There was no need to worry. It was all part of the plan. No reason to panic. No reason to fight. Didn't he want happiness? Didn't he want peace? An end to suffering?

Lucy's eyes blinked. Peace? He clenched a fist on the floor, feeling a spate of desperate laughter bubble in his lungs. Peace? For him?

Peace, for the War to End All Wars! Oh, it was absurd... impossible... It was–

Perspective tilted. The playing field shifted. Real gave way to hyperreal. It was larger there, more evident – a creeping mass of comfort and suggestion, rippling with stolen memories. A creature, glassy and amorphous. A yawning emptiness of sorrow. It coiled within her, tendrils reaching without her, no more native to her many layers of being than he was. Fragments of Lucy's life sparkled within its inner substance: chasing a younger brother around a table in the kitchens, playing at dice on a long night lit by fire, pulling off a helmet once the seals locked and the air cleared, glimmers of a beautiful young woman with eyes of green. Memories that whispered, branches in autumn.

Istvan drew his knife. The Conceptual. That's where they were. The realm of ideas, the perfect geometry of Plato, the plane of existence on which he was bound. Before, he had never been threatened by any other Conceptual anything – he hadn't even known that it was an avenue of attack, much less a place – but now the full weight of what he was churned at the distant edge of his awareness, a horizon just beyond reach.

Chains weighed down his every movement.

They were parchment, only parchment, but inked with words as binding as iron. Arabic calligraphy. Edmund had scribed them. The only Great War Istvan could call on here was the barbed wire that snaked through his bones.

That didn't change the fact that whatever this glassy creature was, it didn't belong here.

He stabbed it. Its substance clung like glue.

"You scorn my offer?" The voice was low and smooth, female, strongly accented with Lucy's American drawl. It sounded surprised.

"Yes." He twisted the knife. No pain: evidently many-misted horrors that resided beyond the physical were acceptable targets for lethal force. Perhaps because he doubted it would be lethal. "Yes, I think I do."

"What a shame that you think that way," it said, its voice deepening with each word until it settled at a low tenor, bordering on baritone. Glowing moments seeped from its glassy flesh: an outmatched tug-of-war with the family dog, a furtive embrace in the trees by the park pond in winter, a sword flashing at his face. The sharp pain of the gashes; the pride in bearing them.

And then... the memory of a young man, slim and delicate, with a well-groomed mustache, grinning like a proud father as he stood with his head inside the scissored maw of an enormous reconstructed fossil fish.

Istvan froze.

How–

The creature chuckled. <When we meet again, Pista, I'm sure you'll reconsider.>

German. Perfect Viennese German.

It blew apart. Darkness rushed in to fill its place.

Istvan stumbled away. Fell back to what was merely real. Tore himself free of aching temples, of a heart that pounded like thunder, of ribs crushed by living weight, and backed up against the dead solidity of the coffee counter, breathing hard with lungs that didn't exist. "What in God's name was that?"

The woman in scarlet jerked away from Lucy's unconscious form. "I told you not to touch!"

Edmund appeared behind her, bits of egg and lobster shell speckling his suit jacket. "What the hell do you think you're–"

She spun around, hefted him by his collar with one hand, and slammed him into the wall. "Sorry, Eddie," she said. "I had to be sure you were the mark, or I'd have showed up earlier."

Istvan choked.

Eddie? *Eddie*? Only one person in recent memory had called the man that, and she was dead.

She was supposed to be dead.

"Grace?" whispered Edmund.

"Yeah." Static sparked across her harness. "We'll talk when you wake up."

She punched him.

CHAPTER ELEVEN

It was her. That speed, that lightning, that freakish strength... it all fit. No one but a Conduit could do that. Istvan had only ever met one.

Grace Wu.

She was sharp and raw and roiling, and her guilt held none of Edmund's mellowed nobility.

"You!" Istvan finally managed. He was still backed up against the bookshelf. He didn't want to get any closer and couldn't retreat. No. No, no. This wasn't... He couldn't...

She heaved Edmund's limp form over her shoulder. "Hello to you, too, Mengele."

Mad doctor – cruel doctor – is that a ghost, Eddie – why did you release something like that, Eddie – how can you be you friends with that thing, that horror, that monster –

He was airborne. "Don't you ever call me that!" he roared, razored and skeletal. He slashed a bloody hand through the air. "I am nothing like that!"

Again, Beldam fled.

"Yeah," replied Grace, "keep telling yourself that."

No widening of her eyes. No tremble in her voice. She was good at hiding it – she was very good, she always had been – but Istvan knew she feared him. She knew he knew, knew he couldn't be fooled, and yet she never let up on that bloody bravado of hers!

She adjusted her grip on Edmund, balancing him so his feet no longer dragged on the floor.

Istvan blocked her path, muddy feathers rustled over and across one another, barbed wire tangling and tearing their vanes. The pain of the Twelfth Hour's bindings dug into his chest, burned at his wrists: a warning which, for the first time in years, he wasn't certain he didn't need. "Where do you think you're taking him?" he hissed.

She sighed. "You have a problem with the couch?"

He glanced back at the living room. Bits of scorched food spattered the doors of the liquor cabinet. The front window was broken.

"I'll clear off any glass," said Grace. "Now, remember, don't touch our femme fatale, all right?" She jerked her head at Lucy. "Remember what happened when you touched her, Doc?"

He cringed. He glanced down at the strange woman, sprawled on the floor in her dress, abandoned where she had fallen. Even now, it was like she wasn't there. Empty. And to force a possession – to... to draw his very substance, like wire, like...

He brushed at his left cheek and jaw, where his dueling scars had been before their near-obliteration by burning, and almost expected his fingers to come away bloody.

"It gets worse," Grace said. "That was just a fragment. A shard. Trust me, it gets worse."

Istvan shuddered. "How is it that you can touch her, then?"

Grace tapped the copper band around her head. Then she brushed past him, still holding Edmund, and laid the man out on his own couch.

"You haven't said why," Istvan said.

No response. She propped Edmund's legs up on a pillow.

Something twisted in Istvan's chest. "Miss Wu, you're back from the bloody dead, and you haven't said why!"

Grace looked up. "Hey, can you make sure no one's come to investigate? I'm good, but I really don't want to deal with an army of smilers right now."

"Army of what?"

She waved at the window. "Torches. Pitchforks. Just go have a look, OK?"

Istvan stared at her. Stared at Grace bloody Wu, standing over Edmund in his own house with a broken window that she'd probably thrown him through.

Then he went to the front door and opened it.

A pair of children ran away, screaming, as children do. The curtains at the next house over whisked shut.

Istvan stepped out. He closed the door.

Pista, the creature had called him. A nickname. A reminder of happier days, cut short long ago. Oh, Pietro had been so proud to see that monster of a fish reassembled and put on display. A magnificent beast, in life. He'd drawn so many pictures of it.

Which do you think, Pista, the blue or the green?

The front steps were clear, and Istvan sat on them, propping his head in his hands and trying to catch the breath he no longer drew. No one had called him that in over a hundred and twenty years.

Edmund came to. Then he wished he hadn't. The wind was too cold, his back ached, and he was half-certain someone had sawed his head open and filled it with confetti. He touched nervous fingers to what felt like the seam. Metal. A thin band of it, all the way around his skull.

He stared up at the ceiling, wondering why there was wind if there was a ceiling there. Was that rain? It had been starting to rain when he'd left. Or arrived. Or... something. He couldn't remember. He and Lucy had been having fun, right? Time flew. Was she ever pretty. What had they...

A railroad spike hammered through one temple.

"Edmund?" someone was saying, over and over. "Edmund?"

Cold bit into his shoulder, a bone-deep numbness that he recognized. The pain receded. He groaned, sitting partway up. Couch. He was on the couch.

Lucy, nothing: this was one of those days, wasn't it? The bad days. Figments and dreams. He didn't feel hungover, exactly, but it was awfully close.

He massaged his face, regretting everything he'd never done. "How much?"

"None at all," said Istvan. There had always been a faint, indefinably distant quality to the specter's voice, but the effect was even more pronounced now. A pat on his shoulder. "None at all."

Edmund finally got his eyes to focus. They were in the living room, which correlated with vague memories of showing Lucy through the front door, and there was a pillow knocked onto the floor near his feet. His kitchen table lay flipped on its side. Burned things spattered across the ceiling and walls. A cold wind gusted in through the shattered panes of his front window. "The hell," he said.

Istvan crouched to his left, as he usually did – from that side, the ghost's scarring wasn't as visible. Before him, the limp form of Lucy in her yellow dress slumped against the upright radio, and before her...

He stared.

Grace.

He wasn't dead. Edmund knew that. There wasn't enough unimaginable torment for that, and anyway Istvan was right next to him and translucent as ever.

That left his list of possible explanations a solid blank.

Grace Wu. Sitting, arms propped on crossed legs, and watching him blink. She wore a new costume now: a real costume, armored, reinforced to keep her from accidentally shattering her own bones. Bright red. Bright yellow. She'd always liked bright colors. Her cowl was off. Her hair, black as her undersuit, was cut to just above her shoulders. Its strands crackled where the wind struck. Age and worry lines were just beginning to show around her eyes. She was still painfully beautiful.

"Grace?" he said.

"In the flesh, Eddie."

Edmund tried to concentrate. Deep breaths. His right hand crept down and held tight to his pocket watch. He was more calm than he ought to have been, he thought. Istvan's presence likely had something to do with that. Good old Istvan.

Grace. Hello, Grace. Long time. Looking good. How are you? Where have you been?

Why didn't you call?

His jaw ached, he realized. "Grace?"

"Yes?"

"Did you punch me?"

"A little."

He rubbed at it. That would bruise, then. That would bruise badly. "Oh."

Grace shrugged. "Had to hit hard reset to make sure you'd clean up right. Sorry."

Edmund touched the metal circlet around his head

again. This didn't feel real. It was like he was one step distant, watching himself talk. "Don't worry about it."

She stood. She held out a hand to him.

"I'm fine," he said. "I can get up myself."

"No, Eddie, I need the tiara back."

"Oh." He took the circlet off and handed it to her.

She set it back on her own head. "Thanks."

He got to his feet, waving off Istvan's attempted assistance. It was automatic, he knew, and appreciated, but leaning on a ghost was ill-advised at the best of times. Luckily, his own legs held him. "Can I... get you anything? Water? Tea?"

She shook her head. "Don't bother making a trip to the well for me. I can't believe you people seriously don't have running water yet."

"It's on the shortlist," he replied.

"I bet."

"There were some issues with flooding. Contamination. We're working on it. Even wizards know practical things, you know," he added, hoping he didn't sound too defensive. "Some of the oldest spells are actually instructions on how to preserve food and the like."

She raised an eyebrow at him. "Don't tell me you have a copy of *Ye Olde Magickal Art of Digging Privies*."

He smiled, despite himself. "Actually, the division between magic and mundane was much less strict in those days, and a few of the records do cite more humble sources. Not much on privies, but–"

"Awesome. Anything on hot showers?"

"The Romans had plumbing," he said, and then the situation caught up to him again. He looked at Lucy. She was breathing, shallowly. He wondered if he was actually going to throw up or if it just felt that way. "What did you do to her?"

"There's a creature," said Istvan, quietly. "Something possessing her."

"She's a smiler," said Grace.

Edmund frowned. "A what?"

"Smiler. She was controlled, Eddie. A puppet. Given a whole new personality. Lucy probably isn't even her name. She was speaking for something else, seeing for something else, this whole time, and never knew it." Grace brushed at her hair, her expression strange and distant. "Had you falling for it, too."

Edmund held up a hand, feeling dizzy. Too much at once. His window was broken and there was rain getting in. "Wait. Wait, say that again?"

"No," said Grace. "You don't know what you're dealing with. Neither one of you knows. You've been kept in the dark, Eddie, and if you want real answers, you'll have to come with me." She bent down, hefting the unconscious Lucy over one shoulder, and jutted her chin at Istvan. "The spook's optional."

Edmund rubbed at where the band had been, one corner of his brain marveling at how effortlessly she moved under the weight. Almost like she wasn't carrying anyone at all. Superpowers, she'd said, are kind of great. Not that I need them to be awesome.

He could agree with that. Though certain aspects of her Conduit abilities had made certain things... interesting.

They hadn't killed her, then. Not yet.

"Where?" he asked.

She turned. "Barrio Libertad."

He took a step backwards. "Barrio Libertad?"

"Yeah."

"The fortress-state? The one sitting in the ruins of Providence? *That* Barrio Libertad?"

"That's the one. Look, I know our reputation isn't

great, but trust me on this one."Edmund wavered, suddenly unsure if his legs were working after all. Grace never had adjusted to magic. Not his, not anyone's... but especially not his. Why not take up with a place utterly isolated from the rest of Big East? A place from which no one never returned? A place that the Magister had blacklisted the instant she'd been elected?

Providence. Ground zero. The place where Shokat Anoushak died in a storm of fire.

Was it something he'd done? Something he'd said? She jabbed a thumb at her chest. Lights flickered behind her goggles. "I'm Resistor Alpha, Eddie. State hero of *that* Barrio Libertad. I'm here for a reason, I promise. Come with me and I'll waive your wizard-ness for the authorities. Nothing to worry about."

Istvan drew closer to him, voice low. "There *was* a creature," he said. "I saw it. I fought it. It... it knows things it shouldn't. Your address, Edmund. The Bernault devices. If you're going with Miss Wu, I'm coming with you."

Edmund swallowed. "Istvan, you can't cross the border."

"I'm coming, irregardless."

"'Regardless,'" Edmund corrected him automatically. "And what do you mean? How?"Istvan looked away. Barbed wire looped around his boots in tangled circles, wound tight. "Providence isn't that large," he muttered. "I don't believe Barrio Libertad is far enough out of bounds to hurt too badly."

Edmund raised an eyebrow, wishing he felt more relieved at the other man's determination. If Istvan was willing to endure that kind of punishment to find out what was going on, well... that left Edmund little choice but to match it. Barrio Libertad. Providence. Last battlefield of the Wizard War. No place he'd ever wanted to see again, awash in rumors of horror and paradise.

Grace Wu, alive.

She was tugging the front door open already. "You coming or not?"

Edmund glanced to Istvan. "Is she…?"

The specter sighed, crossing his arms as he regarded her. If Edmund hadn't known him better – known how badly the scarring twisted his expressions – he would have sworn that was a scornful grimace. "It's her."

Edmund took a breath.

Seven years. Not a word. Not a sign.

He stood. "Hold up, Grace. Let me at least get something to put in the window."

No teleporting. No magic at all. Grace made that very clear: Barrio Libertad, and indeed all of Providence, was under interdiction. Given Shokat Anoushak's example during the Wizard War, it was a sensible precaution… but that didn't answer how it was done, or how means Grace insisted were non-magical could counter the impossible.

She didn't know, either.

"I'm not that kind of genius," she said. "You'll want to ring up the architect for that."

"Are you sure this will work?"

"I told you, only teleportation is permanently blocked and for the rest we've already made an exception just for you. You won't turn into a pile of dust, I promise."

Edmund sighed. Nothing for it. "I'm not a vampire, Grace."

He took them to the rim instead. Two jumps, one to Ganges Station and another to where Providence began, its heat-hazed wastes visible from the station roof, a broken sidewalk baked by the afternoon sun. The razed foundations of the city that once was still bore scars from the blast, parking lots replaced by rough patches of farmland. In the crater, its rim shadowed by the stripped and rusting hulk of a toppled monstrosity, there was only glass.

There was supposed to be only glass.

"Grace, this can't be right."

"Never said it was."

"No, Grace, this…"

Edmund closed his eyes, recalling armies. Tides of monsters that poured through a storm-torn twilight, skittering below hulks that crushed cities in their iron jaws: lions that breathed fire, winged serpents, toothed mockeries of tanks and helicopters, green lightning flashing through pools of oil. Shokat Anoushak herself wheeled on her razor-winged mount, sword and quiver at her belt, dozens of black braids streaming behind her in golden fastenings, arrows sowing reinforcements where they fell.

Run, she'd said.

Her eyes had been a bright, bright, sunken green, like buried emeralds. She wore the archaic regalia of a Scythian queen: a tapered headdress of cloth and feathers, a knee-length dress over pants and boots, heavy cloth worked in bold stripes of patterned color. Golden figures of fantastical beasts glittered about her neck and arms, molten and shifting. She rode like she'd never touched the ground. She spoke a language almost two thousand years dead.

Run, she'd said, *and keep running, as the jaws of fate and madness close on your throat. That's all that awaits you, immortal. That's all you can do.*

Run.

He opened his eyes again, blinking back gentle sunlight. "...how?"

It was a day more suited to spring than summer, warm and fragrant, just enough clouds floating across the sky to be picturesque. A flight of sparrows wheeled past as he watched. Before him stretched a sleepy, sprawling suburb, shaded by oaks, its winding streets marked by the mossy remnants of Colonial stone walls. Each flower-lined driveway held one automobile, similar makes and models as those that cruised outside Charlie's. Each freshly-painted home possessed its own decorative mailbox: some in the shapes of animals, others sporting American flags or sparkling pinwheels.

It was afternoon, but the birds were singing a dawn chorus, just like the one on his aunt's farm. He hadn't heard anything like that since.... well, they'd moved out there after the stock market crash. The Great Depression.

He'd been ten. Eleven, maybe.

Long time.

"How?" he repeated.

"We call it the Susurration," said Grace.

Edmund glanced at her. Lucy still dangled from her shoulders. Beside her rose a ramshackle steel pylon twice the height of a telephone pole and some three times as broad. Strange, twisted antennae jutted from its sides, humming a tone that set his teeth on edge. "What?" he asked. "The neighborhood?"

"The creature that makes you think you're seeing whatever you're seeing. The neighborhood, sure. Whatever you think is most pleasant and peaceful and inviting. The Susurration pulls it right out of your head, whether you want it to or not."

Edmund frowned. He looked back at the neighborhood with a more critical eye, noting the double row of pylons leading into it, the mirage of walls looming far off in the distance. A safe path, she'd said.

What about the glass? The rumored concentration camps? The warnings?

"Grace," he said, "what's really out there?"

A shrug. "Providence." She dropped her voice to a dry mutter. "And don't look now, Eddie, but I think your spook's a little spooked."

Edmund glanced over his shoulder. Istvan hung back, clutching his knife to his chest as he stared, whispering something over and over to himself in Hungarian.

<My God. My God.>

Grace cast the ghost a scornful look. "Wonder what it found for him."

Edmund held up a hand – *just a moment*, a stand-in for words he could no longer safely say without consideration – and turned back, a little spooked himself. He didn't like seeing Istvan nervous. That meant he was in the same general vicinity of something that made Istvan nervous. "Istvan? Are you all right? Is there a problem?"

<It's torn,> came the reply. German, a drawling Austrian dialect that had taken Edmund some time to get used to. Istvan knew he was better with German than Hungarian. <It's the *Ringstrasse* in Vienna, but there's rents in it, holes, like the entire city is nothing but a film or a sheet draped over a model, and Edmund...> The ghost shuddered. <...it's empty. This entire crater is empty.>

Grace propped a fist on her hip. "Care to translate from Nazi-ese?"

Istvan jerked, ripped from fear to fury in an instant. "I was never–!"

"He wasn't, and Grace, please don't," Edmund interrupted. He looked over the neighborhood again.

The perfect skies, the perfect streets. An old woman was watering her roses down there, peering up at him with no evident opinion – only a mild, incurious acknowledgment of his existence. He was very glad, now, that Istvan had come along. The worst horrors were the ones you couldn't see.

Susurration. A whisper, so quiet you barely knew it was there.

Grace was real, though, right? None of this was real but Grace. And Istvan.

And him, he supposed.

"Grace?" he asked, for confirmation, or maybe just to hear her say something in response. She turned, Lucy's blonde locks sweeping over her shoulder like a bullfighter's cape, and strode away. "No loitering, Eddie. If you're coming, you're coming."

He took a steadying breath. "How's the border treating you, Istvan? You'll manage?"

The ghost still clutched his knife. Tightly. "Yes. Go on. I'll follow you."

Edmund nodded, and caught up with Grace's departing figure. She had a point. Wherever they were now didn't seem like the best place to linger exactly because it did seem like the best place: it was peaceful, it was inviting, it was beautiful, and it felt like he could happily spend lifetimes there.

Those kinds of places didn't exist after the Wizard War.

He found himself wondering what Shokat Anoushak would have seen. If she'd seen anything before she died with Providence.

They walked. The path zig-zagged down the crater wall, the neighborhood proper beginning where it flattened out, just as perfect on closer inspection. Heat rose from the pavement, but it wasn't an unpleasant

heat. The flags flapped in a breeze just strong enough
to display the Stars and Stripes at their best. Someone,
somewhere, was playing a saxophone. Solo jazz. Good
enough to be professional.

"The Susurration is what we in the business call a
sapient, parasitic, extradimensional thought-concept,"
said Grace. She waved at the distant crater rim. "We've
got it trapped here, so it can't directly affect anyone
outside – that's what it uses the smilers for – but it's
basically got total control of the rest of the crater. Give
it half a chance and it gets in your head, rifles through
your hopes and fears and most secret memories, and
uses them against you until you break. I mentioned a
safe path? That's the pylons."

She nodded at the next one in line, its antennae
humming. "What these things do is shield us from the
whole conviction-eroding, mind-controlling, preachy
I-am-the-world's-salvation schtick. Leave the path and
you're in the same boat as 'Lucy,' here."

"Istvan told me he fought it."

Grace snorted. "Yeah, well, that's what he does, isn't
it?"

Extradimensional thought-concept, nothing: this
thing had to be Conceptual, if Istvan could fight it. A
representative of Memory, maybe. Control. Peace. How
had it gotten here?

Edmund fingered his pocket watch. "Salvation,
Grace?"

"We'll get to that. What does Doctor Pain see,
anyway?"

"Vienna. With gashes ripped in it."

She laughed. "Yeah, it would have trouble with
him, wouldn't it? Tries to offer something pleasant and
peaceful and normal, but what can you do with a guy

who drools over death and blood, am I right?"

Edmund glanced over his shoulder. Istvan was still there, trailing some distance back, his features wavering between flesh and bone. If he had heard Grace's comment, he gave no sign. "He's on our side, Grace."

"That's what you said when you let him loose."

Edmund grimaced.

"I thought so," Grace said. She brushed a hand across the next pylon in line. "Anyway, these people you're seeing? They're the only thing about this that's real. The pylons throw a bit of a wrench into the idyll, make the disjunction a little more obvious." They passed the old woman from before, still watching with that same incurious expression on her face. Water poured from her hose; she stood like a statue, head barely turning. Grace nodded at her. "There's thousands of them trapped here, Eddie. Hundreds of thousands."

He blanched. "Oh."

"In fact, our best guess right now is somewhere right around half a million."

"Oh."

"We try to warn people off, but the Susurration hamstrings our efforts every chance it gets. Those counter-rumors of paradise you probably dismissed as crazy ramblings? Yeah. It's been growing. More people, more influence."

Edmund tried to pretend that they weren't surrounded by half a million puppeted observers staring in slow motion. He couldn't imagine how Istvan was coping. "I see."

Grace pressed on, relentlessly. "It uses the smilers to find new targets and get close to them, convince them to make a little trip into the crater... and then they never leave, or if they do, it's as a double agent. It's a big deal,

Eddie. Haven't you ever wondered why Big East is so stable?"

He blinked. "Stable" wasn't the word he would have used. "Excuse me?"

She flashed a grin. "All I'm saying is, for being trapped in a post-apocalyptic hellscape overrun with monsters after a war that shattered everything we ever knew about the world, a lot of people are taking it pretty well, don't you think?"

Edmund smiled back, blandly. "How often do you get out of that fortress, Grace?"

She gave him a look.

He shrugged. He wasn't the one who was completely ignoring the efforts of the Twelfth Hour and the other enclaves. They had worked hard to get where they were.

"The Susurration is after you," she said. "It heard about you coming back."

"I didn't know I was so popular."

She spun, prodding at his chest. "It wants you, Eddie. It wants the Hour Thief. The guy who can go anywhere and survive anything and is handsome and charming and so experienced that people just assume he knows what he's talking about even when he doesn't. The guy who's so famous he's got his face on a sign. You were *Magister*, Eddie! Can't you see how that makes you a perfect target?"

Edmund turned his watch over in his hand, still buried in his jacket pocket. No teleporting, but the smoothness of the metal made him feel better.

It was worse than that. The Hour Thief run amok could mean an untouchable, uncatchable, immortal serial killer running around with the favored weapon of marriage proposal. Given time – and privacy – it would be laughably easy to ask for the rest of someone's life.

He'd thought about this. Too often.

"Can the Susurration learn magic?" he asked.Grace's lips thinned. "It's interdicted, Eddie. Magic doesn't work here. You need to stop obsessing over your little time-stealing trick."

"You made an exception for–"

"*I* didn't." She swept a hand at a pylon, at the walls looming closer. They were immense, Edmund realized, stained and dilapidated, like the newspaper photos he'd seen of Hoover Dam while it was under construction. "Barrio Libertad did."

"Grace..." he began, and then everything he didn't want to say rushed in to interrupt.

Grace, how did you survive? Why didn't you call? Grace, I loved you. I still love you. I took that chance, and I spent seven years still loving you after you were gone. Now you're going to make me mourn you twice?

Grace... where were you?

"How did you find me?" he finally asked. He looked away. He was a coward; he knew that already. "How did you know this Susurration creature was coming after me?"

"We have our ways."

"Grace, that's *Barrio Libertad*! What have you been doing all this time in Barrio Libertad?"

She looked at him. A long look, measuring behind her goggles. Her mask. "Fighting the good fight," she said. "Same as you."

"That's not what I meant."

"What? Someone has to do it."

"Grace, I thought..." He pressed his lips together, staring at the walls. Self-defense. She did it out of self-defense. They'd been able to talk, once, without any of that, but now... now, it had been a long time. Why bother? She had to have made up her mind by now. Found someone else. If she'd wanted to see him again, she would have come back, wouldn't she?

Unless... unless something had stopped her, unless somehow...

He shoved both hands in his pockets. "Grace, please understand. I don't know where we stand. I don't know where you've been. I don't know what you've been doing, or with who, or why you..."

The memorial. The candle, floating on the river. Fourteen months an invalid. Had she thought about him at all? How had she survived?

"I've missed you," he said. "I've missed you a lot."

She didn't reply. She walked, Lucy over her shoulder like a loose puppet. The hero, like she'd always been, returning with her spoils. The walls towered before them. Her walls.

"Grace..." he began again.

"I'm sorry," she said. "Eddie, I'm really sorry. I wouldn't have come if this wasn't so important. You would have never seen me again." She still wouldn't look at him. "You're the one who said it would never work out. Not me."

The words escaped before he could drown them. "That was before I fell in love with you, Grace."

She stepped around an oncoming bicyclist, a boy careening forward without touching the pedals, frozen, floating.

"We all make mistakes," she said.

CHAPTER TWELVE

Istvan scrabbled after them, his vision narrowed to twin blurs, a mad dash through the semblance of his home city draped over Hell. Glassy tendrils reached for him, whispering in a dozen languages. Chasms yawned on every side. Buildings ended where they shouldn't; men and women strolled past, clad in his era, like dolls. The emptiness suffocated, smothered, spun apart, whirled into spinning vertigo, and he feared he might come apart with it. Nothing. Nothing, nothing....

Edmund was straight ahead, a mirage of dark silk and faded gold. Not gone – not even mired in such horrors – but distinctly distant, skimming like a fish just below the water's surface. It was all Istvan had. He'd promised he would follow him. He was following. He would follow him anywhere.

They finally reached the wall.

Not wood. Not brick. This was a vast pile of concrete and corrugated steel seven hundred feet high, rough and angular and held together by crude rivets. It curved outward like the hull of a battleship as it rose, terminating in spiked battlements and some sort of radio antennae: strange, twisted, nonsensical structures of bent wire. Faint seams suggested folding panels. The metal was painted in bright reds and yellows, marked every few dozen feet with slogans in English or Spanish or both that read things like "Against the Control," and "Free Thought Deserves Protection." Turrets the size of railway cars, mounted far above, rumbled just below the threshold of hearing as they rolled on their bearings.

Barrio Libertad. Forbidden territory, floating in a sea of terrors.

Istvan stumbled beside Edmund and stayed right by him as they approached the entrance. It was barred, but unguarded. Flanked by two murals. The first depicted fists of every color raised against a pale, amorphous entity composed of reaching tentacles and hints of human faces. The second depicted a shattered lantern, brilliant white light spilling from behind rose-tinted glass. Both were blocky and stylized, laid out with mechanical precision. As Grace approached, the doors between them slid sideways with an electric whine and the pounding of powerful motors. Beyond lay a cavernous elevator.

No one to greet them. Helpful raised lettering on one wall suggested that passengers keep all limbs inside the conveyance, followed by what Istvan assumed to be a similar note in Spanish.

Grace walked in, propping Lucy in a corner and leaning against the wall opposite the notice. Edmund followed her, and Istvan followed him, perversely grateful for Edmund's old, distinctive terrors: their richness was bracing, their mere existence confirmation that Istvan hadn't lost his senses entirely. A focal point. An anchor. That single light in the darkness.

Grace had her own miasma, he supposed, but that wasn't the same.

The doors clanged shut behind them. A boom, like

a weight released, and then the elevator rumbled downwards.

No music.

Grace said nothing. Edmund said nothing. The floor, it seemed, was the most interesting part of the elevator, and neither one of the former lovers had any comment to make on it.

Istvan stayed where he was, so close to Edmund they were nearly touching, and glanced back and forth between the two while trying to pretend he was doing nothing of the sort. They must have spoken during the walk. Only a walk, for them, through a nightmare they couldn't perceive. Grace, much as before, radiated hard resignation, regret, and disappointment, self-loathing she did her best to bury... but Edmund...

Grief. Confusion. A longing, seven years seasoned, old wounds ripped open by a woman's claws.

Istvan wished he didn't feel quite so relieved. So vindicated. Grace was nothing but trouble and she always had been. Edmund had to realize that, now. Poor bastard.

Istvan touched his arm. <It wouldn't have worked, anyhow.>

<You don't know that,> Edmund muttered, but Istvan knew he didn't believe it.

"Rude," said Grace.

Istvan opened his mouth in retort – and paused. It was faint, but he thought he could detect the barest hint of other emotions somewhere beyond the elevator's walls. Real, feeling, suffering, human beings. Particularly anger, which was odd, but in an enclosed populace...

Then, it was as though they crossed a threshold. The whispering presence around him vanished, wiped away as though it had never existed. A weight – no, a pressure, more omnipresent, pressing in from every direction – lifted. But, more importantly, there was pain. Less than in Big East – far less – but to Istvan's starved perceptions it was a great rush of distraction and distrust and despair and domestic annoyance, a grand bounty of human experience laid before him like a flight of wines. The anger was almost overpowering, an acid edge to every interaction, but even that was preferable to nothing. Vastly, vastly preferable.

He laughed in abject relief, leaning into Edmund's side. Oh, to be awash once more in life and living!

Grace edged away, and her fear was icing. "Eddie, remind me again how he's not a B-movie villain."

The elevator shuddered to a halt.

"Good afternoon," crackled a man's voice, though there was no speaker – human, mechanical, or otherwise – in sight. "Welcome to the neighborhood-fortress of Barrio Libertad. State your business, please. It is r-recommended that you consider your current position in a small box suspended over a fall of one hundred forty-two meters." A pause. The statement repeated itself in Spanish. The voice was heavily accented, hesitating in odd places and shot through with static.

"It's me," Grace said. "One to beam up. And... guests."

"Yes," came the reply.

The elevator began moving again.

A short tunnel awaited them at the bottom, as ramshackle as the walls and lit by strips of orange set deeply into the roof. A team of people with a stretcher rolled up, calling for the smiler, congratulating Resistor Alpha on another successful retrieval.

Then they stopped, staring at Edmund. The Hour Thief? What was the Hour Thief doing here? A wizard?

He knew about Diego's stance on magic, didn't he? How did he get past the interdiction?

Edmund tipped his hat to them. Istvan had gone invisible, claiming that he didn't want to start a panic, and Edmund had agreed: under the circumstances, the Hour Thief alone was bad enough. No need to make it look like an invasion.

I'm not an army, Istvan said.

I think they would prefer an army, Edmund said.

Grace waved. Smiled. Handed Lucy over with a gentleness that Istvan asserted she had never shown in her previous encounter with the woman. Explained that the Hour Thief was here because he was Lucy's target and therefore permitted – he was the one the Susurration had taken such a powerful interest in, according, again, to Diego. Whoever the man was, she seemed to think highly of him.

Edmund had a sinking feeling about the whole business.

Once Lucy was taken away – for healing, deprogramming, and rehabilitation, Grace claimed – he and Istvan were finally permitted to leave the elevator. Faint seams in the tunnel walls trembled but didn't split as they passed, marking protective panels mounted over who-knew-what. Edmund didn't ask. Istvan stayed close by him, which was both European and understandable under the circumstances.

The afternoon sun awaited them at journey's end, its glare blazing high over the dark curve of the far wall.

Grace backed up before them, holding out her hands. "Gentlemen... Doctor Czernin... welcome to Barrio Libertad."

Edmund squinted. He tilted the brim of his hat down. Then he reached for the nearest rail as the fortress proper swam into sight.

Dante's Hell. That was the first image that came to mind. Enormous, circular, terrace after broad terrace dug into the earth. Not underground, but in shadow. A tangle of walls and stairs and walkways, homes stacked ten or fifteen high, a perilous maze of corrugated steel, plaster, and adobe painted dozens of different hues. Vast buttresses anchored entire blocks, soaring upwards to the highest terrace and beyond. Rails larger than locomotives ran across the upper edge of the walls, gears and wheels anchoring metal sheets that folded over and across each other like the sails of a steel armada. Strings of lights hung suspended over his head, sloping gently down to a central plaza ringed with mural-covered colonial buildings. The fortress boomed: wind striking the walls, the metallic creaking of gantry cranes, a faint dull thudding he couldn't place.

Something was missing, and after a moment he realized what it was. No cracks. No fallen masonry, no scaffolding, no half-tumbled buildings. No earthquake damage at all.

"Well?" Grace said with a broad grin, "What do you think?"

Edmund leaned over the rail. Yes, that was a garden down there. Or, given the distance, an entire farm. "It's... something."

Istvan peered up at the walls. "Is there a reason everything is covered in spikes?"

"Diego's Chilean. It's the style." Grace started up a nearby set of stairs. "He claims he based the place on his home city, and that it isn't a work of art, because he doesn't do art. He's so wrong." She pushed open a door. "Come on, we're going up."

Edmund picked his way after her, not feeling any

better. The rumors had never mentioned a Diego as the architect, but they had never mentioned Grace, either. Diego or Grace. Diego and Grace. The conjunctions made all the difference.

Istvan stayed right beside him. <It's for the best,> he said.

<It's none of your business, and would you back off?>

<I'm trying to–>

<I appreciate it, I really do, but my arm's going numb. I'll be fine.>

The door led to a box, a tiny room with windows open to the air. Edmund leaned out the nearest, grateful for the view. The contraption sat on a near-vertical rail strung with frighteningly thin cables. It was a long way up... and a long way down.

Istvan took one look at it, said something about transporting wounded men the same way during vicious fighting in the Alps, and announced he'd ride up top. Edmund didn't dispute it. Grace shut the door behind her – she'd insisted Edmund enter first, because he clearly wouldn't know how to lock the device – and banged on the wall. The box started upwards with a creak.

"Cable car," she said. She hung out one of the windows, arms folded on the sill. "Welcome to the city of tomorrow."

"It's something," he repeated. Hat off, he propped his elbows on the window beside her.

"Don't do that."

"Why?"

She grinned. "You'll unbalance the car and flip us off the rails into the abyss."

He stepped away. He didn't believe her, but... well, it was probably better to humor her. "What happens to Lucy?" he asked, staring out the window instead of at her. Trying to. "Is she allowed to leave after she recovers or are these walls one-way?"

A shrug. "She probably won't stay, but most do. Most people never feel safe outside, knowing that the Susurration's out there waiting for them. That if it really wanted it could find them again. Take them again." She readjusted her copper circlet. "Think of it like agoraphobia. You start needing walls."

"I see."

A string of lights rolled past, round bulbs that glowed a soft white-gold.

"Besides," Grace continued, "the Barrio's not so bad. We're completely self-contained – own food, own water, own power, everything, and it's all reliable. Black box, but reliable."

"Black box?"

She looked at him like he was stupid. It was a look that wasn't wholly unfamiliar. "Put something in the box, something else comes out of the box, no one has a clue what happens inside the box. Like your phone, Eddie, but for us future people."

Edmund leaned against the opposite window. In the old days, she would have teased him mercilessly: for the rescue, for his age and infirmity, for his reliance on the magic she claimed could be understood, if you only looked hard enough. She would have washed away the Susurration's horrors with wit and words. Reduced it to a threat that was beatable, with an eye you could spit in. She'd believed that anything could be beaten. Anything could be solved. Anyone could be saved.

We all make mistakes.

"Diego's an engineer, too?" he asked.

She turned back to her view of the fortress. "You have no idea."

They sighed to a halt just below the upper rails, shadowed by the enormous sheets of metal folded against them. Every inch looked worn, old and used, like the mechanisms had been in service for decades.

Grace motioned him out of the cable car. A rickety catwalk led to another tunnel hollowed in the wall, and then to a round of circular stairs. Edmund focused on his feet: the steps were so narrow they more resembled the rungs of a ladder, and the stairwell so steep it came close to being one. Around and around.

Grace didn't speak. Edmund didn't know how to begin. Istvan waited for them four stories up, having managed only a few yards before losing patience with conventional methods.

Grace threw open a hatch in the roof.

Edmund took his bearings. They were on top of the wall, a broad expanse like the deck of a battleship. One of the turrets loomed nearby, the slow tick-tick-tick of odd mechanisms now audible over the deep rumbling of its motors. Close up, it resembled a conventional maritime gun, only superficially – Edmund had seen enough of those in the Pacific theater to know. Beside it ran a narrow catwalk, and beyond that...

A vast grid of identical shelters, encircling the fortress as far as he could see. Acres of white canvas. No structure taller than two stories. The streets were dust, pounded flat, heaps of rubble piled around squares of rough farmland and pushed into once-molten wastes, stone frozen into bubbled whorls of black and grey. People – not all human – sorted through the remnants. Tiny figures worked the fields. No one seemed to be resting, or talking. Hundreds of thousands, Grace had said. Trapped, not because the fortress wouldn't let them in, but because their own minds wouldn't let them out.

The crater wall rose in the distance, glassy and striated, a hulk of ruined towers and broken fangs crumpled across it like a landslide. Beyond that... the river. Dammed.

Edmund looked away. Providence. All of Shokat Anoushak's forces congregated in one place, looking for something she'd never found. Never would find.

He'd never wanted to come back.

"How can anyone live there?" Istvan breathed.

"Work," said Grace. She drew up before them, leaning on the rail of the catwalk. She didn't look at the wastes. "Hard work. Industry is a virtue, I'm told, even if you don't realize you're doing it and sometimes drop dead without knowing why."

"What?" The specter stared at her, appalled. "Why don't you stop it? Why don't you help them?"

"What do you think we're trying to do?"

"They're on your bloody doorstep, woman! Can't you go out and haul them in, one by one, or build more of those pylon devices, or–"

"Istvan." Edmund waved him into silence. "Istvan, we don't know the situation. Grace, if the Susurration goes to all this trouble to collect people, why would it work them to death?"

She shrugged. "As far as it's concerned, people are a precious commodity, in bulk. Individuals tend to get lost in the shuffle. It doesn't intentionally mistreat them, as far as we can tell. It just... well, it's a harsh environment out there. Everyone has to do their part. Everyone gets the minimum required to survive, and everyone's happy – that's what matters, right?"

Edmund winced at the bitterness of her tone. If she could save them, he knew, she would have. The old Grace would have. Before. "What about the outside agents? The smilers? How many are out there?"

"We don't know. It seems to keep the majority here, but we've found smilers operating in Triskelion and as far away as Tornado Alley."

"I see."

"Do you?" She turned to him, even as he turned away. "Do you see what we're doing out here? What we're trying to stop? What the Twelfth Hour should be marking as Number One on the Things We Should Take Down list?"

He stared at a point just behind her. The barrel of the turret. What was there to shoot at, he wondered. "You've made a convincing case."

"Good, because your Magister never even bothered to listen. We need her to do something for us. You were Magister yourself, once – she listens to you, right?"

Edmund rubbed at his face. He preferred diplomacy any day, but usually he wasn't hit in the head before talks. Usually the women he loved didn't come back from the dead with no explanation of how or why or when. "Sometimes."

"What do you mean Magister Hahn didn't bother to listen?" Istvan demanded, "You've approached her before? You've told her of this... this Susurration creature?"

Grace crossed her arms. "I didn't, Diego did."

"Well, in that case, she clearly did listen, Miss Wu: weren't you aware that Barrio Libertad is on our blacklist?"

"Yeah, but did she ever tell anyone why?"

"Perhaps she thought it would cause a panic! You certainly never tried to–"

Edmund held up a hand. "Grace, what was it you needed?"

Anything. Everything. How can I make this right?

Grace, I don't make promises, but if you want one...

"The Bernault devices," she said.

"What?"

She looked out at the wastes, then away. Fixed her masked gaze on him, eye to goggled eye, bold and beautiful and grim. "I'm sorry, Eddie. We need those Bernault devices you intercepted."

CHAPTER THIRTEEN

"You certainly do not," snarled Istvan.

"Grace," said Edmund, light-headed and leaden-stomached, "you realize what this sounds like."

"What, the rogue state asking for weapons of mass destruction? Believe me, Eddie, I–"

Istvan advanced on her. "What sort of ploy is this, woman? Wait until Edmund is the one targeted, drag us here through that horror, play on our sympathies, and then beg for a shipment of the very same weapons the Twelfth Hour has tried for years to bring under control?" He slashed a hand at the sorry shelters beyond the wall. "What were you planning to do? Deal with your little problem by blowing Providence to bits a second time?"

Grace didn't budge. "That shipment is ours, you idiot. The whole trade is ours."

Oh, hell.

Edmund put on a pleasant smile. "I'm sorry, I'm not sure if I heard right. Did you just admit responsibility for the Bernault smuggling ring?"

She set a hand to her forehead. "We're the good guys here, OK? We collect them off the streets, pay a fair price for them, keep them from falling into the wrong hands, the whole deal, and without them that–" She pointed at the wastes. "–gets out."

"So Barrio Libertad is the buyer."

She levered herself off the rail. Reached for him.

Istvan snapped a wing open between them, a wall of decaying feathers and bent wire. "Don't you bloody touch him."

She slapped him. Wing, shoulder, and part of the specter's arm blew apart with a crack.

Edmund shielded his eyes – too little, too late. He blinked away spots. "Grace!"

Again she reached for him and this time caught his shoulder as Istvan slumped against the rail, cursing, bleeding mist and poison. Her grip tingled through her glove. Electric. Literally electric.

Edmund shivered, not from pain. The current wasn't strong enough for that. Not anymore. "You didn't have to do that," he said.

She snorted, steering him towards the inner wall of the fortress. "I didn't have to, no."

Wire snaked around a new framework of replacement bone, a wing already reforming. Istvan didn't follow.

Edmund tried to concentrate on something other than her touch. Now wasn't the time for that. "Grace…"

She stopped. She didn't take her hand off his shoulder. "Look," she said. She waved at the opposite wall, the city tiers, the massive machines ringing the perimeter. "How do you think we're powering all this? How do you think we keep that monster pinned down? Eddie, Barrio Libertad is the only reason the Susurration has borders. We're the only thing standing between civilization and happy, friendly, eternal stagnation with a side of regrettable death. You didn't think Lucy tipped you off to the jackpot because you're pretty, did you?"

Edmund reached for one of the catwalk rails. Shocked himself. Bit back a curse of his own.

Barrio Libertad, behind Big East's most dangerous trade. Barrio Libertad, surrounded by a mind-controlling monster, claiming that they needed weapons of mass destruction to keep it in check and hiring Triskelion mercenaries to acquire those weapons. Losing them to the Twelfth Hour because of a tip from Lucy. Lucy, controlled by the Susurration. No devices, no power, and the monster would get out.

Barrio Libertad wanted him to hand over enough firepower to destroy Providence twice over, so the monster wouldn't get out.

No. No, the woman he loved – who wasn't dead, who was maybe with someone else now, who was still as stunning as ever – was asking for the equivalent of twenty nuclear warheads in a gift box and it wasn't even Christmas.

How was he supposed to explain this to Mercedes?

He shut his eyes, then opened them again. "Did Magister Hahn know about this?"

She let go of him. "I don't know what she knows. But it's a lot more than she's telling you."

Istvan stalked across the catwalk towards them, reformed wings flickering, flaring and fading and flaring again. "More than she's telling us? What about the truth about this place? Springs up out of nowhere, stockpiles dozens of superweapons, we haven't even met the bloody architect–"

"You have," she snapped back, "and if he wasn't willing to–"

"–forbids teleportation, trapping Edmund where you want him, and what about the *rage*, Miss Wu?" He pointed at the turret behind them. The accent he'd stopped trying to hide struck the first syllable of every word like a nail hammered into a wall, sentences hanging skewered in even cadence. "This fortress of yours is seething! Fury, unwavering, unnatural, leaking from the bloody walls! Did you think I wouldn't notice?"

She clenched her fists, sparks crackling through her hair. "Did you think I wanted you here in the first place?"

Istvan bared his teeth. "I never abandon my own, Miss Wu."

"Oh, so you're staking claims now? Eddie, did I miss something?"

"Miss something? Miss something? Only the last seven years of his life, you... you evil, heartless, brazen hussy!"

She lunged.

Edmund caught her wrist, yelped as shock jolted up his arm. Twisted sideways, sending her into the rail, fingers gone numb. She struck with a snarl and spun around. Istvan drew his knife. Another moment spent – another blow expected –

Edmund interposed himself between them, nerves jangling. "Are you out of your minds? Are you both really out of your minds?"

"Me? You're the one who just lets him get away with this stuff, Eddie!"

"She comes back after seven years faking her own death and suddenly I'm the mad one? Suddenly I'm the one who can't be trusted?"

"Suddenly you're allowed to commit war crimes and never pay for it?"

"I never–!"

"You were allied with the Nazis!" Grace spat. "You've personally killed more people across more continents than anyone in the history of ever, and I'm supposed to just sit here and be OK with that?"

"You, Miss Wu, are supposed to be dead!"

Edmund stayed where he was. This wasn't happening. This wasn't happening. Not again. Nothing he ever said had worked – arguments that Grace was a good person, really, to Istvan, that Istvan wasn't a monster, to Grace, that both of them should try talking to each other for once rather than skipping immediately to worst impressions – all of it, useless.

They'd always hated each other. Always.

Then Grace had died, Istvan remained, and it had been over... until now. Until it wasn't. Until they made him choose, again. Until they forced him to weigh up a friendship that would last against a love that was mortal. Assuming Grace would ever take him back. He'd missed her. He'd missed her so much.

He stood there as they yelled at each other, and tried to swallow back the oil in his throat.

He couldn't lose her again. Couldn't bear even the thought of...

"I'm sorry," he said, pushing them apart as best as he was able, "but we should be going."

Grace threw her hands up. "You're leaving? Just like that?"

"Yes."

"I'm not even finished!"

"I'm sure we can meet again at a later date."

"There won't *be* a later date. You go out there, Eddie, and the Susurration will come after you again. It doesn't stop, do you understand? It doesn't stop, ever, until it gets what it wants!"

"Oh, now you worry about him," snarled Istvan.

Edmund brushed a wing away, or tried to. "That's enough. We're leaving."

Grace shook her head. Wonder. Disbelief. Disappointment. "You really haven't changed, have you?"

"You have." Edmund flipped open his pocket watch with his free hand and then remembered: no teleporting in or out of the fortress. He started off down the catwalk. "Istvan, come on."

Artillery thudded over the rush and boom of wind and fortress. Wire whispered across steel. A moment later, the specter fell into step beside him, trembling with a rage that loosened feathers and sent them drifting down behind him. "You're still in love with her, aren't you?"

"Yes."

"Edmund, you can't! You can't let her do this to you!"

"I'm sorry, Istvan, but you don't get to choose who you fall in love with."

Distant guns faded to silence.

"Now," Edmund continued, "do you remember the way out?"

A blue strip of light appeared before them, running over catwalks and around turrets and, ultimately, to the hatch where they'd arrived. It glowed through the metal, like part of the surface had turned to glass. Edmund glanced over his shoulder. Grace was leaning on the rail, staring out at the wastes. If she was responsible for the light, she didn't take credit.

Edmund closed his eyes and turned away. He'd never wanted to know anything less in his life. "Never mind."

"We aren't diplomats, Edmund. This entire matter is out of our jurisdiction. Out of it entirely unless the Twelfth Hour decides to either appoint us or go to war. I sincerely doubt the former, and the latter... well, it has been some years – we've the manpower again, or at least enough of it to make a good showing, and I wouldn't mind a good fight between powers." Istvan laughed bitterly, the sort of bursting expulsion between a laugh and a sob, the sort that should have hurt. "Oh, Edmund, it's been so long. No one fights proper wars anymore. Of course it won't happen."

Edmund wasn't answering. He sat at the righted kitchen table, holding a fork and staring at a plate of pasta he'd made and not yet touched. His hat, cape, and goggles were off. The record player in the other room played the heathen music that he liked but the noise didn't seem to be helping. No cat; Beldam had fled the kitchen long ago.

A cold wind leaked in through the cardboard pasted over broken windows.

Istvan paced back and forth across the tile. What a terrible day. He hadn't had such a day since... well, since Lucy appeared, but today was far, far worse than that. Grace bloody Wu. She'd been nothing but trouble. Mocked him. Insulted him. And now... and now she...

Oh, he hated her. It frightened him, how much he hated her. Beyond words.

He fidgeted with the top buttons on his uniform, feeling shrapnel twist in his chest. "How many Bernault devices are sitting in that fortress, do you think? Dozens? Hundreds? And all for... for what, electricity?" He reached the end of the kitchen. Turned around. Started back the other way. "Edmund, that fortress of hers – the whole construction – that was fury, Edmund. No, that was if someone took fury and strained out all the flavor and then bottled it, alone, nothing else. Flat. Ah... oh, it's difficult to explain, it was..."

"Mechanical."

Istvan threw up a hand. "Yes. Mechanical. Run through a press. Just as unnatural as that Susurration creature, and certainly not the sort of feeling associated with peaceful purposes. Electricity." He snorted. "Edmund, I don't believe that for a second."

Again Edmund was silent. He pushed the pasta around his plate. He had thrown out what was left of Lucy's pies, cleaned off the walls and ceiling, swept up the glass, dusted the whole house, and written a report to Magister Hahn before making dinner. Now the completed document lay beside him, three pages of excruciatingly well-formed lettering that could have been produced by a typewriter. There was nothing in it about Grace Wu.

"She hasn't come back for you," Istvan told him for the fifth or sixth time that evening. "She wants those weapons, Edmund, and I would bet a month's wages if I were paid that she wants to vanish those poor people outside the walls. Any means necessary to control the beast, hm? Living with that sort of horror for that long can do that to a person, Edmund, believe me. I've seen it."

"I need to talk to her again," said Edmund.

"No, you don't. It's over, and once you turn in that report, it's out of our hands." Istvan pulled out his chair and dropped into it. "I don't understand why you can't accept that."

Edmund set his fork down. "Think about how insular Barrio Libertad is, Istvan. Don't you think there's a fair chance she had to disappear because she was given no other choice? Couldn't leave? Couldn't be permitted to talk to a wizard? This could be the first time she's been able to do what she always wanted, and I can't take any chances that it isn't."

Istvan sighed. "Edmund–"

"You were married! You can't sit there and say you

don't understand what I'm dealing with here!"

Istvan turned his ring around his finger. Poor Franceska. A banker's daughter, over a decade his junior. He had told her family that he waited so long because he wanted to become well-established before proposing to anyone. That while there was a palace carrying his name in Vienna, he hailed from a distant bastard offshoot with no titles: what he had built was his alone.

Her family accepted. They both had hoped he'd done it for love.

He left everything to her when he bought that ticket to South Africa. When he returned from the Ceylon prisoner-of-war camp, years later, she hadn't recognized him.

She'd found someone else. She'd deserved better.

"It wasn't the same," he said.

Edmund set both elbows on the table. "What do you mean it wasn't the same? Look, I know you don't like Grace, but I do, all right? Can't you believe for one second that she might be someone worth fighting for?"

"She doesn't want to be fought for, Edmund."

"You can't know that."

Long-denied betrayal swirled over and after the old regrets. The wizard wanted her; knew he shouldn't; knew it was a bad idea to pursue her, and yet he couldn't bring himself to admit it, couldn't concede, couldn't surrender. Even drowning, all those years ago, he hadn't given in. Oh, he was so stubborn.

Istvan sighed. "I can, and I do. Would I lie to you about something like this?"

"About Grace?" Edmund picked up his fork again. "Yes, I think you would."

"Edmund, after what she did to you–"

"Just drop it, all right? That isn't your business, I don't

want to think about it, and I'm trying to eat."

Istvan eyed his plate. "You haven't been eating for the past half-hour."

He stabbed a noodle. "I can't eat while you're talking."

"Then what would you have me do?"

"Stop talking." He bayoneted another several noodles and ate them, chewing like a machine himself. Not looking at Istvan. Not annoyed so much as tired, afraid of what might happen, afraid that he might seem afraid. Almost the usual, if it weren't for Grace Wu. The hurt was rough and bitter, dark with the subdued richness of repetition, salted chocolate and smoke. Denial cupped and distorted it like glass. Ever the stoic.

Istvan held up his hands. He rose, pushed the chair back in, and retreated to the sitting room. Beldam the cat sped away from him with a hiss. Trumpets squealed from the record player. That bloody stupid horseshoe hung above the front door, tilted sideways so the luck wouldn't run out or some nonsense. The bookshelves were full – it was Edmund's house, after all, the lair of a librarian – but turning pages wasn't motion enough, and Istvan had already read everything in English and German, among other things struggling through every volume of Sherlock Holmes. The rest was all French, Chinese, Sanskrit, Russian, Arabic, Latin.

He hated Latin. He'd always hated Latin.

He circled the coffee table, tried sitting on one of the couches, and then circled the table again. Clinking from the kitchen meant Edmund was indeed eating, which was good. The man didn't always eat enough. Drinking was another matter.

Istvan sighed. Oh, this mess was only going to make it worse.

He went back to the kitchen. "Edmund, if I were to

find a different investigation, would you–"

The wizard dropped his fork on his plate. "I'm done."

"No, you're not. You've barely touched–"

"I'm not hungry."

Istvan trailed him as he stood and scraped his food into a bowl. "Edmund, Miss Wu isn't even the question here!" He pointed at the report, sitting on the table. "That is! That whole business with Barrio Libertad, the Bernault devices, and that bloody monster that set Lucy on you. There is a terrible force out there hunting you and it knows where you live – that is what you ought to concern yourself about. Not chasing after a hateful woman who loved you so little she might as well have left you for dead."

Edmund put the bowl in the refrigerator. "I said I'm done talking about this."

"Once you give that report to Magister Hahn, it's out of your hands. Even if you are assigned to the fortress, you're always needed elsewhere and you have no obligation to Miss Wu. Don't you forget that."

"I'll leave that decision up to Mercedes."

"You can refuse!"

Edmund stalked to the door, snatching up cape and hat. "I'm going out."

Istvan grasped his arm so he couldn't vanish. "What? Now?"

"Better than sitting here wasting time. The rest of the world doesn't take a break just because I haven't finished dinner."

"You aren't planning to go out there alone, are you? With the Susurration lurking about?"

Edmund pulled on his goggles. "That depends on whether you're going to keep up a subject you ought to drop."

Istvan stared at him.

Then he grabbed at a belt and bandolier that hadn't been there before, dangling from one of the hooks. Habit, hanging them up in the house. It made little practical sense and he knew it.

He'd half-expected to be denied, to be pushed away. To be told that he couldn't come and that he'd been replaced. Instead... oh, Edmund was doing it again, knowing or not. That thing he did. He was the Hour Thief, immortal if not invincible, and once his mind was made, he wouldn't be stopped. Not by anyone. He was the most delicate, most fragile, most inevitable juggernaut Istvan had ever met. The Man in Black made flesh.

He'd been the real thing, once. At the loosening of Istvan's chains.

The bandolier was a relic from the Boer War, an affectation and a reminder of the few battles Istvan had fought in life. He buckled it over his shoulder and donned his field cap as Edmund retrieved his watch, trying not to feel so stupidly grateful. "I can't let you take all the credit, you know."

CHAPTER FOURTEEN

"That's it," said Edmund, "That's the flat. Six complaints about nightly disturbances, all centered here – fire, chanting, and robed figures. It's been on my list for a while now. I'm surprised no one's had a look yet."

Istvan watched him adjust his goggles. Water streaked the lenses, scratched from dozens of close calls. It was freezing cold and pouring rain and yet Edmund didn't seem to mind. Didn't even seem to notice. His cape pooled in dirty puddles as he kneeled, and while it was made of a heavy sort of material, Istvan knew it wasn't waterproof. "I doubt anyone had the time."

"It's lucky someone does, then."

They were on the roof opposite the flat in question, peering down at a window full of wilted plants in flower boxes. It was one of the more dangerous districts: Fourth and Black, a warren of dilapidated tenements controlled by an ever-shifting pack of gangs and lit by odd drifting filaments of pale cyan, wrapped around poles and power lines and trailing off luminously into the night. Behind the window pane flickered tiny fires, like candles... and wound all through the surrounding miasma of disgruntled despair was a thin, trembling thread of sugar-sweet fear.

"Edmund, I think they've found themselves a captive."

"Ah. That would be the virgin sacrifice."

Istvan rolled his eyes. "Oh, of course. Nothing like kidnapping a hapless girl on a night with pouring rain and... Edmund?"

Beside him lay only the fading golden glow of a teleport. He cursed. This was the third time.

He unfurled bony wings, preparing to leap from the roof –

– and then Edmund dropped out of thin air, mid-somersault and trailing fading embers, righting himself with a graceful pirouette that kept the ragged boy with him from falling off the edge. He straightened his hat. "Are you all right?"

The boy nodded. His eyes were like dinner plates.

"Good. If anything else comes after you tonight, go ahead and take a moment to get out of the way."

He vanished. A pair of figures ran past the window and then hurtled backwards in the opposite direction. What had once been a single thread of terror became six or seven.

Istvan exchanged an exasperated glance with the boy, who shrieked and bolted behind the boxy metal shelter of a roof fan.

"Stay there, then," he grumbled. Pain sparked in his awareness, none of it Edmund's. The bastard. Istvan dove off the roof, barreling through the closed window on folded wing. The sorry room beyond held a couch, a table, and a bewildering maze of colored chalk lines, scuffed out in places and centered around clusters of candles, feathers, bells, bones, and other offerings. Six figures in costume robes lay sprawled on the floor. The wallpaper smoldered. "Edmund..."

A tattooed young man, hood askew, ran through him and into a right hook.

Istvan spun around. "Edmund!"

The wizard caught and lowered his last victim to the ground, tracing a sign over his chest. "What?"

"Would you stop it?"

"I just did."

"That's not what I meant and you—"

Something dark, leathery, and with a number of wings he couldn't quite count sprang out of nowhere, blazing like coal aflame. Istvan didn't so much draw his knife as lunge with the blade already in his—

A crack. It wasn't one sound. It was at least five in quick succession, blows delivered so quickly Istvan could only make out the cumulative effect. The creature yelped. Staggered sideways. Lashed out with a tongue, or perhaps a tail. Missed what wasn't there. Edmund darted from behind it, scuffing out the chalk lines. Had already scuffed them out.

A shriek. The creature shattered like ice.

Istvan shouted something wordless. Not fair. Not fair at all.

Edmund kicked a piece aside, woefully massaging his knuckles. "Now I've stopped it."

"Edmund!"

"I'm sorry, they were more finished than I thought. Did you leave the kid on the roof?"

"I—"

"You left the kid on the roof."

For probably the hundredth time that evening, he vanished.

Istvan slammed his knife back in its sheath. Oh, for—

"Edmund," he snarled, alighting beside him in the rain, "If you expect me to—"

The boy opened his mouth to yell. Edmund dashed forward. Both vanished in a gold-rimmed blur.

Istvan threw his field cap down. No splash. Bloody hell. He picked it up again and sat against the fan, legs drawn up and wings draped around him like a ghastly curtain. Couldn't keep up. Istvan was the Great War, the very embodiment of violent conflict, but try as he might he couldn't keep up. Edmund was doing this on purpose. How better could he put the lie to the romantic notion of fighting side-by-side than ending battles before Istvan could draw steel? Before he could finish a bloody sentence?

Edmund had always gone where Istvan couldn't follow – given time, taken time, spent time where Istvan had none – but it had never felt quite so much like he was running away from him. Away from the one who'd stood by him. Away from the only friend that would never leave him. Monster that he was.

Istvan slapped at a puddle and this time it splashed, clouded red.

Bloody American children, anyhow. The country wasn't old enough for ghosts. Girls and boys in Europe had come right up to him, tried to touch him, asked which war he'd died in. But here? Oh, no. Not enough battles. Not enough respect.

Edmund reappeared a short while later. "That could have gone better."

"Could it have? I wasn't aware. How do you think it could have gone better?"

Edmund brushed rainwater from his shoulders. "Don't be like that."

"Like what? Utterly useless?" Istvan threw his hands in the air. "That's three times, now, Edmund. Three bloody times!"

"Would you rather people get hurt?"

"I..." He did. He always did. As a particular someone kept reminding him, kept goading him. He hadn't killed anyone since the Wizard War! Hadn't fought in a real, conventional war since the Gulf! Soldiers, only soldiers, only ever soldiers...

He took off his glasses. "Damn you, Edmund."

Edmund shrugged, a font of barely-concealed exasperation. "I never said you had to come. I can take care of myself."

"Like you did with Lucy?"

The wizard clenched his fists. "Istvan, we are not talking about this again."

Istvan scrambled to his feet, jamming his glasses back on. "You don't want me here at all, do you? You would rather I left and you played the hero alone, bait for that bloody monster, so you would have an excuse to go back to that bloody fortress and see that bloody woman again!"

"The only excuse I need is a lack of information, and whose fault is that?"

"She left you, Edmund! She left you years ago! She lied to you, she manipulated you, and she only came back because she wanted something from you, not because–"

"We're lucky she showed up when she did!"

He was angry now. Oh, it was so difficult to make Edmund angry, but now he struggled to keep it from rolling off him in waves of spice and citrus. Istvan tapped the hilt of his knife on the man's breastbone. "That's what she wants you to think," he leered.

Edmund slapped the knife away. "Don't touch me."

Real anger. Tart, full-bodied. Seasoned with denial and self-loathing; oh, it was so much better than that horror at the fortress. All the horrors of the day. Cold fury. It was best cold.

Istvan drew closer, and closer still. Still holding his knife. "I fought the Susurration," he said. "I drove it off, not her. Lucky she showed up, Edmund? Lucky she only did what I could have done?" He wasn't touching him. So close, and not touching him. "Lucky, Edmund, that you were saved by a woman?"

Edmund's face twisted into a masked smile. "What?" he said, and his teeth flashed perfect in the pale light. "Jealous?"

Istvan punched him in the jaw. Edmund, more startled than hurt, lashed out with a return uppercut that whistled harmlessly through the specter's head. Istvan hit him twice more. Again in the jaw. Once in the gut. As fast and as hard as he could, one after the other. Edmund only stepped backwards, holding his arms up in bewildered defense against nothing.

Istvan found himself laughing. No use. No use at all. Edmund couldn't touch him, and Istvan... oh, he'd boxed once, and in life he'd have been stronger than the other man, and heavier too, but he couldn't hit hard enough anymore to even bruise. Relic force. No more than the memory of a blow once thrown.

Edmund dropped his hands to his sides, anger tempered by embarrassment. "Well," he said.

"That really doesn't work at all."

"No, it doesn't."

Istvan inspected his knuckles. "I was quite good in my day, you know."

"I'm sure you were."

They stood a moment, in the rain. The pale glow of drifting filaments glistened across brick and steel.

Edmund straightened his hat. Straightened his jacket.

Kicked at the rooftop, and Istvan was suddenly reminded of when the man had been younger. Brighter. Fool enough to think there were any winners in a European war. He'd tripped, in that riverbed, but still managed to dodge the next sweep of the knife. "Istvan?" he said.

"Hm?"

"How about we call it a night? Your people are probably looking for you in the infirmary and I'd hate for Mercedes to accuse you of neglecting your duties on top of everything else. I won't stay out." He shook his head. "I may have hurt my wrist in that last bout, anyway."

He hadn't. Istvan knew he hadn't.

"You're right," he agreed. "You oughtn't strain it."

Edmund pulled out his pocket watch. Homeward-bound. Rest, sanctuary, and a precious few hours of peace. After today, he deserved it. Veteran that he was, battered and brave, he always deserved it. But now... now peace held its own dangers, in glass and creeping whispers, and Istvan couldn't always be there to ward it off.

He couldn't sleep. Hadn't for a hundred years.

"Do be careful."

"I will."

Edmund vanished.

CHAPTER FIFTEEN

Static. Broken glass razored the air. A pair of stone lions with golden antlers didn't bother trying to dodge a falling radio mast; a crash, and they vanished from sight. Green streaks shot overhead. The horizon reared up, roaring, and every remaining window shattered.

Edmund huddled behind the twitching iron hulk of a crushed tank, clutching at his soaked undershirt with tie askew. Sparks and smoke hazed his vision. His chest rattled with every dull boom. Not good, with a hole in it.

"So I'm curious..." Grace shouted. She hurtled over the top of the tank and dropped down beside him, electricity crackling through her black hair. Her voice was hoarse, raw from inhaled soot.

He winced. "What about?"

"Well," she said, "for one, how much black you have in your wardrobe."

"Maybe a third."

"Two, can I pick you up?"

He squinted at her through the smoke. "What?"

"I know the guy is supposed to make his move first, but–"

A helicopter slewed sideways overhead, insectile jaws

gnashing beneath its cockpit, mantis claws tucked in place of landing skids.

Pain burst in his chest as she yanked him upward. Threw him over a shoulder. Took off running, at a dead sprint he knew she could beat a dozen times over alone. Jets of acid burned into the dirt as she skidded into an alley. Sunbursts popped in his vision. "Grace," he gasped, trying to brace himself and hold on to his hat all at once, "you are aware I can teleport, right?"

"I'm faster!"

The helicopter slammed into the corner. Pieces of brick and other things showered all over the street. He covered his eyes.

"Hey, one last question," she said once both of them could hear again.

"Yeah?"

"Can I call you Eddie? You look like an Eddie."

He laughed. He instantly regretted it. "Haven't heard that in a while."

She grinned at him, slung backwards as he was. "So..."

"Sure. Sure, Grace, that's fine." The claw hadn't pierced anything vital – his time hadn't run out yet – but lately he was starting to wonder if maybe something had. He tried to stop laughing. God, it hurt. "Been a long time. Can you please put me down now?"

"Edmund?" someone else interrupted. "Edmund?"

Blackness hazed the edges of his sight. "Grace," he tried to say. "Grace, this isn't... this is a bad...."

"Edmund!"

He awoke to Death.

"Goddammit, Istvan!"

The ghost ignored the pillow flung through his chest. "They've found it," he cackled. He brandished bloody hands, his cuffs rolled up to his elbows, heedless of the exposed burn scarring on his left forearm. "They've found the beast!"

Edmund picked himself up off the floor. "What beast? What are you talking about? What are you doing in my room?"

"The ice monster, Edmund! The one responsible for mauling all those people and the last investigations team!" He shook Edmund's shoulders. "They've found it and I've volunteered us to catch it!"

Never before had Edmund been more grateful that he'd had the presence of mind to put on pajamas. "Out of my room."

"You'll have to eat quickly," Istvan continued, his words almost tripping over each other, "It's taken up residence in Cheerful Gardens, they said, and we need to capture it before any visitors arrive. Miss Justice said that all the information you need is somewhere on your phone."

"Istvan, out. I've told you not to come in here like this and I can't get dressed with you standing here."

The specter laughed. "I'll put on the water, then!"

He turned – almost a pirouette, balanced by the shadow of wings – and skipped through the door. Bloodstains and bullet holes flickered across the wood, then faded.

Edmund brushed at his shoulders. There was nothing there. He eyed the bottle of gin on his bedside table, then collapsed back onto his sheets, staring at the cracks on the ceiling. He hadn't touched his glass last night. He'd promised himself he wouldn't drink over any of this last night. If he drank anything now, Istvan would notice and he wouldn't hear the end of it.

Dishes rattled in the kitchen. Clinks and scraping. The

rush of water. A humming, half-sung words he couldn't make out, the sort of simple marching melody the ghost favored when he wasn't arguing for the radio to be switched to waltz. If Janet had already made the arrangements...

Edmund sat back up, dragged his pocket watch off the table, and snapped it open. The light coming through the curtained window was faint and pale, a washed-out orange that didn't bode well but was enough to make out the clock's face. Five. Barely five. He mouthed a few choice obscenities to himself. He'd slept less than three hours.

He rubbed at the puncture scar on his chest and gazed across the room. Closet, wooden floors, flowered wallpaper. His time ledger lay open on the top of his desk, forgotten after he'd finished tabulating time stolen and spent. That wasn't right. He couldn't be doing that. He got up to put it away. He'd promised himself he wouldn't drink over this. Not over Grace. Not anymore.

But... an ice monster? At five in the morning? After everything that had happened yesterday, Istvan wanted to go on a hunting expedition?

He shut the ledger in its drawer. Scrubbed his hands across his face. Eyed the bottle again.

Just one. Istvan wouldn't notice just one.

Edmund took a moment to get dressed.

A figure in black slouched down the hallway.

"There you are," Istvan called. He saluted with transparent cup and saucer. Coffee, in an earlier age; now nothing but habit and memory, something to hold that steamed. "I've put the water on, as promised. It was boiling a moment ago."

Edmund squinted at the lights. "That's very kind of you."

"You know, that's what you said when I made *Fiakergulasch* last Thanksgiving."

"So it is."

"You hated it."

"So I did. It was still a kind gesture." Edmund retrieved a cup and saucer of his own, and scooped a spoonful of furled leaves from the tea tin. "Now what's this about an ice monster?"

Istvan laughed as barbed wire looped in sweeping curves around his feet, glittering red and silver. Fresh and new. What luck to bring this news, and what a bloody night it had been! "Oh, the latest team came back an hour or so after I arrived. Frightful, Edmund, absolutely frightful – they thought they were tracking it, but it was tracking them, and you can imagine the carnage. I stabilized the lot, and while everyone is defrosting, you and I are to chase the beast down and return it to the Twelfth Hour for study and safekeeping. And…" He leaned forward, eyebrows raised in conspiracy. "… they're saying that it doesn't match the usual spellscar creatures, Edmund. It might be from further north. Perhaps even the Greater Great Lakes."

Edmund poured the water so thoughtfully provided into his cup and set it down to steep. "Ah."

"A straggler from the Wizard War, after all this time!" Istvan set his own cup down so he could gesture with both hands. His sleeves were still rolled up, unbuttoned, original surgeon's cuffs. "Oh, it sounds a terror, Edmund – frostbite, clawing, internal laceration from bits of ice broken off in the wounds, some of the victims hurled or dragged great distances – it ought to be great fun taking it down, wouldn't you say?"

Edmund set out a frying pan. "I don't know that I would."

Fear stirred and sweetened his affect, and Istvan knew why – there weren't supposed to be any stragglers, not in Big East, not after Providence, not after then-Magister Templeton had hurled the last remnants of the Twelfth Hour into Death's teeth. They'd kept Shokat Anoushak busy. Distracted. Hour after hour, until whatever strange stratagem Mercedes Hahn had prepared was ready – and she called an immediate retreat, for what good that had done.

Big East was safe now, as much as a fracture region could be. All of its monstrous armies lured to Providence and destroyed with Shokat Anoushak herself.

Istvan couldn't remember anything but a blur of brilliant euphoria, blasts and shattering, blood spun in lazy arcs through smoke. He had managed to stay on the defensive for a short while, but according to Edmund he had followed orders for only the first quarter-hour or so, and then gone off on a mad tear through anything his bindings would permit him to kill. He was the World War! The First! The Great! The crack and roar of guns that never ceased, machine-driven death that dealt in swathes and droves, all the discoveries of a grand and hopeful age bent to ending it in mud and rot and bloody snow.

He hadn't retreated in time. He'd gotten better.

He reached over to shake Edmund's shoulder, still chuckling to himself. "Oh, don't be so melancholy, Edmund. It's only a single ice monster. Something like a bear, I'm told. Surely the Hour Thief can handle a bear."

Edmund opened the refrigerator door, selected two of the remaining eggs, and closed it again. "I wouldn't know," he said. "Hard to take time from an animal that doesn't know what you're asking."

"But it isn't an animal."

"Does it talk?"

"I suppose we'll find out, hm?" Istvan picked up his coffee again, congratulating himself on a successful distraction. The man would have no cause to think of Grace Wu now. "Don't worry so, Edmund. There isn't a beast alive, magical or not, that can best me."

"Not that we've met."

"And stop dragging your feet. I know you're better than this."

Edmund rolled his eyes – and then he'd cracked, cooked, seasoned, and thrown the eggs onto a plate. Tea retrieved. Fork selected and seated in the closest chair to the stove, facing the doorway. He was a decent cook – he had to be, planning as he did to never have a wife – but nothing extraordinary, Istvan knew. "Happy?"

"Cheater."

"And a thief." Edmund bolted down his breakfast.

Istvan turned his face, hiding his scarring as he smiled. Oh, it was like the old days again. Like it should be.

After all, it was Istvan who had helped him through the worst. Istvan who had requested to be paired with him on all official assignments. Istvan who ensured his shellshock remained under control. Istvan who had become so closely affiliated with him that even though Edmund were more famous it was in a Gothic sense: the masked mystery in black who ought never be crossed, lest he reappear with his terrifying winged partner.

He didn't need Grace any more than he needed poison. All that had to be done was remind him of that.

Cheerful Gardens was silent. The great glass dome over the trees shielded them from fitful winds, the steam and smoke that drifted from the Generator district passing over in wisps and ribbons. Much later in the day, the place should have played host to dozens of Big Easterners – former New Yorkers, former Bostonians, former townsfolk of innumerable smaller cities and towns from across New England – taking a respite from their labors. Walking, flinging Frisbees, sitting on benches formed of scented wood, trying to decipher any one of a dozen signposts written in what was almost Japanese. The misplaced habitat dome had become a haven, a refuge from the twisted realities of the outside world. It was safe.

It should have been safe.

That was before two picnickers turned up missing. Then, days later, not missing: found with great bloody gashes ripped in their flesh, limbs torn off, blood flash-frozen in their veins. A new caller had come to town... and it wasn't interested in reading signs.

Edmund crept beneath the pines. Pocket watch ready. Neck hair raised. He'd downed two cups of something caffeinated at the Twelfth Hour before they left for the scene of the crime, but now it seemed he wouldn't be needing it. Birds flitting through branches and needles crackling underfoot were enough. He focused on his own breathing, slow and regular. On every errant motion between the trees. Istvan was only a step ahead, silent save for the faint rushing slither of barbed wire, stopping at odd intervals to peer in one direction and then another before stalking off on a new route.

"It's here," the ghost muttered, stopping yet again to look around. "I know it's here."

"That's what you said an hour ago."

"I'm no bloody good with animals."

"You said it wasn't an animal."

"It's like an animal, then. Enough to make this difficult!"

Edmund brushed away a branch the other man had walked through before it hit him in the eye. "Istvan, I was looking forward to some sleep before I had to turn in that report. Not all of us are restless spirits and no one is awake this early." He winced at the wooden crack of one of his own footsteps. "No one sane."

Istvan grimaced. "It's stalking us, I think." He jogged up a rise, leaping a guardrail to a footpath marked by floating lamps of red and gold.

Edmund followed him, soft loam giving way beneath his shoes, cursing the specter's unnatural tirelessness. He himself was in decent shape, thanks to his habitual patrolling, but Istvan was a tough act to follow – especially uphill. "That's what you said an hour ago."

"No, this time it's closer. It's..." Istvan turned slowly around, scanning the trees.

Edmund glanced up at the great angular stone that marked the park's center. Dark granite. He was sure they had circled it at least twice. His pocket watch was smooth and reassuring, though not as secure as it could have been. Despite the coolness of the park, he was sweating. "It's what?"

"What would you have me say? It's hungry? That isn't anything, Edmund. I can't work from that. It's so watered-down, I...." Istvan looked back to him, expression twisted, almost pleading. "I had hoped it would be more man-like, Edmund. Please, believe that."

Edmund squinted at him. "This doesn't have anything to do with–"

Istvan flinched. "No! No, not at all!"

"–what you are, does it?" Edmund finished. He waved at the woods, suppressing the thought of last night. No more fighting. Not over that. If Istvan wanted to keep worrying over Grace, he could do it alone. Edmund had used up his gin allowance for the day. "Most animals don't go to war, Istvan. I was just thinking that might be why you have so much trouble with them."

Istvan stared at him. Then he drew his knife and resumed his search of the trees, muttering, "Perhaps."

Edmund followed his gaze. Mist curled through the ferns. Pine needles shivered. "Does it seem colder to you?"

"You know, now that you—"

Branches cracked. Edmund spun around. A maw that could encompass a human head gaped wide, fangs glistening like icicles. The ground below enormous paws froze solid. He yelled. He took a moment to run – and slipped. Scrabbled on the ice. Fell over, scrambling backwards while his brain gibbered about six-inch canines. A hurricane of snow-pale fur hammered into his chest. At least a thousand carving knives slashed into his left forearm. Blood flew, froze, and pattered down like crimson hail.

Istvan was shouting. Hungarian. Nothing Edmund understood but his own name, over and over, and a plethora of curses. Wings beat around his head. A blur of cloth and uniform piping. The flash of a blade. The beast roared. Icicles shattered on Edmund's skin. Black spots danced across his vision. The stench of rotten meat seemed to have frozen inside his nostrils.

Was his arm gone? He couldn't tell. Would it hurt like that if an arm were torn off? He had never lost a limb before. It was different from drowning, he was pretty sure.

The beast whirled about, yanking him sideways across the dirt.

Arm still attached. OK. OK.

His top hat tumbled away. Frost blew past, followed by

frozen pine needles and showers of stones and branches. He couldn't feel his face, or his hands. He flailed his best approximation of a teleport –

– and slammed into a tree.

Blue-striped death hurtled towards him. Not a bear. A tiger.

CHAPTER SIXTEEN

His fault. This was his fault. His idea, his insistence, his fear of the Susurration's return, his blood-hazed delusion that if only he and Edmund could fight together, everything would be rendered right. If the creature was one of the last survivors of its kind, a relic of the Wizard War, ought not Edmund – the perennial last survivor, the impossible soldier, the unwilling general who had overseen every battle, every loss, been there for the final act at Providence – be the one to capture it? He and Istvan, a war himself, together?

Closure. The man deserved some bloody closure.

Not this.

Istvan threw himself before the beast and it barreled straight through him. Teeth and cold – killing cold, worse than his own touch in its permanence. He spun, throwing out a wing before he toppled sideways, grabbing at anything he could. His fingers sank through fur and muscle and hooked around the lowermost part of the beast's ribcage. His other hand found its spine.

He had a moment to reflect that this may not have been the wisest decision.

Then he was airborne. Dragged on the ground. On

the beast's back, scrambling over churning hindquarters, a tail as thick as his arm whipping through trailing wire. Branches rushed at his head. Flecks of ice and snow ripped through his greatcoat. He cursed. He'd ridden horses. This was nothing like a horse. A glimpse of Edmund's face – startled, pain-glazed, his agony the fiery rippling of a drink savored – and then Istvan threw himself forward, jamming his knife between the beast's teeth.

It roared, whirling around in a shower of dirt and frosted needles, rising to its hind legs and then slamming back to the ground. It had shoulders like a bear. Claws like a bear. Pines splintered as though shell-struck. Istvan held onto its spine, still cursing, trying to find its unnatural equivalent to human nerves. They all ran in the same places, but the chemistry was off and the frame was so much bigger–

A snarl. A spin. Another splintered tree, springboarding them both back around to the only living prey in the park.

Istvan gave up and cut off every impulse he could find.

The beast slapped at nothing, then struck the ground with a crack and a shatter, its shoulder carving a trench into frozen earth. A snarl died in its throat. Istvan almost fell on his head before he remembered he had wings.

He righted himself, kicked at the creature to be sure it was incapacitated, then took off running. "Edmund!"

The wizard leaned against a broken pine. Standing, but barely. "I'm all right," he said, and that was a lie because he was clearly in shock, flesh chapped and burnt by cold, and he cradled a left forearm soaked in congealed blood just beginning to run liquid. His cape lay in a heap beside him, rent and torn. "I'm all right," he repeated.

Istvan was at his side in an instant, tracing his fingers across the wound. A bite. A deep, frozen bite, all the way to the bone. All the dragging around had almost dislocated his shoulder. The pain of it was intoxicating; Istvan reflexively siphoned it away even as he despaired at his own reaction. Taking any pleasure at all in the poor man's agony wasn't right. "Why didn't you teleport?" he demanded. "Why didn't you take a moment to escape?"

Edmund slumped as the pain faded. "Lost my hat," he muttered.

Istvan glanced around and discovered it laying in the dirt some paces distant. "Edmund, why are you still here?"

A shrug. "Have to catch the monster. 'Less you can carry it." He stumbled forward, weaving side to side.

"Edmund, stop it. You can't—"

The wizard tripped on a fallen branch.

Istvan's hands went through him. No use. No use at all. He swallowed. "Edmund, if you fall, I can't help you. You know I can't help you."

Edmund wavered away. Towards the fallen beast. "I'll be fine."

Istvan followed him, aching to draw beside him. Take his arm. Put it over his shoulders. Be there like anyone else in the world could be there, so the poor man wouldn't have to wobble forward, stump by stump, edging perilously across each dip and rise in the icy ground. Oh, fighting monsters was easy. Istvan could fight anything. He should have come alone. He should have let Edmund sleep.

It took days to reach the fallen hulk. Weeks.

Finally, Istvan crouched beside the beast's enormous skull as Edmund leaned on its shoulders, calculating teleport measurements. Clouds of mist rolled from lungs like glacial bellows. Those scarlet-smeared canine teeth were longer than his hand. Edmund was shivering. Istvan had a coat – it was cold enough to warrant one, as cold as the Italian Alps – but he couldn't offer it. There was nothing to offer.

He stripped the thing off and hurled it aside.

Edmund glanced up. "I think I have it," he said. His handsome face was blistered, red and raw. Dirt dusted his goatee and sideburns. He hitched his chewed arm at his side, clenching and re-clenching fingers Istvan knew he couldn't feel. "I hate to ask, but... my hat?"

Istvan fetched his hat.

He sat, embroidering. Steel striking, fabric parting, thread leaking from a thousand wounds. A stain of petals. Poppies, this time. Red. No pattern, no plan. Grand maneuvers always ground to stalemate. The point of the needle was all that mattered, all that determined what came next and where. The rest was inertia.

Istvan had run out of follow-up cases long ago. Grown tired of wary eyes and worried whispers. The beast was gone, locked in a secure cell, and its victim slept in the bed beside him, a heap of blankets and drug-dulled misery. Hours had passed since the attack. Since Edmund had staggered across the frozen ground, bruised, bleeding, and bare of all that made him look bigger than he was. Hat. Cape. Confidence. The man had collapsed moments after returning to the Twelfth Hour, and someone else had caught him.

Now Istvan sat. Waiting.

Beauty spread before him, inch by bloody inch.

He was three-quarters through his thirteenth pattern when Magister Hahn ducked through the ward's curtains. She wore the same too-large jacket as always. Men's clothing, acceptable in this day and age for reasons he no longer cared to fathom. Worry simmered just below her hard facade, fears too rich to be recent, too deep to be passing. Exhaustion pooled beneath her eyes. "How is he?"

Istvan finished off the black, slicing the thread on the blade of his knife and tying it off. Thread weighed almost nothing, like him. "He'll live. He always does."

She gazed down at the bed. "Cowardice is his great talent."

"He isn't a coward, Magister, and with all due respect if you say that again in my presence I can't speak for what I might do."

Her lips thinned. She didn't ask what had happened. She wouldn't. The only time the Hour Thief returned from a mission in such a state was when he made a foolish mistake. When someone close to him made a foolish mistake that encouraged more mistakes. Three hours of sleep. Dragged into a tiger hunt after Lucy. After meeting the Susurration. After finding Bernault devices at Barrio Libertad. After learning Grace Wu was alive, had been alive for all this time, and had never once called. Istvan hadn't blamed him for sneaking that drink. Hadn't said anything.

Hoped.

"Full recovery?" she asked eventually.

Istvan jabbed the needle into a half-finished poppy and set his work on the bedside table. "Yes. In fact, he ought to be clear for release by the end of today. He won't have full use of the arm for some time, of course, but the rest is in working order." He watched the rise-and-fall of breath under blankets. "No thanks to me."

"I read his report."

"Then you know that Barrio Libertad is surrounded

by an uncommon horror, and intends to make a second Providence of it."

"I know that is a possibility, yes."

Istvan let out a breath. "Magister, what Edmund neglected to mention is that the fortress holds a card over him. Grace Wu."

The Magister raised an eyebrow.

"I don't know how she survived, Magister, but she has. I've tried talking to Edmund, but I don't know that he can be trusted to make impartial decisions in this matter. And, ah... in his condition, I... I wouldn't care for leaving him alone. Not with this Susurration creature about and still after him."

The Magister pulled a pen from her hair. Tapped it against her pockmarked cheek. "Doctor, Mr Templeton mentioned in his report that you fought it. I was hoping you could provide details."

Istvan brushed at the remnants of his dueling scars. "Details, Magister?"

She nodded.

He couldn't remember what Edmund had written. He had read the report over Edmund's shoulder, but... oh, the man didn't know everything. He couldn't.

"Magister," he began, "Miss Wu said that Barrio Libertad contacted you at least once. That they spoke to you about the Susurration. Did they not?"

"The name is new to me," she replied flatly.

He nodded, not believing her, but with little say in what she would and wouldn't share. "Of course, Magister. The Susurration is, as near as I can tell, a sort of ethereal presence that lives in the crater at Providence. Trapped there, if Miss Wu can be believed. It controls people, creates mirages from their memories, and is trying to capture more of them. It has... There are a lot of people out there, Magister." Istvan tried not to think about the overwhelming emptiness of the place, the wrongness of it. "Edmund thinks it's Conceptual."

"Like yourself."

"Yes, but rather opposite. Peace, order, nostalgia... that sort of vein." Edmund shifted beneath the blankets. The medication was wearing off. Istvan reached through artificial wool and cotton to pat him on the shoulder. "I'm told it was only a fragment, but to be perfectly honest, Magister, I'm surprised I could attack it at all. I suppose horrors like that aren't on my list of–"

Edmund flinched away, shivering.

Istvan snatched his hand back. Damn his touch. Cold layered on cold, distilled despair and death. Always unpleasant, always distasteful, always unnatural. No sane man could take comfort in the embrace of a corpse.

"Doctor? You mentioned a fragment?"

"Yes. Yes, my apologies." He dropped his hand in his lap, blinking behind his glasses. "The, ah, Susurration was inhabiting Lucy, rather like a spirit itself, and I... may have driven it off. I'm not certain. Grace Wu called her a 'smiler,' a sort of agent, and insisted that what I fought was only a small part of the creature controlling her – and on that count, I'm certain she was telling the truth. The whole is far worse." He shuddered. "I do believe that if only fragments can leave its territory, I could prevent it from affecting Edmund again. Or discourage it, at least."

"Hm." She inspected him a moment, then continued, "Did it say anything to you?"

He stared down at his hands.

When we meet again, Pista...

"It... offered peace. Nonsense, of course. All nonsense. I don't think it knew what I am."

"And you drove it off."

"As I said, I'm not certain. Perhaps."

The Magister propped her elbow on a crossed arm, hand at her chin, peering down at Edmund again. Thinking.

"The fortress is a sort of presence, as well," Istvan offered. "Not like the Susurration, I don't think, but certainly not inert and not at all peaceful. Nothing I would trust with Bernault devices, to be sure."

A nod. Her affect had changed: still worried, but lessened, more calculating. No surprise at anything he'd said. Of course, she was the Magister: the office came with a frankly unnerving degree of power, and access to all sorts of information that even Edmund had refused to share with anyone.

But even Edmund didn't know what had happened at Providence. No one did. No one but Magister Mercedes Hahn, who had somehow destroyed Shokat Anoushak and an army of horrors in a single mysterious stroke.

"Carry on," she said. She nodded at Edmund. "When he wakes, inform Mr Templeton that both of you are to back off. No deal on the devices. No dealings with Barrio Libertad until I tell you otherwise. Continue confiscating Bernault devices as you encounter them, and if the Susurration or any of its agents appear again, you are to bring the matter to me."

Istvan rubbed his wrists. Direct orders. "Yes, Magister."

"Oh," she added as she turned to leave, "and tell Mr Templeton that he should be more suspicious of strange women from this day forward. You never know what they might be carrying."

The curtain swung back into place behind her.

"Yes, Magister," he muttered.

He reached for his embroidery again.

●●●

Edmund winced as something realigned itself in his arm. It didn't hurt, numb as it was, but the dull slither of internal motion wasn't pleasant. He grasped his own bandaged wrist, trying to keep it steady.

Istvan stopped. "Too quickly?"

"Would you please stop fussing and get it over with?"

"You nearly had your arm bitten off by a tiger – I believe I'm entitled."

"It wasn't nearly bitten off, I'll be fine, and as I recall, when I was run through by that sword-claw and stuck in recovery for three weeks, you acted like it was a paper cut."

"That's because I've dealt with sword wounds. More at university alone than you've ever seen in your life. Some of them mine." He shifted something else. "This is different."

Edmund gritted his teeth. Being crushed between fangs and then dragged at high speed through the dirt hadn't done his arm any favors, and he understood the need to get rid of any bits of rock or bone or whatever else that had lodged in it. That didn't mean he had to sing the experience any praises. "Happy to provide a learning experience."

Istvan snorted.

Edmund tried to focus on something else. He would have to fix the sleeve of his shirt and jacket. Patch a cape trodden on by claws and torn off its fastenings. He had a few spares, but it was getting harder and harder to keep his ensemble in good condition. Double-breasted suit jackets and replacement opera capes weren't a typical consumer demand these days.

He should have teleported. Dodged. Something. How was he supposed to do his job with a bum arm? Istvan kept blaming himself, but Edmund had agreed to come.

Stupidly, but he'd agreed. It was already arranged. He'd done more on less sleep before and he was needed.

Maybe he'd hoped that going along would take his mind off Grace.

Finally, Istvan withdrew his hand, wiping away the memory of blood. He dropped a tiny fragment of something on a tray for tiny fragments. "I believe that's all of it," he said.

Edmund tried to sit up straighter, then realized putting any weight on his wounded arm was a bad idea. He would have to spend some time recovering, for sure.

He mentally tabulated what he had listed in his ledger, and what increment would be best suited to the task. He had time. He healed no faster than anyone else, but his days weren't limited to twenty-four hours.

Legendary resilience, and all a sham.

"Was it one of hers?" he asked, thinking of Shokat Anoushak and Providence.

"It was." Istvan pulled a length of gauze from beneath the tray, white spangled with red and black flowers arranged in almost liquid flecks and spatters. "How the beast survived so long, I've no idea. I expect I'll be looking it over soon, but..."

"But?"

"Oh, Edmund, I'm so sorry."

"Would you stop apologizing?"

"Edmund, you don't understand! With you in such pain, and I... The... the way I am, Edmund, all this time, I've been enjoying it! It isn't often you're hurt this badly, and it's... it's..." He tugged a needle from the fabric, threaded it, and jabbed savagely at the material. It kept him in practice, went the claim. Edmund doubted he'd ever had cause to perform surgical stitching so intricate. <I hate it.>

Edmund leaned back on his pillows. Istvan would never complain about his abilities in front of his staff – he performed miracles with them, after all – and that left only one person to talk to about it. It was a conversation so old Edmund knew it by rote. <You can't help it.>

<I still hate it.>

<If you didn't, I'd be...>

The tray rattled. Istvan stopped his work. Edmund almost told him to stop kicking the bed before he remembered that the specter couldn't, that it wasn't a poltergeist responsible for the swaying lights overhead, for the rumble of rolling wheels, for the crashes and cries beyond the trembling curtains. The tray rattled to the edge of the table. Slid and fell.

Oh, hell. Not another one.

Edmund clutched the edges of the mattress as the bed bucked like it was trying to throw him off. Istvan did manage to catch the tray, but not the curtain support that fell through him. Chrome detailing pinged off the pillars, stained glass cracking. Dust showered from the ceiling. The ground rolled. The way ground shouldn't roll, floor and earth and rock no longer stable and no longer certain. If rock wasn't certain, what was?

It was nothing like the swaying deck of a ship. Nothing like the sudden tilt of catastrophe.

Nothing like. Nothing like.

Edmund squeezed his eyes shut. Books. Some of the Twelfth Hour's books would be falling off the shelves again. Probably the ones on the upper story, where the shaking would be more severe. He didn't need both arms to shelve books.

He was running a mental catalog of written inventory by the time the earthquake subsided.

Istvan set the tray and embroidery back on the table.

"Edmund, stay here. You're in no shape to help with emergency response."

"I wasn't about to volunteer." He released his death grip on the bed. "You know, Istvan, I'm really starting to get tired of these. We never had earthquakes before. Not here."

"You aren't released until I tell you," Istvan continued. "Don't go home."

Edmund sighed. "Istvan—"

"Don't go home!"

The specter took two running steps forward, spread tattered wings, and shot through the infirmary doors.

CHAPTER SEVENTEEN

His house was intact. Only a few new cracks, running through the hall and bathroom. Hairline. The broken windows had lost a few more shards of glass, but the cardboard patches remained attached. The horseshoe Istvan hated still hung in its place above the door. The lights weren't working, but they sometimes didn't.

He lit some candles. The stove was working, one of the benefits of not being electric. He drew some water from the barrel outside and put the kettle on.

"If anyone comes by, I'm not home," he told Beldam.

She made one of her usual lazy attempts to trip him. He sidestepped the cat's efforts and made for his room. His damaged cape, jacket, and shirt went on one side of the closet, to be repaired or used to make replacements when he got the chance. He had three spare jackets and one spare cape left. Five shirts. It would have to do for now.

He took a shower, put on his robe, put his arm back in its sling, and made a cup of tea. The gin could wait until later, when the bite started to hurt again in earnest. Alcohol was a painkiller. He'd have a drink then, for that reason. Maybe two. It depended on how badly it hurt.

No one at the door for dinner. Istvan worried too much.

Edmund finished his second cup of tea. He'd shelved most of the fallen books and made note of those missing, but he did have some archival work waiting in the vault. It was technically on hold, what with his recent return to duty, but was something Mercedes did want finished, eventually, under the usual supervision. He could do that tomorrow. That was a good plan for tomorrow.

Tomorrow was the Fourth of July, and that meant dressing for the occasion. He returned to his room.

His desk was locked, but he knew how to find the key, and in short order he had the left drawer open. Packed in the back were photographs of his family. Letters from friends. A sampling of both from lovers, some yellowed and some fresh as yesterday. He ignored them all like they weren't there. He pushed aside the Yokata family tanto. Didn't look at Grace's picture or the signed photo of Rita May or the keys to Dan's car (entomologist to his etymologist, they'd always said, close as brothers). Beneath that hideous tie with clocks and cats he couldn't bring himself to either wear or be rid of, he found his old American flag pin. He pulled it out, and shut the desk.

The pin went on the lapel of the first of his spare jackets. Below the clock-and-crescent of the Twelfth Hour. Whether or not the United States still existed as such was a fine question, but the pin had always gone there and so that's where he put it.

He regarded it a moment. Then he went back to the desk and retrieved Grace's picture. Round. Framed. Just a tad larger than locket-sized, printed on poor-quality paper. She was smiling, her dark eyes exposed to the world, a gash on her cheek stitched closed the day before.

Long after his sword accident. Two months before she'd been killed.

He poured himself a glass of gin on the way out.

Back to the kitchen. He set Grace's picture on the table, face-down. Then he pulled out his chair and sat in it. Beldam quested up beside him, tail flicking side to side. He scratched her behind the ears. A matter of seconds and then the enormous cat was in his lap, purring, cutting off circulation to both legs.

He regarded his glass.

He looked at the living room, where he'd once tried and failed to teach Grace how to dance foxtrot. It wasn't that she was a slow learner.

Is this Sinatra? Why do you have to be so old, Eddie?

I'm thirty-five.

Show me.

He regarded his glass again.

Grace Wu. Scarlet lightning. Dynamite on rails. Probably smarter than he was, and the only gal he'd ever met who could keep up with a time wizard in more ways than one. Istvan had feared for his safety, citing her speed, her strength, her generation of potentially killing current, all the unknowns of Conduit physiology. Edmund had reminded him that in the event he broke a few bones or came down with a case of St Elmo's fire, he knew a good doctor.

Less than a year they had been together. Spring and summer and into the fall. The leaves had turned and then she was gone.

The leaves had turned in 1941 and then he was trapped.

He downed his glass.

It wouldn't have lasted. Nothing lasted, not with him. That was what she'd said about Istvan – that the only reason Edmund kept him around was that the ghost was one of the few things that would last as long as he would. He wished he'd been able to argue that it wasn't true.

Beldam squirmed in his lap. He realized that he'd stopped patting her and resumed, muttering an apology.

The picture sat before him, face-down. It was over. She'd all but said it was over.

All but said.

He shouldn't have – he knew he shouldn't have – but he flipped the picture face-up. Stared at it.

Grace Wu. She'd come from New York City after the Wizard War changed it into what it was now, clawing her way out with the aid of that strange power that surged through her flesh and bones: power she was just learning to use, power that as far as anyone knew would kill her before the year was up. She'd lost everything.

She'd refused to let it stop her.

She'd called herself Shandian, "Lightning" in Chinese, even though she didn't speak the language and neither had her parents or grandparents. She'd thrown herself into the business of fighting the Wizard War with vigor and laughing wit, racing ahead so she wouldn't dwell on what was behind or before her, believing all the while that they could somehow win what didn't seem winnable.

She'd been like him, in his earlier days. Costumes. Code names. She suddenly had superpowers and she had grown up with same four-color influences that had inspired him to take up his own mantle all those years ago. Glossier pages, but the same.

Grace had become Shandian, and Shandian wouldn't take no from anybody. Shandian took what she wanted. Shandian never gave up.

He didn't know who Resistor Alpha was.

Edmund had been the Hour Thief since the mid-Fifties, when he'd realized what he'd have to do, where he'd have to find his time, how he should present himself so he didn't feel like a predator. Like a leech.

Edmund didn't take time. That was someone else, someone both better and worse than he was, someone strong enough to bear the pressure when he couldn't – and, so very often, he couldn't.

It was the Hour Thief who was famous, not him. The Hour Thief who was really employed by the Twelfth Hour, who had led so many of its members to destruction. The Hour Thief who formed the leading half of a strange and public partnership, paired with a much older and foreign friend who thought the whole business was faintly ridiculous.

The Hour Thief.

Edmund blinked. He set the picture down.

Oh, boy. Oh, this was a bad idea, but if he could just talk to Grace again...

Barrio Libertad was a rogue state. This was established. Mercedes had forbidden him to have anything to do with it – him and Istvan both – but who, exactly, was *him*? Who was Edmund Templeton, to the public? Who was forbidden to visit the fortress?

He stood, dumping Beldam off his lap. Wobbled on numb legs.

She grumbled at him.

"Sorry," he said.

She sniffed a disparaging remark about his manners or parentage and minced away, tail in the air.

He snatched up picture and glass, empty now but no longer needed, and headed back to his room. That flag pin was on one of his black jackets, but it could be moved. The sole requirement for the Fourth of July was that he had it, not that he had it on that particular lapel. Only about a third of his wardrobe was black.

The Hour Thief was down for the count. Bound by orders. Forbidden to interact or intervene, and unable to throw a proper punch.

Maybe Edmund Templeton could get some answers.

He had gone home. Istvan knew Edmund had gone home. If there was one thing the man couldn't be trusted to do, it was abandon routine. He'd gone home, taken a shower, made tea, read a book, had a glass of gin, and gone to bed at midnight. He always did, on off days, and with his arm in that condition and his heart not yet recovered... yes, very much an off day. He'd gone home and done all the usual small things Edmund did when Edmund was able. Even when he oughtn't.

Oh, Istvan hoped he was all right. The Susurration was all too insidious for his tastes. Too gentle. Too quiet. A creeping, smothering doom, like snow.

<Please be calm,> he said. His Vietnamese was rusty and his accent as terrible as ever but thirty years in Indochina took some time to erase. <Help is coming. I will tell them where you are.>

A cough in the darkness, the air close and stifling and the fallen beams of the apartment block closer still. Three people trapped in a small pocket, two adults and a child, as near as he could tell, barely enough room to breathe. Istvan himself crouched in the rubble, electrical wire and broken concrete scraping through his ribs. All three of them were afraid, but not of him. Not once he told them who he was.

<Thank you,> one said, a low rasp choked with dust. <I didn't think the stories were true.>

<Oh, I don't know that they all are,> he replied. He

finished staunching the last of the bleeding, navigating torn arteries by touch alone, a leg impaled by rebar. It would hold long enough. Already the scrapes and clinks of digging filtered down from above. <Be brave, now, and shout as best you can once they've come closer.>

<We will.>

He patted a knee he couldn't see and then departed, angling upward through the collapse. Shoddy construction, all of it. Built of rubble itself. They were lucky it hadn't tilted into the nearest spellscar – that had been a horror, runaway magic cracking new shafts into the ground, leaking phosphorescent growth that changed to moss where it touched flesh – but, in survival alone, they would always be lucky.

Gradual settling, indeed. The earth ought to make up its mind and be done with it.

Lamps cast sallow light across exhausted faces laboring in the rescue shaft. A circular ring of white and blue hovered further above, weightless, a craft of some sort parked above operations and lifting away the heaviest beams with slender tentacles, strange assistance without a sound. Istvan told the man who looked to be coordinating efforts about those trapped: three directly below, two huddled in a doorway some ten meters off, several others beneath desks or tables, some wounded and some not. First efforts ought to be turned towards these people, and then these. *Save as many as you can. Do your best.*

Agreement, noting down the locations on a chart he carried. Their best was all they could do, no?

Istvan winged away. More searching. More circling, straining the air for that distinct variety of helpless terror, descending and rising and descending again, bound by contract and simple human obligation to help. He couldn't lift anything himself, not anymore.

He hoped Edmund was all right.

Edmund slept better than he had in a long while. No earthquakes. No nightmares. No midnight surprises. Istvan didn't show for breakfast, but Edmund could put on his own water and he did, turning on the radio to catch nothing but faint static and then putting on a record instead. No requests for classical or waltz. The sun was out and he could dust his bookshelves without anyone making fun of him. His stolen spellbook was still there, still safe, and still distinctly less appealing than the book beside it, which seemed a far better read for anyone browsing.

He put out a new set of bowls for Beldam, washed his dishes, and mulled over the decision of last night with the satisfaction of knowing that for once he could do something about someone he'd lost. Grace might be over him, yes. She might be with someone else, yes. But he didn't know any of that for sure and people did change. He had to try. He'd done worse things for worse reasons.

His civilian ensemble was a bit musty, but serviceable: pressed khakis, vest, dress shirt, tie, and suspenders. Navy-blue instead of black, except the tie, which was red. The flag pin went on his lapel, next to a sprig of flowers.

Before he left, he wrote a note so Istvan wouldn't worry and stuck it to the refrigerator. *Extenuation*, said the word magnet. It was a good word to know.

No teleporting to Barrio Libertad. He thought, instead, of Providence. Murals painted before immense double-doors. Those pylons that made his teeth ache, that cleared a partial path through the Susurration and its pleasant illusions. Through perfection. Through peace.

What else could frighten an avatar of war so badly?

He snapped his pocket watch.

The sun was out there, too, and the breeze ideal. The walls of Barrio Libertad loomed above him, ramshackle immensity topped by turrets aimed at nothing. He approached the doors and they slid open, just as they had before. *Keep all limbs inside the conveyance*, said the walls. English and Spanish. Raised lettering.

The doors slid shut.

Edmund leaned against the rail. He adjusted his tie.

The elevator didn't move.

"Good morning," crackled the same heavily accented, stuttering voice from before.

"Good morning," he replied. "This is Edmund Templeton. I was hoping to meet with–"

"You are ducks. Your current position is in a small box suspended over a fall of one hundred sixty meters."

"Excuse me?"

Something crashed into place behind the walls. The elevator shuddered.

He clutched at the rail. Barrio Libertad. Insular, paranoid, and so staunchly thaumophobic that he required a special exception to enter with a single passive spell intact. Right. "Look, I'm not here to cause trouble, I promise." Who was he talking to? "I just want to meet with Grace. Grace Wu. Resistor Alpha. Is she available?"

A clanging. A ripping. The air contorted around him, mathematical patterns gonging against the backs of his eyeballs.

He took a moment to yank out his pocket watch... to shout...

The elevator bent inwards and outwards at the same time and then he was where he shouldn't have been.

●●●

Istvan winged northward over rubble, finally free. All night. All morning. Well into the afternoon. After six earthquakes it had become clear that his particular skillset – tireless, immaterial, fast enough to cover enormous swathes of territory – was invaluable in the initial stages of disaster. He couldn't remember how much surveying he had done. No chance at all to check on Edmund. He had eventually pleaded mental rather than physical fatigue: he could manage thirty or forty hours at a stretch, and would later if he had to, but couldn't stand to worry any longer.Now the sun blazed to his right, clouds billowing across the sky like gunpowder given a match. The twisted spire of the Black Building loomed over former Manhattan, a solid sheet of dark steel that rushed towards and then past him, unscathed by the many lightning strikes it had suffered over the years and untouched by the earth's violence. It swayed during quakes, nothing more.

He banked over Edmund's neighborhood, the pagoda on the hill a little worse for wear. The man hadn't seemed to be at the Twelfth Hour, as expected. He'd probably woken early, dusted, read another book. He was probably perfectly fine. Moping a bit over Grace, perhaps, but...

Istvan alighted on the roof, skidded down the shingles, and swung through the living room wall.

No Edmund.

Istvan didn't panic, precisely. He did check every room in the house multiple times, terrify the cat, startle several neighbors, and finally find himself standing in the middle of the kitchen, wanting to tear off in search someplace else, and not moving because it felt like if he did he would fly apart in all directions. Edmund was probably off on some legitimate business. Edmund had managed just fine on his own for many years. Edmund didn't need help or protection, not like that and certainly not from the likes of Istvan. He was fine. He was fine. He had to be fine.

Istvan was debating his chances of taking on the full weight of the Susurration one-on-one by the time he noticed the note left on the refrigerator.

Gone out, it said, *will be undercover at Barrio Libertad for Fourth of July festivities. Hoping to find some answers. Should be back late tonight or tomorrow. Please don't look for me.*

Don't look for me.

Please don't–

<What?> Istvan hissed. He read it again. Then a third time. Edmund was supposed to be the rational one. The sensible one. The reasonable one, with the steadiest temperament and the greatest devotion to duty any man could have. He wasn't wild and violent, like Istvan. He was a wizard who had seen too much. A librarian who led armies. A man who knew better, who respected his own dignity, who'd kept to the same routine for seventy years. He knew his place. He followed orders.

Will be undercover? Not returning until tomorrow?

Istvan crumpled the note in a fist and threw it. Looking for answers, oh, no – looking for Grace Wu. She had been here. This was her fault. Edmund wasn't like this. He wasn't supposed to be like this. He was disobeying direct orders – direct orders! – and gallivanting off in pursuit of a woman who didn't even care for him anymore. Who maybe never had!

She had no right to do this to him!

He was Istvan's Man in Black, not hers!

Istvan snapped open his wings and shot through the wall. Wood. Electrical wiring. Insulation. Wood again. He skimmed the hedge, slashing a trench through the top. Out. Up. Focus on climbing. On wingbeats. On clouds above and then below, faster and faster, winds that screamed through him like solid barriers, air that turned to ice. The sky shaded to purple. Black. Focus on something else. Anything else. His chains burned, taut and choking, tugged in a dozen different directions by conflicting mandates of uncertain priority: watch Edmund, stay away from the fortress, don't tell him of this conversation, help with the earthquake, do whatever you think is prudent, *stay within bounds...*

The stars hardened into unblinking points, distant and unsympathetic.

Barrio Libertad was a rogue state. Magister Hahn had given Edmund the direct order to avoid dealings with it. Edmund had chosen to attend a Fourth of July celebration at Barrio Libertad. That was more than insubordination. That was consorting with the enemy. That was treason.

The Magister had to be told. That was what mattered. Nothing else.

All the world curved below, forbidden.

Istvan dove.

CHAPTER EIGHTEEN

"He's not going to contaminate the place, I promise. I'll make sure he keeps his ducks to himself."

A panel hissed upwards before him. Red lights. The tang of salt and ozone. His mouth was dry and he still heard ringing. Crashing. The rush of water, maybe, somewhere far off. He was on his back. He lifted a hand to shield his eyes.

Grace leaned over him. No cowl, no goggles. Just Grace. The light was above her and it made interesting highlights in her hair. "Eddie," she said. "What are you doing here?"

He tested his tongue. "Came to see you."

She sighed. "That's what Diego said."

"What?"

"Come on," she said, "let him up."

The panel below him tilted upwards, becoming a chair and then a wall that retreated and vanished. More panels drew away to either side, angular petals rimmed in sawtoothed latches, hooking over and around each other to form a small room out of... well, out of the presumably larger room that had been there before. A sphere of orange rust. Somehow, no seams. Edmund kicked cautiously at the floor. It seemed solid.

"Grace…" he began, and then he realized she wasn't alone.

A man clad in a red T-shirt glowered beside her. He was shorter than her, stocky but bony, almost painfully thin. The flesh at his neck was dark brown and deeply scarred, interrupted by a haphazard array of metal support bracings and other things: a ribbed tube plunging through his esophagus, bolts driven into his collarbone, a grille embedded where his voicebox should have been. Above that…

…Above that sat a crude, roughly skull-sized device more akin to a camera, or perhaps a tabletop radio, than a human face. No ears. No nose. No mouth. Cooling fans in tubular mountings hummed at each side. Five lenses spun, focused, and re-focused, irised "eyes" of sky blue, all different sizes and arranged with no sense of symmetry. All staring at Edmund. Machinery whirred with each tiny motion, balancing a weight never intended for the human spinal column.

"Cameraman," Edmund croaked.

"I can't believe you tried to just walk through the front door," Grace was saying. "I thought we had a reputation, Eddie. Or did you forget the whole rogue, incommunicado, magic-hating city-state thing?" She pointed at at his lapel. "And if you say that's thyme instead of lavender, I might have to punch you."

Edmund made sure he still had his pocket watch. He did. "Grace? Who is this?"

"Hm?"

"Your… friend."

She glanced at her companion. "Oh, right. Sorry. I thought you knew." She gestured from one to the other and back again. "Diego, Eddie. Eddie, Diego Escarra

Espinoza. You've actually met already, just not in person."

Edmund froze. The architect? This was the architect she'd kept going on about?

He took a moment to straighten his jacket. Always better to be composed in a situation like this.

"Pleased to meet you," he said.

"They devour the numbers," replied Diego. He crossed brown arms covered in faded tattoos of flowers and hummingbirds, a motion rough and sharp and teetering just on the edge of coordination, like a vengeful marionette. Mismatched lenses clicked and swiveled disdainfully in their mountings. "The pattern collapse to the accommodation of possibility is n- not sufficient."

Grace flashed Edmund an ear-to-ear grin, the kind she usually reserved for showing off her powers or her genius. "Isn't he weird?"

"Yes," Edmund said. "Yes, he is." He waited for a response and received none: Diego simply glared at him. "What... is he?"

"A computer. Well, a cyborg. Or an android, really – there's no fleshy bits left above the neck – but he calls himself a computer."

"A computer," Edmund repeated flatly.

"Fastest in the world."

"What was that about ducks?"

"Mathematical substitution. A way to bypass anything that doesn't make sense. He's figured out magic, Eddie, and that's how."

"Why ducks?"

"Why not ducks? Eddie, all you need to understand is that Diego here is so far beyond genius that we don't have a word for it. He built this entire fortress out of dust over a period of about two months. Those cameras of his can see anything, and I mean anything: past, present, future, subatomic, around corners." She dropped an arm around Diego's bony shoulders. The android didn't flinch or, despite his emaciated frame, buckle like Edmund half-expected. "This, Eddie, is a guy who runs simulations of worldwide weather patterns out to centuries and down to single snowflakes, and does it in massive parallel between every word we say because he's bored."

The words emerged on their own. "I didn't know you had a thing for chrome, Grace."

She started laughing. "What?"

"I don't know. You tell me."

"No," she choked, still laughing, "No, Eddie, that would be the worst – I love science, Eddie, but not like that."

"He has no sense," said Diego. "There is no purpose to r- remain."

"Besides," Grace continued, "he's not interested." She pulled her arm away but didn't relinquish her touch, hand remaining on Diego's shoulder. Easily. Casually. Like she didn't even notice she was doing it. "Look, uh, would you excuse us for a second?"

Edmund stood there as she tugged the other man through the room's circular door. "Sure, Grace."

A machine. Diego was a machine. Grace's architect friend, if not lover, was an artificial brain stapled onto a flesh-and-blood body that didn't even act like it was human.

And she complained about Istvan?

Istvan winged to a running landing over the cracked remnants of a sidewalk. The stoplight leaning over the equally root-shattered street was shedding leaves unseasonably early, thin round things that blinked red and green. Axe marks marred its trunk, to no avail.

The mountainous curves of the edifice itself towered before him, its broad steps lettered with old poems, its Grecian columns festooned with imaginative sculpture that, thus far, remained uncensored. Chips of fallen stone lay scattered across its lower levels. Some of its windows were cracked. According to Edmund, the upper library had once been a small three-story affair converted from an old church, a wholly ordinary structure with a weather vane in the shape of a crescent moon. No longer.

Istvan took the steps three or four at a time. The door was glass and steel, modern shelves lined with modern books visible beyond. A labeled handle invited entry: PULL.

He hammered at it with the hilt of his knife. "Doctor Czernin. I've vital information regarding the Hour Thief. Do you mind?"

The label changed to PUSH.

He did, not paying attention to his own lack of mass and barely remembering to mutter thanks. The shelving beyond the glass didn't change, but the shelving revealed through the doorway was wood instead of metal, stained dark, inlaid with glass and chrome. Another library, basement-built with no basement access. Until now.

The place was crowded as always. More earthquake victims and their tenders, New Haven farmers carting in boxes of tomatoes, Twelfth Hour wizards and watchmen reporting back from spellscar patrol, visitors from the Magnolia Group inspecting tangles of electrical wire. A family of ravens browsed the shelves. The giant lizard was back, stumping along on a stout cane. All sorts of people. His only concession to common courtesy was to fly over rather than through the majority of them.

"Magister Hahn," he called. He banged on the heavy

door at the end of the hall. "Magister Hahn, this is Doctor Czernin. It's about Edmund, he's gone and... Magister Hahn, are you there?"

The wood sank into grooves before his eyes. *Busy*, it said.

Istvan cursed. He hammered at it a second time. "Magister Hahn!"

Do Not Disturb, the door informed him.

Istvan sheathed his knife and tried to charge through it, only to strike it as though he were solid – and not with enough force to break it down, either. He cursed again. Faint murmurings drifted from behind the door, but it always did that and he couldn't make out any words. She had read Edmund's report. She knew what was going on with Barrio Libertad and the surrounding horrors. The Susurration. Edmund. Grace bloody Wu. All of it. Of all the days to be absent!

He turned, took a breath, took a step... and then whirled about and assaulted the door again, a surprise attack that only resulted in a prim *In Urgent Conference*. No use. No bloody use at all. What on Earth was she doing?

Were there smilers in the Twelfth Hour? Had it all been compromised? What manner of coincidence was this?

The sensation of a heart hammering where he had none, he sprinted back down the hall. Telephone. She had a telephone, and though Edmund's hadn't been left in his house, someone else would have one.

As it turned out, the Magister gave very few people her personal number. It made sense, he supposed, but it wasn't a sense he wanted to hear at the moment.

Istvan made a beeline for the Department of Modern Technology and Such.

•••

Barrio Libertad, in two days, had transformed itself into a riot of red, white, and blue. Streamers fluttered from every surface. Rows of tiny flags strung up on lines zigzagged above bridges and walkways. Larger flags flapped from windows. Most were the American standard, but others bore a simple diagram of the fortress in place of stars, and only two stripes. The streets were spilling over with people, and someone, somewhere, was cooking sausages. Stands, stalls, carts, and performance stages choked the central plaza below. Firecrackers burst on the sidewalks.

That Barrio Libertad was an independent city-state built by a Chilean didn't seem to factor into people's minds: it was the Fourth, and the Fourth was and always would be an excuse to gather, carouse, barbecue, and light off colorful explosives in mass quantities.

Edmund wondered where they had found all of the meat.

He followed Grace across one of the bridges, far enough away from the main mass of festivities that they could hear each other talk. The rails looked like steel but weren't – no more than the adobe was adobe, the canvas umbrellas were made of canvas, or the murals were painted in paint. Grace claimed that the entire fortress was built of materials he couldn't imagine and no one else could replicate, mutable and nigh-indestructible.

"It's thyme, isn't it," she said.

He touched his lapel. "It is."

"You're the worst."

"It doesn't bother you?"

"I can handle puns, Eddie."

"No. Not that." He glanced uneasily up at a looming gantry, scaffolding laced between support columns for a spiraled stairway. High-tension wires trailed downward from the nearest wall. Strings of flags flapped from every corner. It didn't look like any of it would hold up to a stiff wind... but, high above, one of the enormous turrets turned with the ponderous grace of a whale.

After what she had told him, the buttresses along the walls put him vividly in mind of a tremendous steel rib cage.

"Grace," he said, "how can you live here?"

She shrugged. "It's better than the alternative."

He bit back a sharp retort. That's what he had said. That was his answer, for why he did what he did and how he lived with himself. She had to realize what she was doing. "Grace, you said Diego can monitor everything and everyone here, controls everything down to the color of the murals, and can reshape entire sections at a whim – that he *is* Barrio Libertad in every way that counts."

"That's right."

He caught her arm. "Does that mean that anger Istvan was talking about is him? Is it because I'm here?" She pulled away; he held tighter. "Not all wizards can be blamed for the Shift, Grace – if it was the war that caused it, it was Shokat Anoushak, not the rest of us. We aren't all like her, Grace. Please, believe me. We aren't all like her."

Not me. Not yet. Not ever.

Grace looked at him, and he couldn't tell what she was thinking, and he didn't want to speculate.

"It's motivational anger with a side of grim determination," she said. She pried his fingers off with almost contemptuous ease. "And Diego's always like that. He chooses it. Says it's his most productive setting. Magic has nothing to do with it."

"So what–"

"He can see it, Eddie."

Edmund stared at her. Seeing the effects of magic, fine. Seeing magic itself... oh, boy.

Oh, boy.

"Grace, are you crazy?"

She walked away.

He chased after her, fingers closing around his pocket watch. All of Providence was under total magical interdiction. He'd never learned how. "Grace, do you know what you're saying? Nothing human can see magic. Nothing even close to human, not without becoming something else, something like a... a god, Grace, the kind that exists outside the world, the kind that you don't *want* to give a damn about you or your life or anything you care about, ever!"

He took a moment to skid to a stop in front of her. "Grace, please, trust me. There are some things you shouldn't tempt."

"You're one to talk," she muttered.

"I am! I know what I'm talking about!"

She brushed past him, leaving the bridge and making for a spiked gate. The wrought-iron archway overhead resembled curling leaves, and she made as though to push the gate open... before halting, one hand still resting on the bars. The other combed through her hair. Straightened her T-shirt. It looked good on her. Everything looked good on her.

A garden lay beyond: roofed, meticulously geometric, lit bright as daylight. Green and white. Everything not leafy or fruiting was tile, pale and glowing. It smelled like the forest behind the old farm house, after rain. It was her sort of garden.

"Grace," he tried again, "you can't stay here. It isn't safe."

"I'll decide that," she replied.

He reached for her. "Come with me?"

She looked at his hand.

"I know we don't have running water, but we're working on it." He tried a smile. "I'll haul the buckets."

She looked away. "I'm sorry," she said. "I really am. Eddie, I know what I did. I know what it must look like. I wish it hadn't worked out this way, I really do, but Eddie, I couldn't leave. I still can't. I'm Resistor Alpha. I have a job to do." She closed her fingers around the bars. "And before you ask, I ran. That's how I survived. I ran and ran and didn't stop running until I was miles away."

His lips moved. "Is there someone else?"

She shook her head. "Even if there were, it's been years. I know what you're hoping, and I'm sorry, but it's not going to happen. We're over."

He knew it. He'd always known it. They always said that, eventually.

"Why?"

She sighed, and he realized that she had to be thirty-six, now. A year older than he was... than he told himself he was... than how old, physically, he was. Just on the edge of lines, depending on the harshness of one's experience, not yet to greying. Istvan was in his mid-forties and weather-beaten; Istvan would never look any different.

Grace would. Everyone else would. Photographs, shifting and sliding and slipping away from his own unchanging portrait, forever–

"You drink too much," she said.

Edmund took a steadying breath. "I know."

"When we met, Eddie, I didn't know anything. I didn't know you. I didn't know me. I didn't know what would happen and I didn't know how long I'd have, and when you swept in like Zorro, I figured I'd make the best of it. And it was pretty good." She cast him a brief smile, and then the expression faded. "I know myself better, now. I've got a place. I've got a cause. And... Eddie, I can't."

He waited. He had time. He always had time. She pulled away from the gate, not looking at him. "You've given up on yourself," she said. "You talk about your great mistake and then you don't do anything about it. You go, and you sit, and you drink. I can't deal with that."

"You let me think you were dead."

"It was easier."

"Easier than what?"

She let go of the gate, pale fingers sliding away from dark iron. Then she turned, without a word, and started across another bridge.

Edmund clenched clammy hands, trailing after her. Almost dizzy. Almost floating. "Do you know what you did to me? After you died – disappeared, whatever happened – I stopped thinking again. More than usual. I just did what I had to do, and when it was finally over, we held a memorial service. They read your name."

She stopped.

"They read your name," he repeated. He blinked, and looked down at the bridge. "I was a wreck for over a year, Grace. Couldn't do anything. Could barely leave the house. Istvan was the only person I could stand to have around. I'd threaten anyone else, run from them, go into fits. I... I couldn't..."

She wasn't saying anything.

He kicked at the bridge, wishing he hadn't said anything either. "Look, I know you don't like him, but Istvan does know what he's doing. He got me through it. I went back to work. Same-old, same-old."

"Not so invincible, then," she said.

He lifted his bad arm, still in its sling. "Never was."

Firecrackers popped below. She glanced over the rail. Glanced at him.

Walked back, and took his good arm.

"Come on, Eddie," she said. She waved him forward, down another path. "You went to all this trouble to get here and I haven't even offered you a Fourth of July hot dog."

CHAPTER NINETEEN

The corridor Istvan followed now hadn't been there eight years ago. The Magnolia Group had rigged it with power and lighting but the earthquakes hadn't been kind: many of the visible carvings were riddled with cracks.

The door to Modern Technologies and Such was ajar. Istvan stepped through. <Miss Justice? I need to reach the Magister. It's very important.>

<Doctor?>

<Yes. It's... it's about Edmund.>

<Back here,> came the reply. It remained a schooled and very German sort of German, but she had gotten much better over the last few years and it was something of a comfort that she spoke it at all. <One second.>

Istvan started towards the back of the room. Scaffolding stretched eight and ten feet high. The hum of machinery permeated the air, omnipresent, much like the many hundreds of multicolored cables snaking across the stone. Holes drilled in the walls supported shelves full of odd devices and personal knickknacks. Precautionary wards flickered across an enormous crack in the ceiling. The air was cool and dry, supposedly the perfect environment for computing machines, though he doubted the dust from broken plaster was doing it any favors.

Lists of names scrolled across screens at the far end of the room, marked with numbers. Boxes appeared and disappeared. Columns of light slewed across one of the panels, detonating multicolored triangles in starry bursts. A celery stick sat in an empty coffee cup before a well-padded swivel chair, currently occupied by a different sort of wizard.

Janet Justice.

She glanced back at him with a hesitant smile before returning her attention to her electric magic. <You know,> she said, <I was supposed to meet with Mr Templeton yesterday. What happened?>

He told her.

He probably shouldn't have gone on the way he did, or been quite so insulting of the man's taste and intelligence, but Edmund deserved it. A note? *Don't follow me*?

Miss Justice finally held up her hands. <Doctor, I'm only catching about half of what you're saying. You're talking really fast and some of it doesn't sound like German.>

Istvan came to a halt, worrying at his scarring. <Sorry. I simply... oh, this isn't really your business.>

<You're pretty worried about him, aren't you?>

<No!>

She raised her eyebrows.

<Yes,> he admitted. He jammed his glasses back on. <Would you please just see to it that the Magister hears of what he's done? I'm going to... I'm going to make sure he is where I think he is. Thank you, Miss Justice. For the help. And, ah... pardon my language. Soldiers, you know. Not the best of polite company.>

She shrugged. <I've heard worse.> A glance at her machinery, and then back to him, her dark eyes glittering with blue and green reflections. <A favor for me?>

He paused. <Yes?>

<When you find him, let him know that the conjunction he asked me to watch for is coming up on the seventh, this month, 7 pm, provided that what's up there in space still holds true. It should. I think. And... well, over the last few days there's been a small but notable spike in goat trafficking.>

Istvan blinked. <Goat... trafficking?>

A shrug. She struck a key.

A map appeared on another screen, a copy of the larger one on the Twelfth Hour's wall and its constellation of pins.

Miss Justice pointed at the upper part of Triskelion, deep in the spellscarred mountains of former Pennsylvania. <I've got reports of livestock coming out of there where it never has before. All goats.>

Istvan leaned over to get a closer look. Triskelion? That was the home of those mercenaries, the best in Big East. Stealing goats was surely far below their purview. Men who dealt in Bernault devices had better things to do with their time. <Edmund told you to watch for this?>

<In conjunction with the conjunction,> Janet replied, confusion well-leavened with the cautious dread characteristic of most who worked with the Twelfth Hour, wizards and laymen alike. <Some other things, too. Amber, for instance, and certain kinds of pigments.> Another shrug. <I didn't ask.>

Of course Edmund hadn't told Istvan, or explained to him, or even taken care to warn him, if there were anything to warn him about. At this rate Istvan would find a note about this, too. Goat trafficking, indeed.

Bloody wizards.

Miss Justice made the map disappear again. <Good luck with your search. And be careful. I've checked again; the satellites still can't see Barrio Libertad. It's like that entire area has been erased.>

Istvan sighed. <Oh, I'm not the one to worry about.>

He departed. Back through the stone corridors, through the library, through the door of glass and steel that opened both ways to two different places. He wasn't following Edmund, not precisely. Not all the way. He would only make certain that Edmund was in fact at Barrio Libertad, and not... elsewhere.

The Susurration knew where Edmund lived, after all. Could likely find a way inside. Even fake his handwriting, if it wanted. The creature dealt in memory and impersonation – Istvan had no way of knowing for sure if the note was genuine. If it was, Edmund would be in terrible trouble, yes, but if it wasn't, it was easy enough to drop charges.

If it wasn't, the man was in terrible trouble of a different sort.

Istvan wasn't following, wasn't chasing, wasn't worrying overmuch, he was... he was being sensible. Rational. Proper man's logic. He had to be certain.

He felt no additional pain at the border. The Twelfth Hour's bounds ended some miles short of where Providence began, steering well clear of the blasted landscape, and he alighted there. The street was rough and cobbled, and terminated abruptly before the husk of a fallen monstrosity, the decayed concrete and iron bars of an immense tail attached to the greater beast heaped in the distance. Past the boundary, it rose as an angular framework and nothing more, stripped to what passed for its skeleton. The work of men and women who had no idea what they were really doing. Dreamers, walking.

Istvan searched for the pylons. That was where the Susurration began. That was where the horror started.

Just past the beast.

He took a breath.

Hesitated.

He turned away, pacing across the street. What would the Susurration have to gain by leaving a note like that? Misleading him? Why put a return time on it, if it meant to keep him away? But... the alternative was that the note was real, and Edmund had done what he'd done, and that Grace... that he and Grace... that Grace had come back and...

Istvan kicked at the tail. It didn't matter. It wasn't supposed to matter. It wasn't supposed to hurt this much.

Bloody shrapnel. Bloody woman. Bloody–

"What are you looking at?"

Istvan started. Turned around. "Pardon?"

A man in a grey business suit leaned against one of the flickering street lights, a suitcase on wheels propped beside him. Blonde. His smile was hesitant, but kind. "You've been pacing around for a while now, staring," he said. He gestured at the ruins, at the vast ribcage stark against the orange sky. "Some waste, isn't it? I'd hate to meet one of those things alive."

"Do you know what that waste is?"

A shrug. "Sure. You just looking, or looking for someone?"

Istvan blinked back a sudden upwelling of what he knew wasn't the pain of the bindings, punishment for overstepping his bounds. Maybe it was the smile. Maybe the concern. That was rare, among anyone who didn't know him. He swallowed. "I've a... a good friend in there," he muttered. He fiddled with his wedding ring. "Somewhere."

"Maybe you should go after him," the man said. He drew up beside him, abandoning his suitcase beneath the streetlight, peering out at the restricted borders of Providence with his hands in his pockets. Not afraid. Not even nervous, so close to a ghost. "I mean, friends are pretty valuable, right? You don't want to lose this one. Not like you lost Pietro."

"Excuse me?"

A rueful shake of the head. "Best of luck."

The man walked back to his suitcase, took the handle, and strolled away.

Istvan could have stopped him. Could have sped after him, caught him, and demanded to know why he could shake his head ruefully but evidence no emotion of the sort, why he wasn't afraid or even slightly discomfited by the cold, why he was empty–

Instead, he stood, and watched him go. He could do nothing else.

They had met at the University of Vienna. Pietro was there on a scholarship, Istvan on what was left of his father's good graces. They had shared a flat to save rent. Pietro had resolved to show Istvan every park in the city – he was a native, he knew everything – and Istvan had tried to teach him Hungarian. They became a regular fixture at the coffeehouse near the museum: the loud one with the exotic accent and dueling scars, and the quiet one with intense eyes and that sudden wit, who drew long-dead monsters on scraps of paper and would sometimes sketch caricatures of unwitting customers.

Oh, they had been inseparable.

It was all so long ago.

●●●

She offered him a hot dog. It wasn't real, she said, but what was these days? He agreed: hot dogs had never been real anyway. She offered him lemonade, a walk around the plaza, an introduction to acquaintances (most former smilers, most conversing only briefly). Edmund accepted it. All of it. What was there to accept.

Followed her.

She talked about her work, intercepting the Susurration's agents both closer to home and far afield, trying to decode Diego's strange speech and stranger technology, trying to keep morale up as best she could. It sounded difficult and he said so. He ate more of the hot dog, which she informed him was a product of that technology: all of it powered by the Bernault devices they needed to keep the Susurration in check.

"You know," she said, "you're the only one who can help us. The only one who might listen. Your Magister is the one who declared us off-limits, isn't she? Are you sure you can't convince her to turn over that shipment? Or, failing that, bring them in some other way..."

"I'm not a criminal," he said.

"You probably aren't supposed to be here," she said.

He stopped talking, then, because he knew: he was a thief and a criminal and that was why she had left him. Drank too much. She drank her lemonade; Istvan drank pain; he, Edmund Templeton, drank lives and then drank over them, doing nothing but try to forget how deep down a well he'd fallen. Grace was right. Why had he ever tried to get her back?

Over. It's over. I'm sorry.

Why was she still talking to him? Was it over, really? How could she do this to him twice?

Finally, she took him back up atop the walls, another ride in one of the deceptively fragile cable cars. The sun was setting, throwing Providence and all the Susurration's prisoners into shadow, a darkness distorted by the hulks sprawled about like fallen mountains. Hundreds of thousands trapped, and no lights to see by. Did they work at night? Did the Susurration drive them on, blind?

He asked. Grace shrugged.

Around them stretched walkways and turrets and more walkways, all crowded with people. Families. Groups of friends. Couples. All of them seemed to have brought blankets and chairs. The whole fortress, setting up for quite the spectacle.

Music drifted up from the dark. Sousa marches.

Edmund rubbed at his bad arm. "Grace, what's going on?"

"I told you. Fireworks. It is the Fourth, Eddie. You can't leave without watching some fireworks."

"Shouldn't everyone be facing the other way?"

She swung herself up onto a turret. "Nope. Now get up here, before someone else takes it."

He dropped his hand to his pocket, already running through the parameters for a short teleport – and then dropped the hand to his side. Not here. He eyed the barrel, wondering what caliber something like that would fire, and how far. Forty miles? Fifty?

It wasn't that high up. Maybe if he got a good start...

"Oh, right," Grace said. She dropped back down beside him.

"Don't pick me up," he said automatically.

She chuckled. "Here, I'll give you a leg up."

It took some doing, and he bashed his bad arm against metal once or twice, but he managed. There was plenty of room on the turret proper, and he sat there. The surface warmed as he touched it. Not metal, then, and controlled by Grace's machine friend, like everything else. "I could have done it if I'd had two good arms," he said.

Grace sat beside him. "Sure."

"I was mauled by a tiger."

"I believe you."

She was close, but not too close. Not close enough. A friendly distance that scorched the air between them. She'd said they were over. She'd sounded like she meant it. Istvan certainly seemed to think she had no feelings for him anymore, and, despite personal bias, the specter did have a certain insight into such matters. But if that were true, why was she doing this?

Edmund took his hat off. "You're sure we're facing the right way?"

"Absolutely. The Susurration puts on a hell of a show."

He froze. "The Susurration?"

"Yup."

"Why?"

She leaned back, putting her arms behind her head. "No idea."

The sun set as he hovered, high above the horror. No more hesitation. No more weakness. No way in but through. A moment within the fortress walls ought to confirm Edmund's presence, and then Istvan could be off again. That was all. He could tell Edmund of this mysterious conjunction and its stolen goats later, once the man had finished being a fool. No need to stay, no need to reveal himself. No need to dwell on what he oughtn't.

Istvan steeled himself. If he flew fast enough, maybe the Susurration wouldn't have time to affect him.

He tilted into a steep dive.

Vienna yawned around him, rent and torn, human shells on noontime promenade, whispering filaments of glass twisting just beyond his perceptions. Empty – empty – the fortress the target on a range, the rings beckoning –

He covered his eyes – and slammed into a wall.

A barrier. A Conceptual barrier.

Istvan wobbled away, tumbling drunkenly across a solid nothing. A vast crowd gathered on the walls below, none of them looking at him. None of them feeling anything. Blocked. Empty. Surrounded by blankness masquerading as substance. Edmund. Where was Edmund? He had to find Edmund, had to–

Istvan regained his wings and angled straight at steel.

This time the report blew him backwards in a fuzzy haze of flickering mists and tangled wire.

Dazed, reeling, he tumbled past the walls. Striking the walls. Solid. All solid. How was it solid?

<Welcome,> someone said, and it was a voice he hadn't heard in over a century, a low tenor bordering on baritone, perfect for singing if only the man had ever bothered to try.

It struck Istvan's heart like the shock that had killed him.

No. No, no, no....

He lunged for the fortress once more but it had gone, receding, replaced by a rippling like waves on the ocean. Curtains. Scrollwork. Tree branches and vines, hypnotic intricacy, winding about and about in a lattice of whispering glass that smelled of rain and coffee and old leather. Waltz, but wrong. There were holes in the rhythm... and it was empty.

"Edmund!" A yelp more than a warning. He didn't care. "Edmund!"

<My dear Pista,> said Pietro Koller, long-lost, long-beloved. <I hoped you would come. I was looking forward to another talk.>

The Susurration dragged him down, drowning.

At precisely ten o'clock, the first rockets streaked heavenward. A thump and a whistle, repeated a dozen times across the horizon – and then the sky burst into sparkling fury directly above them. Thirteen ribbons of red and white. An offset flash of crackling blue, stars tumbling through stripes even as the image of the flag itself unfurled upwards. It lasted only an instant before collapsing into a great shower of sparks, but it was enough to startle him into a whispered, "Holy..."

"We're still not sure where it finds them," she said.

"It's all half-starved smilers, running this?"

"Yup."

More rockets were already on their way. Rings within rings within rings. Ovals laid out in zig-zags whose final edges barely touched. Patterns of tiny bursts sketched out like a field of blooming flowers. Screamers tuned to distinct chords. The detonations were so close he could feel the roar through his back, rattling the metal beneath them.

"Think how it looks from the other side," Grace mumbled.

"Hm?"

"The show. You've seen the difference. It looks good from here, but outside... their skies are clear, Eddie. No glare from Barrio Libertad. Stars that go on forever. Smoke that highlights those colors just so, like a painting. That screamer that just went off? A choir of angels." A sigh, almost wistful. "Absolute perfection."

He turned to look at her, a silhouette outlined in

red and gold. She lay with her hands behind her head, one knee up, chest rising and falling in gentle rhythm. The music had changed to a medley of strident patriotic tunes, and the night had deepened to a greater cold. Was she shivering?

He edged toward her.

She didn't look away from the heavens. "Don't. Please don't."

He rolled to his side. "Why not? Why did you keep me here, if you don't want me around?"

"Because I need you," she said. She dropped a hand to the surface of the turret, and it warmed at her touch: a radiant heat, like coals. She propped the hand behind her head again. "Just... not like that."

"Right," he said.

"Besides, I thought you'd like the fireworks."

He rolled onto his back again, wishing he'd brought a pillow. Wishing a lot of things. "And keep in mind what's firing them, Grace?"

"That, too."

CHAPTER TWENTY

She had one more thing to show him after the fireworks were over.

"Come on," she said. "Let me tell you a story."

"OK," he said. What else could he do? He'd followed her all day, listened to what she had to say all day. Not very well, maybe, but he had. It was almost worth it, to be close to her.

Istvan would have told him he was in denial and been right, too, but Istvan wasn't there. Edmund would take what he could get.

She led him back to a cable car as the crowds dispersed. "Remember how I told you it took two months to build this place?"

"I do."

"Those were the two months after Providence. After the fallout settled."

He leaned against one of the window slats as the car started downwards. "The dust."

"That's right." She took up position on the opposite side, watching strings of lights as they passed. "That explosion that leveled the city, killed Anoushak and her–"

"Shokat Anoushak. Names are important. Get them right."

"Yeah, whatever. Listen: that was us, Eddie. That was Diego."

Edmund scrubbed a hand across his eyes. It was too late for this. "Grace, that makes no sense."

"Shut up and let me explain. Barrio Libertad was a combo deal: a bomb and a prison cell, all in one package. The fortress, the pylons, the whole shebang. Aerosol dispersion. The Susurration didn't even realize what was going on until it couldn't go anywhere – and it was here, Eddie, all along. As far as we can tell, it was here before Anoushak, maybe even since the Wizard War began."

"Grace," Edmund repeated, more slowly, "that makes no sense."

"No?"

"Not unless Magister Hahn has been taking credit for your..."

Grace raised her eyebrows.

Edmund leaned more heavily. Mercedes had never mentioned anything like this. She had never detailed what she did to end the Wizard War at all.

But... then again, she *was* the Magister, however she had attained the title. It was almost a requirement for the position, to be distrustful and dangerous and, as the years wore on, just a little crazy. Magister Jackson had won the vault in a card game with God-knew-what, after all, with consequences no one cared to ponder if he had lost. Mercedes was far from the worst.

Besides, if the Susurration had always been here, and if Diego had really...

He watched the great metal sails overhead recede. "Grace, are you saying that killing the most powerful wizard of all time was *incidental*?"

"No, I'm saying that we did our part and that now we need some help to do our part again. Just wait for it, Eddie – I'm not done."

"You're not?"

The cable car stopped and she led him out. Out and down, down, down to a large circular structure standing apart from the living blocks, far away on the lowest terrace ring. A sign in both English and Spanish declared it to be "The Center for Existence Improvement," which sounded grand enough, but rows of decorations strung across the door suggested that no one came or went on a regular basis.

Edmund ran a finger across the doorknob, expecting dust, but the metal was spotless. "Grace, what is this?"

She tugged the streamers down. "You'll see."

The interior resembled the halls of a battleship. Gunmetal-grey. Exposed piping. Strange depressions in the walls, man-sized, filled with jointed steel arms and sheets of filmy material. Most of the machinery clustered around the head region. Several of the wires and needles looked as though they were meant to be inserted inside the skull. Edmund stayed close by Grace, focusing on breathing. The walls were plenty far apart and there was no water. No motion. No need to worry. At the back of the building Grace waved him into another elevator.

He hesitated. "Grace?"

"You'll see," she repeated. "I just need you to not panic, OK?"

That was never a promising request. Edmund followed her in and took his fedora off, trying to pretend he wasn't as tense as he was. "Grace, you know what I do for a living."

"I also know what you do when you remember that for yourself."

He flinched. "That wasn't what I meant."

She didn't reply. She struck a switch on the wall and they plummeted.

Edmund clutched at his fedora, wishing he'd brought his top hat instead. Wishing he had his cape and mask. He was a librarian with one good arm – he was fine for watching fireworks, but this? Don't panic? Make sure your shoes were tied before enacting the ritual? Grace could say what she liked; this place was sounding more and more like magic all the time, and as the Hour Thief he'd spent the greater part of his career combating magical threats. The very worst kind. After Magister Jackson, the Twelfth Hour had realized that having an immortal on roster meant having someone who could be sent on suicide missions more than once. He was an expendable asset guaranteed to came back.

He'd seen things. Don't panic, hah.

He still wished he had his other hat.

The doors slid open. A soft blue-white glow spilled from beyond, pooling in the air as though each particle were illuminated from within.

Edmund knew that light. He knew it very well.

He stepped forward – and Grace slapped an arm across his chest. "Don't," she said. "Stay in the elevator."

He backed up again, straining to see past the glow. It wasn't coming from spheres, he thought... more like filaments, or tubes, lines that ran straight but seemed curved. Maybe the other way around. The elevator trembled with the same indefinable hum that emanated from the pylons outside. He gritted his teeth against it. "This is the part where you tell me what you really do with the Bernault devices, Grace?"

"No," she said. "This is the part where I tell you that Barrio Libertad was designed from the ground up to collapse the Susurration's home dimension into this one and then blow it and its entire domain straight to Hell."

He hadn't heard that right. He couldn't have heard that right.

He turned to stare at her. The blue light made it look as though all the blood had drained from her body.

"Do you understand now?" she asked.

Edmund opened his mouth. Closed it. She reached for him. He backed away, dizzy, his pocket watch slippery in his fingers. The deck trembled beneath him, the smell of grease and diesel filling his nostrils. She looked dead. The light made her look dead. She was dead.

"Look," she said, and he didn't, he couldn't, he reeled around to face the light so he wouldn't have to, "we need those devices, Eddie. We need to keep the Susurration under control or a lot of people are going to die. The option to fire the weapon comes up every year and we've voted it down every year and it's gotten worse and worse, and Eddie, Diego isn't going to wait anymore. You saw how many smilers are out there. Do you understand now? Eddie? Eddie, are you listening to me? I know you don't want to hear it, Eddie, but I'm serious. If you don't believe me, I can show you. Here."

A switch clicked. The elevator pitched forward.

Water ripped through the shredded hull. Ship foundering. No light. No air. Decks lurching crazily beneath him, walls becoming floors and then ceilings that dragged him down beneath them. His lungs screaming. Himself, screaming. Bubbles he could feel but not see. He floundered through the darkness, seeking a hatch or a ladder or anything, anything that would lead out, lead up – and touched hair.

The corpse hugged him.

He yelled. Jerked away. A star-spotted yank at his

bad arm brought him up short, dangling. Before him –
below him – stretched metal supports that tapered and
vanished, bands of elaborate latticed wafers suspended
by nothing, bolts of blue-white particulates sheeting
across vast mechanical vertebrae, an overpowering
electric tremble that stood every hair on end and tasted
of oil. Oil in water.

Istvan. Istvan. He had to find Istvan. Istvan could fix
this.

He scrambled for his watch. No thought spared; the
calculations for home slotted themselves into place by
instinct.

A snap –

– and he vanished.

He fought. Oh, how he fought, across one world and
then another, scrambling between what was and what
had been, fleeing from what might be. He was dead,
but not gone. He wasn't wholly a man, nor wholly an
event. Istvan Czernin was a patchwork crux of warring
ideas who (as multiple past and extant foes could attest)
was extraordinarily difficult to catch, much less be rid of
forever.

Most opponents, however, existed in but a single
realm. They weren't able to attach themselves like a
glittering leech to his psyche. They couldn't strip away
layer after layer of self-definition and rifle, relentless as
the War itself, through his memory for ammunition.

The Susurration could.

Istvan fought and he fled, tripping over the rasping
parchment of his chains.

<Oh, Pista, don't be like this. All you must do is
listen.>

"Stop calling me that!" He refused to speak German.

It hurt too much in German. "You have no right to call me that!"

Pietro appeared before him again, seated on one of the benches in a park that gaped with sickening holes. His jacket shimmered, like stars in blackness, and his eyes were soft, his smile kind. Brown eyes, with flecks of yellow, ringed with a dark rim like a section of oak. He was slim, not thin. Delicate fingers. Hair to match his eyes, half-hidden beneath that bowler hat he'd taken such a fancy to in the last year. <Don't I?> he said, and his Viennese was flawless. <I know you just as well.>

Better than Istvan's own family. Better than Franceska. Better than Edmund.

"No!" Istvan skidded about, wings trailing broken feathers. One of his chains caught on his ribs and snapped him backwards, through the grass, into the dirt and past it, face-to-face with Pietro again. Dead bones. Like him.

<Istvan!> shouted another voice, short of breath and dashing after him as he left his practice. <Istvan, I'm sorry, but you must know! Pietro... Pietro is dead, he hurled himself from a window, he–>

Istvan tripped over himself. <What?>

Janos – it was Janos, disheveled and miserable – reached out to steady him. <I just heard. I'm sorry. I'm so sorry.>

Istvan drifted sideways. Sit down. He had to sit down. He felt like he'd just lost a boxing match and was newly awoken from a concussion. He couldn't see straight. <What?> he repeated. There was a flight of stairs nearby; he half-fell onto them –

– and then fell again, tumbling backwards into snow.

<Pista, Pista....> sighed the Susurration. The monster, the memory-stealing horror, not Pietro. Not dear Peti. <You are different, aren't you? What can I do with you?>

Istvan lay there, coughing. He wore a greatcoat now, torn and bullet-riddled, but it didn't seem to matter. It shouldn't have mattered. Oh, it was cold. "You can't do to me what you do to everyone else, can you?" he rasped. "Catch them? Control them? Work them until they die?"

Pietro, now clad in a greatcoat himself, crouched in the snow beside him. <My people are as my children, Pista. Do you not think I would better provide for them, if I were able? Do you not think if I were free of this wasteland, I would do everything in my power to ensure their safety? Their security?> He shook his head, his expression a familiar quiet anguish. <All I can give them is happiness, and you condemn me for it?>

Something whistled. The snow shifted beneath him. Istvan scrambled away, sprinting behind an outcropping as shellfire exploded where he'd just been. Where Pietro still was. Where he wasn't, any longer.

Chips of rock ripped through Istvan's fleshless bones; when he held up a hand, he was bleeding.

<I am the end of suffering,> came the pronouncement. The cheerful notes of a Strauss waltz rang behind the words.

The sky snatched at Istvan's chains. Yanked him upwards. Hurled him against frozen stone. It was too late. The guns had already fired, the shells had burst among the Austrian column, the pass cracked and boomed and the snow roared down and down and down–

<You brought me here. You cried out, and I came.>

Istvan couldn't save them all. He couldn't even find all of what was left of them. The worst part was that he felt almost nothing, that there was so much pain and yet it didn't overwhelm him with euphoria, that – two years in – he possessed a tolerance for suffering so high that he could weep at the losses of one or a dozen or a hundred men. How much greater agonies were yet to come? Was this his sentence for demanding answers, for cursing the Almighty, for dying as he'd done? Torn to pieces... and returned, to watch others suffer the same?

<But you, Pista, you scorn my gifts. You struggle!>

Starry emptiness reached for him, the space between grown solid. Echoes.

Istvan stabbed it.

Laughter. Pietro's laughter, deep within his chest. <Do you think I'm afraid of you? Devil's Doctor? War to End All Wars? You are a house of bones bound by barbed wire, dancing to the pull of bloody strings.> The emptiness oozed around his knife, towards his hand. Climbing. <You, who can offer no happiness to anyone, who has become all that he despised, who has no future but the lonely thunder of guns? Why would I ever be afraid of you?>

Istvan tried to rip his knife free. Couldn't.

<That honor, Pista, falls to the one you love most.>

Istvan froze. Past experiences used against him, fine. That was little different than what he could do to himself, that was guilt, it was all over and gone in the end. Over and gone. But this...

"No," he said. "Stop it. And stop calling me that name!"

<The one who has replaced your dear Peti,> the creature continued, <all unknowing, and who will only loathe you all the more should he ever learn of it.> A sigh, low and wistful. <How much suffering are you willing to endure? Chained for good cause, sowing nothing but horror, witnessing naught but destruction and glorying in it, only to hate all that you are when the bloodlust ebbs. Haven't you ever wanted to end it, Pista?>

So soft. So gentle. It was wholly sincere, in Pietro's voice, and only wanted to help.

It had to know that he'd tried. Once. In life. After he'd lost his closest friend, his constant companion, the man who he had betrayed in the name of respectability. The man who had forgiven him. The man he'd loved more than anything.

In a matter of days Istvan had found himself aboard a passenger ship, signed up as a volunteer fighter in a war on another continent he knew nothing about, having given up everything he'd owned, and signed away the rest. No warning. No goodbyes.

He wouldn't be coming back.

But then, when he had... when the British had sent him home years later... scarred and destitute, addicted to morphine, fevered and angry and desperate and with no one to blame but God himself...

He still didn't know if the Susurration had Edmund.

Istvan threw himself off the mountain.

He was home. He flipped on the lights. Nothing happened.

That was enough.

Hours later, Edmund lay on the couch, candles burning on the table beside him, a bottle he hadn't touched through some heroic effort toppled on the floor below him, Beldam purring thunderously as she sprawled on his chest. He'd thrown up until he couldn't taste oil anymore and now he'd finally stopped shaking. No Istvan. The specter had obviously given up on him, just like Grace. After all, who would bother being around a guy whose entire existence came at the expense of others? Who survived only because he stole time from its rightful owners, and squandered it on fits of nightmare, on terror, on self-loathing so powerful he wished he'd drowned... and then he remembered there was nothing there for him, either, there was no way out even at the extremes of torment. He was damned. No way out. He would be the only one left, over and over, forever, and it was his fault. His stupid fault.

Shokat Anoushak herself had confirmed that, hadn't she?

Run. Forever.

That was it. That was all. So much for being a hero.

He looked dully down at the bottle again. He hadn't touched it. Somehow, he hadn't touched it. He'd promised he wouldn't, not over Grace, and yes he'd slipped up with the tiger but this time...

Well. That was something.

Beldam twitched. He scratched her ears. "You're squashing me," he told her.

She purred louder.

Istvan was... he was probably at the Twelfth Hour. He usually was, at this hour. That made sense. Besides, there was that whole matter of Barrio Libertad being one enormous bomb built by the camera-headed aberration who had singlehandedly killed Shokat Anoushak and didn't have any qualms about repeating the process.

That was kind of important. Someone had to hear about that. Someone who had ordered him not to look into the matter. Someone who was sometimes up and about this late, in an office she may have won through a barefaced lie.

Edmund reached down and picked up the bottle.

Just a little. Just enough to wash out his mouth, and maybe a few memories. Istvan wasn't around. He wouldn't notice.

Really, if any situation merited a drink, this was it.

He nudged Beldam. "Let me up."

The cat didn't move.

He put the bottle back down. "I appreciate it, I really do, but I can't stay here." He prodded her again. "I have things to do."

She grumbled something obscene and slouched off, tail switching side to side.

Edmund got up and away before he could reconsider. He shucked his rumpled civilian clothes in the washroom, brushed his teeth, and put on the black. Gloves, cape, aviator goggles. His top hat hung on its peg by the door, and after he set it on his head he checked himself over in the mirror. None of the stitching was visible. That was good. Bum arm still, but that couldn't be helped.

He tried a smile. He was the Hour Thief.

The Hour Thief could do this.

"I'll be back in two shakes," he told Beldam. She sniffed at him. He pictured the Twelfth Hour, ran the right almost-calculations, and vanished.

Istvan wasn't in the infirmary. In fact, he wasn't anywhere in the building, and his staff had no idea where he'd gone. Out sulking, maybe – he wasn't taking events well, either. The note probably hadn't helped. Taking advantage of a loophole in direct orders probably hadn't helped. Grace, more than anything, wasn't helping.

Yes, the ghost had to be off burning steam. There was still a lot of earthquake damage out there and the combination of fear, pain, and flying was just the ticket. Flying always helped, he'd said. The one undeniable positive of his condition.

That left Mercedes. The matter of Barrio Libertad. The revelation of a weapon that could kill hundreds of thousands of innocents along with their eerie jailer, its trigger in the hands of an entity just as inhuman and frightening as the presence outside the walls. One who had broken the back of the greatest sorcerous army the world had ever seen. No wonder the Susurration was so desperate to escape.

Now all Edmund had to do was fess up to his visit.

He strode down the picture hall, eyed the Magister's door, and tapped it with a shoe. "Mercedes? This is…"

It swung open.

"…Edmund."

No one sat at the Magister's desk. Candles ringed the moons-and-clock emblem set into the floor, three clustered at each cardinal point. A labyrinth of chalk lines crisscrossed the floor, offering bowls spaced wherever they intersected, most of them filled with the usual odd knick-knacks and one or two with blood. Some of the flames flickered into signs and sigils as he watched. Mercedes' phone lay in the center, resting atop a seven-pointed star made of cables and wire. Someone was chanting, long slow syllables in a tongue he recognized as ancient Aramaic.

He frowned. Since when were phones standard summoning foci? "Mercedes?"

The chanting stopped. Mercedes stuck her head out from the window seat. "Don't stand there," she said, "you're letting in a draft."

He stepped in and shut the door behind him, making sure not to scuff any of the lines. "Mercedes, were you aware that Barrio Libertad is actually a transdimensional superweapon designed to wipe out the Susurration and all half a million people trapped in that crater with it?"

"Is it."

Not a question. She didn't sound surprised.

He waited for her to ask what he'd been doing there. Why he'd gone there. What authority he thought he possessed, to pursue a forbidden investigation against direct orders. He was the Hour Thief. Fine china. An heirloom passed from one figure of power to the next, one who should never have taken up the Magister's mantle, even once.

The skull of Magister Jackson stared at him. *You damn fool Templeton. Learn your place.*

Mercedes said nothing. She stayed in the window seat, barely visible.

Edmund edged around the circle's perimeter. He didn't like having that phone in it. That meant part of the ritual was new, and innovation in magic was akin to innovation in falling. You could only try so many times from so many heights. Sometimes it was the first one that killed you.

Not for the first time, he wondered about her missing finger.

"Mercedes," he began again, "I understand that I shouldn't have been at the fortress at all. That was a mistake on my part. I'll accept whatever sentence you dictate."

She wrapped a scarlet-stained bandage around her left hand. Her jacket was rumpled, its sleeves rolled up and a coffee stain spilling down the front. The pens remained in her hair, but strands had come loose, frizzing about the sharp angles of her face. She looked like she'd slept about as much as he had. "But?"

No buts, he wanted to say. *None at all.*

But... why wasn't she surprised? Why wasn't she laying down judgment? What was she doing so late at night with a ritual circle like this?

Magister Jackson stared. Edmund looked down at a chalk line running before his shoes.

Barrio Libertad put an end to Shokat Anoushak and her

armies, Mercedes. Not you. Not unless someone else is lying here. If you didn't, why claim it?

You became Magister after all this, Mercedes. You declared Providence off-limits. You barred further investigation.

A telephone as a focus, Mercedes?

"Spit it out, Mr Templeton."

He steadied himself. "Barrio Libertad was built from dust by what I dearly hope isn't some kind of nascent machine god. It – he – goes by Diego Escarra Espinoza, and if what I've learned is true, he's responsible for both the Susurration's confinement and the blast that wiped out Providence. He finished off Shokat Anoushak. Now, you claim to have done that. You were elected Magister after that. You've done a fine job and I'm not looking to reclaim the position, by any means, but..."

The chalk line lay before him. *Don't ask. The wizards who survive are the ones who don't ask.*

He stepped over it. "Mercedes, I'd like to know what's going on here."

CHAPTER TWENTY-ONE

She tied off the bandage with a wince. "An explanation, Mr Templeton? I thought you knew better than that."

"Frankly, Mercedes, I don't think the Twelfth Hour can afford to sit back on this one. If that weapon goes off, we're losing a lot of innocent people, and right now that's the best outcome on the table. If you know something – if you can refute any of what I heard – I'd be grateful to hear it." He turned his hat in his hands, wishing Istvan weren't off... wherever he was. Some backup would have been nice. "I'm looking for a solution, not a witch hunt."

"Mm," Mercedes replied. She waved at the lines, the candles, the sputters of sigils in the fire. "What do you think this is?"

"I wouldn't know."

"Mr Templeton, I can assure you that I'm aware of the delicacy of the situation. I don't blacklist entire nation-states without reason. If I had authorized wizards to enter Providence, years ago, what do you think would have happened?"

He shook his head. "I can't say what might have been. I can only say what might be."

"What might be," she repeated. She swung her legs around to face him, waves rolling behind her. It was night on the Atlantic, moon-lit, droplets of salt spray rolling from the window panes. A studying gaze – he knew the routine – and then she clasped her hands together, a maimed gesture, uneven. "What do you expect me to do, then?"

Providence. The last battle. A convergence of Shokat Anoushak's forces from across the globe, all searching for something never found, all destroyed in that blast. He had always thought it was Mercedes' work. She had taken advantage of the strange decision, was all. Shokat Anoushak was mad, pulling so much of her forces into one place, but... well, she was mad.

A lot of people had died at Providence. Too many.

He did his best to hold Mercedes' eyes. "As I said, I'd like to know what's going on."

She shook her head. "Wouldn't we all."

"Mercedes…"

"Mr Templeton, has it occurred to you how the Susurration operates? You were already targeted once. Compromised once. Led your friend Doctor Czernin into a fight with it once. You've just returned from Barrio Libertad – an explicitly unauthorized visit, during which time you could easily have been intercepted – and, after all that, Mr Templeton, you expect me to trust you?"

"No," he said. "But one can hope."

"Don't."

Edmund tucked his hat under his arm, resigning himself to ignorance. That was that. The Magister had spoken; the Hour Thief obeyed. That was how it had always been. That was how it had to stay. The alternative was all too thinkable, and she had a name.

How much memory led to madness?

"One question before I go," he said. "I've checked with the infirmary and no one seems to know where Istvan's gone off to. I was wondering if you might know where he is, or when he'll be back."

"Doctor Czernin?" She frowned, glancing at her telephone. "You didn't meet him at the fortress?"

Edmund bit back a curse. He'd left a note, hadn't he? *Don't follow*? *Don't look for me*? He could take care of himself just fine, especially in something so personal. Istvan always worried too much. "I wasn't expecting to, and I didn't."

Mercedes stood.

"Wait, are you saying he hasn't come back?"

She stepped around her drawn lines, making for the door. "How much do you care for your friend, Mr Templeton – on a scale of one to 'would kill him myself'?"

<I never wanted to end them,> said Pietro. Said the Susurration, pursuing him through the pews. <Shokat Anoushak, her creatures, those misguided souls who worshipped her – Pista, I wanted to save them. Save all of them. Redeem them! Give them what they sought, spare the world their misguided ravages, end it all with a whisper. Doesn't everyone deserve another chance, Pista? Doesn't everyone deserve happiness, no matter how monstrous?>

Istvan vaulted the last wooden back, sprinted for the doors –

– and found himself again on the other side of the church, scrambling over the altar, back where he'd began. Three times, he'd tried. Three times, failed. There was something biblical in that, something damning, like all the rest. He was tired. He was so tired.

He set his eyes on stained glass. Ran again. Leapt,

wings churning... tripped, tangled in his own chains, for how many attempts he couldn't remember. No escape. No end.

Pietro offered a hand to help him up, as he'd done a thousand times before. <I was bound, just as you are. I didn't want to seek out such a terrible weapon but I did, and I didn't want to bring poor Shokat Anoushak to it, but I did, because I had no choice. Even now, I have no choice. I would keep my people safe forever, if I could!>

Istvan ignored the hand. Struggled to his feet. Missed a stair. Stair?

Tumbled.

Landed with a thwack, skidding on his back through the dust, his glasses cracked, bullets pelting the hill beside him. Men shouted in a tongue he didn't know, a twisted cousin to German warped by long exposure to the South African frontier. The Transvaal. One of his own farmer-militiamen lay before him, a Boer, blood bubbling over weather-beaten flesh torn by British artillery fire.

Istvan couldn't stop the bleeding fast enough. He could barely see through the dust.

<How many soldiers did you save, Pista? How many of those men returned to war, fought again, suffered again, died where you couldn't help them?>

A whistle. Close. Too close. He threw himself over the wounded man before it hit.

Fire.

<How many yet suffer?>

Faded lines of Arabic. Loops and dots. Words penned at the fall of the Sassanids, crumbling, a tale of ancient horrors wrought by the simple act of living too long for too high a price. The dust plugged his nose. He sneezed. The pages turned. A picture, flattened and stylized, painted by hands long gone, fell open before him: a man in a black cloak and top hat, a corpse in a bridal veil at his feet.

A smile, faint and pleasant. Eyes turning, remorseless–
Istvan yelled.

Pietro caught him. Leaned him against the park bench as he shook and shivered.

<I can help him,> he said. <I know what haunts him, Pista, and if you help me free myself from this miserable waste, I promise, I can help him.>

Istvan swallowed. Tasted dust. He couldn't breathe, for the dust.

<Please,> pleaded Pietro, <All I need is enough time.>

Edmund dashed after Mercedes as she made a beeline straight for the vault. "Why didn't you tell me you'd done this earlier?"

"Would you have approved?"

"Has my approval ever mattered?"

"It was a case of need to know, Mr Templeton," she called over her shoulder. "Need to know!"

They slid to a halt in front of the enormous circular door. Startled faces stared from further down the hall, bleary-eyed latecomers who hadn't yet made full use of the Twelfth Hour's coveted caffeine reserve. No worries regarding interference: Magister Hahn was involved in whatever it was, and if she were involved, it was Serious Business that shouldn't be interrupted.

She set her palm in the central depression and the door rolled back with a crash. "D Section," she said. "Things We Really Oughtn't. Look for a mahogany case with scorch marks on it, about this big." She held up her hands to indicate something roughly the size and shape of a lunchbox.

Edmund hesitated. "You aren't coming?"

"Mr Templeton, you can search far more quickly than I. Magister Jackson's mysterious countermeasures remain in place in the event you take anything you shouldn't, and I'm not accepting any of your ill-gotten time." She jerked her chin at the blackness beyond. "Go. I'll set up the rest and have the vault open again when you reach the exit."

Well. He couldn't argue with that. "Any labels?"

"'Security Deposit.'"

"Right."

He went.

The vault sections remained nearly constant, but individual locations could and did change with unnerving frequency: any attempt to re-locate an archived item was a monumental task in and of itself. Time, even considering Edmund's powers, was of the essence.

For three stolen hours he walked alone through the bones of a dead beast dreaming.

When he finally found the box, it was labeled, just as Mercedes had said, and closed with a brass lock, for which he was grateful. Locks had a way of removing options.

Mercedes was right: he hadn't needed to know.

He brushed the dust off the wood, picked it up – it was lighter than he'd expected – and tucked it under his good arm. A walk of any length with its contents wasn't an appealing prospect, but the vault had a way of being smaller on the way out. He reached the massive stone door within ten minutes. The Demon's Chamber was another five.

By the time he got there, Mercedes had drawn a familiar ashen summoning circle around the pillar in its center and activated the wards that circumscribed each wall. Salt, cedar, iron. The shackles that had once held Istvan fast gaped in their mountings, fangs etched with faint Greek inscriptions. They had been cast to control more traditional dangers, in the founding years of the Twelfth Hour, and looked it.

Edmund checked his watch. It had been about a half-hour, Mercedes' time.

"Put the box in that empty space," she ordered, producing a brass key to match the brass lock.

He did so. "Anything else?"

"No. I'll get it open and we'll go from there."

She kneeled beside it. No muttered words, no ritual incantations: the key turned smoothly and the lid opened with nary a creak. Inside, resting upon a bed of cushioned red satin, was a blackened human jawbone. Part of one. Edmund was no dentist, but if he had to guess he would have said it was from nearer the ear than the chin, and it was missing about two molars. The blackening was clearly from fire. Scattered around it was a few ashes, or pieces that had come off.

Concrete details. He had to focus on the concrete details.

Mercedes sat back on her heels. "There we go."

Edmund remained standing just outside the circle. He didn't want to get any closer. Every moment spent staring at that sorry piece of bone was another moment reminding him that the man who was, at this point, his closest friend in all the world, was dead. That he had been dead for over a century. That he had died, in horrific galvanic agony, almost two decades before Edmund was ever born.

It was one thing to know that while trading jibes with Istvan's spirit-shadow. It was quite another to look at what little was left of him.

He swallowed.

All of his friends were dead.

•••

<No,> Istvan said. <No. I can't. I can't. I'm sorry.>

He pulled away.

Pietro caught his wrist. Memories long-faded flared like photographs given color.

Morning meetings at the coffee house, matches of chess that Istvan almost always lost. Pietro's total ineptitude at Hungarian. That perfectly awful flat they'd shared. Arguments over this matter of nationalism, the ridiculousness of that Freud character, and whether or not heavier-than-air craft would ever be viable. Istvan's struggle with Latin anatomy, assisted by relentless drills and bribery. Pietro watching, from the second row, Istvan's long-awaited betrothal to Franceska; Istvan watching, in turn, Pietro's wedding, and applauding as any good friend ought. That dreadful year of attempting to avoid one another, to do their respective duties, to forget and pretend and fail, and meet again as failures. They'd been failures for eight years already – why stop now?

Most of all, those precious, few, forbidden dances after public festivals, joking over who ought to take the woman's part and whirling, hands clasped, in laughing circles about the empty tables...

Istvan hugged himself, elbows tight against his sides. Like his own knife had split him open. Like ravens had ripped out his intestines, leaving nothing but a gaping, wind-whistled ache. His eyes floated in their sockets. <Please, no.>

<If you loved me, help me.> Arms encircled him, drew him close, like he were solid, like he were living. A warmth that didn't care he was disfigured, that he was awful. A warmth that didn't flinch away. A voice he hadn't heard in over a hundred and twenty years,

that had told him his cheekbones were lovely. <Oh, my poor Pista,> whispered Peti, <Help me.>

He broke.

Mercedes raised her eyebrows. "Mr Templeton?"

Edmund ran a hand across his face. His own jawbone was there, the muscles surrounding it clenched beneath his skin. "OK," he said. He was acutely aware of his tongue against his teeth, the vibration of vocal cords deepened by past decades of smoking within his throat, the exhalation of a deep breath from living lungs. "Show me what I have to do."

CHAPTER TWENTY-TWO

He couldn't look away.

There was no other route to use. He had done the best he could. It was all for good reason, and better than the alternative. It was the last sympathetic connection between bone and spirit, and Mercedes knew what she was on about. It all made perfect sense.

That didn't change the fact that Edmund had just helped condemn the only friend he might be able to keep for all of forever to a second agonizing death. Sundered spirit. Torn to pieces. His soul left shredded and drifting, awaiting the terrible energies of a world war to pour between its cracks and settle, solidify, revive him whole and forever changed from what and who he might have been.

Edmund owed it to him to not to look away.

Electric arcs flashed and spat across the specter's remains, the pitiful bit of bone twisting and jerking in the air like a living thing. Ash whirled through the storm – more ash than the box had ever contained – collecting along distinct and disturbing lines like iron filings across a magnet. A spine. An upheld hand. A full skull, now, jaw agape in what Edmund knew to be a scream. He couldn't hear it over the sizzle of killing current.

He didn't look away. He couldn't. He wouldn't.

Smoke and flames stung his eyes. The stench of charred meat assailed his nostrils. A complete skeleton now writhed within the circle, shackled, wreathed in the burning remnants of its own flesh.

Mercedes opened her hands, as though in greeting, and spat a final phrase in Greek. <Istvan Czernin, Devil's Doctor, Great War to End All Wars... I never expected to see you again.>

Barbed wire snaked around the ashes, binding together each bone. It was translucent as they were not, and where it touched they ignited and vanished, power spent. Electric arcs gave way to ragged fabric and tattered wings. The storm sputtered out. Istvan tumbled to the ground, form flickering wildly between man and avatar, shuddering like an invalid. The chains that bound him glittered just at the edge of vision, contractual links trailing back to toothed shackles. Only a small part of his jaw was solid: the bone used to bring him here, re-affixed to its proper place even as it crumbled.

Mercedes lowered her hands. Done. It was done. She nodded to Edmund, then tottered to the nearest wall and sat down.

Resigned to what would come, Edmund knelt beside the circle. "Istvan?"

The specter mumbled something in German, wheezing. Edmund couldn't make out the words: they were too faint, weak and slurred by shock and pain.

<Istvan, I'm sorry,> he told him, <We had to do it.>

A shuddering cough. The sickly smell of chlorine mixed with the lingering stench of charred meat. Istvan was still mumbling, still shaking.

Edmund switched back to English. When he'd been at

his worst, for all those months, Istvan had spoken to him in German, and that small extra effort it took to change tracks had sometimes helped bring him back. "It's all right," he said. "It's over. You're here now. It's all right."

Istvan stared up at him, recognition flickering somewhere far back in his eyes – then flung himself at him, burying his face in his shoulder.

"Peti," he said, repeating, over and over. "Peti... Peti... Peti..."

Edmund tried not to pull away from the cold. A name. It had to be a name. Istvan had mentioned his wife a few times over the years. Franceska. A petite, patient woman, he'd said, over a decade his junior. Common enough, in his day. Edmund knew almost nothing else about her. If she'd had any nicknames, pet names, private names... he had no idea. It wasn't his business. He hadn't asked.

Istvan hung off him, twisting his fingers through the front of his jacket.

Sobbing.

Edmund extended his good arm, awkwardly. Patted where the other man's back would have been. His fingers brushed only air, numbed by a chill both more and less than physical. "It's all right."

Mercedes rose. She moved bent, holding her bandaged hand, and stepped over the lines of ash, salt, and iron filings with a weary heaviness Edmund understood all too well. "I'll be back in a few minutes," she said. "Have an errand to run somewhere convenient."

Edmund got him home. Established him on the couch. Saw the bottle left behind from earlier, and put it away where it belonged. Took a few moments to return to the Twelfth Hour, run to the infirmary, and retrieve what embroidery equipment he could find. Istvan didn't sleep.

He couldn't. Edmund had always been a bit envious of that, but now he wasn't sure. The specter seemed grateful for the offer, when he returned, but didn't touch any of it. Just sat. Stared at nothing.

Edmund sat beside him. Tried talking to him, like Istvan had talked to him so many times before. Not about anything in particular. Just talking. Istvan clung to his arm, fingers sunk deep inside to a pulse, but that was all.

Edmund kept talking.

At some point – he didn't know when – he fell asleep.

Istvan twisted thread between his fingers, unable to hold a design in his mind. Unable to start. Unable to concentrate on anything but the presence beside him, the gentle rhythm of living breath, the warm, sleep-dulled pain of a recent wound and the merciful release of almost all else to smooth, drifting blandness, undisturbed by nightmare. Edmund, sprawled where he had fallen, stretched lazily across the greater portion of the couch like the cat he kept. His mauled arm rose and fell with his chest. His neck was tilted at an unfortunate angle, propped against the arm of the couch. Both legs dangled off the side. He had never taken off his shoes.

Istvan sat apart. Not far away – not in full retreat, not pressed against the opposite arm – but far enough to keep the hideous, unnatural chill of his presence to himself. He had turned the lamp off hours ago. A candle burned on the table, but of course its heat wasn't enough and its light barely sufficed to see by, work by... if only he could start.

Edmund breathed beside him. He didn't seem nearly so weary when he was asleep. So remorseful. So ancient. Pietro, too, had been something of an old soul, a man of deep and placid intensity, a seeker of bones who drew wonderful pictures of terrible beasts long gone. We both return life to the dead, he'd said once. The only difference is that my patients have more teeth.

He'd wanted so much to go to America. Wyoming. South Dakota. Colorado. He didn't know English, of course – he wasn't very good with languages, not like Edmund, but...

Istvan realized that the thread had become a cat's-cradle. He wiped at his eyes. He couldn't untangle it if he couldn't see.

Oh, this was all Edmund's fault. Bloody Edmund, chasing after that bloody woman. He should never have gone back to that fortress. If he hadn't he would have never left that note, and Istvan would never have found it, and wouldn't have gone to find him. Hours of worry, all night, all morning, worrying. Waiting to see him again. Hoping he was all right, that he hadn't done something stupid.

He was so smart, but... but that didn't keep him from being so stupid.

So...

Istvan dropped his head in tangled fingers, forcing regularity on lungs that didn't exist. He couldn't get the thread off. He couldn't see to get the thread off. Oh, Pietro. Peti, Peti. Fifteen years, thrown away. He didn't know why. Over a century of battles and he still didn't know why. He would never know. He had died trying to pry the answer from God, struck down and torn apart by a power he hadn't realized he had called, and he would never know.

That last memory the Susurration had revived in him burned his eyes as Edmund breathed.

Dear Edmund. He was so foolish, so thoughtless, a man

placid and incurious and dull, brave and indomitable,
beautiful in the quiet, the one who now had saved him
twice. Embraced him willingly. Once. Under extreme
duress. He was so like Pietro. All unknowing.

Istvan wanted so badly to touch him. He loved him so
much, and he couldn't touch him.

It was all Edmund's fault.

A kettle whistled.

Edmund sat bolt upright. Eighteen fishhooks sank
themselves into his flesh. He yelped. Cursed under his
breath. Clutched at the furry mass clinging to his jacket
front.

Cat. Cat on his chest. Cat not letting go.

"Beldam," he told her, unhooking her claw by claw,
"Beldam, ow."

She oozed sullenly onto his lap and stayed there,
folding her weaponry beneath her. He was forgiven. This
time.

He took stock. He was still fully dressed and still on
the couch. Istvan was nowhere to be seen. Laid across
the far arm of the couch was a length of gauze, attached
to a frame but almost untouched, a needle jammed
into the side of a single, jagged, unfinished red petal. To
Edmund's untrained eye it looked as though the stitches
had been ripped out more than once.

He looked to the kitchen. His tie had come loose in
the night; he pulled it off, patting Beldam in chastened
apology. "Istvan?"

The whistling petered out.

Edmund leaned to the side to try and get a better look.
"Istvan, are you…"

The ghost appeared at the divider between the two
rooms, bare of cap, belt, and bandolier, rigid collar

unbuttoned. The fabric of his uniform was stained and threadbare, as though he'd been on muddy campaign for months. He didn't look at Edmund. He brushed at a line of bullet holes across his chest and they vanished. "I put the water on," he said.

"I heard that. Thank you."

Istvan stayed there a moment, like he wanted to say something else, then turned stiffly back into the kitchen without another word.

Edmund took a breath, long and low. At least Istvan was up and walking. Talking, some. That was a good place to start. After that summoning, and after whatever the Susurration had done to him, it was a miracle he was functional at all.

The thought was no real comfort. Istvan was... well, he was Istvan. Invincible. Immutable. The unstoppable force behind Edmund's unstrikable object. A fixed point that Edmund would always be able to rely on, a friend who would always be there. Istvan. Full stop.

The Susurration had shattered him in a single night. He had fought it – and lost.

He'd lost.

How was anyone supposed to fight something Istvan couldn't?

Edmund convinced Beldam to let him up and walked into the kitchen himself. Istvan stood next to the stove, watching steam curl up from the tea kettle, hugging himself with arms tightly crossed. His expression was impossible to make out: all Edmund could see was the stretched grimace of his scarred side. The wire at his feet was just as tight and tangled, wound barrier-like as though to protect him from oncoming armies.

"I'll listen if you want to talk," Edmund told him.

Istvan shook his head.

There was a tea cup and saucer sitting on the counter next to him. Edmund picked them up, reaching for the tea tin.

That name. Istvan had kept repeating that name. Edmund didn't usually care to pry – what was in the past was best left in the past – but Istvan was a ghost. Memory was all he had. Memory was what the Susurration twisted, tore at, blurred and rebuilt and replaced. If it had used some treasured part of Istvan's long history against him...

Edmund measured out a portion of curled tea leaves. He was running low; it had been some months since his last run. "You know," he said, "it's all right if you miss her."

Istvan stared at the steam. "Edmund, I don't want to talk about it. Please."

"All right. I'm sorry." Edmund poured some water, carried his cup to the table, and set it down. It was just past nine and his bad arm ached. He smoothed his sleep-worn jacket. "Before anything else happens, I think I'm going to get dressed. Will you be OK?"

"I'm dead."

Edmund kicked himself for poor choice of words. "Right. I'll be back."

Some hundred-forty seconds later, he had undressed, showered, seen to teeth and hair, dashed across the hall in his bathrobe, dressed again, removed the flag pin from his lapel, put it away, and tossed his rumpled clothes from last night in the hamper where they belonged. He strolled back into the kitchen clad in one of his Hour Thief spares. No sling. His arm still hurt, but it didn't have to look it.

Istvan sat in his usual place, form flickering. His glasses lay on the table beside him, his head in hands that wavered between whole and skeletal, clean and bloodstained. His shoulders were hunched, his wings raised: a curved wall of dark and ghostly feathers that didn't quite mask him from sight. No shaking. No sobbing. That was good. Seeing him once in such an unnervingly vulnerable state had been enough.

He had never maintained wings in the house before. Edmund wasn't sure if he even realized he was doing it.

He didn't ask.

A test revealed that his tea had cooled to something drinkable. He downed some of it and then went in search of breakfast. He still had that bowl of leftover pasta from a few nights earlier. That would be enough.

"Edmund?"

He paused in his search of the refrigerator. "Hm?"

"Will you grant that I am your closest friend?"

Edmund peered over the open door. Istvan hadn't moved. "Of course."

Why was he asking a question like that? He knew that. His only possible competition would have been Dan and Esther Rose, but they had vanished in the late Seventies. Something to do with the Russians. The Cold War. Edmund had long resigned himself to the reality that he would never see them again.

And of course there was Apsara before that, Stella and Chiyuki and...

Well. The past was past.

Edmund pulled out the bowl, retrieved a fork, and made for his own chair. It was blocked by one of Istvan's wings – the specter's wingspan was enormous, eighteen feet tip to tip, and would have been very awkward if he were solid – and Edmund waited for him to draw it out of the way.

He didn't.

"You're afraid of me," he mumbled.

Edmund closed his eyes. Oh boy. Of course trying to stifle his dread over the whole affair hadn't been enough. The prospect of facing the Susurration alone, of dealing with Grace alone, of piecing together the case alone... he hadn't flown solo on something this big since the relapse. Since some idiot had woken something up beneath Lake Erie in '82.

"Sometimes," he said.

"I'll leave, then."

"No. Don't." He steeled himself, then stepped through the obstructing wing. The shock of the cold was jarring and ugly, and he hoped it wouldn't make things worse. "Istvan, I can honestly say that I don't know where I'd be without you."

Istvan froze, wing still outstretched.

Edmund set his pasta on the table. "I don't know what the Susurration said or did, but it's wrong. We may not have started out on the best foot, granted. We might have our rough moments, granted. You are what you are, fine, but Istvan, you're a doctor. Before everything else. Before anything else. In these thirty years I've known you, you've worked miracles. I'm one of them."

"Edmund–"

"I'm glad I took you up on coffee all those years ago. I'm glad I was brave enough to show up. I'm glad I made such a friend out of such an enemy, and after what I've found... Istvan, Barrio Libertad was built by a would-be machine god who killed Shokat Anoushak and is looking for any reason to pull the trigger again. Grace wants the Bernault devices so she can delay him. The Susurration, whatever it's after, knows the situation isn't survivable – and Mercedes won't talk to me about any of it." He sighed. "It's a mess, Istvan. Whatever happens, I'm going to need help, and I can't think of anyone better to have at my back."

"Not even Miss Wu?"

"No."

Istvan drew back his wings, slowly, folding both behind his back. He brushed away a new line of wounds across his chest. Not a word.

Edmund swallowed. He hadn't brought any of it up earlier. It hadn't been the time. He wished it still wasn't. She needed him, she'd said – just not like that, not anymore, he drank too much. "We talked."

Silence.

Edmund pulled out his chair and sat in it. "It's over. She made that very clear. You were right and you're the one I want to have around right now, more than ever, because nothing past this point will be easy." He looked down at his pasta, left over from an earlier battle. "Not for either of us."

A chill brushed his mauled left arm, brief and hesitant. The ache receded.

Istvan drew his hand back. "I'm sorry."

Edmund rubbed his arm. "So am I."

Breakfast suddenly didn't seem appetizing. It wasn't the noodles. He would have felt the same if it were anything else.

He picked up his fork anyway. He had to eat.

"I'm sorry," Istvan repeated. He pushed his chair back, one of those things he could only do if he wasn't paying attention, and stood. "Edmund, I... I've work to do. With the earthquake, and the ice monster, and God knows what else. I was expected back long ago. I shouldn't have stayed here so long as I have."

"You're always welcome here," Edmund said, and he meant it. He hoped Istvan could tell that he meant it.

"In fact," he continued, "I'll be heading to the Twelfth Hour myself shortly. I have an archival backlog that I've been meaning to take care of. Probably some books to re-shelve. I can take a few moments to eat and go with you, if you'd like." He stabbed a noodle. "Unless you feel like flying. I wouldn't blame you if you did."

Istvan wavered. He flickered, still, but less – only the shadow of wings, flesh more often than bone. More himself. "Oh, Edmund," he said. He sat down again, dropping his head back in his hands. "Edmund, what on Earth am I supposed to tell them?"

"Nothing you don't want to."

CHAPTER TWENTY-THREE

The infirmary went quiet when Istvan walked through the doors. The dust and chips and flakes of fallen ornamentation were gone, swept away soon after the earthquake, and toppled monitors and partitions stood once more where they belonged – newly secured, in most cases, with bolts or lengths of rope or tape. Fewer patients now, only the more severe or stranger cases remaining. It was still ostentatious, still a grand meeting hall, but nearer and nearer to his old battlefield haunts with every disaster. He wondered when the roof would fall in.

Edmund had promised that he would be around. He wasn't going anywhere. Never mind that he could finish in a matter of minutes what took other men hours; no need to waste time like that now. A check revealed that he was puttering about the library, trying not to worry. Not going anywhere, like he'd said. His presence was unique among all others, damaged and fearful and so very old, and Istvan wished he didn't find it such a comfort. Wished he had possessed such powers when it might have mattered.

"Doctor Czernin." Someone he didn't recognize, a

long-haired woman with a sharp nose, locks pulled back in a braid. Not one of his people. She was afraid of him, too. "I'm Doctor Orlean. I was called in to help with the shortfall." She extended a hand, hesitantly, then withdrew it. "I'm sorry, I don't know how you–"

"Where's Roberts?" he asked.

"Coming," she said. She dropped her hand to her side. "I'm told you usually work every night."

"I do." There was an official infirmary hierarchy of some sort, he knew. He'd never bothered with it. He was the Devil's Doctor. If he was present, it was his infirmary, with Roberts as preferred liaison. He hadn't missed a night like this, so soon after an emergency, in....

Oh, it was depressing to contemplate. And now they'd brought in some woman to replace him?

"How was your Fourth?" she tried.

He checked on Edmund again. Still there. "Not enough mortars."

He did usually enjoy the Fourth. It was a celebration of Independence, after all, which meant it commemorated a war and the men who'd fought in it. Any holiday of that nature was the best sort of holiday, especially when it included fireworks – explosions that everyone could enjoy without fear for their lives, a small taste of how all such things were to him. Look at that! Long might the night blaze in fire! Long might sacrifice be remembered!

Not this year. Not for any reason he could explain, not in generalities to the public and not in specifics to anyone.

He took off his glasses, rubbing a hand across his face. "How soon is 'coming'?"

"Doctor!" Roberts rounded a corner with surprising speed for his bulk, clipboard in hand. "There you are – the Magister came down herself and told us you'd be indisposed until further notice. I'm glad you're all right."

"I'm fine," Istvan said. Then he realized he sounded like Edmund. He put his glasses back on. "Rather, I'll be fine once I've something to do. That will be all, Miss Orleans."

"Orlean," she said. "*Doctor* Orlean."

Istvan meandered over to look at Roberts' clipboard. Surely one woman hadn't attended to everything, or even several things. Who else had been brought in? "Regardless."

A huff. Sharp irritation mingled with the fear, a green and pungent hurt at being dismissed out of hand. The sensation had a smoothness to it that suggested it wasn't a new one, that she was tired of it, that she'd almost been expecting it from the likes of him...

He sighed. Sometimes he wished that sense were more selective. "My apologies."

Roberts cast him a worried glance. "Sorry, he's... not usually like this."

"I'm usually far worse," Istvan muttered.

Orlean backed away, shaking her head. "I can imagine."

Disappointed. She was disappointed. What kind of legend was he, anyhow? The Devil's Doctor himself, oldest and greatest surgeon in the world, slouching about like a lovesick idiot, betrayed and pining over a friend who always preferred not to know. Who would turn his back if he did. Who would never be a true replacement for the one so long gone, never mind the similarities, the wit, the patience, the kindness.

Istvan found himself checking the library again. Oh, they were so similar. As if one curse wasn't enough.

He took the first step of a mock charge.

Orlean quadrupled her speed of retreat, tripped over

herself, recovered with startling agility, stammered something about being relieved of duty, and ducked behind one of the partitions. Rather less disappointed, now. Terror had a way of clearing one's priorities.

Roberts stared at him a moment, then let out a belated chuckle. "You must not be doing too badly, then."

Istvan inspected a hand gone skeletal. Fresh bone. It was always fresh and glistening, newly flensed, his fingers bloodied. "Doesn't it bother you?"

A shrug. "It helps if I pretend every day is Halloween."

"Oh."

He knew that holiday. He rather liked that holiday.

"By the way," Roberts continued, "you might want to have a look at that ice monster you brought in day before yesterday. It's awake, it's stopped trying to claw people, it's eaten probably two tons of meat and meat-like products... and it talks."

Istvan startled back to flesh. "Anoushak's beasts never talked."

"This one does."

The beast in the holding cell lay broodingly on its stomach, a bright orange rain poncho draped over its prone form. What remained exposed were its head, its enormous paws, its neck and shoulders. Flecks of ice tipped each hair of its thick coat. Clouds of its breath rolled through the open bars, coating them in frost. Even the floor around it, bare concrete, shimmered.

A small portable heater and a keyboard lay before it. Wires snaked out of the bars and connected to the back of a small screen positioned some distance away, black with green letters. *Can't type fast*, it said. *Please be patient*. A white bar blinked at the end.

"What is this?" asked Istvan. "You said it talked."

Roberts shrugged. "Near enough. Vocal cords like that aren't really built for human speech."

The beast growled low in its throat, a raspy, forced sound. Its eyes were brilliant yellow against blue-striped white, and it gathered its great paws as Istvan watched. Rising – slowly, haltingly – to a crouch. It reached one massive paw to the board, tapping out letters one clumsy stroke at a time.

Remember you. Sorry about attack.

"That was my own bloody fault," Istvan said, feeling faintly foolish. Talking to a beast. A tiger. "If I'd come alone, you wouldn't have been so lucky."

The line jumped downwards. *Maybe,* the beast typed.

"He's fine, I'll have you know. Edmund. The Hour Thief. You did nearly break his arm and he won't be healed for weeks, but he is fine."

"He knows," said Roberts.

Istvan crossed his arms, a strange desperation rising in his throat. "It's a he, now?"

The beast bared scything canines. Keys clacked, one by one. *Call me William Blake.*

They didn't talk. Shokat Anoushak's creatures didn't talk. They didn't have names, they didn't remember any shred of human identity, and they certainly didn't have the intelligence to use a typewriter. All those that Istvan had killed – he didn't know how many, he'd never counted – had been utterly lost. Transformed and mindless.

Or so he'd thought.

He turned away, tugging Roberts to a safe distance. "It can't be a survivor, Roberts. It isn't possible. It must be the victim of a spellscar, or a Conduit, or something. Not one of Anoushak's." He gestured at the contraption before it. "Whose idea was this... this typewriter business?"

"That would be mine," rasped a voice from the stairs. That lizard. That giant lizard, in its purple parka, propped awkwardly against the wall, its cane hooked over one arm. It bobbed its head at the ice-coated holding cell. "He seemed lonely."

"He," Istvan said tightly, "is impossible."

A shrug. "There's a lot we still don't know about what happened."

Istvan spun around. "You're proposing that all of those creatures were slave soldiers! Thinking minds, trapped inside monsters! That death wasn't a mercy, that they could be... that I–" He hurled his knife at nothing in particular. It spun, bounced off a wall with a clatter, and skittered into a corner. "Oh, I couldn't have been permitted one guiltless massacre, now could I? Just one!"

Roberts raised his eyebrows. "Doctor–"

"Don't! Not a bloody word!" The lizard flickered its tongue. Istvan caught at the fastenings at the creature's throat. "And don't you dare put your tongue out at me!"

The tongue vanished.

A growl from the cell. The keyboard started clicking again.

Istvan half-drew his knife, back where it belonged through means he could never determine, and then realized what he was doing.

Pietro wouldn't have approved at all. No, he would have been terrified, appalled, utterly disbelieving; his Pista, so willing to start a fight, or finish one, showing up at the door bruised or bloodied over one slight or another, *Ah, but you should have seen the others!*; his Pista, foolishly combative but not cruel, no stomach for even the idea of hunting; his Pista, so very changed, rabid as the beasts he'd thought he dispatched.

Not Pietro's Pista at all. Not anymore.

Istvan let go.

The lizard adjusted its parka, tugging the furry hood over a head too long-necked and frilled to be fully covered. "We think he was frozen, all this time," it said. Its affect was distant, muted, inhuman. Like the beast itself. "Maybe something changed. We don't know. He doesn't remember. But, since he is what he is... ask him about Anoushak, eh?"

Istvan flinched. The Susurration hadn't wanted to kill her. It had been compelled to end the Wizard War – chosen, not choosing – and had delayed as long as it could, mourned the loss of her armies even as the weapon fired. All Pietro had wanted to do was help. Save them. Redeem them.

Oh, that voice.

Istvan sought out Edmund again, a convulsive reflex like a hand closing on another's wrist. Still there. Real – very real – and still there.

"Doctor?"

Roberts. Dear, faithful Roberts.

"I'm fine," Istvan lied. It was an easy lie. He supposed that was the reason Edmund so often used it. "I'm... tired, is all. The, ah, earthquake, you know."

The nurse didn't believe him – he was too unnerved for that, knew Istvan's proclivities too well – but he did stay where he was, turning his clipboard in his hands. He was... he was married, wasn't he? Worked grueling hours. Seemed proud of his position, but sometimes resentful. Why? His work? His treatment? His schedule, or rather lack of one? Had Istvan never been appreciative enough of his help, never told him how grateful he was that he always seemed to be around when needed?

That would have to change.

"Mr Blake's trying to talk to you, Doctor," said the

lizard. It sounded wary but faintly disappointed, just like Orlean. This dangerous, distractible idiot was the War to End All Wars? "In a manner of speaking."

Istvan turned. The beast crouched in its cage, its speech glowing green before it.

I am right here, said the screen. *Please be civil*. And, below that, the line blinking at its end: *The Immortal was interested in your friend*.

Istvan swallowed, trying to keep his mind from straying to boiling hordes and bloodied hands. "What do you mean? What do you mean, 'interested'?"

New talent leads to new methods. The beast fixed him with a yellow eye. *All she ever needed was enough time*.

Edmund meandered through the glittering shelves. He had returned all the fallen books to their places after the quake, more or less, and the rest was the usual maintenance. Correcting mis-shelvings. Making sure all that belonged was still present, and that what didn't was properly examined. Noting any new arrivals. Reinforcing the wards. Checking some of the more notorious books for victims.

The greater part of the work that needed doing was in the vault, but he doubted Istvan's senses could reach across dimensions, he didn't want to risk another panic, and asking about vault permissions would be testing Mercedes' fragile patience with him. Best to stay in the main stacks, all around.

He started up the next ladder. It was a slower climb with one bad arm, but it had to be done. Inexcusable Mathematics almost always had something in the wrong place, as of late.

"Edmund!"

He paused, one foot halfway between rungs. "Istvan?"

The faint clamor of guns came in reply, barbed wire slithering across wooden floors.

Edmund turned, still on the ladder, some four feet in the air. No cape to flick out of the way: he'd learned his lesson about capes and ladders years ago, and it hung on a well-worn peg three aisles over. "Istvan, what is it?"

The specter stood at the foot of the ladder, breathing hard, as though he'd just slid to a stop and still breathed. <It wants your magic,> he said in German, <Your black magic.>

<What does?>

<The Susurration,> Istvan replied miserably. <It knows it can't survive whatever Barrio Libertad intends to do. It doesn't want to lose anyone, not again, and...> His voice cracked. He took hold of the ladder. <Edmund, you can't be killed. So long as you have time, you can't be killed.>

Edmund concentrated on balance. A ladder wasn't the right place for this sort of news. <Right. Let me get down.>

Grace had said that the Susurration didn't want his magic. It was interdicted. It wouldn't be able to use it. Why bother?

But...

More people like him. Leeches. Uncatchable. Unkillable. Armies of them, striking faster than the eye could see, exchanging moments like water. The Susurration with complete control over the distribution of every second of everyone's lives, and under no obligation to ensure that everyone received an equal share. Anything could be done, given enough manpower... and enough time.

Willing martyrs.

Wedding proposals.

The fortress had made an exception for this spell, and

this spell alone. Did it not matter who used it? Did the Susurration know something Grace didn't?

<Istvan, who told you this?>

Silence.

Edmund immediately regretted the question. <Never mind.>

Rusted wire crept up the ladder like vines, twisting and thorny. He told himself it wasn't real. He told himself they had time to figure this out, that this particular ritual required a very precise set of conditions to even attempt. Most rituals of that power did. He lowered one foot, made sure the rung would hold, rested his weight on it. Lowered the next.

Right. Left. Right. Left. Seven rungs to the bottom.

Seven.

He stopped.

Oh.

Oh, no.

He'd forgotten. With Lucy, and Grace, and the tiger attack, and everything else, disaster after disaster coming at him so quickly... he'd forgotten what he'd asked Janet to do. Forgotten that she'd called, and that the time was here.

Conjunction. Seventh day of the seventh month, seven at night, provided the stars were right and you were sincere about giving up your soul. All it took was a lot of blood.

<Edmund,> Istvan said, quietly, <men have died for worse things than eternal peace on Earth.>

Edmund swayed on the last rung. "Yes. They have."

CHAPTER TWENTY-FOUR

"Why didn't you tell me?" Istvan demanded as he fled back through the Twelfth Hour's shelves. "Something like this coming up and the Susurration may have already taken your... Edmund, you could have told me!"

Edmund snatched his cape up and swung it around his shoulders. "I could have."

"Why didn't you?"

"You didn't need to know." He fastened the buttons as quickly as he could without spending any extra time. The cape was designed to tear off, should he catch it in something. Better than being strangled. There was no worse feeling than no air. "I thought you didn't need to know."

"Edmund, if I had known that was what Miss Justice was on about..."

"You talked to Janet?"

"While I was looking for you, yes! She wanted me to tell you about this conjunction of yours and a plague of stolen goats. I didn't think..." His expression twisted, somewhere between hurt and disgust. "*Goats*, Edmund."

Oh, hell.

Edmund fastened the last button. "We're going to see Janet."

"That's all you have to say?"

"You didn't know."

He took a step.

Bony phalanges jabbed through his sternum. "Don't you dare forget that this is all your fault."

Edmund froze. A trickle of phantom blood ran down the front of his shirt.

"If you hadn't been such an idiot," Death hissed, "none of this would have happened."

Edmund swallowed. Just Istvan. It was just Istvan. "I–"

The specter leaned closer... and then let go, shaking. Feathers drifted loose. "I was out of my mind with worry after you left that note."

He retreated. Fading loops of barbed wire trailed past and around the nearest shelf.

Edmund wiped clammy hands on his jacket. OK. It was OK. If Istvan were really leaving, he would have flown out, and he hadn't. It had just been a hard night.

It would be OK.

He tipped his hat at the nearest lamp, just in case it was watching, and then followed the wire. "Istvan?" He switched to German. <Istvan, I'm sorry. I wasn't thinking.>

The ghost stood not far down the aisle, his back turned.

Edmund stopped at a respectful distance. <If you don't want to come along, I'll understand. It's a lot to ask.>

<I'm bloody well coming along.>

Edmund let out a breath. <Thank you.>

Istvan brushed a mostly-fleshed hand over his eyes, then his scarring. <Don't run off and leave me a bloody note again.>

<I won't.>

The Department of Modern Technology and Such remained exactly where it belonged, which was a relief. Things staying fixed in their places was always good. There were only a few new cracks.

Edmund pushed the door open. "Hello?"

"Be right there," replied Janet.

She was still here. Sometimes he wondered if the woman ever slept.

He stepped gingerly into the room, taking his hat off and turning it in his hands, trying to think about anything but what he was doing. What he'd done. The recent earthquake didn't seem to have damaged any of the equipment, though dust coated the tops of some of the machines. The crack in the ceiling seemed wider. Golden web filaments drifted from its edges. He hoped, when it did give way, it wouldn't be too little, too late.

Istvan followed him. He stood further away than usual.

<I truly am sorry,> Edmund told him.

The specter shook his head.

Finally, Janet Justice strolled out from behind one of the partitions, gliding over and around strewn cables and protruding shelves with an easy, weighted grace. She was tall for a woman, an inch or two over Istvan, and the grey in her hair glittered red and green, backlit by the clutter of her equipment. She glanced uncertainly at the reticent ghost, then nodded to Edmund. "So, the guest of honor finally shows. I was starting to worry."

"It's been a busy few days."

Her eyes darted to Istvan again. "So I understand. Did Doctor Czernin tell you?"

"He told me enough." Goats, plural. Amber, too, probably, and all the other trappings of belief, sincerity, and deliberation. Nothing would listen unless you were serious. "Have you figured out where it's all going?"

She struck a key. A map appeared on the nearest screen.

Edmund shut his eyes. Of course. Of course it would be Providence. No way around it. No way out. There never was.

Run.

This was a problem Barrio Libertad could solve itself. They didn't need him. They had the means, the motive, and the power, and no compunction against using it.

He'd seen too much of that kind of problem solving in '45.

He nodded. It felt like someone else was doing it. "Thank you, Janet."

"Sure," she said. She raised her eyebrows. "Do I still not want to know what this is all about?"

"You don't."

He turned to leave with what he hoped was a suitably self-assured flick of the cape.

"We ought to tell the Magister," said Istvan.

Edmund tripped over a cable, suddenly dizzy. Tell Mercedes? Tell her what? That he was the Hour Thief for a reason, and that he had forgotten about the conjunction? That meant he would have to explain that, and then explain the ramifications of that, and then explain how it worked, which meant he would be explaining what he had done. Remembering it.

Rituals of that sort weren't meant to be remembered. Even the memories burned.

It had seemed like such a good idea at the time.

"No," he managed. "No, we're not telling her."

He was back in the hall. It was cracked. The walls were carved with foreign figures, the bodies and faces of deities, and covered with cracks. He backed away.

Wishful thinking, the idea that they looked like that. Human. Anything close to human.

His had come from the lake.

Ice gripped his shoulder. "Edmund."

He realized he was sweating. Mind racing. Heart racing. Oil rising in his throat. The Navy, too, had seemed like a good idea at the time. Freshwater and saltwater weren't the same. Any other service might have landed him back in Europe.

"I can't tell her," he said. "I can't tell anyone."

The grip tightened. "Edmund, she is our superior officer by any measure, you have already disobeyed her orders at least once, and this is a matter of dire import. If you can't tell her, I will."

Edmund swallowed, counting his breaths. He wished he'd never found that book. Never studied the only other immortal in written history. That way he wouldn't know the price for sure.

It was always better not to know.

"Istvan, what if I'd done something terrible?"

The ghost regarded him a moment, not bothering to turn the ruined side of his face away. "You would be in good company."

"Does that make it any better?"

"No. It doesn't."

"All right."

Istvan stayed where he was until Edmund's heart slowed to something more manageable. Then he drew back, fiddling with his wedding ring before hooking the offending thumb in his belt. "Now, will you tell the

Magister or shall I?"

Edmund steadied himself. "No, this is my fault. You shouldn't have to do more than you've already done." He donned his hat. It helped, a little. It always did. "I'll tell her."

Janet pulled the door closed. It clicked.

Istvan stayed a step behind Edmund as they hurried past the last of the shelves and into the long lantern-lit hall with its alcoves. It was the proper thing to do, taking this to the Magister. It was what they ought to have done long ago. Whatever she was on about – whatever Edmund claimed she may or may not have done – she still held the title, and had steered the Twelfth Hour well enough for long enough to deserve it.

She had rescued Istvan from the Susurration, not Edmund.

The Susurration.

Istvan tried to drive that voice out of his head. Of course it wanted what it did. Of course it would do anything to get it. Trapped against its will in a horrid waste for years, laboring betrayed and unappreciated under constant threat of destruction – men broke under such circumstances, went to staring, went to fits. Why should it be any different for the Susurration? What better way to survive than ensure that it couldn't be killed?

But... how?

Edmund had never explained by what means he learned his time magic. All Istvan knew was that the man had stolen a book, sometime before the Second World War, and done something awful. That was all.

Beyond that, it hadn't mattered, really. Edmund was simply the Hour Thief. It was part of him, as much as the cape or the watch. Istvan had always considered it to be less terrible than what he himself did. It wasn't nearly so final, or so direct, or bloody – it was wholly bloodless, in fact – and, after all, Edmund didn't *kill* people, now did he?

Could he?

Had he?

Istvan tried to look at him without looking like he was looking at him. The man's expression had fixed into a forced calm, even a bit of a smile, but nothing else about his presence supported it. His terror was wonderful.

It was still all his fault.

Istvan clasped his hands behind his back. "Why did you ask Miss Justice to attend to this conjunction business anyhow? Stars and planets? Sorcerous alignments? I know something of what her machines can do, but she isn't a wizard, Edmund."

"Exactly."

"Why didn't you tell me?"

Edmund walked faster. "The less anyone knows about how it's done, the better."

They reached the Magister's door. Edmund tapped the toe of his shoe against it, needlessly cautious as always. "Mercedes? It's Edmund. I'm sorry, but something new has come up. It's important."

The door cracked open. Magister Hahn darted out of it, a messenger bag slung over her shoulder, and slammed it shut behind her back before Istvan could make out more than the smell of burning camphor. Her hand with its missing finger was bandaged and she looked exhausted, as she had for days, not helped by her pressed but too-large jacket. Pens strained at her hair. "Gentlemen."

"Mercedes," said Edmund, flatly, as though he'd

rehearsed it, "we have good reason to believe that the Susurration has learned my time theft ritual and will be enacting it less than two days from now."

She stared at him.

"We thought you ought to know," Istvan added, trying not to sound too prim about it.

The wild, apprehensive, doubtful churn of her presence roared into a storm of dread to match Edmund's. "Mr Templeton, what's your evidence for this?"

Edmund shoved his hands deeper in his pockets. "It wouldn't be collecting sacrificial goats if it didn't know what it was doing."

Istvan choked. "Sacri–"

"It's traditional."

"You *sacrificed* a *goat*?"

"I was twenty-one."

"This is worse than that bloody stupid horseshoe!"

"Istvan, no one's going to mistake me for a nineteenth-century European peasant."

"It's ridiculous!"

"Better safe than sorry!"

"You're a man of letters, for God's sake! Don't you know what you…" The Magister started forward. Istvan dodged out of her way before she could stride through him. "Magister?"

She adjusted the Twelfth Hour pin at her throat. "We're picking up those Bernault devices."

"We're what?"

"Mr Templeton, are you familiar with Braunland Observatory?"

Edmund fell into place behind her. "Yes."

She switched her bag to her other shoulder. Istvan wondered what was in it. "I want you to take me and the devices there."

"May I ask why?"

"I'm sending a message to Barrio Libertad. I want at least one representative to meet me there – in person – and if Triskelion is working so closely with the fortress as it seems, I want the ear of whichever warlord they have contracted as well. The observatory is far enough away from the territories of all parties that it should be acceptable." She grinned tightly. "I know you two aren't much for politics, but in this case…"

"We're for politics."

"I thought so."

Istvan trailed them both, feeling whatever satisfaction he'd gained from finally acknowledging the chain of command slipping away. "You're giving them the Bernault devices."

"They'll make better use of them than we will." Her pace had quickened; they were nearly a quarter of the way back down the hall now, just passing the alcove for 1930.

"You're telling them about the ritual, too?"

"Yes."

"You can't do that," said Edmund.

"Why not?"

"The weapon. Mercedes, if you tell them they have two days to stop this, they'll stop it."

She eyed the candles burning for 2015. "Mr Templeton, the last thing we need is another Hour Thief, and one without your scruples. I'd rather not risk what might happen if we don't tell them."

He fell silent.

"Doctor Czernin," she continued, "notify your people that you won't be available for the rest of today. Conferences like this require a certain kind of showing."

Istvan rubbed at his wrists. Never mind that he would

do that already. Never mind what had happened last time. Never mind how badly so many directives had twisted and tangled. He was what he was, and every casual word from that woman was an order clad in molten iron.

He found himself wishing for mortars. It would be so much simpler if there were a war on.

"Yes, Magister."

It was afternoon when they finally had it all assembled. Representatives of the Twelfth Hour, Barrio Libertad, and Triskelion gathered peaceably together in one place for the first time. It was just past four. It wasn't late.

The sky above the observatory's crumbling dome blazed with stars.

"I guess this is it," Edmund said.

"I suppose it is," Istvan agreed.

They stood just outside, waiting for the last of the security detail to roll into place. They were in the mountains now, further to the west than he'd ever been able to fly without pain, Big East's industrial cityscape giving way to ragged foothills and finally blasted and smoke-wreathed peaks, storms from Tornado Alley breaking over their stony backs. Beyond lay Triskelion, the nearest region broken into true warfare he had never visited.

He could almost hear the report of rifles, the clatter of wheels, the shouting of the supply trains hauling ammunition over snow-choked passes, the roar of emplacements echoing peak to peak to avalanching peak...

Oh, it wasn't to be. For the best, he knew, but he did miss it, in that terrible guilty sense that one missed anything one oughtn't.

Edmund sighed. "What the hell am I supposed to do?"

Istvan realized he was sighing to himself as well, and stopped. "What? This is the Magister's game now, as it ought to have been days ago: all you must do is speak when spoken to."

"Not that."

"You were a fine leader, Edmund, under the circumstances."

"Not that, either." The wizard swung his pocket watch in a circle before catching it. Stared at the distant city skyline. His affect churned, lidded but not hidden, grief and frustration and terror boiling like goulash. "Istvan, there was one time years ago – her name was Marianne – she'd moved on, but then so had I, mostly, and it's somehow different when you know she's alive. The letters just stopped coming, was all. That happened to a lot of fellows. But this… Istvan, how am I supposed to deal with this? Has anything like this ever happened to you?"

Grace. Bloody Grace.

Istvan glanced back at the observatory. A Triskelion mercenary stood guard at the door. Others formed a perimeter, idling on foot or at the guns of strangely baroque armored vehicles, machines wide enough that they had been forced to inch up the steep mountain roads one by one. The representatives were already inside. Grace Wu, in her peculiar guise as Barrio Libertad's "state hero," was among them, because of course she was.

"Dealing with a woman who doesn't love you back, Edmund?"

"Yes."

"I can't say that I have."

"Right. Sorry. This isn't the time." The wizard ran a finger over brass. "Forget I asked."

Istvan cast one last wistful glance at the embattled mountains. "It should be starting soon," he said, "We ought to go in." He hesitated, then patted Edmund's shoulder. "Don't worry, I'm sure you'll manage."

"I'm sure."

CHAPTER TWENTY-FIVE

The mercenary at the door rested a hand on the pommel of his sabre, his voice with its indefinable accent blaring brassy and metallic. "Hour Thief. All fares well?"

"No toll yet," the Hour Thief replied, "but thank you for asking."

"Attend closely, and guard well your vengeful spirit."

"I'm sure he'll behave himself."

Istvan, at his side, sighed.

They followed the man inside. A catwalk hung suspended over a sea of rusted mechanisms, enormous wheels and motors Edmund assumed were meant to position the equally enormous telescope that reared skyward in the center, a flaking hulk with broken mirrors. Clicks and mechanical chattering echoed from lifeless consoles. According to Janet, the place still published nightly reports on the state of the heavens: charting new phenomena no one could place, tracking constellations that never existed. The only light was foreign, rigged over a platform riddled with bolt holes where components had been removed. A circular table sat there now. Occupied.

Mercedes nodded at them from their section. She didn't smile.

Edmund made his way across the room, Istvan close by his side, and focused on being the Hour Thief. Walk smooth and easy. Smile: faint, pleasant, and self-assured. Don't look too long at any one person, except for effect. Stay tall. Stay calm. He could do this.

Don't look too long.

To Mercedes' right sat the contingent from Triskelion, a trio of armored figures in familiar style. The man in the center wore an elaborate breastplate, a crimson cape, and at least two greatcoats, his pauldrons a cascade of golden spikes. He still wore his helmet, as did his men: crested, skull-faced, a horsehair plume trailing off the back of his chair. A broadsword lay propped on the railing behind him. One of the warlords, no doubt.

Across from him, behind a redundant placard labeled "Barrio Libertad," she waited.

She was, once again, Resistor Alpha. Cowled, goggled, and clad in that harness that strapped around her arms. Bright red and yellow. She wore the same copper circlet she had once placed on Edmund's own head, when this had all begun. Only a few days ago. It felt like years.

No Diego. Evidently mortal deliberation was beneath his attention.

Mostly mortal.

Edmund hung his hat on his chair and sat down before he could somehow make a fool of himself. Istvan took up position beside the box of Bernault devices. No one present would want to go through him to get at them, or so Mercedes had reasoned. It didn't hurt to be cautious.

The Triskelion warlord leaned forward. "So," boomed the man to his left, raising a gauntleted fist, "this is the hero who harried the armies of the dread wizard lord Shokat Anoushak to their downfall. Hail, Hour Thief. The great and magnanimous Lord Kasimir hopes that your esteemed successor will demonstrate such courage at these deliberations."

Edmund smiled politely. "I'm certain she will."

Mercedes folded her hands, not quite hiding the bandages. "Thank you all for agreeing to attend, but our time is limited. It has come to my attention that the Susurration is preparing a ritual that will allow it to duplicate Mr Templeton's abilities."

Grace swore.

"It will be ready in less than two days," Mercedes continued. "The seventh day of the seventh month, seven at night."

"You could have said something earlier," Grace snapped. "Eddie, if this thing was coming up, you should have said something."

"You're right," the Hour Thief said, "I should have. I forgot about it. I'm sorry."

She swore again, dropping her head on a fist. "I should have known," she muttered. "I should have.... God, I was so *stupid*."

Lord Kasimir drummed his fingers on the table. "A dire predicament!" boomed his spokesman. "But my most intrigued and uncanny lord finds himself wondering, Resistor Alpha: could you not simply make use of your ultimate weapon? Surely ending the beast in flames would bring an end to these fears of sorcery?"

She looked up, eyes hard behind her goggles. "Most of us have problems with the idea of murdering several hundred thousand innocent people."

"Is not more at stake?"

"There's this thing called 'principle.' Ultimate weapon isn't on the table."

"Barrio Libertad mounts impressive weaponry, and our forces are highly skilled. Given knowledge of the sorcery's location, perhaps a conventional bombardment would suffice?"

"Given the nature of the Susurration," Mercedes said, "I doubt there will be only one ritual attempt. How many goats, Mr Templeton?"

He shook his head. Janet hadn't said. "Enough to notice."

Lord Kasimir tapped a finger on his helmet chin-plate.

"Couldn't you counter it?" Istvan asked. "The magic. Barrio Libertad has Providence under interdiction, doesn't it? If it can counter teleporting, couldn't it–"

"That would be fine if Eddie hadn't teleported out of the fortress yesterday," Grace said.

Istvan opened his mouth again. Closed it. He leaned on the box.

Edmund reminded himself to breathe. The elevator. The panic. He hadn't even thought about it. The spell was practically second nature now and he'd had other things on his mind afterward, like cleaning up the bathroom and confronting Mercedes and seeing to Istvan and dealing with the kind of deadly geopolitics he'd hoped he would never have to juggle again.

At least Grace hadn't mentioned the circumstances.

"Mine is different from Shokat Anoushak's," he said. Then, because she didn't look convinced, "She left a significant body of work and spawned a host of imitators, but the majority of the known canon was developed piecemeal by single individuals desperate enough to have a go at breaking reality. They're all different."

"Who developed yours, then? You?"

"Of course not."

"And I guess the time-stealing thing isn't Anoushak's, either."

"No. And it's *Sh*–"

"Which brings us to the matter at hand," said Mercedes. She tapped a pen on the table. "Ms Wu, in return for seeing this ritual stopped, I'm prepared to loan you the use of my two best operatives, the Bernault devices we confiscated, and any other assistance you would care to accept."

Grace set an elbow on the table. "I need an evacuation."

"Excuse me?"

"Magister, while I'm glad we finally caught your attention, stopping this ritual thing isn't enough. Even a new set of Bernault devices doesn't solve things. It just puts us back to square one: us, the Susurration, and a lot of people caught in the middle."

Mercedes' lips thinned. "I'm sorry, Ms Wu, but I can't pull a mass exodus out of my hat."

"Yeah? I bet he can."

Edmund realized Grace was pointing at him, took a moment to compose himself, and then kicked himself for proving her point. He wasn't even wearing his hat. He wasn't that kind of wizard. "No."

Grace leaned forward. "You've got time to spare, Eddie. Think about it."

"I am. That's too many people. I'd burn through everything I have before I got them all out." He shook his head, hating himself for it. "I'm sorry. I can't."

She sighed.

Edmund tried to look at the banks of old machinery behind her rather than at her. Coward. Thief. Even she had given up on him – and she didn't give up on anyone, not the Grace he remembered. Anything could be solved. Anyone could be saved. Seven years gone by or no, he should have known she'd seize on any opportunity to try.

He wished he still had her optimism.

He wished he wasn't so quick to take the coward's way out.

Mercedes turned a pen between her fingers. If she thought anything of the exchange, she wasn't showing it. "Returning to what is *feasible*, Ms Wu, I can offer you twenty Bernault devices. Given that, would you be able to weaken the Susurration's grip on the area long enough for the ritual sites to be properly dealt with?" She nodded to Edmund. "You have time for that much, I would think."

Grace frowned. "Twenty?"

Lord Kasimir looked to the armored figure on his right.

"The four devices required for Site Two evaded detection," came the reply, sounding subdued and tired even through the electronic filter. "My lord's subtlety remains unmatched."

"They burst," Istvan muttered.

"Sorry," added Edmund. When the visored helmet turned to him, he shrugged. "Maybe you should invest in better crates."

Grace tilted her head, as though she were listening to someone beside her. "I don't know how weak we can manage," she said. "It would burn the Bernault devices out pretty quick and anyone going would have to wear a circlet, at the very least, which rules out the spook. Though... he might not need it." She considered. "Hey, Eddie, if we sent–"

"No," Edmund and Istvan both said at once.

"No," Istvan repeated. He looked as though he'd just seen another ghost.

Grace looked between them oddly, but Edmund didn't care to explain. If Istvan wanted to talk about it, that was his prerogative; if he didn't, no one else should.

"You know," she said, "if we got everyone out, we wouldn't be discussing this."

Edmund closed his eyes. "I know."

"The Susurration is using those people as a shield, don't you realize that? That's the only reason it's lasted this long. Get the people out of the way, and bam!" She slapped the table. "No Susurration, no ritual, no problem. Everybody wins."

"Grace, believe me, I know!"

He couldn't. He couldn't risk it. None of that time was his and he hadn't earned it and he had no right to it, but he had it now, and giving up so much, even for a good cause, wasn't possible. He cared – boy, did he care, he *had* to care – but he couldn't do it. Not even to stop another Hour Thief.

He turned polished brass over and over in his pocket. He'd had the watch since the start. The hourglass engraving on its front had worn off once already.

Every second over that seven-year buffer was a second he wouldn't get back.

"You would simply kill it, then?" asked Istvan. There was a strange note in his voice Edmund couldn't quite pin down. "No warning? No chance at all to surrender?"

Grace rolled her eyes. "That's what an ultimate weapon is for, genius. I mean, I'm sorry there wouldn't be more pain and suffering, but–"

Istvan marched to the table. "You can't."

Mercedes' pen cracked in half. She glanced down at it, blue ink staining her remaining fingers, then folded her hands as though nothing had happened. "Doctor, this isn't a traditional engagement."

"Don't you bloody lecture me on the Geneva Conventions," he snapped. "The Susurration is terrible, yes, and I would see it stopped as much as anyone, but it didn't choose what it is. It didn't even choose to *be* here.

It has as much right to a fair trial as anyone – you can't sit about and plan to murder it like this."

Everyone around the table stared at him.

Then Kasimir's spokesman leapt to his feet, pointing with a roar. "Remove this shrinking daisy of a peacemaker!"

The specter bristled. "A flower, am I?"

"That was the wrong metaphor," Edmund said. "Wrong flower, too."

"I could fight you all! I could put you all under the flowers in an instant, if I wanted!"

"Doctor Czernin," warned Mercedes.

Grace stood, electricity crackling. "What is this? You're *sympathizing* with it now? You? Doctor Awful?" She looked to Edmund. "What happened? If he's compromised–"

"If he has no doughty spleen for what must be done, he has no place at the table of the stern and terrible Lord Kasimir!"

Edmund dodged the sudden flare of wings. Well. This was going downhill faster than a sled. This was the worst. What did Istvan mean, it hadn't chosen to be here? "If we could please–"

"Terrible?" Barbed wire snarled across the floor, rusted and stained. "Terrible?"

The observatory door crashed open.

One of Kasimir's mercenaries strolled across the catwalk, carrying a flat white box. "Jailer, betrayer, and beloved, all together," he called. "I never received an invitation, but I'm sure you meant to send one. I forgive you. I will always forgive you, if you allow it. I've even brought you a pie."

He lifted the lid.

"It's apple."

•••

"Hand the traitor!" Kasimir and his men leapt from their chairs, the latter drawing sabers and the former taking up the broadsword that lay against the railing, "The just and unwavering Lord Kasimir will not stand a forced turncoat in his ranks!"

Grace Wu was already charging.

Istvan threw himself before her – and ran into Edmund. Through Edmund. He hadn't seen the wizard move. A rush of warm and wet, bone scraping through bone, a nauseating doubling of organs where they didn't belong.... and shock. Utter shock. Istvan, what are you doing? Defending the Susurration? Seeking peaceful solutions? What's happened to you?

Istvan, the cold...

Istvan scrambled away. "I'm sorry! I'm sorry!"

"Wait," called Edmund, "I want to know why it's–"

Grace bolted to the right. Edmund, indomitable, blurred to meet her, a mobile obstruction too quick to strike or bypass. The others stood, shouted, closed in – and the wizard stalled them all, shouting in return the need to listen. Oh, he was wonderful to watch. Wonderful.

Only Magister Hahn remained at the table, white-knuckled, a great wellspring of loathing and terror, remorse and regret. Perhaps the Susurration could be granted mercy after all. Perhaps reason, for once, would win out.

Magister Hahn.

Istvan bolted for the door.

"Doctor Czernin, silence the smiler. Now."

His chains snapped taut. Wrists, ankles, neck. Shackles that burned. Hooks that dug into his stomach. He slewed sideways, choking, crashing into and partially through the catwalk's rusting rail. Too slow. Too late.

He snarled to himself. Oh, this was Edmund's fault.

Edmund whirled around. "Mercedes, what are you doing?"

"What I must."

Istvan clung to the rail, thoughts spinning. The Susurration, gone, without even the chance to surrender; even the chance to explain what it was on about. It hadn't had a choice in the matter. All it wanted was peace. A second chance. A measure of happiness, for everyone, however misguided.

War wasn't the calculated extermination of the helpless and confined. That was something else.

He was awful. He wasn't that awful. He couldn't be that awful.

The chains winched tighter. He strained backwards, resolving to make every inch as hard-fought as those on the Western Front.

"Mercedes Hahn," called the Susurration's agent, "still you silence the truth? You lie to your own people, as you lied to me?"

She stood. "Doctor Czernin!"

Lightning. Fire. White phosphorous. Chains of parchment calligraphy blazing around his bones.

He let go of the rail, stifling a cry. Silence him. Silence the smiler. Now. He leapt for the mercenary's spine, reaching –

– and struck steel. No further.

The man's armor was solid. Just like last time, at Oxus Station. Just like Barrio Libertad.

"I came when you called," the Susurration said, grief ringing in its host's processed tones, "and now you force others to assault me when I arrive unasked? You conspire with those who seek to destroy me?"

Shouting. Everyone was shouting. Edmund at the

Magister. Grace at Edmund. Kasimir's spokesman at everyone, amplified accusations of obstructing justice. Himself at nothing, as his chains burned. Through it all sizzled the Magister's terror.

"Doctor Czernin, silence it now! Silence it!"

"Mercedes! Mercedes, think about what the hell you're doing!"

Istvan drew his knife.

The mercenary brought up his sabre, lights flickering through the eyes of his helmet. "You wanted peace, desperate one, oath-breaker, shaper, betrayer – and I brought it."

"Mercedes!"

Let it talk. Please let it talk. Sometimes, it spoke in Pietro's voice.

Istvan lunged.

"I did as you commanded," the Susurration proclaimed, parrying, empty. "I destroyed in sorrow, and saved what I could. Why should anyone else have to die? Why should anyone else suffer?"

Blade striking blade. He had sheared through metal, once, the armor of tanks and airplanes, the cold skin of sorcerous mockeries that fell from the heavens. He couldn't, now. He couldn't. He couldn't.

Don't kill it.

"I did what you wanted," it said. "Soon... I'll do what is right."

The mercenary trembled. The sabre fell from his grasp, a flash that tumbled from the catwalk. Clanged. Tumbled further, whirling over and over, vanishing into the rusted depths. Its owner slumped, a heap of nerveless armor.

Silenced. Not by Istvan's hand, but silenced.

Istvan sheathed his knife and sank down beside him, clutching at his wrists. The man was unconscious... but not empty. The Susurration was gone. It had given him up. Freed him. Judging from what Kasimir's spokesman was shouting, would it be enough to avoid a summary execution? Traitor, traitor. Deal with him. Take him away.

The pie box lay crushed, its contents spilled and dripping.

Edmund drew up behind him. "You all right?"

Istvan watched the fluids fall, pale syrup and cinnamon. Apple. It was apple. "I miss pastries."

"You wouldn't want that one anyway."

"It's American, isn't it? Apple pie?"

"As much as baseball and men in funny masks. Would you like a hand up?"

It was a pointless gesture. A formality. Silly, offering such a thing to a ghost.

Istvan took it.

"Magister Hahn," said Grace Wu, "I'm starting to think you weren't being level with us."

Lord Kasimir and his spokesman stood beside her, the third mercenary making his way across the catwalk towards their "traitor."

The Magister remained at the table, sitting down, slowly. Terror yet churned, hidden. An old fear, old grief, old desperation. "It lies," she said. "You've fought it this long. You know that."

The mercenary drew closer, blade drawn, intent on the fallen man.

Istvan tapped the butt of his knife on his breastplate. "Harm him," he hissed, "and terrible things will happen."

The mercenary sheathed his sabre.

"Mercedes," said Edmund, ignoring the altercation and, to his credit, not edging away, "blaming you for its very existence here doesn't sound like a minor fabrication to me."

"It intended to disrupt our efforts and that it has done," she replied. "I suggest we return to discussing the ritual we–"

"You say you stopped the Wizard War," interrupted Grace, "and if the Susurration was your plan, what was the plan for afterward, huh? What if we hadn't been there to stop it? What then?"

"Ms Wu, your fortress will be facing a terrible choice less than two days from now and you are dwelling on may-have-beens."

Grace slammed her fists on the table. "Because this is all your fault!"

The catwalk trembled. Dust sifted down from the ceiling. The telescope groaned, the deep bongs and pops of stressed metal.

Istvan drew closer to Edmund, curbing the urge to take hold of his arm but unable to stop the protective shadow of a wing. She hadn't hit the table that hard. She was strong, but not that strong.

Grace lifted her hands away. "It's doing what?" she asked the air, as she'd done before. She backed up. "I thought it was dead." She searched the floor: the platform, the mechanisms below. "Diego, I thought they were dead!"

"Earthquake?" asked Edmund. He looked down, too, reaching for his hat.

"No," Istvan said. "No, I don't think so."

Edmund stared at him. "Oh, hell." He turned to shout at the rest of the room. "Everyone, take a few moments to get out of the building, now!"

The ground exploded.

CHAPTER TWENTY-SIX

Edmund ran for Grace. Mercedes was more important, in a geopolitical sense, and the mercenary who had fallen couldn't flee, himself, but Edmund ran for Grace.

The machinery below rolled upwards, roaring.

He ran. Grace was faster.

She snatched up the fallen mercenary and bolted for the door. Right past Edmund. Eyes wide open, but not looking at him. Shouting, but not to him. He couldn't make out what she was saying over the sound of the building falling apart.

He spun around but couldn't touch her. Istvan swept through her path, mid-leap, and she didn't stop. Didn't pause. Electric arcs crackled along the rails, the door slammed open, and both she and her armored ally were gone.

Wheels and motors and rusting braces crashed into the catwalk – and kept going. Upwards. Pierced by jagged pillars of iron, curved, the light sparkling on smoky serrations of glass. Sparks spun away from smashed bulbs. The telescope toppled ponderously towards the platform, its underpinnings severed. The box of Bernault devices rolled towards the edge, one side shattered, spilling blue-white globes that tumbled in a dozen different directions. It wasn't the machinery that roared.

Lord Kasimir and his men vanished in a clang and a tearing of dust-choked air.

Mercedes remained. Magister by unanimous vote, never asked and never explaining what she had done to earn it. The end of the Wizard War. The beginning of a new world, battered but breathing. Not the blast. The convergence. Shokat Anoushak's strange, mad decision to cross the ocean with an entourage of armies, to search for something she had never found – until the last.

Peace.

The Susurration.

Mercedes jabbed an elbow into his hip. "Mr Templeton, are you looking to be re-elected?"

"No," he said, glancing back at where Grace had gone. Istvan was rushing toward them, reaching, bony jaw wide open. "No, I'm not."

He snapped his pocket watch as the observatory crumpled between iron teeth.

Istvan wasn't fast enough.

Time for everyone but him. Not possible, granting it to the dead man. That would be resurrection. That was well beyond Edmund's powers. No, instead he would give it to Grace – and the rest – and they would flash off, all at once, abandoning Istvan to the monster that burst from below.

He was what he was, after all.

It didn't matter.

The catwalk ripped through him. More machinery followed, cold steel and colder glass, a vortex of rough and jagged and rattling, stone breaking, waterfalls crashing, the tumbling-down of bridges and towers, noise so loud it was solid and solidity that drowned.

He tore at it. Beat forward. Up or down, he didn't know.

Dust. Part of the telescope whirled past him. Rubble sheeted through his wings, torn from the observatory and from the rock, a tornado screaming through a vast rotten ribcage. Glimpses of the mountains below and beyond spun through the gaps.

He dove. Out. Up. Cracked sheets of concrete and glassy scales sped past, elevator cables and guy wires dangling from exposed vertebrae. Telephone poles fringed a twisted maw of scythes and crushing mandibles. Emerald lightning boiled in a cavernous eye socket.

It ignored him. He doubted it noticed him.

The beast heaved itself halfway out of the mountain, rock running like water. It didn't move any further. It crouched there, its storms scouring away the peak, and complained to itself, a moaning millstone squall that echoed cliff to cliff and brought down landslides. It looked as dead as he was. A skeleton. A relic, falling to pieces. Even its lightning flickered. A crest of broken towers lined its hunched back, trailing smoke from three immense wounds blown through them end-to-end.

Nothing like the monsters Istvan remembered from the Wizard War.

Nothing left of the observatory.

He banked lower, searching for the others. They had all gone. A baroque Triskelion tank slid down the mountainside, empty.

The rents in the great beast's rusting sides blazed blue-white. It screamed.

"And you left me there!"

"You're fine!"

"That is entirely beside the point and you know it!"

"What was I supposed to do, come back and try to punch it to death?"

"No!"

Edmund knocked his head back against a scraggly tree growing out of the mountainside, his irritation a thin layer of spice over a richer turmoil. "Then what would you have suggested?"

Istvan snarled to himself. How was he supposed to know? How was he supposed to know anything anymore?

He kicked at the trail. A pebble spun down into the new valley below. Heaped towers lay there, the serpentine curve of enormous ribs, the splayed claws of at least five stout limbs half-buried in landslides. Whatever force it was that animated the beast had sputtered out, leaving it silent, blackened, and still burning. He didn't know how many of the Bernault devices had detonated inside it, but he didn't want to delve through it again to check. Even Shokat Anoushak's sorcery had limits.

The Susurration had sent it. The Susurration had tried to kill everyone at the conference and destroyed any chance of using the devices to buy time – all after Istvan had tried to defend it! After Istvan had fought to let it talk! After Istvan had... had hoped, that, somehow...

Oh, he didn't know what he'd hoped. He didn't want to know.

He picked up another pebble and threw it.

"There's nothing we can do, anyway," Edmund muttered.

"The Magister–"

"Istvan, it doesn't matter. The ritual, Mercedes, the people out there, whatever the Susurration has planned – none of it matters. Diego still has that weapon and he's going to use it. All we've done is move up the timetable.

Two days, Istvan. That's it. It doesn't matter what we or
Grace or anyone else says. The Bernault devices were
the only thing we could offer. The only thing. It's over.
We're done. We tried."

He hitched his bad arm around so he could cross it
with the other, leaning back against the tree and staring
darkly at the next peak over. "You know that old saying
about living long enough to become a villain."

He was giving up. Overwhelmed. Paralyzed. Plunged
into that deep, yawning pit of despair and grief, resigned
to drowning. If anyone did something wrong, it would
be his fault. If a decision couldn't be reached, best not to
make one at all. Grace was alive, and she had left him –
him and the conference both – and she had taken all of
his confidence with her. Oh, he was so foolish.

Istvan kicked at the dust. "We can't sit here."

"I know we can't sit here."

"Have you no ideas at all?"

"Istvan, no one wants to cooperate. Mercedes
stonewalled me when I got her back and no one else will
want to talk to us again. I don't know what we can do if
no one wants to cooperate."

"That's because they don't understand! They don't
understand what they're doing! Edmund, I've seen
it. I am it! If we do nothing, and they do nothing, it's
precisely the same as agreeing with the present course
of action. The talking stops and all the rest rushes into
action with banners and parades and before you know
it you're invading Italy and it's awful and no one has
any idea how it happened or how to stop it or what the
fighting is for, and it's all inertia from there. Nothing is
ever the same afterwards. And then no one learns and it
happens again. Over and over."

He blinked at his hands. His dead, bloodied hands.

"All these years, Edmund, and I've never done anything to... Not once have I... We can't let that happen here, Edmund, we can't. It isn't right. It isn't right at all. I might be this... this horrible thing, but... but I – Edmund, I can't..." He ripped off his glasses with a curse, turning away to wipe viciously at his eyes. Soft, he was, after two bloody days with the Susurration, overwrought and womanish and weak. "Oh, I hate this."

"You've seen me worse."

"Yes, but you're..."

Shellshocked? A proper man at heart? Irresistible when in pain; handsome, tragic, and brave?

Istvan hooked his glasses on his bandolier and rubbed at his face. Flickering again. Not right, indeed. "I'm sorry."

Edmund shook his head. "Don't apologize."

"I... I simply want to find some other way, Edmund. For once. Something that isn't a massacre." He leaned back against the mountainside, suddenly wrung-out, weary as the wizard beside him. He turned his ring around his finger, thinking of the tiger locked in its cage. <Peti wouldn't have wanted a massacre.>

Edmund was silent.

Another landslide gave way, crashing and bonging down the fallen rocks. Metal glinted within it. Part of the observatory, Istvan thought. Would it still report its view of the heavens, even now?

"Maybe we should talk to Mercedes," Edmund said.

"You said she didn't want to explain herself."

"At this point it seems there's not a whole lot of room for want, Istvan. If the Susurration was telling the truth – and there's no reason to believe that it wasn't, given what I've seen – she might be our best bet."

Istvan blinked at him. "You don't mean to..."

Edmund stood, turmoil yet churning but crushed beneath purpose. A blur: hat on, jacket straightened, cape cleared of bark and dust, snapping in the breeze. The Hour Thief. The impossible soldier. The Man in Black. He was bigger than he was, and Istvan still couldn't understand how he did it.

The man who had been Magister swung his pocket watch around his hand, caught it, and sighed. "Like I said. Not a whole lot of room for want."

CHAPTER TWENTY-SEVEN

The ritual circle lay drawn where Edmund last remembered it, still intact. The offering remained in their bowls, old blood congealing beneath Chinese lanterns. Only Mercedes' phone was missing... and Mercedes herself.

"You can teleport into the Magister's office?" demanded Istvan.

Edmund picked his way across the chalk, making sure not to scuff any of it. The window was open, for the first time since he recalled, and he had a sinking feeling he knew where Mercedes had gone. There had always been something odd about that window. "Unfortunately."

"But–"

"I took the wards down for convenience's sake and never got around to putting them back up. I'll talk to Mercedes about it first thing after this is over, I swear." He reached the seat below, set a knee on the cushions, and leaned forward to push the window open. It swung away on hinges, twin panels of glass reinforced by weathered wood and strips of iron. The waves roared. Salt spray stung his lips. Open ocean, as far as he could see.

Istvan skimmed over the ritual circle, alighting beside him. "You don't really think she went out there, do you?"

Edmund tugged at the curtain rod. Solid. He held tight to it with his good arm and swung through the window like it was a shipboard hatch.

His feet struck wood. He staggered. The drop had been much shorter than he'd anticipated, and the position of the window seemed to have reversed itself: the waves were, once more, outside, though the inside he now occupied was vastly different. Before him stretched a carved wooden railing, curving back around to both left and right before leading down a spiral stairway. Above him, slats radiated outward from a conical roof. A tremendous heat burned at his back: heat, and a brilliance that nearly blinded him when he turned to look.

A lighthouse.

The window sat incongruously between two panes of glass, looking out over the same ocean as all the rest. He peered over the railing. Whitecaps broke on barnacle-razored rocks below.

Istvan burst backwards from the window, pinwheeling, like he'd tried to dive through and it had hurled him in reverse into elsewhere. His spine struck the lighthouse lamp; he staggered away from it with a curse. "Edmund, what is this?"

The stairs creaked.

"Do tell," said Mercedes.

Edmund whirled around, automatically pulling off his hat. Istvan snapped to attention. Mercedes stood at the top of the stairs, holding a chipped mug and clad in a blue fluffy bathrobe. Her hair was wet, down, and lacking its customary pens. Her pockmarked face – and her eyes – were sharp as ever.

Whatever Edmund had been planning to say flew out of his head. Did she live here? She'd gone home, after that conference, and taken a bath?

Could he blame her?

I'm sorry, we'll come back at a better time. We didn't mean to bother you. I'll get right to fixing those wards – we shouldn't be in here at all, I know. Sorry. Forget we were ever here. You're the Magister, not me.

"I imagine you're here about the Susurration," she said.

Edmund took a deep breath. "That's right."

"I didn't know you could teleport into my office, Mr Templeton."

"It's a loophole from my tenure. I'll show you how to put the wards back after this is over, I promise."

"I'll hold you to that." She started back down the stairs. "Come on, then."

Edmund realized that Istvan had remained ramrod-rigid throughout the exchange, staring straight ahead with his field cap clasped in one hand and the other clutching his own wrist. All normal but for that last detail. He frowned. "Mercedes?"

"I don't like the idea of taking chances with the ones who will be telling stories about me after I'm gone. Besides," she called as she vanished from sight, "I took a shower. I always think better after a shower."

Edmund looked to Istvan.

"So long as I'm not ordered about again," the specter muttered.

"I'll see what I can do."

They followed her down the staircase, a tunnel of brick and iron that spiraled around and around at dizzyingly steep angles, creaking. Edmund watched his step. Istvan followed closely behind.

Mercedes strode ahead, cup in one hand and the other on the rail. Her feet were bare. "I didn't create the Susurration," she said. "It was already there, waiting to be given form and purpose, and a way into the world. I gave it that. I brought it here, and I tasked it to kill Shokat Anoushak and her armies. Bring peace. End suffering. Save us all. You can see the problem already, I'm sure."

Edmund thought of perfect clouds. How wonderful had Lucy been, while it lasted? Before he realized what she was doing, what she was? No more fears, no more abyss lurking behind every too-close wall, every person who grew too familiar, every drop of water in the dark. He could talk to her about anything. Laugh. Feel normal again.

Wasn't that almost worth living in a realm of birds and sunlight and boys on bicycles while his body toiled itself to rags?

"It wants to finish what you brought it here to do," he said, more to himself than anyone.

Peace, over the whole world, a final end to suffering. An indescribable toll lurking just beyond the illusion. But if no one knew, what would it matter?

Jailer, betrayer, and beloved...

"Bingo," she said.

"Mercedes, it's Conceptual. It's like Istvan. You gave it a goal like that and then let it loose, and hoped it would stop at Shokat Anoushak?"

"It seemed like a good idea at the time."

He ran a hand across his eyes. "It always does."

She chuckled darkly. "They say you're not a real wizard until you regret it."

"It didn't want to kill her," murmured Istvan.

She glanced back at him. "I know."

Edmund watched his feet. How many circles had they descended now? Two? Three? At this point he wouldn't be surprised if there were seven... or nine.

"Mercedes," he began, "you didn't seem surprised by anything I said about Barrio Libertad. I can see now why you took credit for the blast, but as far as I can tell you've left everything else up to the fortress since it appeared and, conveniently, you've never been mentioned by anyone there – even though the Susurration has to know who summoned it."

A blue-robed shrug. "Your point, Mr Templeton?"

"Diego."

"What of him?"

"He must have come from somewhere."

"I'm sure he must have."

He spent a moment to step in front of her. "Mercedes, I've been in this business for a hell of a long time and I'd really like to know if we're being somehow double- or triple-crossed here. How long have you known about Diego?"

She looked down at her cup, which was mostly empty. She sighed. "After my election, Mr Templeton, I received a single text message from Barrio Libertad, with an aerial photo of the Providence crater attached. It said – and I quote – 'Keep Out.'"

"That's all?"

"This was before we restored power," she said. "Before I had a working phone. It turned on, flashed the message, and then went dead again. I figured we had an agreement and blacklisted the fortress the next morning."

"What about the smilers?"

She waved a hand. "What would I have done about

the smilers? Made an announcement? Started a witch-hunt? Caused a panic?"

He exchanged glances with Istvan. "So you let people disappear."

"Smilers don't become tyrants," she said. "Whatever danger it poses unchecked, the Susurration is still a creature of peace and order, Mr Templeton. Don't forget that."

She stepped past him and started back down the stairs. "I almost worry about what might happen to Big East without it."

Edmund rubbed at his forehead. Grace had said something about that. That things were too stable. That people were adapting too easily. That it shouldn't be like that after something like the Wizard War, and that he should have noticed that something was wrong.

He'd hoped things were just getting better.

"I didn't recognize that ritual circle in your office," he said.

Mercedes kept descending, step by step. "Two powers can't occupy the same metaphysical space," she replied. "When I realized that Doctor Czernin can fight it – deal with it on its own level, resist its temptations by the simple virtue of being something it is not – I thought I might replicate the effect. Send others into the Conceptual realm to engage with it and then, once it was weakened, re-bind it properly." She finished off the last of her drink. "You've done that yourself, as I recall. I was hoping to do the same on a larger scale."

Edmund almost fell down the stairs. It had taken a lot of archival searching to come up with the means to do that. He was no binder or summoner or portal-walker. It was a wonder it had worked at all, and even then he hadn't done it alone. Most people back then had liked the idea of getting Istvan out of the besieged Twelfth Hour – and into battles, to turn the tide where living defenders could barely hold their own – and the ritual itself had required five wizards to complete. Five, to send one.

Mercedes, alone, had tried to do the same? Bigger?

He shook his head, steadying himself. "You know, you could have asked for help."

She held up her bandaged hand with its missing ring finger. "I did."

Edmund realized Istvan was no longer behind him. The specter had paused where he was, one hand clenched tightly on the rail, not looking at either of them. Edmund started back up towards him. "Istvan?"

Istvan shook his head, blinking. "Nothing. It's nothing."

"All right."

Edmund stepped away. Istvan followed him. Good enough. Maybe it was just as well Mercedes' solution hadn't gone through – if the Susurration could damage its complete conceptual opposite so badly, Edmund didn't dare guess what it might do to an ordinary person translated into its realm. To Mercedes. To him.

They reached the bottom after four revolutions, passing into a sparse, small sitting room paneled in weather-worn pine. A tiny kitchen occupied one side, barely enough room for burners. Other doors led off into yet smaller areas. A drum of water occupied one corner. A chess board and a mostly complete set of pieces sat atop the lone bookshelf, which held a plethora of what looked to be mysteries, manuals of forensics and astronomy, cases for movies or maybe games, and the complete works of HP Lovecraft, none of it organized according to any clear system.

Edmund resolved to stay away from it. Her problem, not his.

She paused beside a round glass table, its edges cracked. "Now you know," she said. "I was hoping it wouldn't come to this. That it wouldn't come so quickly." She set her cup down. "Are you so certain you don't want the position back, Mr Templeton? It might be for the best."

"That wasn't my plan," he said, focusing on the kitchen behind her.

"Then what is? What would you have me do? The Bernault devices were the last thing I could offer that might have made a difference before the conjunction. If the Susurration is so set on its course that it will raise monsters, so powerful that the fortress can no longer prevent it from doing so, and so impossible to dissuade by the threat of that weapon, how am I supposed to keep everyone it's captured over the last seven years from paying for my mistakes?" She gestured back to the stairway, to her office. "I never did figure out how to translate any more than a single person, and even if it were you, Mr Templeton, I doubt you could fight the Susurration to a standstill in its own territory."

Edmund tried to meet her eyes, and couldn't. He swallowed. This was practically her house, as far as he could tell. She was wearing a bathrobe. Her hair was wet. He had broken into her house to tell her he didn't like the way she was handling her office. He, Magister Jackson's damn fool Templeton, interfering in what he shouldn't.

What would you have me do? Tell us, immortal, what we must do.

Run.

What was he doing? What was he doing here?

A chill touched his arm.

"We don't... have a plan, precisely," Istvan admitted. He drew his hand away, wavered, and then stayed where he was. "The grand sum of our intentions was speaking to you. We were hoping you might have some insight on how to, ah, convince it to abandon its plans, perhaps, or some weakness we could exploit, or... or, ah..." He looked away. "Magister, if you brought the creature here, you must know it better than anyone. All I know is that we can't stand by and watch Barrio Libertad massacre all those people, and the Susurration, too. It isn't right and I expect you know that."

"Is that tea?" Edmund asked.

Mercedes looked down at her cup. "Of a sort."

"I can put on more, if you'd like."

She raised an eyebrow at him. "Please do. Only one cabinet for the tableware, pot's on the stove, the tin's right beside. Thank you, Mr Templeton."

He started for the kitchen. Something warm to drink always helped. It was something to hold. Something to concentrate on. You couldn't plan a good counterplan to mass murder without tea, or tea of a sort. Grace hadn't agreed with that, but she'd been more of a coffee person anyway. She probably still was.

She would thank him when this was done. She didn't want to set off that weapon, either.

He wasn't leading anything. He was assisting. Enabling.

The Magister didn't serve tea.

"I don't know," said Edmund. "I thought everything was interdicted, but there are plenty of monsters scattered outside the effect. It might have sent a team of smilers to raise one of those. Within Providence... well, I'm pretty sure I still have that exception, though I don't know what Barrio Libertad would think of us showing up to hit the ritual sites ourselves. They're probably prepping for a bombardment or something. Grace won't be sitting idle."

He sat on a bench across from Magister Hahn, cradling his steaming cup in his hands, the glass table drawn up before him. His goggles were off. He looked perfectly composed, smooth-faced save for the expected creases of thought and concern, but was still nervous, still prone to sudden flickers of a more powerful fear. The tea had helped. Distractions always did.

Istvan sat beside him, cleaning his glasses for the third time.

"We wouldn't make a parade of it," mused the Magister. She adjusted one of the pens in her hair. She had dressed while Edmund busied himself in the kitchen, darting into one of the many doors and reappearing less than a minute later in her usual men's garb, the Twelfth Hour emblem affixed once more to her throat. "I think, if we were careful, most of the trouble would be the Susurration itself. You realize, Mr Templeton, that you wouldn't have nearly so effective a defense as Doctor Czernin."

"I know."

"He's native to the plane. Part of this world, part of that one. You aren't. Last time you visited the Conceptual, as I understand, you weren't there for long and you weren't under attack from anything living there, much less anything like the Susurration." She drummed her fingers on the table. "Being able to perceive and communicate with it doesn't mean you can fight it."

"I think we're all aware of that," Edmund muttered. He blew at the steam.

Istvan sighed, holding sparkling lenses up to the light

and feeling immensely useless. He wasn't a wizard. He didn't know anything of rituals or celestial conjunctions. He wouldn't be able to help the Magister with whatever she meant to do, and Edmund refused to hear of him facing the Susurration again. No. No, I can't ask you to do that. Not after what happened.

Istvan couldn't bring himself to argue with him.

Worse, he kept getting distracted.

The Man in Black was the logical one for the task. Edmund was. The man couldn't be killed. Knew what he was on about. Bravery in spades, enough to face the worst and come out of it, and keep going, damaged but dauntless. If anyone could infiltrate Providence from the Conceptual realm and shut down those ritual sites, it was him.

It was foolish – he knew it was foolish – but Istvan almost yearned to go with him. It would mean facing the Susurration again, yes. Facing Pietro. Facing… all of it, yes, but how was that any different than usual, really? Edmund strove for what he'd become every time he put on that cape.

Oh, he'd been magnificent. Istvan wished none of it had ever happened.

"I could do it," the Magister said. A strange certainty filled her presence, tinged with terror. "I'd be able to get a better idea of the Susurration's current state if I did. Besides," she added with a tight smile, "I suspect I'd hold its attention better than both of you put together."

Edmund shook his head. "If anything goes wrong, I'd prefer to have you in a position where you could do some good. You're the only one who knows the Susurration like this."

"Diego," she pointed out.

"A lot of help he's been." He gazed out at the room.

"I appreciate what you're offering, Mercedes, but before anything else, you're the Magister. We can't afford to risk you."

She picked up her cup, fear receding, self-hatred rushing into its place. Steam rose in whorls. "I thought you might say that."

Edmund didn't reply.

Istvan jammed his glasses back on, trying to get the memory of a bloodied blade and the taste of the pain that accompanied it out of his head. Pain suffered willingly. Suffered for him! "Is there nothing I can do?"

"You could go with Mr Templeton," the Magister said shortly.

"I–"

"You don't require a ritual circle to accompany him, you've fought the Susurration three times now and emerged sane, and – whatever else you might be, Doctor – you are a one hundred and fifty year-old Conceptual avatar of trench warfare."

He swallowed, suddenly acutely aware of the knife hanging at his side and sickened by the idea of drawing it on Pietro. "I'm... aware of that, Magister."

"Damaged or not, given the proper orders and enough incentive, I think you would pull through well enough. Mr Templeton may not agree with me, but Mr Templeton is convinced he can single-handedly evade a mind-controlling, memory-stealing, psyche-eroding extraplanar genius loci by *running* from it."

Edmund didn't respond to the goading. Something new churned within him, the glimmerings of a deep uncertainty and horror. It didn't seem like the start of another episode, but...

Istvan eyed him. He was staring at the chess board atop the bookshelf.

"Mercedes," the wizard said after a moment, "You play chess?"

She shook her head. "It's ornamental, is all. Now, I know the state your friend was in when we summoned him back, but–"

"We need to play chess."

The Magister looked at him oddly. "Mr Templeton, I said I don't play."

He leaned forward, setting down his cup. "No, no, we need to play chess. That's what the Susurration's done. That's what we need to do, too."

Istvan frowned. Edmund enjoyed the matches, but he wasn't a compulsive player by any means; he enjoyed metaphors, but this one made no sense. "If the creature is playing chess, Edmund, I should like a rematch with better oversight. It hasn't played a fair game at all – it's always bringing in new pieces and changing the rules to... Oh."

"Right?" said Edmund.

Istvan sat back. "Oh," he repeated.

"Istvan, we need a zeppelin."

"I should think Barrio Libertad was the zeppelin."

"Is it?"

"It's the largest single piece, the primary object of terror among a confined civilian populace, and a wholly civilized means of waging war so long as you pay no mind to what you're actually doing."

The Magister looked back and forth between them. "Zeppelin?"

Edmund held up his hands, tracing half-formed pieces in the air. "Right, if that's that, then we... We need... your knights. Istvan, your knights. Same piece, acts differently, more powerful."

"Yes, but what–"

"Park the zeppelin, give it different munitions, modify the terrain to our advantage, and instead of taking corners, we charge straight. What was it you said that time you fielded fifteen cannons?"

"Something about 'desperate times call for more cannons.' But Edmund, we don't have…"

Edmund leapt to his feet. "We have a zeppelin and a *battleship*, Istvan. A dreadnought. We just have to flood the field."

"Gentlemen," said the Magister, "I'd say this is no time for games, but I'd dearly love to be mistaken."

Edmund turned to her, eyes wild for all their permanent look of exhaustion. "Mercedes, if this works, I think we can pull off Grace's evacuation, Istvan will get his chance to press for surrender, and we can cripple the Susurration badly enough that you might be able to bind it properly."

She raised her eyebrows. "Go on."

"Yes," echoed Istvan. An evacuation? A dreadnought? He had never used a piece like that save for shore bombardment and he could only think of one possible equivalent. Surely Edmund didn't mean to raise one of Shokat Anoushak's monsters himself.

"Mercedes," the wizard continued, "you know how to bind the Susurration but can't weaken it or stall it enough because you can't hit it on the right scale. Diego can. The weapon itself might be lethal but some part of it collapses the physical and the Conceptual together, and that would put *everyone* on the Susurration's level, wouldn't it? All the smilers. Who, like you said, can't fight it, necessarily, but might be able to resist it long enough to get themselves out of Providence."

"How long is long enough?"

"Let me worry about that."

She set her cup down. "Mr Templeton, are you saying–"

"I am."

Istvan stared at him. An evacuation. All of those people. All that time. He couldn't, he'd said. That would burn through everything he had. He couldn't risk it.

He couldn't.

"You weren't so eager to volunteer your time earlier," said the Magister.

Edmund shrugged. It was a loose shrug, broad and exaggerated, the type of shrug Istvan had seen from airmen in the days before parachutes. "It won't kill me."

He didn't know that. How could he know that? He'd never done this before! Thirty-five for seventy years, and he'd never–

"Edmund, you can't."

The wizard brushed at his shoulder, and Istvan realized that he'd grabbed at it, that he was half-standing, that he was trying to shake him but of course it wasn't working. He sat down again. He couldn't bring himself to let go. "Edmund, think, please. You can't know what–"

"It won't kill me," Edmund repeated, "and I'm not done." He turned to the Magister, almost conspiratorial, caught up again in that strange surge of desperate vitality. "Mercedes, you have to talk to Diego. See if the collapse can be separated from the weapon, or stalled, or reversed, or whatever else would give us an intact Providence merged with the Conceptual. No killing. Just the collapse. I don't know anything about how that works and I don't want to go any further with this until I know that's possible."

The Magister glanced from him to the chessboard. One hand dropped to her jacket pocket, where she kept her telephone. "What guarantee do you have that Barrio

Libertad will agree to this?"

"I don't. But it's been seven years since you and Diego last exchanged words, so I think it's about time for a good conversation between you two about the Susurration." Edmund picked up his cup again, glanced at its contents, and then tossed the remainder down his throat. "I mean, hell, it's worth a shot."

It was tea, not gin, but the similarity in the act was unmistakable.

He'd done this before. During the last days of the Wizard War, he'd been little more than a driven husk. Nothing to do but what had to be done. Nowhere to go but forward. No one and nothing to dissuade him, like a tank rolling into battle over wounded men: allies, enemies, anyone who couldn't get out of the way, smashed into the mud with all the others.

Istvan knew that had happened. He remembered it. He knew their names.

His grip tightened on the man's arm. Through it. Into it. Blood pounded past his fingers like the stroke of an engine, burning hot. "Edmund," he said, "there are hundreds of thousands of people in Providence."

"That's right."

"Diego didn't come to the conference," said the Magister.

Edmund smiled. "I know how to find him."

CHAPTER TWENTY-EIGHT

They teleported into Barrio Libertad from the Magister's office. Edmund could do that. He wasn't supposed to be able to do that, but a combination of enemy negligence and past power could lead to a great deal of possibilities that weren't supposed to be.

It won't kill me.

That was all. That was all he would say. Over and over, like a mantra.

And that smile… oh, it was the one he wore when he fought, when he distanced himself from himself, and Istvan didn't like that at all. He changed when he smiled. They stood atop the wall, that tremendous barrier that separated Barrio Libertad from the Susurration, and from Providence. Fields of dust. Fields of glass. An orange sun setting over the jagged spines of dead beasts. Hundreds of thousands of innocents trapped, unaware, pawns in the same great game played between well-meaning powers since the dawn of time.Hearts and minds. Bodies, if that didn't work.Istvan clasped his hands tightly behind his back, trying to focus through the choking fog of ambient rage that seeped from every surface. There were so many of them. How could Edmund think to evacuate so many? The Magister crossed her arms over the strap of her messenger bag, staring out at the crater walls, the canvas shelters, the great skeletons heaped like mountains, the only remnants to survive the blast. If there were any pride mixed with the rest – the grief, the dread – Istvan couldn't detect it.

"Well," she said.

"That's about right," said Edmund. He turned, eyeing the turrets and walkways, cape swept in the wind. "Now, let's see if this works." He knocked on a nearby railing. "Diego?"

Something clanged. It wasn't the railing.

"Diego, I'm sorry about the short notice, but Magister Hahn would like to speak with you and–"

The clanging struck like a train, a rush and clatter. The air turned to crystal.

Magister Hahn disappeared.

The clanging faded.

A path of glowing blue lit up beneath their feet.

"Right," muttered Edmund. He started off down the line.

Istvan trailed him, wishing the fortress' ambiance didn't make it so difficult to concentrate. It was like forging through clouds of acid, and he wondered how in the world no one else noticed it. "That was the mercenary teleport."

"Yes, it was."

"What do you suppose will happen to her?"

"No idea. Hope for the best."

"How did you know that would happen?"

Edmund walked faster. "I made a mistake once."

The light led to a cable car. It was difficult to pick out the fortress populace with much precision, but they seemed to be on a wartime footing: crowds milling far below, fire teams setting up defensive positions all across the walls and walkways. What for? Was something looking to get in?

Istvan peered out the nearest window as the car began to move. Given the way the fortress was built, anyone or anything who appeared in the central plaza would be an immediate target for the upper terraces, provided anyone could shoot properly, and it took hardly any imagination at all to picture craters punched into the mosaics, steel roofs and adobe walls toppled into rubble, defenders manning makeshift emplacements that fired with a flash, a shock; short-lived suns that burst with scorching fury. Such an enclosed space would be ideal for gas: the wind couldn't blow it away, and thus trapped it would spread, and settle, seep down into all the warrens dug out below…

Whatever else you might be, Doctor…

He felt sick again. He stared down at his hands instead. Then he unbuttoned his cuffs and rolled up his left sleeve. The burns on the underside of his arm were there, rough and taut and twisting – as he knew they did – up and across shoulder, chest, neck, face. A reminder of the one war he'd fought in life. How it really was. What it really did.

Franceska hadn't recognized him. Pietro was dead.

Edmund rested his elbows on the window beside him. "Istvan?"

He rolled his sleeve back down, wanting to touch him again, to feel that blood burning beneath his skin, to remind him how precious it was and demand to know how he thought he could save all of those people by himself – Edmund, you mad, brave, selfish *fool*. He didn't. "What dreadnought did you mean, back at the lighthouse?"

"It doesn't matter until we know the fortress can play its part."

Istvan tugged his cuff straight, brushing away fraying hems. The buttons had gone dull. He shined them. "Glory is all fine and well until you find yourself hung rotting on a wire, Edmund, do you understand?"

Edmund stared at the strings of lights as they flowed past. He was close, but so distant – again like he had divorced himself from himself, and someone else was speaking. "It won't be like that," he said. "I'm far too much of a coward for that."

"How can you propose a plan like this and then claim to be a coward?"

"Leave it, will you?"

"If anything, this is precisely the opposite. This is… This is recklessness, Edmund, and you–"

"Leave it."

The cable car came to a stop and he stepped out of it, cape fluttering.

Istvan called after him. "We don't even know where that line goes!"

He didn't stop.

The line of light led along deserted streets, narrow, vertiginous, hemmed in by mismatched sheets of corrugated steel. They passed a mural of white birds painted around someone's door. Wind chimes twirled above their heads, hung from strings of globular lamps. It was as though the fortress purposefully led them away from the crowds, away from preparing citizen-defenders who might otherwise halt their work, whisper, stare.

Edmund tried not to look for ducks. Tried not to wonder where Mercedes may have been taken. Tried to follow the line to the letter, because it was something to follow, and tried not to think about what he would have to do to the man who followed him.

If this worked.

That was leadership, wasn't it? Convincing people to trust you and then convincing yourself, when the day was done, that it wasn't betrayal. That you did your best. That the candles were enough.

He walked. Istvan followed. They crossed a bridge and came to a domed structure, its doors propped open. The light darted up narrow stairs, glowing beneath the metal, and halted, pulsing. A stuttering command crackled somewhere inside, drowning out the quieter murmur of other voices. Five people? Six?

Istvan hesitated. "Edmund..."

The reply was automatic. "Don't worry about it."

He started up the steps –

– and Grace strode through the doorway. Her cowl was pulled down, her goggles dangling about her neck, her articulated harness whirring with each swing of her arms. She descended three steps and then halted, propping a fist on her hip without much conviction. "Eddie."

"Grace," said the Hour Thief, noting distantly that Istvan had drawn up beside him, "I don't know what you've been told, but we might have an alternative to your superweapon."

She blinked. "*Now* you come up with this?"

He nodded. There was a smile playing around his lips that seemed to have put itself there. Part of the act. Put people at ease. The Hour Thief was a charmer; everyone knew that.

Grace descended the rest of the stairs in a near slide. "I was just talking to the People's Council about artillery strikes and mass kidnappings and militia defense – we don't know if it has your teleport, either, we don't know if it can raise more monsters, we don't know *anything* anymore – and if you've got something better, I'm all ears." She swung closer to him, voice dropped to a low mutter. "Diego's reporting a pleasant teatime chat with your boss, Eddie; that was quick. Who's running this operation?"

"She is."

"Riiight."

"Grace, if I am, we're going to collapse two planes of reality together, evacuate everyone from Providence, and hurt the Susurration so badly Magister Hahn will be able to chain it down like she should have done years ago."

She stepped back, incredulous. "On whose time?"

"Mine."

"But you said–"

"I know what I said." He realized he had retrieved his watch, and spun it around by its chain in the most nonchalant fashion he could. "It won't kill me."

He didn't feel quite as concerned as he thought he should, and he chalked that up to the nature of the beast. He wasn't going to execute this plan, the Hour Thief was. That was how the Conceptual realm worked. It took what you were and made it more so, and for better or worse, that's exactly what the Hour Thief was.

That's what he was for.

She stared at him. Then at Istvan, who crossed his arms and looked away. She mouthed something under her breath. "Eddie, when I asked about using your time, I didn't mean all at once. We had the Bernault devices. I figured we could space it out, we could give you time to–"

He shook his head. "No. Never from allies."

She smacked her forehead. "I mean, wait for you to pull it off in installments, or something. Eddie, there's half a million people out there! You're planning to get them all in one go? Alone?"

"Istvan's coming, too," he said.

The specter started. "I'm what?"

"Oh, that's real helpful, I'm sure the dead guy's got lots of time to spare." Grace spun on her heel, throwing up her hands. "Eddie, this is…"

"This is what, Grace?"

"It's just… this is *you* we're talking about. You don't *do* things like this."

He maintained a brittle smile. "Things like what, Grace?"

She spun back around and jabbed his sternum. "Listen, if you're still trying to get me back, pulling some kind of stupid sacrificial stunt isn't the way to do it."

"That's precisely what I told him," Istvan muttered.

"See? Even Doctor Awful agrees and we never agree on anything. And what do you mean he's coming? Remember what happened at the conference?"

Edmund tried to push her hand away. "You don't know the whole story."

"He's compromised! You can't risk–"

Istvan caught her wrist. "Risk what?"

They both looked at Edmund.

He backed up a step. "I didn't say this would be easy."

"You haven't said hardly anything," said Istvan.

"You've said," Edmund corrected him.

"He's said what?" demanded Grace.

He was done. He was done with this now. He'd been done with this for eighty years.

"A double negative!" he shouted, "That was a double negative! 'You haven't said hardly anything' should be 'you've said hardly anything' or it isn't right, and I keep telling people things like this and they never listen and they should know better anyway! I'm doing the best I can!"

He jammed his watch back into his pocket. Faces peered from the doorway at the top of the stairs. He glared at them and they vanished.

"Really?" said Grace.

"Do you want a way out of this or not?"

She sighed.

Istvan crossed his arms again, rusted wire tangling around a nearby railing. "Edmund, I should like to know my part in this."

Edmund lifted his goggles so he could run a hand across his face. "No, you don't."

"I believe that I do."

"No. Trust me, you don't. Not until we're sure that the fortress can come through."

"Oh, we're sure," said Mercedes.

Well. That was that.

"Great," he said woodenly.

Mercedes took the steps down from the domed structure two at a time. "Remarkable place. I hadn't realized that its layout followed such familiar principles, though turned about and run through several additional dimensions than is usual. This architect isn't a god, Mr Templeton, but there comes a point when the difference is in some ways academic."

He frowned, well aware that said architect was listening. "What do you mean by that?"

"She means you need to read more science fiction," said Grace, stepping around him. She propped her armored fists on her hips. "So, Magister Hahn. I'm told you had a change of heart and you're running things here. What's the plan?"

"That depends."

"Depends on what?"

Mercedes grinned a tight grin. "According to Mr Diego Escarra Espinoza, this superweapon is nothing more than an abrupt end to the planar merger. Collapse two paradigms together, immediately cease any attempt to make them agree with each other, and watch them turn local truth into Swiss cheese."

Grace goggled. "You understood him?"

"I summoned the Susurration. Of course I understood him."

"But–"

Mercedes held up a finger. "He says that abrupt end is optional. He can mitigate it – monitor every corner of the merged plane and adjust as needed to maintain stability, if you can imagine – but he can't weaken the Susurration for us. That weapon is all or nothing."

"So…"

Mercedes nodded at Edmund. "That's your flooded chessboard, Mr Templeton. Let's see that dreadnought."

Edmund pointed at Istvan.

Hazed. It was all hazed. So hard to concentrate.

"I can't," Istvan said.

The Magister turned a pen between her fingers. "Mr Templeton, we discussed this."

"No, we didn't."

"Last night. Ash and lightning. I'm sure you both remember. While I still believe he could cover your evacuation, and I'm touched by your confidence in his abilities, the problem remains one of scale. Doctor Czernin would be impossibly outmatched."

No inflection in Edmund's voice. "I'm unchaining him."

Devil's Doctor. War to End All Wars.

Istvan backed away. To the railing. Partway through the railing, a fall beyond. "What?" – *a house of bones bound by barbed wire, dancing to the pull of bloody strings –*

"This is your plan?" demanded Grace. – *chained for good cause –*

"Out of the question," said the Magister. – *no future but the lonely thunder of guns –*

"Mercedes," said Edmund, "it's what I have. It's all we have."

Do you think I'm afraid of you?

"Mr Templeton, do you realize what unchaining him while the physical and Conceptual are collapsed together will do?"

That honor falls to the one you love most.

"I do."

Istvan fled.

Along the rail. Back across the bridge. Into the alleys.

Edmund raced alone, Grace and Mercedes left where they stood. There were walls now where there hadn't been walls before, sudden turns and dead ends he didn't remember. Something beneath the streets rumbled.

"Istvan," he called, "Istvan, stop!"

The specter arrowed upward. An awning swung out to intercept him, striking one wing with a shockingly audible crack.

Solid. Just like the armor, before. What the hell was everything made out of?

Istvan spun sideways and slammed into a window. The mural of white birds scattered into clear sky. More awnings closed in overhead, roofing the alley in cheerful filtered reds and yellows.

Edmund caught up to him as he tumbled to street

level in a confused heap. "Istvan?"

The ghost rolled onto his back, staring upwards through a canopy of his own broken feathers. "Those were thinking beasts," he said.

"What?"

"During the Wizard War. Shokat Anoushak's creatures. Slave soldiers, all of them."

Edmund let out a breath. Great. "If that's the case, you didn't know it then."

"You know it wouldn't have mattered. I would have enjoyed it anyhow. I always do. You, of all men, ought to know that." He shuddered. He was flickering again. "You, of all men."

"That was a long time ago."

"Edmund, how can you ask this of me?"

There was a bench nearby. There hadn't been before, but now there was. Edmund sat on it. A flock of painted white birds settled on a painted wire above him.

Fire to fight fire. Suffering to put an end to the end of suffering. I'm sorry, but all you can do is what you'll hate and regret. That's all you're good for.

He didn't have enough time for the evacuation, he knew. There was only one way to get more.

I'm sorry.

Edmund shut his eyes. "I need someone to cover my back and keep the Susurration occupied, and when it comes down to it, two powers can't occupy the same metaphysical space. It's like Mercedes said, and I hate to say it, but you are what you are. All it takes is one shot to trump peace, and you represent enough firepower to level Europe."

Istvan mumbled something.

"Your war left survivors," Edmund told him. "It won't kill the Susurration and if I miss anyone – and I'm sure

I will – they still stand a chance of coming out of it. We'll be crippling. Badly, but only crippling, and then Mercedes can do what she needs to do."

"I asked if you had any idea what you're proposing."

"It isn't a proposal."

Λ metallic rush: the specter staggered to his feet, barbed wire scraping phantom wounds into supposed brick and steel. "Edmund, you can't."

Edmund felt that familiar hollowness settle in his stomach. They had less than two days. They didn't have time for this.

He was the Hour Thief, and even he didn't have time for this.

"There's no other way," he said tightly, "This is it. This is all we can do before they pull out the band and the banners and end it just like you said they would."

Istvan rounded on him. "Why are you trying to convince me? What have you to prove? I've no bloody choice in this and you know it! I never do! No one listens to Doctor Czernin, oh no, he's no idea what he's talking about, it's perfectly fine and well to use *the* Great bloody War to assault what is literally a living embodiment of peace and happiness–"

"Istvan."

"–that is perfectly moral and right, isn't it, and damn whatever he gets up to afterward, unchained, free to do as he likes, just as he's done for the last century of murder–"

"Istvan–"

"Edmund, have you ever seen half a horse dangling four months dead and twenty feet up in half a tree, and thought to yourself, 'well, at least he's holding up well'?"

"Istvan!"

"Oh, no, you're far too good for that, you're far too

busy martyring yourself for the cause, you… you bloody, blinkered *vampire*."

Edmund shot to his feet.

"Quiet."

Istvan choked.

Mercedes strode up the street, the much taller Grace keeping pace on her left. A lone white bird flitted across the wall beside them, landing beside the ones perched on the wire above, preening its painted feathers, and then halting as though it had never moved.

"Doctor Czernin," Mercedes said, waving further down the alley, "a moment?"

Istvan gaped. Coughed. Slashed his hands through the air before him, fingers clawed in frustration.

"I'd rather not make that an order, Doctor."

The specter stomped away.

"I'm not a vampire," Edmund muttered. He glanced back at Istvan. "Grace, Mercedes, I'm sorry, but I knew he wouldn't take it well. Please, let me explain."

"We know," said Grace.

Edmund sighed. "A little bird told you?"

"Actually, a huge robot fortress, but yeah."

Mercedes waited until both muddied bootprints and loops of bloody wire had vanished, the booming of artillery faded to little more than a rush of wind. Then she looked to Edmund, one hand resting on the strap of her shoulder bag. "Mr Templeton, I would call your friend a dangerous man, but that would be doing the magnitude of what he is a disservice. It took eighty years for anyone to identify, track and capture him; nothing I would care to retrieve from the vault can destroy him; and the same force that drew Shokat Anoushak and her forces to their deaths has only managed to hurt his feelings. If this is our only option, it's our only option, but I need to be very, very certain that cutting him loose isn't a terrible, terrible idea."

Edmund remembered fleeing down that riverbed, the last survivor for the first time in his long career. The knife that barely missed. Assisting in the capture of that same horror, years later, and watching it… him… *Istvan* freeze at the sight. *You,* he'd said. *I've thought about you often. I remember you. The impossible soldier. I never miss, but I missed you.*

Then they'd bound the dread Devil's Doctor tight and left him shackled alone in the Demon's Chamber, only an invitation to remember him by: *if ever you'd care to drop by for coffee, Mr Templeton… we could have a lot to talk about.*

Almost thirty years ago. Edmund had never known him when he wasn't chained.

"I trust him," he said.

She closed her eyes. "Mr Templeton, I hope you're bearing in mind that I'd hate to be the Magister who lost the fine china."

He fingered his pocket watch, not looking at Grace. "Don't worry about it."

Nothing had changed. Nothing would change. Istvan would still be Istvan and a little time lost wouldn't matter in the long run. He had to believe that. The alternative was… was nothing he should be thinking about now. Not if he meant to go through with this.

"Don't worry about it," he repeated.

"You know," said Grace, "this isn't the kind of mercy plan that nets you a Nobel Prize, Eddie."

"I never expected one."

Mercedes checked her telephone. "Will I have to encourage Doctor Czernin to do as he's told?"

Edmund looked to the ghost, pacing far down the

alley. No choice. He knew he had no choice. Not while he was chained. "He's a military man, Mercedes. I think you can answer that one yourself."

"That's that, then." She put her telephone away. "If this goes as planned – and if I can be provided with the necessary materials, Ms Wu – you will have the honor of witnessing the largest contractual circle I've ever drawn in operation. If not, I suppose we get to test your contingency plans."

"Yeah," said Grace. "We've got those." She didn't sound happy about it.

"I'd like to have everything up and ready by tomorrow. Mr Templeton, I'll need you to help me move a few things from the Twelfth Hour, and after that... do what you have to do."

Edmund swallowed. Right.

That.

Istvan wouldn't want to talk to him. Istvan would probably never want to talk to him again.

He couldn't blame him. The only one to blame was himself. The only one to ever blame for what he'd done was himself.

A few moments. Some time. A little while. That was what his ledger said, how many phrases of time he had stored away. To move half a million people, he would need more than that. He would need enough time. Enough for everyone. More than enough.

All he had to do was collect.

CHAPTER TWENTY-NINE

Istvan paced around a corrugated rooftop, silent despite the hobnails in his boots. He'd never been in the fortress for so long. Hours upon hours. Rage boiling off every surface. He couldn't pick out anything, anyone, through the miasma anymore. Couldn't concentrate long enough to try.

Couldn't leave, not with the Susurration still out there, lurking behind the great dark shadows of the walls, waiting for its next chance at kindness.

Trapped.

Bloody Edmund. He'd known.

Even the Magister hadn't once come by to give him orders beyond "tomorrow." What would be the point? There was nowhere to run. No other option.

A cannon, he was, waiting to be loosed.

Granting leeway, as in the Wizard War, was one thing. That had allowed him only a greater range of motion and specific permission to combat a specific foe. Facing the Susurration again was another matter, one he wished he were more opposed to, one that promised another glimpse of the Man in Black as well as other, worse, unspeakable things, but at least he'd done it once already. As he was.

Unchaining the Great War outright was something wholly different.

And Pietro!

Oh, Pietro. How could anyone expect him to... to...

But he couldn't tell anyone about that. No one could know anything about that.

He shook away traitor thoughts – the Susurration would listen, it already knew everything anyhow; that was where Pietro was, even if he wasn't – and took wing, swooping to a higher terrace and alighting atop a gantry crane. There he sat, one leg swinging free, fuming because that was better than any weaker alternative and his embroidery was still at Edmund's house. Beyond the walls. Unreachable.

He retrieved his trench knife instead, turning it over and over in his hands.

It wasn't his. Not really. He'd found it, back in those early days, a point of deceptive safety to hold onto when he blundered into barrages fired by his own side and startled at the sight of his own wings, and a weapon to drop in terror when he realized he didn't remember how he'd gotten where he was and that no one else could have killed all those Serbian soldiers. It was fine steel, but shouldn't have been able to rip through tank treads or tear the wings off fighter jets. It didn't look at all as though it had seen a hundred years of use.

He balanced it on a finger, and that, too, was far easier than it perhaps should have been. Hadn't he proven, over and over, that he was what he was?

And now Edmund planned to use that same blade to unchain him.

Don't worry. The cause was just. It would be all right.

It would be over by Christmas.

He flipped the blade over and stabbed savagely at the gantry crane. It struck with a concussive crash, sinking to the hilt. Sparks spun away and fell to the roofs and walkways below.

Istvan froze. He tugged the knife back out. No damage.

He looked to where he'd struck. The wound was already gone. Blue-white hexagons flickered across the surface and faded.

<Was that to make me feel better?> he demanded.

"Hey!" called a familiar voice from below.

He peered over the edge of the crane. Grace Wu. Grace bloody Wu.

She waved her arms. "Get down here, will you?"

He debated the merits of refusing, staying where he was, and perhaps suffering a visit from Magister Hahn. He sighed. He sheathed his knife. Then he swung both legs off and tumbled into the air again, circling once and landing beside her, wings only half-folded. "What do you want?"

"I want you to go find Eddie."

Find him? He wasn't here? He hadn't said anything, just like he'd done before, after all that had happened, and now Grace Wu, of all people, wanted Istvan to go find him?

He turned away. "No."

She frowned. "What do you mean, *no*?"

"Precisely what I said," Istvan snapped. "Whatever he's on about, I'm sure he doesn't want me following him. He never does." He eyed a higher terrace. "If you're so worried, you go find him. You have legs."

"What? No, listen, I–"

He took off, two wingbeats to reach the terrace and the third to bring him to the top of what seemed to be some sort of radio tower, its joined steel spars a decent replacement for the gantry crane. He took hold of the nearest bar and swung around it to a landing. Away from Grace Wu. No further from the fortress's seething rage.

Find Edmund, indeed. The man had the freedom to go where he pleased and the plan to justify it. He was probably out patrolling. That was what he did, after all. Tear away time from others and then use it for his own ends, year after year after year, justifying it with a hat and cape, so terrified of telling anyone how he'd done it that he'd come to the edge of panic just *thinking* of telling the Magister of that bloody ritual, that goat-sacrificing young man's mistake he claimed to regret.

He couldn't have enough time. Not for tomorrow.

If that was what he was doing, why…

Istvan shook his head. No. No, he wouldn't want Istvan along. Istvan couldn't keep up, after all. Couldn't help him at all. Wasn't needed.

Not for this.

The "Hour Thief" had made his decision. Now he had to live with it.

Don't follow me.

No note. Not this time. Just as he had promised.

Oh, how had someone so supposedly intelligent brought himself to sacrifice a goat?

A crash. The tower rattled as though struck by a sledgehammer. "Doc, you get down here and listen to me, right now!"

Istvan sighed. The woman was far too quick for her own good. "No."

"*Your best friend* took off the second the Magister didn't need him, he hasn't come back for hours, and in case you hadn't noticed, we need him for any of this to work," she yelled. Another blow, harder. "This is the second time he's freaked out and run off like this!"

The second time?

Istvan dropped away from the tower before she could hit it again. "What do you mean? What are you talking about? What did you say to him?"

She closed on him as he landed, electric arcs crackling between her clenched fists and the tower's metal supports. "What kind of cure have you been working, anyway? You claim to care about him, sure, but then you leave him like this?"

Istvan bristled. "Miss Wu, I–"

"He's broken! He's broken and he's hurting and you're a doctor, all right? A doctor!" She punched the nearest support, armored gauntlet striking with a deafening clang that reverberated as she turned, hair crackling like static. "Why don't you fix him?"

She was worried. She was genuinely worried. She had known Edmund before his relapse, when it was hardly evident at all that he suffered what he did, and the number of times she had spoken to him since could be counted on one hand.

She didn't know what it was. She didn't know how deep it ran.

Istvan stepped away from the sizzling arcs jumping across the supports. "I can't."

"Then you should refer him to someone who can. A psychiatrist. Something."

"He would never agree to that." She tried to speak; he cut her off. "Never. I know shellshock, and I know Edmund, and I will have you know that he has made dramatic improvement from where he was seven years ago. That's all you can expect, is improvement. If you're looking for a cure, there isn't one."

"Bullshit."

"Miss Wu, last year was his hundredth birthday. As a veteran and a wizard both he's seen more awful things than I would wish on anyone. He still won't speak to me of what happened at the Great Lakes, much less what he did to attain his magic in the first place. I've done what I can."

She looked at him for a long moment.

"If you can locate a functioning clinic with a lead on some permanent form of rehabilitation," he said, "point me to it."

She crossed her arms, partially, like she couldn't decide what to do with them, and then propped them on her hips instead. "So you'll go find him?"

Edmund hadn't had enough time. He'd left to acquire more time. Alone.

Once that gruesome task was done…

Istvan glanced up at the darkened sky, that invisible barrier that separated the choking ambiance of Barrio Libertad from the stars and the terrors. Part of him clamored to leave the man, let him suffer, let him stew in fears of loosing flame and genocide, but…

Oh, if Istvan couldn't do anything, it was turn away from suffering. Even now. Even if it were for all the wrong reasons.

"If I leave by elevator," he asked, "that path we traveled – the one with the pylons – is it safe?"

This time she crossed her arms. Tightly. "As long as you stay on it."

"Stay on it," he repeated. He'd done it once. He knew, now, the consequences for attempting any other route. He readied to leave… and then paused. There had been a strange note in Grace's voice, a strange sourness in her veneer of confidence. He glanced over a wing. "Miss Wu, you're able to leave. Why come to me?"

She didn't look up at the sky. "Just go find Eddie, will you?"

Find him. He already had a good idea where to look.

Istvan stepped up onto the terrace railing and leapt off.

Edmund claimed that Charlie's was an old place. A piece of the past, he said. Exotic to most, home to him, the only place outside his own four walls and the Twelfth Hour where he could feel like he belonged. No one had stools like that anymore. No one had a mechanical cash register anymore. Drove automobiles like that anymore. Wore hats like that. Those electric lamps hanging from the pressed tin ceiling burned dim and yellow, smoke-fogged, a light worn and comfortable.

Old past. 1939. Edmund's place.

It looked like the future to Istvan.

A group of young revelers caroused and cheered around three tables pushed together as he walked through the doors. Something about a birthday, or perhaps a departure. One of them saw him, and all celebration ceased. Some darted glances at the far corner.

"Pardon me," he said.

He walked past, trailing wire, to Edmund's booth. It was always the same booth. Always same side of the booth. The left: the one that offered a clear view of the door.

Edmund wasn't looking at the door now.

Istvan came to a slow halt at the head of the table. He set a hand on it. "Edmund?"

The wizard sat collapsed, head pillowed in his arms.

A glass of gin lay before him. His presence rushed and roared like floodwaters, ancient oaken bitterness burst through to despair and self-hatred, the rationality he prized caught whirling in old fears of failure, of death, of darkness, all distinction lost and drowning. His breath came in wheezing gasps. His shoulders trembled.

"Edmund," Istvan said, "I'm going to sit down." He switched to German. <I'm going to sit down, all right?>

Edmund didn't look up. He clenched both hands into fists.

Istvan slid into the booth opposite. The glass was almost empty; he pushed it aside and then reached a hand across the table to touch a shaking forearm, as lightly as he could. Edmund flinched, muffling a cry. He was sweating. Nauseous. His breath was sour, vomit washed down with gin and chased with more gin. It all tasted like oil, he'd said, sick during those long nights; the water was full of oil.

How long had he been here? Where on Earth had he patrolled?

How much time had he stolen?

Istvan touched his arm again, wishing he could think of any reassurance beyond "it's all right." Edmund didn't take well to claims that he had no choice, or that it was necessary, or that it would go to good use, or that it wasn't his fault. It was his fault, he always insisted. He chose it. He had no right.

Istvan murmured what he could. "It's all right. It will be all right."

"They're all going to die," came the reply.

"No, they won't. No one's going to die. It's all right."

Edmund crushed his eyes into sleeves darkened by the tears he couldn't show. "No, it isn't. It's all my fault.

No one's ever going to forgive me. They'll all be dead. Istvan, they're all going to die. They're practically dead already. Istvan, Istvan, they're all dead."

Some of the revelers were staring. Istvan threw up a wing to obscure the view. Nothing to do but keep talking, keep maintaining contact, and wait. He'd seen worse, though not in the last several years.

Oh, he should have insisted on accompanying him, terrible plan or not. Pure selfishness, staying where he had. Pacing. Brooding. Edmund had done all he could do. Done what needed doing. Tomorrow, again, he would be needed. He would always be needed.

That was the problem.

It's all right. It's all right.

Finally, Edmund stopped trembling. He didn't stop hiding his face.

"I can't do this," he slurred into his hat, "Istvan, I can't do this."

"You can."

"It's too much. I've done too much and it's all in my head and I can't... Istvan, I can't give it back. It's too much." He tried to rip a napkin out of the dispenser, ripped it in half instead, and didn't seem to notice. "I... I can't not think about it, and I can't think about it, and if I mess this up, it's all for nothing." He wiped the general vicinity of his nose with the half a napkin, then prodded it gingerly into a pile of them on the edge of the table. Even drunk, he couldn't stand disorderliness. "It's all for nothing anyway, the punching. Doesn't help. Crime's an illness of society, that's what she said, and she's right. You're right, too, Istvan, I'm a... a vampire. On patrol. Don't even do it for the good fight."

Istvan patted his hand. That much, at least, seemed to

help. "Yes, you do."

"No. No, it's all my fault. If I'd... if I'd done my job, Istvan, if I'd remembered the conjunction and the... the Bernault devices, Istvan, I messed that all up and you're never going to forgive me. She's never going to forgive me."

"You did what you thought was best."

Edmund sniffed. "Never should have let myself fall in love with her. Knew this would happen. I... Istvan, I knew this would happen. Always does. They always leave, they always..." He blinked, a rapid flutter, and reached for another napkin. This one ripped, too. "Stupid. Istvan, I'm so stupid. I'll never be with anyone, not really, not ever. Should act like it. Don't deserve it. Should've... should've given up a long time ago."

Istvan swallowed back an old ache of his own. "Edmund..."

"You're lucky. You were married. You did that. You just... you did that. You found someone and you kept her. You got to know what that was like, and... and I... I'll never..." The wizard dropped his hat, elbow slewing through the pile of napkins, and buried his head back in his sleeves. "Never should've tried," he croaked between shudders, "I never, never should've tried..."

A chair scraped across the floor. Istvan glanced back through his yet-upraised wing. The revelers were leaving, pushing glasses away and abandoning gifts of makeshift currencies, notes of contracted service in exchange, and an odd brass lantern on the table. Those who couldn't walk quite straight leaned on those who could.

What time was it, after all? The building had no clocks.

Istvan slid out of the booth, allowing muddied feathers to dissipate. Edmund stayed where he was, head down, wet napkins fluttering off the table. Istvan set newly-fleshed hands on the man's shoulders as they shook. "Come on," he sighed, "Let's get you home."

Edmund mumbled something unintelligible.

"I know you can get us there – I've seen you do it very nearly in your sleep. Come on, get up." He held on to him as the wizard slouched out of the booth, trying a few times to find his top hat and then perching it precariously on his head, swaying. "That's right."

"Have to get my watch," said Edmund. He fumbled for his pocket, leaning heavily into Istvan's side.

"Wait. Wait, no, Edmund, you can't…"

The bartender peered over the counter at the thud.

Istvan crouched down, putting up a wing again. Good Lord. "Oh, Edmund," he chuckled even as he cringed at his lack of substance, "you know that doesn't work."

Edmund blinked fuzzily at the ceiling. "Huh," he said. After another moment of consideration, he added, "Huh."

Istvan followed the gold chain into the wizard's right pocket and found his watch, then handed it to him. His fingers were slack; Istvan folded them safely around it, clasping Edmund's hand in both of his. "There you are."

"Thanks."

Istvan waited until he was sure the man had a good grip on it, then let go. The device stayed put. He shook his head. "You'll have to get yourself to bed, I'm afraid."

Edmund inspected the brass casing, prying it open with some effort and holding it up from his spot on the floor. "I'm a big boy."

"I know."

"Stay… stay with me?"

"I will."

Edmund wiped at his nose. "Oh, good."

He snapped his watch.

He made it to bed. He even managed to sleep.

Then Shokat Anoushak came for him. The Kamikazes. The watcher in the deep, black and oily, the water that drowned everyone but him. Last survivor. No one left.

Alone, forever.

His fault.

Run –

When he woke, thrashing, Istvan was there. Just like he'd promised. Just like he'd been there, all those times before. Someone to stop the shaking. Someone to stanch the terror.

Someone to be there, like he'd promised. The only friend a sinner could keep.

"I'm going crazy," Edmund told him, face-down in his pillow, unable to stop the tears and angry that he couldn't and tired of it all but unable to end it, and most of all grateful for the dark, "I'm going to hurt people, Istvan. I already hurt people. I'm going to be like her."

The specter sat beside him, a faint translucence, his presence alone a chill that numbed. Too close for comfort, perhaps... but close enough for comfort. "You aren't going crazy."

"You know what they call it now, Istvan, officially. Post-Traumatic Stress *Disorder*. That means crazy."

"That only means you need help sometimes, Edmund, and that's why I'm here. I won't let you go crazy, I promise." A hand rested on his back. Achingly cold but familiar, a faint memory of living pressure. "You won't be like her."

"You promise?"

"I promise."

A few minutes more – softly-spoken reassurances repeated in that accent like Dracula's, maybe, but too trusted to be threatening, almost musical in its cadence –

and Edmund drifted back to sleep. Good old Istvan. War itself. Already dead. Not even Edmund's curse, dogging him now and forever, could harm Istvan.

He'd come for him.

He'd come for him, after everything.

CHAPTER THIRTY

The cure to gin was a glass of gin.

That was a fact. That had been a fact for seventy years.

Istvan insisted on pitching in as well – "I know you like to torment yourself, Edmund, but we do need you as capable as possible" – and Edmund gave up and let him. An end to pain and dizziness wasn't really the end to pain and dizziness, just a delay, but a delay was all he could ask. He could collapse later. He probably would.

Grace wasn't ever going to forgive him.

He didn't dare spend any time for recovery. He'd need that time later. He'd need as much time as he'd taken.

He realized he was staring at a breakfast plate and finished off whatever was on it. Food, of some sort. Istvan had insisted.

"Istvan?"

The specter looked up from prodding at Edmund's phone. He didn't look much better than Edmund felt, but his scarring never helped with that and at least there weren't any bloodstains or bullet holes. "Hm?"

"Istvan, please tell me this plan is a good idea."

Istvan looked back at the phone. "It's, ah…"

Edmund stood. Picked up his plate. Walked a few

steps and retrieved a dipper from the bucket next to the sink. "You don't have to be honest."

"Ah." Istvan folded his hands on the table. "Well, then, in that case, I think it's a splendid idea, putting all those people on the same field as the Susurration, using up all your time to help them run away, and then cutting my chains so the Great War itself can blow peace and happiness to tiny pieces for the Magister to collect." He went back to tapping at the screen. "Absolutely a good idea. The best."

Edmund put his plate away. He'd washed it, hadn't he?

He checked.

He had.

"Thank you," he said.

"Of course." Istvan fiddled with the phone a moment longer, then stood. "Now, come on. I've sent a message to the Magister, I think, but I'm not certain it went through." He handed the device to Edmund. "We ought to be at the fortress as soon as we can."

Edmund glanced at it. *Recovered*, it said, *on our way presently stop*

He never had understood the appeal of sending what amounted to fortune cookie messages when you could simply call, but Istvan, all things considered, had caught on shockingly quickly. "Right."

Be at the fortress. Be what he needed to be, do what he needed to do, and don't panic. Grace would never forgive him even more if he panicked.

His head didn't hurt but he knew it should have.

He dropped the phone in his pocket, wiping wet hands on his jacket. "We need to stop at the Twelfth Hour for some things first. I left them in Mercedes' office. Knew I'd be out most of the night."

Out patrolling. Laid out. Out of his mind.

Years, stolen.

How can you sleep at night?

Istvan nodded. He knew what Edmund meant – he had to, after so long – but he didn't mention it. Didn't dwell on it. Didn't treat him like he was broken, or weak, or not trying hard enough. In less urgent times, he would always leave Edmund to his misery when he requested it. "Come on, then."

Edmund retrieved his hat and cape.

They went.

The fortress roof was closing when they arrived. Barrio Libertad had a roof, it seemed – and it moved into place with a deep, groaning, almost naval rumble, immense wheels rolling on their rails with shattering bongs and crashes. The folded steel sails along the walls weren't folded any longer: they rose and turned and swung across one another, ignoring the wind that rattled against their broad sides, splitting the sky into bright triangles and the city below into sweeping columns of light and shadow.

The walkways trembled.

Edmund tensed. Istvan set a hand on his shoulder. <It's all right.>

The man's next breath came easier. <Right.>

Istvan sought the guiding line that had always appeared before, but there was no sign of it. The inhabitants of the fortress bustled behind spiked railings, stringing last-minute perimeters and taking down hanging laundry, vague figures in the place's choking emotional haze. Murals displayed maps and instructions. Emplacements fabricated who-knew-where nodded from balconies, blunt muzzles swiveled to point down at the central plaza. Istvan had to wonder if the adobe down there could handle the weight of fire pointed at it.

Yesterday, Grace Wu had mentioned in passing that if they failed, the epitaphs for all the casualties would be stenciled on the exterior walls. That seemed proper. Names and dates, all in their places. A paragraph or so for the unknown. Speeches. Monuments. Promises to remember.

Poor compensation, yes, but it was something.

"This is a good idea," murmured Edmund. He rifled through the satchel he carried, checking for what he had put into it at the Twelfth Hour: a silver knife, iron filings, notes and instructions from Magister Hahn, ink mixed with ash. The first time he had managed with less, but this task was different. Cutting the chains, not rewriting them.

He had said something vague and noncommittal when Istvan asked about the ash.

"It's what we have," said Istvan. A readied fire team watched from a nearby balcony, the shadow of a sail creeping towards them over bridges and gardens. He nodded at them. "They wouldn't stop us, you know."

Edmund let the satchel be. "What wouldn't?"

"The defenses. If the Susurration refuses to surrender, Edmund, if this doesn't work – or if it does work, too well. You know what the creature can do. What we can do." He touched the handle of the knife sheathed at his side. "I've thought about this, Edmund. Those people are preparing for *us*."

"It won't come to that," Edmund said. He sounded like he wished the idea had never come up.

Istvan shrugged. He tossed the fire team a salute. He wondered what their names were.

They waved back, hesitantly.

The last columns of sun shrank, slivered, and streaked

upwards across the walls. Fleeting. Fleeing. Then the roof thundered shut. Spotlights pierced the echoes, blazing to life one after the other in a blinding ring around the perimeter.

Edmund reeled, sagging onto the nearest rail. Istvan did what he could.

The last spotlight lit as the last vestiges of sound faded.

Footsteps marched along the walkway towards them. Golden boots, golden pauldrons, a crimson cape and spikes. The masked helmet was no skull-faced visage: that was unique to Triskelion warlords, as far as Istvan could tell. This one was slitted, and blank.

Edmund squinted. "Istvan, I haven't seen a blue line anywhere, have you?"

"Perhaps this time we merit an escort," Istvan replied, stepping before him to meet the mercenary himself, just in case. "Pageantry before the storm."

"I'm not made of glass," Edmund grumbled.

Istvan stayed where he was.

The mercenary halted two sabre-lengths away from them and slammed a fist on his breastplate. "Hail, Hour Thief, wizard-general of the last war."

"Thanks," gritted Edmund.

The mercenary dropped to a knee. "Hail, Doctor Czernin, butcher of dragons, to whom I owe my true life and my revenging gauntlet."

Istvan blinked. "Ah…"

The mercenary pulled off his helmet.

Her helmet.

"I," proclaimed Lucy, "am Second-Among-Twenty, Banner-Bearer, the Crashing Blade Who Casts the Slain Against the Rocks, and I grant you here the right and honor to look upon the last of my masks. I am myself, once again and truly, thanks to your intercession." She bowed, setting her helmet against the walkway. "My might is your might, should you have need of it."

Istvan opened his mouth. Closed it.

"Are you quite certain you're in fighting trim?" he asked. "You were terribly thin to be swinging a sword about."

"I will regain my strength once I have regained my honor," she boomed.

"Of course."

"Follow. I will show you to our council."

She replaced her helmet on her head, stood, and marched away.

"I'm still amazed this kind of thing doesn't bother you." Edmund said, faintly.

Istvan shrugged. He wasn't sure why it didn't, himself, save that he could recount the exploits of a number of female soldiers of his war from automatic memory and had met enough others (overt and not) that it was somehow no longer as remarkable as it ought to have been.

A Triskelion mercenary. That made their involvement in this affair rather more personal than he'd thought.

He caught up with Lucy – Lucy? – as she led them across a bridge that might have been familiar. "Why were you permitted to remain alive?" he asked. "What happened to the smiler at the conference? Wasn't he shot?"

"Our alliance with this place spared his life and sanity," she replied. "We brought him here, and here he remains, awaiting his recovery from memory's maze."

"I see."

"Our great lord moved quickly to secure assistance once the true magnitude of this threat became clear... or so I have heard. Some years are lost to me." The helmet turned, blank visor just visible over her armored shoulder. "I sought to thank you at the summit, Doctor, but fate brought us another path. Another of Shokat Anoushak's great horrors for your trophy hall. Your fourth, is it not?"

He frowned. "Fourth?"

"The pennant-backed serpent of the obelisk that laid waste to the southern shores? The crocodile of bridges, its star-towers lying dead across the bay?"

"How would you know—"

"The storm-wrought scourge of dread Chicago! They say you felled it after eight hours of single combat! That you hacked its skull from its shoulders and it fell like thunder and lo, there it remains!"

Well, that wasn't all *quite* true, but...

Edmund muttered to himself.

Istvan glanced back at him, unsure whether to feel flattered or unnerved by the attention. "Did you say something?"

Edmund shook his head. "No, no. You two are perfect for each other."

They approached the domed building from the night before, this time ascending its narrow stairway with no interruptions. It led to a balcony, crowded with spectators who fell back before Lucy's spiked presence, drawn sword, and amplified voice.

"Make way! Make way!"

Edmund put on a smile and followed, trying not to look to either side. Trying to focus on the cold presence of Istvan behind him, on the round steel table that emerged into view below, on the painted circle of hands that marked the dome above. Were those concertina lines on the walls?

The Hour Thief, the crowd murmured, *It's the Hour Thief. He doesn't look so good, does he? I saw him with his arm all bound up on the Fourth. How does he figure he can save everyone by himself?*

He's not by himself. Don't get too close. If that ghost walks through you, you die.

"Silence amongst the rabble!" Lucy commanded. She elbowed aside someone in a long patched overcoat who didn't move fast enough. The voices hushed.

"Our apologies," Istvan muttered.

Lucy bullied her way through the last of the crowd and ushered the two of them down a spiral staircase. There were a lot of people seated at the table Edmund didn't recognize. Mostly people – the hummingbird seemed to have a seat to itself, and he wasn't sure what the creature three seats over was (though it, too, had feathers, he thought). Six men, three women. Maybe two of them from different Earths or futures or pasts. Barrio Libertad's governing council?

The skull-helmeted Lord Kasimir was familiar, at least, accompanied by the man who spoke for him.

Mercedes sat two seats away from Grace. "Good morning, gentlemen." Her hair was up, her oversized jacket as pressed as it ever looked, her sharp, pockmarked face somehow wistful. She wore a messenger bag slung over one shoulder, packed full of supplies for her own task: beads and glass shards and drawing materials, a Greek mathematics text, her telephone, stripped wire, and a number of other, stranger things. "Slept well, I trust?"

"Sit," commanded Lucy.

Edmund found himself prodded into the empty chair next to Grace. He tried to decide how he felt about that and then decided it was better not to. He set his satchel down. "Morning, Mercedes."

"Eddie," said Grace. She was Resistor Alpha just as he was the Hour Thief. She wrinkled her nose as he sat. "You've been drinking."

"Just one this morning."

"Yeah, right. You hang this whole one-man miracle plan on yourself and then you go out and get hammered. Bravo."

"I'll manage," he said. He held his own hands down to keep them from shaking. She wouldn't forgive him. "I'm sorry," he added.

"At least you made it," she muttered.

It wasn't forgiveness. It didn't always feel right, being right.

All dead. All dead.

<You've come this far,> murmured Istvan.

Lucy slammed a fist on her breastplate and withdrew, joining the other mercenary standing behind Lord Kasimir and falling into parade rest.

Edmund dropped his head in his hands. Too loud. Everything was too loud. <Istvan, this isn't going to work.>

<Do you have a choice?>

<No.>

<Then you know how I feel. Now sit up. You're the Hour Thief. Act like it.>

Edmund winched his head back into position. Someone had started talking. One of the people he didn't know. How many smilers would he be able to rescue, did he think? What did the Hour Thief think? Did he have a number?

Istvan nudged him.

"All of them," the Hour Thief said. He smiled. "I'll be giving it my damnedest, anyway."

Whispering in the balcony.

"Did you have to put it that way?" hissed Grace.

He shrugged.

"How long?" someone called. "How long is this wizard plan going to take? If it doesn't work and the Susurration takes them both over…"

"We should just set off the bomb," called someone else.

The whispering exploded into a cacophony. *Let the wizards try – why are we letting wizards dictate what we do – the Shift was their fault in the first place – we can't just kill everything if we have a choice, we discussed this – us or them, isn't it – we were them – we were all them, don't you remember – what if it were us –*

Edmund covered his ears.

"Order," crackled Diego's voice, echoing from everywhere at once, "The vote is decided. Order or r-removal from the chamber."

The walls turned. Shifted, somehow – something to do with the acoustics – and the shouting faded, diffused. Foiled, some of the spectators departed. The rest stayed. Their mouths moved, no sound reaching the table.

"Grace," Edmund muttered, "I'm sorry, but your 'friend' is frightening as hell."

"We really did vote," she muttered back.

"Yeah? Who tallied it?"

A different councilman held up a hand. "Hour Thief. Doctor Czernin. We're all aware that there is no further decision to be made here. There is no aid we can offer you. I can't even assure you that the idea of 'letting the wizards try' was popular, but it seems to be the best plan we have, and we called you to this summit to wish you both good luck."

"Thank you," said Edmund, rather wishing they hadn't.

<Couldn't let it go without a bit of pageantry,> Istvan said.

The councilman nodded at Mercedes. "Magister Hahn, the People's Council holds contingency plans three and nine on standby, as you suggested. We're as ready as we'll ever be. Lord Kasimir?"

The warlord waved a hand. "All requisitioned forces are in position," declared his herald. "The bold and cunning Lord Kasimir awaits only engagement, should we have need of it."

Mercedes looked to Edmund and Istvan. "Gentlemen, it seems the rest falls to you."

Istvan stood, snapping to automatic attention as he did. "Magister."

Edmund rose to his feet more carefully, picking up his satchel of equipment and slinging it back across his shoulder. Getting up too fast would only make him dizzy. "Do we parade off somewhere or does transport come to us?"

"Remember where I showed you?" asked Grace.

"Below the fortress?"

"That's it. You need to go there. Go, jump off, do whatever you need to do."

Something boomed beneath their feet.

"Right."

"No matter who or what you see," Mercedes said, "don't stop until you're finished. Don't stop. The Susurration won't play fair and it won't pull punches. If it can use anything you've done or lost against you, it will."

Edmund glanced at Istvan. The specter was staring at the wall.

"The smilers should be translated into the Conceptual individually, according to their own self-images,"

Mercedes continued. "When you find them, you'll know, but *don't linger*. Make one circuit of the fortress, offer escape once to whatever you see, and then cut Doctor Czernin's chains. You'll have to use his knife on the last link, remember."

"Right."

Istvan would be up to it. He had to be up to it. All he had to do was keep the Susurration occupied, just long enough... Edmund reached for his pocket watch.

Someone grabbed his wrist. Grace. He didn't remember her getting up. She took his hand in hers and pressed something into it. It tingled. "Good luck."

He looked down. Her headband. She'd given him her headband. It was warm. "Grace," he said, "you know I still love you, right?"

She sighed. She didn't look at him. "I know."

He took his hat off and put the headband on. If it helped, it helped. It was over.

He could collapse when this was over.

Grace stepped back. "Keep some names off the walls for me, will you?"

Edmund fitted his hat back over the headband, fixing on half-remembered impressions of a vast pit, crackling with blue-white lightning. The Hour Thief and Doctor Czernin. *Make way*, Lucy had said. *Make way*.

No need for that now.

"I will."

It was to the brink he took them. That sickly pale light strung through tubes, an illumination dead and almost underwater. That humming, teeth-gritting, oil-tasting, that shivered up his neck. Those enormous vertebral constructs stretching down, down, down, dizzying, forever. If any machine could collapse what wasn't real into what was, this was it.

Don't stop until you're finished. Don't stop.

Istvan stood beside him – as he always did, as he always would – tracing spectral fingers through his bitten arm. The pain could wait. The hangover could wait. There would be time for that later. There would be time.

He had to trust that there would be time. He always had time.

"Zero," crackled Diego's voice. "Collapse."

Nothing changed. Edmund swallowed back oil. They were jumping.

Of course, it would be a jump.

"Istvan," he said, "you'll be all right?"

Istvan touched his shoulder. "Oh, Edmund," he replied, "I have wings."

"Right. Well. Istvan, I…" He held tighter to his pocket watch. It should have been harder to breathe. "Watch for me, all right? I'll finish this and cut your chains. Last link, your knife. I promise."

"I promise," the specter echoed. He lingered, a phantom pressure, fingers the barest whisper of sensation –

– and then turned, and dove.

Don't stop. Don't stop.

Edmund had jumped out of an airplane before. This wasn't an airplane. This was nothing like an airplane. This was crazy.

His lungs hammered. Nothing for it.

He clutched his satchel to his side and leapt after Istvan.

CHAPTER THIRTY-ONE

Armies stumbled their blind and groping way through Peace.

Istvan winged among them, wreathed in chains and wondering. He was bone and wire, mud and poison... they were whatever they thought themselves to be, a strange cavalcade of self-concepts translated in one broken instant to something real. Pride in Simple Things was there, as was Lost Tableware and Wishes She Could Remember. The Tall One, and The Wants-To-Be Taller One. The Animal. The Animator of Dust.

Smilers, translated to the Susurration's own level. Half a million of them.

Providence had become greater than itself: a maze of glass, molten when he wasn't looking, the ghosts of trees hovering on the edge of memory. Mountainous skeletons slouched through the ashes, destroyers themselves destroyed. The walls of Barrio Libertad towered amidst the fading shades of a demolished skyline, exactly the same as they were in the normal world.

Beyond that, distances dissolved. The Great War lurked just beyond an unseen divide, as it had done since he was chained.

No sign of Edmund. No sign of the Man in Black.

No sign of Pietro.

Istvan couldn't decide between dread or disappointment. He alighted on the misted ground, set a hand on the hilt of his knife; couldn't draw it. "Edmund?" Glass whispered. Rain. Coffee. Old leather. Tendriled ripples, like waves on the ocean, somehow frantic. The Susurration, reeling at a blow struck by what it couldn't understand.

Footsteps. Istvan turned.

Pietro hurtled across a garden path that hadn't been there before, the pond behind him rippling as though from several thrown stones. <Pista,> he cried, <what have you done?>

Istvan stepped backwards and almost tripped over a park bench. <I ->

<They're all gone, Pista. Torn away, to suffering – all alone, all removed, all gone.> He buried his face in Istvan's collar, an embrace that shook. Dead leaves blew over the path. <Pista, they'll be so unhappy. What have you done?>

Istvan hugged him back. He couldn't help himself. <I'm sorry. I'm sorry, please, listen–>

<What are you allowing to happen? Pista, your chains! Don't you know what will happen?>

That voice; that beautiful voice. Istvan blinked back tears. Oh, he missed him so much. <I do,> he said, <I do, and I'm sorry. Please, listen to me. It's hopeless. You can't finish what you've set out to do. There are so many plans drawn against you.>

The grip drew tighter. <I know.>

Providence had gone. There was only the park, now, deep in the grip of autumn... but the sun still shone, and not all of the leaves had fallen. They rustled, red and gold.

Istvan tried not to remember. Remembering only made it worse. <If you... if you surrender, give up all those people, perhaps...>

He trailed off. He stared at his hand, clasped around Pietro's shoulder. Fleshed. Living. The usual pale grey of his sleeve now had proper blue in it, its piping gone brilliant scarlet. No shackles. <Perhaps... we...>

A whisper in his ear. <I can't, Pista. You know I can't.>

<But...>

<No. Not now.>

Istvan closed his eyes. <Please, don't.>

<I should say the same to you,> came the soft reply. The embrace shifted: a brush against the back of his neck, fingers playing through his hair. <Oh, Pista... I should say the same to you.>

Istvan was the stronger of the two. Always had been. Broader. Taller. A duelist and brawler, with the scars to prove it. He could escape any time he wanted.

Any time.

Where was Edmund?

Pietro broke away. <You deny me?>

Istvan refocused. "I..."

<Oh, Pista, you hurl me away so easily before another?> Delicate fingers caressed the scarred side of his chest, his neck, his face. The voice trembled. <Am I really such a burden? Am I really so terrible that you would rather be rid of me?>

Istvan tried to close those fingers in his. "No, Peti, I–"

Pietro drew back, clutching at his breast. <You would rather see me dead.>

"No!" Istvan reached out a hand... and froze, staring at bloodied bone, bound and shackled in blazing calligraphy. Oh, God.

Oh, God.

<I'm more cherished to you, dead.>

Istvan caught his wrist. <That isn't true, Peti. That isn't true!>

A shell burst between them. Istvan reeled backwards, blinded and then buried, mud oozing through his bones. Something rolled over him; a heavy, ugly thing, steel that screamed; crushing – and then he breached the surface, gasping, and it was a waste, all of it, no trees left and a severed hand lying crab-like beside him, blown off at the wrist. It had a ring on.

<You're letting it all happen again! You don't care about me! You want to be loosed, so it can all happen again!>

Istvan floundered. He couldn't find him. Whose hand? Where was he? <Peti!>

He tumbled into a trench, wire ripping at his uniform. The mud stung, caustic with the residue of a gas attack, wisps swirling at his landing. Not tear gas. Phosgene. This was phosgene. He struggled to his feet, slipping. The shock of another strike hurled him sideways.

Something soft. Wet.

<You drove me to it,> said the dead man, slumped, shrapnel-torn, against the barricades. His eyes were soft and brown, flecked with yellow, irises ringed with a darkness like oak. <It was your fault, Pista. Your fault.>

Istvan scrambled away, his front smeared with blood. It wasn't real. It wasn't real. He could… he could go flying later, he could hide, he could…

Something. Oh, God, something.

He held up his hands, chains dragging in the mud. <Peti, I – I know what you are, you're not–>

<I'm not what? Worthy?>

<No!>

<I don't want your help,> Pietro said. <I don't want

your remorse, or your remembrance. Your apologies. Your touch. I don't want you at all. I never did. Remember what you are, Pista, before anything else.>

Artillery thundered.

Istvan staggered. Sat down, hard, on a worm-eaten ledge. <You can't.>

Those soft eyes gazed at him, pity and hatred and pain. <Remember what you are.>

Edmund fled.

Chasms yawned beside him. Below him. Above him. Before and behind. Storm winds lashed his face. He stared down, at his feet, without trying to look down. He couldn't – down would look back, and pull him under. It was water, he knew it. Like the lake. His shoes slipped on a knife-edge, a strand barely wide enough to balance, cutting into his soles.

There was a pun there. The worst pun.

Istvan hadn't… he wouldn't…

A shadow fell overhead. Edmund skidded, backpedaled, and dove away as one of Shokat Anoushak's terrors spun into the ground, crumpling, seams bursting, rotors snapping off, mantis claws curving like descending sickles, its scream reduced to a labored, moaning howl. Its tail stabilizer was gone.

A pale horror plunged after it. Before it. Veered around at an impossibly sharp angle, ripped a long, jagged, sparking gash through its metallic flesh – and shot away, turning a barrel roll and then vanishing into the storm. Grinning. Laughing. Violence for the sake of violence: gleeful, prancing, and delivered with the explosive brutality of a bronco. Nothing personal, but nothing better.

Istvan.

He was frightening enough standing still. He was frightening enough in his right mind.

"Edmund, do you know what you mean to unleash? You've seen it, Edmund, all those years ago, but perhaps you've forgotten?"

Another flier crashed down. The woods caught fire. Edmund tripped on a root that hadn't been there before, tumbling down a riverbank as he held onto his satchel for dear life, stones ripping the skin from his hands.

He couldn't breathe. It felt like he'd been running forever.

Laughter, somewhere above. "Shall I show it to you again, Edmund?" Thunder through the canopy; vulture's wings arrowed across the stars. "Shall I spark your memory?"

The Susurration had gotten to him.

Istvan was drunk.

He was drunk, and he struck with surgical precision.

Edmund scrambled away from the flash of a knife.

Istvan covered his eyes as another shell struck.

He never had choices. He was what he was: all else flowed from that, irredeemable. There was nothing he could do. Even his face was twisted, and the wire that followed him. He deserved to be hated. He did.

What would Pietro have said, had he known what he was now? What he had become?

Remember what you are, Pista.

Before everything else. Before anything else.

I can honestly say that I don't know where I'd be without you.

The last mud pattered down around him. Istvan whirled and threw his knife.

It thudded into Pietro's shrapnel-torn chest. His heart.

A cleaner end than what had really killed him, so very long ago.

"I'm a doctor," Istvan said. English. A language he and Pietro had never shared. A language he had learned later, from conquerors and jailers. A language less dear and less powerful. He tugged at the band on his arm, the red cross he always carried. "I'm a doctor, and Pietro knew that. If you mean to use his memory to keep me from helping others, as a doctor ought, then you're not even close to representing the man he was."

The Susurration – it was the Susurration – looked down at the handle. Touched it, as though it couldn't believe it. Didn't fall. <This is how you help others, Pista?>

Istvan gestured at the battlefield. "This is how you win my sympathy?"

<You are what you are.>

"Yes. I am. I am your only ally and advocate, regardless of all that you've done, because you were brought here unjustly, trapped, and abandoned. I tried to speak for you at the conference. I tried to argue against what we mean to do now. I am trapped and chained, like you, and I am offering you one last chance to surrender. Give up those people you've imprisoned, and I'll see to it that the victors aren't the only ones who dictate what comes next."

Pietro brushed at his chest, fingers coming away scarlet. <I can't save you, then,> he said, wondering. <Pista, I tried. I tried so hard.>

Istvan stepped toward him, slowly, reminding himself: it wasn't Pietro. It wasn't.

It wasn't.

"Please. Even if this plan works, people will be hurt. Your people."

<You've taken them all away from me.>

"They're still yours, aren't they?" Another step. "You care for them, don't you?"

<I would keep them safe forever, if I could.>

"Then let them go."

Half the distance. A quarter of the distance. The mud clung to his shoes and sucked at the chains he dragged behind him. The guns seemed to have fallen silent. Pietro gazed at him, unmoving. Blood now soaked the entire front of his jacket.

Istvan reached out a hand, pretending it wasn't shaking as badly as it was. "If you care for them, let them go."

<How did you resist me?>

Istvan stopped. He shouldn't have thrown the knife. He shouldn't have. Why had he done that? Oh, God, there was so much blood.

He struggled to find words. Couldn't. Looked away. "Pietro... my Peti, when he..." English wasn't good enough, not for this; Istvan switched back to German. <He would have never said such things to me. Never, no matter how we quarreled. That isn't love – and he loved me, just as I loved him. Just as I'll always love him.>

<You've replaced him.>

<No.>

<Replaced me!>

Istvan lunged. Before he could think. Before he could hesitate.

He grabbed at the knife handle and drove the blade deeper, twisting, an agony burning in his own chest. <You will not do that to me again. You will *not*!>

<He'll hate you,> Pietro hissed, <He'll run from you, your Man in Black. He did once, and now, when he sees the full measure of what you are...> A chuckle. It

gurgled in his throat. <He won't want you near him ever again.>

Istvan stared at him. Edmund. Edmund was here, too. Edmund hadn't ever faced such a foe before, and he was alone.

The Susurration was stalling.

"I like to think we're better friends than that," Istvan said.

He tore out the knife.

The sound was terrible. It always was. Memory bubbled from the wound, glassy, congealing.

"In fact," he added, wiping the blade on his uniform hem, "I think he would have liked you. He loves books, you know. Dreadful ones. You could have formed a club."

A roar on the horizon. Incoming shells whistled.

Oh, Peti. It was high time this was over.

Istvan took wing.

"The worst is living with what you've done," Istvan said, still grinning that deathly grin. He struck: once, twice, steel flashing faster than Edmund should have been able to follow.

Edmund jerked his head out of the way just in time to keep his left eye. The tread assembly of the overturned tank slid away with a crash, interior wheels spinning. Edmund ran around it and came face-to-skull with the specter again. Ducked.

The blade scored his cheek.

Couldn't spend time. He couldn't spend any more time. Couldn't move any faster.

Couldn't escape.

Istvan leered at him. "How is it, living with what you've unleashed?"

Edmund backed up against the tank, holding tight to his pocket watch. Don't. He needed all the time he could get. There were people that needed it. He couldn't spend it.

"You're not like this," he tried, "I know you're not like this."

"Oh, I'm not talking about me," the ghost replied. He flicked the blood from his knife. It spattered across Edmund's jacket. "I'm talking about you. The Hour Thief himself! You're the man who decides who gets all the time and who doesn't, aren't you?" He leaned in closer, the stench of poison gas burning Edmund's nostrils. "Who gave you the right?"

The book was just sitting in the vault.

He was curious. It wasn't a crime to be curious.

What if it worked? At least one other person had done it. What if it really, actually worked?

Really all of forever…

Such a good idea at the time. Such a good idea. Since then, he'd heard it argued that the universe might never end, only cool into a dark and dead expanse of drifting ashes.

Edmund fought down the old panic. Not now. Please, not now. "No one gave me the right."

"No one," Istvan echoed. "No one… but you."

"Istvan…"

"You took it," the specter continued, leaning closer still, close enough that Edmund shivered. Poisonous mists swirled around him, obscuring the forest, the river, the sky. "You didn't want to be like the rest of them."

Edmund's fingers slipped on his watch. He couldn't breathe. "Istvan, stop it."

"Small. Weak. Withering."

"Istvan!"

"Finite."

The mist swallowed him. He fell into dust. Choked on dust. Tried to claw his way out, tried to reach for the hands that sought him, but everything he saw turned to dust. Everyone. It smelled like the archives – *his bloody dust obsession*, Istvan had called it, and he was right – and now there was nothing but the records, words written and rewritten in fading ink, illustrations of ancient ruin, paper that crackled and fell to pieces in his hands.

And her.

She plummeted toward him on a beast of her own making, its harness jangling, sword and quiver buckled at her belt. Dozens of braids whipped behind her, jet-black, capped in gold, each one longer than she was tall. Bright green, those eyes, almost glowing. Mad.

Shokat Anoushak.

CHAPTER THIRTY-TWO

Edmund hit the deck.

Just the Susurration. Just the Susurration. It was only the Susurration.

<Is it, stripling?>

Scythian.

Oh, hell. Oh, hell, oh, hell, oh, hell –

Hot breath on his back. A growl, lion-like. The sweep of steel-shod wings. A chuckle, unamused and uncaring, an expression by rote. <I am Glory Everlasting. Empire after empire has known my name. The Persians, the Romans, the Sassanids.>

He was hyperventilating. Too much dust. He couldn't breathe, for all the dust.

<We, you and I, are eternal. We cannot be subsumed. Your Magister's pet, for all its command of mind and memory, can barely contain my essence.>

He tried to get up.

A huge paw slapped him down. Into the dust. Into the ages.

His ribs creaked. He coughed.

Inevitable. It was all inevitable, wasn't it? Who could stay sane for all of forever? Who knew better than anyone the price of reaching too far? It was only a matter of time.

Everything was a matter of time.

Run, immortal. That's all you can do.

So much for that.

Something thudded.

The beast atop him whirled, crushing him deeper. He wheezed. Scraps of paper whirled past his face. A snap: an arrow loosed, two of them. A roar, definitely leonine.

What was coming...? That was a strange, mechanical hammering, like...

Edmund covered his head.

The impact shattered the ground beneath him. Glass cut his hands. An abyss yawned below, black and infinite. He pinwheeled. Voices filtered from above. A Scythian curse. Shouting, mostly Hungarian that he couldn't catch. His own name.

The abyss ended, with a crack to his collarbone, only a few feet down.

He wheezed, stars sparking before his eyes... and then he saw them. Emperor For a Weekend and The Baltic Chef. The clasped hands of the Twins. The obsidian-tipped blades of Purpose in Precision. Wears That Sweater, in plaid and purled glory.

Thousands of them. Hundreds of thousands.

The walls of the fortress rose behind them, solid amidst a landscape of mists and molten glass. The fading outlines of destroyed buildings stood amidst the even fainter memories of forests. He could see where the roads of Providence had been, if he squinted hard enough.

The Conceptual.

Whatever Diego had done, it had worked.

He looked at his hands, gloved in darkness. Here, he was like them. Like Istvan. Conceptual. An idea. He had become the recurring role in so many stories: liberator, lover, thief, mysterious rogue who always meant well; motives and origins hidden in the dark of the cloak he wore; he who went by many names and none – the Man In Black.

That had been Istvan, back there, on the attack, shattering the Susurration's illusions. It couldn't have been anyone else. Snapped out of it, maybe, or at least distracted. For now.

No time to worry about that.

Edmund found his feet. He still had his satchel, tightly closed, and everything in it. He still had his pocket watch.

The self-images of half a million trapped smilers milled around him, no doubt mired in illusions of their own.

Time to change that.

"Take as long as you need to escape Providence," he told the nearest Concept, Yellow-Souled One, an anole in lightning. Then he moved on to the next, Girl With a Braid, her hair a serpentine body of its own. "Take as long as you need to escape Providence."

Thunder roared through the clouds, leonine. Cracks etched themselves in the glass beneath his feet. He tried to pretend he couldn't see ghostly snarls of barbed wire, jagged and fading, burned across his eyelids where there should have been lightning.

He moved to the next smiler. And the next. English, Japanese, Arabic, German, Latin, Chinese, Russian, his terrible rusty Farsi. On and on, mystery swirling around his feet.

"Take as long as you need to escape Providence."

Years stolen. It would have to be enough.

Istvan tumbled through a fire that wasn't the red of sunset, tangled with the immortal that wasn't his. It wasn't her, either – the real Shokat Anoushak had been a baleful beacon, a breath drawing ever-inward, a well of feeling so deep and so ancient it was almost alien, bitter and overwhelming – and this... this shadow of her was hollow, like the rest. A memory.

A fury!

She plunged and wheeled, her winged steed lion-like and snarling, its claws tearing at his tattered feathers and catching in his chains. He struck where he could; she met each strike with steel of her own, a sword with a tasseled pommel and an edge serrated like a shark's tooth.

"Why should the Hour Thief alone possess such magics?" she demanded in twisted English. "How can you condone what he has stolen, and what he squanders?"

Istvan tried to tear himself away from her. He couldn't linger here. He had to return to the ground, find Edmund – the man had vanished, fleeing, hopefully to do what he ought, but...

He ripped a score along her mount's side. It shrieked, bleeding gold. An opening.

He dove.

Shokat Anoushak caught his chains.

"How is it," she hissed, whirling him scrabbling in a tethered arc, "that a monster like you hopes to defend a monster like him?"

Istvan fought to right himself, wings churning. His knife struck sparks on entangling links of parchment. "He isn't!"

She snapped his chains, whip-like, over her head – her strength as inhuman as her longevity – and Istvan with them. Her mount rushed to meet him, claws and fangs and fire.

He stabbed it in the eye.

It reared, claws tearing more gashes in his already ruined uniform. He slashed his blade across its face and rolled away, folding his own wings tight, diving as fast as he could: no subtlety, no grace, merely flight by the raw will to fly, ripping through the air like a modern jet fighter.

An arrow sped past. The ghosts of serpents writhed and spat in its passage.

Then a rolling thunder like an avalanche blasted from below, a roar that split horizons end to end, that shattered windows in their frames and then carried the frames away, that turned weaker matter to pulp, that far too many had only heard once. Briefly. Grating, metallic, rising...

Jaws the size of a stadium lunged through the clouds.

Istvan slewed sideways, skidding between steel teeth and entangling cables and flashes of actinic green, escaping the maw just before it snapped shut with a shock that sent him tumbling. Oh, not this. Not here. With the realms collapsed, such a monster would cause hideous devastation in what was real.

He shouted at it. "I thought you cared for your people!"

<I do,> came the reply, everywhere at once.

The beast fell back to earth, horned head swept low before hunched shoulders, its many legs squat beneath the impossible weight of the city cresting its crocodilian back. Stone and brick, peaked roofs of faded red, dense blocks and narrow cobbled streets broken by skyscrapers of modern glass, copper-green domes and park walks torn up with the skeletons of trees, all ringed about by the cracked ribbons of highways. Broken tiles tumbled from the mosaic-laden roof of a Gothic cathedral, its sides soot-stained, its south tower immense and knobbled and surmounted by a familiar double-headed eagle supporting a double-armed cross.

St Stephens.

She hadn't. Oh, she hadn't.

<Waste and ruin, War to End All Wars. I seek only to end it... but you *are* it. What do you think will happen to them if you're unchained?>

A tail swept at him, studded with thousands of broken gravestones.

Edmund staggered, ears ringing and jacket coated in dust, trying not to look up. It wouldn't help to look up. Up there wasn't his business.

He looked up.

Oh, hell. Oh, hell. Just a roof. It was just a roof. With legs. An earthquake. A walking disaster. One of hers. The Susurration could animate them here?

Or was it her?

Oh, hell.

"Take as long as you need to escape Providence," he shouted. He didn't know if anyone could hear him, but he couldn't stop. He had a job to do. He'd promised.

He leapt across rubble and kept running. He tried to keep Barrio Libertad on his left: its walls were the only solid navigational markers there were.

"Take as long as you need to escape Providence."

Again, and again, and again. Some of the smilers didn't take it. Some of them didn't move, still trapped, the Susurration seeping over warped and weakened selves like whispering amber. Most were confused and huddled, too dazed to understand what was happening just above their heads. Freedom, after months or years enthralled, in such a strange place as this... he couldn't imagine.

The monster stretching across the sky bellowed; he shouted louder. Bricks cascaded like hail and he moved faster. *Take it, take it, run, go.*

Keep the Susurration occupied, Istvan. Keep it off me. He was going hoarse.

Istvan reflected that Lucy's cited feats of glory on his part were, sadly, somewhat hyperbolic. He had killed one of these monsters, once, but that was after it had suffered days of assault and had been driven to a more pastoral area, trapped and held there at considerable cost. He was dangerous. He wasn't *that* dangerous.

Not chained.

What if Edmund was wrong? What if there were no survivors?

<You're a failure,> the Susurration whispered. <This is your better way? This is your kinder way? You've always been a failure, all your life and after.>

The remains of Vienna's Central Cemetery slammed into him. Through him. Istvan clawed through absolute darkness. Dirt and rock scraped across his skin. Beneath his skin. Within his stomach, his throat, his lungs. It didn't hurt, but that made it all the more unnerving. He tried to imagine he was swimming, or flying, but that didn't help.

Some of the rock wasn't rock.

<*Istvan! Istvan, why didn't you tell me?*>

<*Full retreat – call a full retreat!*>

<*Doctor, he's gone.*>

<*Late again, Mr Czernin?*>

<*I don't know you. I don't know you any more.*>

They reached for him. Tore at him. Grabbed at his chains and hauled him backwards, dragging at his wings, hands he couldn't see and voices he wished he couldn't hear. Friends, instructors, wartime allies, family he'd fled from, colleagues he'd decried… and Franceska.

<*You've done enough. Please, go.*>

He burst from the other side with both hands clutched tightly around his wedding ring. He was upside-down. The glassy ground sped towards him. He couldn't correct himself in time.

<You'll kill him,> said the Susurration. <If he doesn't kill himself first.>

"Take as long as you need to escape Providence," Edmund said, and suddenly he knew.

It didn't hurt. It didn't feel like anything pulled away from him, or out of him, or through him. There was no taste, no texture. Not even a temperature. All those many tongues he'd studied, and he knew only one way to describe it.

Time, running out.

A bloody horror slammed into the ground beside him, rolling, tattered. Bony fingers hooked into his jacket front. "Edmund! Edmund, you mustn't!"

Edmund dodged the wild beating of wings. Snapped his watch. Teleported.

Shokat Anoushak no longer pursued him. She didn't have to.

Circle the fortress. Offer escape, and run.

Run.

All the time he could give, and more. They took it: gauzy figures of silk and fans, souls shivering like branches in autumn, hard-edged brilliant outlines of neon – how they were, how they saw themselves, strange and beautiful. He had a promise to keep.

He would have collapsed long ago if he wasn't the Man in Black.

"Take as long as you need to escape Providence," he said, and he kept running.

CHAPTER THIRTY-THREE

Edmund turned to sand in his hands.

No.

No, no.

Istvan spun away, grasping at nothing, landing paralyzed on his back. Was that what happened? No time left? When he ran out of time, he simply... he...

Something landed beside him. Skittered across the glass.

Istvan picked it up.

Edmund's pocket watch. Brass, well-worn, the hourglass etched into its front ringed by lettering Istvan didn't understand. It wasn't magical. Edmund had said so. It didn't do anything but tell time. It was something to hold, no more.

Nothing else.

Istvan sat there. Flicked it open. Flicked it shut.

A golden lion winged to a landing beside him, paws settling softly in the sand. "A shame," said Shokat Anoushak. "He was handsome."

Istvan vaulted up and over her mount's head and plunged his knife into her throat.

A monster reared to his left, some horrific cross

between a bull and a crocodile, and he killed it. One similar to the talking tiger, leaping – he killed that one, too, and then another, and another, the glassy crater of Providence falling away to what it had once been, seven years ago. A city embattled, its streets full of shrieking horrors.

He sped to meet them.

A wailing fury plunged toward him, rotors whirring, oil drooling from shark-toothed jaws. He tore it open from stem to stern, cables of gold and greenery spiraling outward like freed intestines. It thrashed like a living thing, which it would be until it struck the ground.

He didn't wait for it. He couldn't.

He dove.

A column of tanks roared below, black eyes glittering in the recesses of angular plating.

Not tanks. Those weren't tanks.

He barreled into the first, ripping at every component he could reach in a blind frenzy. Mockery of his war! Hideous duplicate of what his battlefields had demanded!

It bled black, crude oil not suitable for use in an engine, not running through where the fuel lines should have been. He knew where they went. He knew where everything went. He knew every detail of its ancestral construction, who had developed it, who had fought in it, who had died in it, who had crawled out of wrecks stalled or burning to fight again – and this... this thing wasn't even close!

<You dare,> he shouted at it as it screamed, <you dare!>

It had four seats for no reason, all empty. A turret with insides that boiled molten. Its roof was the top of a shell, peeled open, the ghost of a sun to shine on its false innards, sparking and broken. It thrashed. He savaged it until it couldn't.

"Istvan," called someone else, someone he knew. "Istvan, stop!"

He laughed. He was the suicide of nations, the end of empires, the long death by suffocation in shell-churned mud and snow and ruin. What was done couldn't be undone. All that remained was attrition: the relentless, pitiless, senseless murder of generations.

Stop? Stop *him*? Hell itself wouldn't have him!

The greatest monster of all loomed above, murdered Vienna sunk into its back. He leapt for it.

The Man in Black caught at his arm.

Edmund. Whole. Impossible.

Istvan whirled.

Desecration. All that was beloved and beautiful, despoiled and turned against him. First Pietro and now Edmund. It was, perhaps, fitting, in the end.

Another trick. Another illusion. That's all there ever was.

No more.

Istvan lunged.

Edmund dodged around the blade. Barely.

Not the time. This wasn't the time.

There weren't any more smilers he could help – he had ringed the entire fortress, he could barely talk – and this last task was all he had left. *Istvan, it's done. Istvan, it's over. Istvan, what are you doing?*

Please, hold still. I can't finish this if you don't hold still.

"Istvan," he croaked.

The specter didn't seem like he'd even heard him. <Not you,> he said, voice cracking through the strange German of his home city. <Not you.>

His chains burned, calligraphy in white phosphorous. Smoke streamed from their shackles. He pursued well enough but he was slashing about wildly, a far cry from his usual precision.

Out of his mind. What had the Susurration done?

Edmund kept dodging. He'd done it before. He could do it again. No need for panic, not now, not until this was over and he'd gone home and had a shower and finished off two glasses of gin to start. Then he could panic. He would set some time aside for it.

Time.

He sweated cold. He was burning his own time, now. Unique. Irreplaceable. Go home? Take a shower? No, when this was over, he'd have to go back out, thief that he was, and what time he'd lost he could never–

Istvan ripped a gash in his shirt.

End this quickly. End this quickly.

Edmund pulled off his hat. Pulled down his goggles. Forced the words through his raw throat. "Istvan, it's me. It's really me. The impossible soldier, remember? You could never hit me then, you aren't hitting me now, and you aren't going to hit me anytime soon." Keep dodging. Don't think about the time. "Istvan, do you know anyone else like that? Istvan, can you hear me? Please, calm down."

The ghost slowed.

"I need you. I need you more than ever."

"You're afraid of me," Istvan said. He seemed surprised.

Edmund tried a smile. It wasn't his best. "Sometimes."

"Oh." Istvan looked at his knife. He blinked. He dropped it, blade clattering on the glassy ground. "Oh, no."

Edmund let out a breath. He wasn't shaking. He

didn't know how he wasn't. Maybe because the Man in Black didn't. Here, after all, he was the Man in Black. He stepped closer, unslinging his bag from his shoulders. "It's all right."

"Edmund, I..."

He reached for Istvan's shackles. "Just hold still."

Calligraphy blazed beneath his hands.

Once before, Istvan had seen him as he strove to be. When the Wizard War took its turn for the worst. When Istvan's chains trapped him, useless, within walls that might shortly cease to exist – and him along with them. Contractual oblivion.

Then... then, he'd met a figure of darkness, but not of threat: less nights of knives and more of whispered words, withheld violence, river crossings, sudden departures just before the dawn. Salvation at the last moment, one who (when thanked for the risks taken, the wounds suffered, the day won) waved away the praise and vanished with a promise: *I'll be back when I'm needed.*

The Man in Black.

In one hand, he held an owl's feather pen. In the other, a silver ritual knife. He bent silently to his task and parchment links fell away, rewritten and struck out and cut. Faster than any eye could follow. Watching him was like watching a mirage, just beyond real; to be near him was to wonder who he was, from where he had come, how long he would stay before he vanished (not long). Become, in perilous passage, purest Concept.

Edmund. Merely doing his duty, and fulfilling his promise.

The blade glistened, poppy-red, with his blood.

So sudden. So odd, to stand there, watching, and

nothing else. So little Istvan could think but this: it was at once a thrill and a terror to behold such a strange and beautiful aspect of the man he loved so well.

Each scrap that fell burned. A bloodied horizon crouched in wait.

...except when such actions would stand in violation of the provisions of section 28. As detailed in paragraph 9 section 62, the Binder (the Innumerable Citadel, magisterial membership, [and] the Twelfth Hour) hold all rights to use, disposition, and disposal of...

Edmund had studied law at first, almost eighty years ago, before his focus shifted to language, and contracts of the metaphysical were no different once past the arcane writing, past the consequences. It was written, and it could be rewritten. Mightier than the sword, indeed.

Link after link. He took his time. It was his time, now.

It had to be done right.

Only when one last link remained, did he finally slow – finally allow himself to end at the same rate as anyone else.

"Istvan?" he croaked.

"Edmund," the winged and skeletal horror before him confirmed.

Edmund set the ritual knife down. "Are we always this interesting?"

Istvan knelt and retrieved his own blade, wiping it on the hem of his uniform before handing it to him. He was a doctor. It would be all right. "Oh, yes."

Edmund slit a palm already bleeding. All the most powerful magics were paid for in blood freely given. That was the fine print. "I'm just a man, you know," he said. He dipped the pen in the wound. "The rest is all bad choices and good press."

Istvan clasped his hand and the pain faded. "I know."

Edmund carefully wrote in the terms of cancellation and annulment. He knew his Classical Arabic. Translating the old works of the Innumerable Citadel, he'd had to. He was good at it. He swallowed, wondering how many people he'd missed. "Did what I could."

"You did."

"Are you...?"

"No."

Edmund slid the bloodied knife through parchment. The lettering flared red, sputtered, faded.

"OK," he said. He swayed on his feet. "Take it away."

Istvan caught him.

Solid. He was solid, here – War brushing skeletal fingers across a cape black as the man claimed his soul to be, in endless debt – sinking down as Edmund fell and, wondering, kneeling, pressing him tight against a rotten breast, no heartbeat save in feeling. He breathed, yet. Oh, he breathed.

Istvan looked up to Pietro, delicate fingers holding closed a gash in his chest, watching forlornly as the last scraps of chain fluttered into flame. The Susurration.

Something thundered.

<I'm sorry,> Istvan said.

A whistling...

He ducked, hugging Edmund as closely as he could, blanketing him in wire-tangled wings that ripped and tore.

The first shells struck through a sea of poison.

They didn't stop.

They didn't stop.

They didn't stop.

•••

Four years forever. Armies crushed. Empires broken. Dreams and certainty dashed, families gutted, the future resting in the hands of the most ruthless, the most wronged. For the first time, mankind could destroy himself utterly – and he had.

Edmund, alone, was still breathing. Istvan dare not let go.

He could hold him, once in all the time he'd known him, and he did, not looking up. Not until smoke faded back to sky. Chlorine and mustard gas to something breathable. Shouting and bullet-chattering and tanks roaring and mountaintops collapsing and always, always the pounding of artillery... to silence.

It was then that Edmund slumped through him, onto the rubble.

Istvan shifted aside, kneeling beside him instead. Mud and worse things stained his handsome face, his eyes red and swollen, his skin burned from poison. Bloody scratches marred his cheeks and forehead, the results of barbed wire made solid. Istvan wished he had sheltered him better. He wished he could prop the poor man's head on something more comfortable than stone. He tried to prod him over more into dirt, and then he saw it. His left temple.

A shock of grey.

Istvan brushed immaterial fingers through it. "Oh, Edmund..."

Edmund coughed, an ugly sound full of phlegm. The gas hadn't done him any favors. "What?" he croaked.

Istvan took his hand away. "You're all right. I'm... I'm glad, that you're all right."

The wizard coughed again, rolled over – Istvan got out of the way – and spat into the dirt, scrubbing at his lips. Flakes of dirt tumbled from his goatee. His hat fell away, the headband Grace had given him sparkling in its place. "Don't feel all right. Maybe… maybe quasi-right."

He tried to sit up and Istvan couldn't help him. He was hurting, and that Istvan could do something about.

"Hell of a job you've done with the place," he said, blinking out at Providence.

Istvan busied himself lessening his headache, trying to ignore the agonies of many, many others wandering about, dazed, with the same problem or worse. Lost smilers. Too slow, battered and blinded. He would have to attend to them, too, once Edmund was safe. All of them. As long as it took. "Not an uncommon comparison," he muttered.

A slam. The ground shook. Bits of broken glass and other things skittered down the slope beside them.

Edmund hit the dirt. Istvan shielded him – a pointless gesture, here, now, arm and wing outstretched, crouched just over the man's prone form to intercept destruction that never came – and looked to Barrio Libertad.

A monstrous corpse lay sprawled across the closed roof, barely recognizable. No cathedrals. No cobbled streets. It was skeletal, its claws vast scythes of steel, and somewhat resembled a strange crustaceal crown, perched like that. Blue-white smoke leaked from molten caverns in its sides. Barrio Libertad's turreted guns had seen some use after all. Hovercraft bobbed near the creature's crests, rickety things like those in Triskelion, zipping backwards every time it twitched.

"Do you suppose…?" said Istvan.

"No," said Edmund. "I think they got it."

Istvan drew back away, wings dissolving. He squinted. He wasn't sure if he was imagining it or not, but it looked as though someone in spiked armor were planting a tiny flag on its head.

A figure in red and yellow picked its way across the wastes, jumping trenches and shell craters, scrambling past shreds of sheltering canvas. It moved much faster than a normal human. Istvan tried to summon malice, or at least disgruntlement, and discovered he couldn't.

"You two all right?" asked Grace Wu, jogging to a wild-eyed stop.

Edmund, still prone, reached for his hat. "Quasi-right," he said.

"Yes," Istvan echoed.

Grace wavered, uncertain, clasping and re-clasping her hands. Nervous, wary, horrified at the destruction... but no hatred, no anger. Sorrow, at what and who had been lost. Any positives, Istvan couldn't tell. She kicked at the earth. "Nice redecorating job, Doc."

Istvan didn't care to look at it. He knew. Just as he knew that through it, the maimed and wounded stumbled.

Edmund hadn't saved all of them.

"Miss Wu," Istvan said, patting the wizard's caped shoulder, "could you... could you help him back?"

She stared at him.

He passed a hand through Edmund's torso.

"Oh, right," she said. "Sure."

"Ow," said Edmund, but there was no heart in it. He rubbed his side.

Grace crouched beside him. "You look terrible."

"I feel terrible."

"Can I get my tiara back or do you want to keep it?"

He gave it back.

Istvan left them, as Grace levered Edmund's bad arm over her shoulder – and then, after protest, his good arm instead. She would see him back safely. She still cared for him, after all, though their affair was over, and she was quite capable in her own way. It would be all right.

Istvan was a doctor, and he had work to do.

CHAPTER THIRTY-FOUR

The first grey always came as a shock. That was what they'd told him: his parents, his aunt and uncle. *You expect it*, they'd said, *but you never really expect it.* Edmund had believed them, but... well, he'd never expected it.

It wasn't supposed to happen. Not to him.

He turned his head, examining himself in his bathroom mirror. Cuts he could handle. Dirt came off. Chemical burns were worse, but as long as he didn't turn out like Istvan, he'd be fine – and, according to Istvan, they would heal. There was nothing wrong with him that wouldn't heal.

Nothing but the grey streak at his left temple.

He prodded it. It didn't feel any different, though he half-expected it to be brittle.

Yesterday, as soon as he could walk straight and while Istvan was away on that new battlefield, he'd made a beeline for the nearest overcrowded gang enclave. Before washing. Before anything else. Before he could spin into a flat panic.

More time stolen. Starting over from zero... with a loss.

He'd told himself that the toughs he'd jumped

wouldn't miss just a few moments, but he knew that was a lie.

After that, and only after that, had he washed off the worst and slept the whole rest of the day and most of an exhausted, mostly dreamless night. Somehow. Now morning had come again – as mornings did – and he supposed that in addition to a new name plate his next five-year Twelfth Hour portrait would look different. Greyer.

Older.

A knock. "Edmund?"

"Door's open, Istvan. I'm not doing anything."

The specter stepped through. His hat was off and folded; his belt and bandolier missing. He halted at Edmund's face in the mirror. "It doesn't look so bad, you know," he said. He ran a hand through his own hair, grey on grey. "It's... distinguished, I think. It suits you."

"It hasn't gotten worse. That's something."

"As battle scars go, it could certainly have been worse."

"I know."

They regarded themselves, together. Edmund turned again to see the grey streak better in the light. He wouldn't dye it, he decided. Better to keep as a reminder. Time, for once, spent honestly.

Istvan traced the parallel ridges where his dueling scars had been. A caress, almost. His expression – what he could move, what wasn't twisted – was distant, not quite sad, and Edmund suddenly realized that the other man had lived a normal life for much longer than he ever had, absent magic and absent world wars, married and everything.

No wonder the Susurration had used that against him. He'd really had something... and Edmund barely knew more than her name.

"Did it hurt?" Istvan asked.

"No."

"Did you know? Did you know it was happening?"

"I did."

Istvan made as though to reply, then fell silent. "Oh," he said after a moment.

Edmund frowned. "Istvan?"

The specter shook his head, dropping his hand back to his side. "The Magister wanted to meet with you. She's used what she can of the materials she brought, and among other things would like some assistance transferring more from her office. Her, ah, lighthouse, rather."

Something small and dark shot into the bathroom and twined around one of Edmund's legs, hissing at Istvan. Beldam. Irate at the lack of attention – and food – over the last thirty hours, no doubt. Edmund bent down to scratch her ears, grateful for the interruption. "Is that all?"

"I don't know." Istvan rubbed at his wrists. "You saw it, Edmund. What I did. What I... Well, she was rather hesitant to talk to me at all, and with the chains gone, I..."

Edmund nodded, trying not to think about any of what had transpired and not doing so well on that. Istvan, unchained. The Great War freed once again to inflict itself upon the world. A Conceptual maelstrom, past horrors churning, trapped in amber. "I'm sure we'll figure something out."

Cat. The cat needed her bowl refilled. Do that, then go meet Mercedes.

He had time.

Edmund stood back up. One last look at the mirror – it couldn't be helped – and he started for the kitchen, Beldam zipping past with hair on end.

Istvan followed him.

•••

"So," said Mercedes, "I need you to chapter a new branch of the Twelfth Hour."

Edmund choked on his Barrio Libertad coffee. "What?"

"After all that's happened?" demanded Istvan, stepping before him with a suddenness almost violent, "He hasn't hardly recovered! Do you know what that magic of his might have done to him, running wild like that? I don't! I think we ought to…to…" He trailed off, suddenly uncertain. "…Magister?"

Mercedes tossed another length of copper wire into her bag. "Expecting an order, Doctor?"

The specter backed away, worrying at his wrists.

"As I was saying," she continued, "Someone has to keep an eye on Providence and I don't want it to be Barrio Libertad."

Edmund finally found his voice again. "Mercedes…"

"There's no telling what that fortress will do, and you have a good idea what it can. I don't want another crisis before I've finished locking away my own mistakes."

Edmund wiped at the cup before anything else could drip on the floor. He'd spilled coffee on the floor. If it really was coffee. Grace had called it coffee.

Mercedes zipped the bag shut and set it on her enormous inherited Magister's desk. She didn't look very rested; he supposed rebinding the Susurration was a good excuse for that. At least she was still missing only a single finger. "You're the Hour Thief, Mr Templeton. You have leadership experience, people listen to you, you're not likely to need replacing in the next few years, and you get on well with Barrio Libertad's liaison."

He grimaced. "You had to use that word, didn't you?"

"Everyone knows you're back on duty, now, Mr Templeton. I suspect you'll find yourself with quite a flock once you start recruiting."

"No. No, Mercedes, this is a bad–"

"This is what I should have done a long time ago." She spread her arms, encompassing the room he'd once held himself. The shelves, the lanterns, the portrait of Magister Whitfield and the tentacle that held the man's hat for him, the open window in the alcove that led elsewhere. "You've always had this kind of stature, Mr Templeton, this kind of authority, whether you like it or not, and it's about time the Twelfth Hour puts you back to full use."

Edmund swallowed, tearing his eyes away from the skull of Magister Jackson. In his day, he'd finally hung a tablecloth over that bookshelf to blunt the staring. "I haven't always."

"You have for long enough that it doesn't matter, and you act it. Now, you'll have the title and the duties to match. How does Director sound?"

"Better than Magister."

She chuckled darkly. "One can only hope."

"I'm going with him," said Istvan. "If you're going to lay all this on him, I can't very well let him do it alone." He paused, then added, "Re-chain me if you like – and you ought, if you can – but at least grant me that."

"That isn't an option," she replied.

He reached for Edmund's arm. "But…"

"Rebinding you, Doctor, would be a task on the same order of magnitude as rebinding the Susurration, and I had the benefit of a preexisting anchor for that. I can't tell you where to go. I can't tell you what to do. If you decided to kill me right here, I wouldn't be able to stop you. Do what you like." She cast a significant glance at Edmund's grey streak. "Any consequences are on Mr Templeton's head."

Istvan followed her gaze.

Edmund fought the urge to put his hat back on. It wouldn't be right.

Finally, the specter looked away, clasping his hands behind his back. "I... I know what I am, Magister, and I know what I did, and necessity or coercion or not, that does make me responsible for the survivors, if nothing else. I'm sure Roberts and Miss Torres and, ah, Doctor Orlean and the rest will manage perfectly well day-to-day without me. They're all very accomplished, very skilled. Nerves of steel, most of them. I couldn't have asked for better help."

She regarded him a moment, then nodded. "I would suggest you tell them that. In fact, Mr Templeton, why don't you go with him? I'll find you once I'm finished here."

Edmund checked to make sure he hadn't spilled any more coffee. Director Templeton. All that responsibility. All that paperwork. He didn't know paperwork, not really. Not like that. He hadn't done any paperwork when he'd been Magister, and the rest was all Dewey Decimal and the Inexcusable Index.

"Who's going to look after the library?" he asked, faintly.

Mercedes picked up her phone. "I'm sure you'll find time."

The door shut and latched behind them with seven ratcheting clicks. Wrought-iron lanterns shone on old photographs. The Twelfth Hour's seven founders. 1895.

A middling year, as Istvan recalled. An election year. His practice had become a modest success, though not what he – or Franceska – had hoped. Well enough. Better than what would come later. Pietro had found another fossil fish that year, and Istvan remembered him chipping it out of its shard of rock with his own collection of "surgical instruments" while the two of them discussed Karl Lueger's grand plans for the city and the recent imprisonment of Oscar Wilde.

Be careful with that drill, Peti, you wouldn't want to kill the poor creature.

Kill it? Fish are my specialty, Pista. It won't feel a thing, I promise.

"Well," said Edmund. He put his hands in his pockets, succeeding after two attempts. He'd donned his hat again and now it was tilted somewhat to the left in a vain attempt at hiding the grey. His aspect churned.

"You'll make a fine Director, I think," Istvan tried.

Edmund shook his head. "You don't have to come with me, Istvan. Hell, you don't even have to stay here. You could leave."

"I couldn't."

"You could. You can go anywhere, now. How long has it been since you've seen Vienna?"

Istvan twisted at his wedding ring. He hadn't told him. They had hardly spoken of what had happened yesterday, either of them, much less described what they had seen. Vienna perched atop that monstrosity. Pietro dead on the Western Front. Shokat Anoushak. The rest.

Oh, the rest.

"Edmund?"

The wizard started briskly down the hall. "Never mind. You're right, we should get this over with. Mercedes won't want to be kept waiting."

Istvan followed him. "No, Edmund, listen. Back there, at the fortress, after we jumped–"

"It doesn't matter."

"It does." Istvan took a breath. As always, both

necessary and not. He had to say something. "Edmund, I thought I'd lost you."

The man tilted his hat further to the left.

"I thought you'd used every moment you had," Istvan continued. "That there were so many to save, and that you were so determined, and that perhaps you had... perhaps you were..." He swallowed. "I know you aren't a coward, Edmund. I do. But... please tell me you aren't so brave as all that."

Edmund stopped. "Istvan, you know where that time comes from."

"And where did it go? Edmund, there are people who would have given their lives to do what you did. So many who would have lost theirs, if you hadn't."

"Don't remind me."

Istvan touched his shoulder before he could start off again. "Edmund, I'm not condoning the means, but this once... allow it to be a victory. Please." He drew his fingers through the man's mauled arm, living blood rushing through his substance, tracing arteries along their courses. For the pain, of course. It wasn't yet healed.

For the pain.

He drew back. "I'm glad you didn't go to dust."

Edmund worked the arm, his motions less stiff than they had been. "Same here." He started back down the hall. He passed the alcove for 1940. He walked faster.

Istvan stared after him. A nervousness seeped from the man's presence, a wariness that hadn't been so overt in years. Bad memories. The past, recently made all too recent.

"I wouldn't," he said. He caught up to Edmund, not looking at the pictures for 1945. "Edmund, whatever it is you saw, I would never."

"Tell me one thing," the wizard said as they passed

1970. "Are you any different? With the chains gone. Do you feel any different?"

"I don't know."

"You're still Istvan, right?"

He thought of Pietro. He rubbed at his wrists, where no shackles burned. Edmund had never known him unchained. Never known him living. Never known him any other way.

Istvan. Edmund's Istvan.

"The very same."

Edmund looked away. "Good," he said. After a moment, he added, "I like Istvan."

"Truly?"

"Truly." The wizard swung his pocket watch around his hand. Caught it. Inspected the hourglass on its front... and then put it away. "You know," he said, "if you stick around, you'll have to put up with Grace."

"So will you." Istvan hesitated, then elbowed his ribs. "Mr Director Templeton."

Edmund sighed, but Istvan thought it a solid sort of word for a solid sort of man – a title that suited him, something to remind him of what good he'd done. Much better than Magister had ever been.

Better than "Hour Thief."

They walked. The candles in the last alcove were still burning when they stopped to look them over. Istvan's photograph was still black-and-white.

He regarded it a moment.

"Your cheekbones are fine," said Edmund.

"It isn't that."

"No?"

Istvan tugged at a sleeve, recalling what had been. "Do you suppose," he said, slowly, "that this year I could ask for my photograph to have colors on? It wouldn't take much, only a bit of watercolor, and it would be splendid."

Edmund raised an eyebrow.

Istvan shrugged. "I never wore so much grey when I'd the option."

"Wouldn't hurt to ask."

"I shouldn't think so."

A sigh. "You realize what you're doing to me, right?"

Istvan glanced at him. There was a smile there, torn and scratched and tired but wry, and genuine. The Man in Just Black. He chuckled. "Oh, you've a choice, you know."

"I do," said Edmund. He hesitated, then straightened his hat. "I suppose I do."

They ambled into the library.

ACKNOWLEDGMENTS

There were a number of people especially instrumental to *The Interminables* as it developed, some more directly than others. The original project grew out of a desire to preserve some of the characters developed by myself and friends in the MMORPG *City of Heroes*, which shut down in 2012 – the end product is very different, but credit goes where credit is due.

To my brother Hagen: thank you for donating what became the Susurration, Lord Kasimir, the entire country of Triskelion, and probably a full quarter of the plot to the cause. I have no idea how many hours we spent throwing ideas around, but they were well-spent.

To *HairlessRN*, whom I have never met in person: thank you for all the medical fact-checking advice, the insightful commentary, and the inspiration for this book's talking tiger/bear/blizzard.

To *PropBob*, whom I have never met in person: let's just say that Grace Wu wouldn't have been who she is without you.

To *Warpshaper* and *Kusim*, whom I have never met in person: thank you for all your help in early plot development and brainstorming. Tornado Alley still looms on the horizon.

To *Flashtoo*, whom I never met until two years ago and now we're together and you're watching me write this: you know what you've done.

Lastly, I would like to thank all involved parental and grand-parental units, other brothers (biological and bonus), the population of Targhee dorm (2013-14), the *Virtue* server, and, of course, the inestimable Mrs Zapatka, for their inspiration and support.

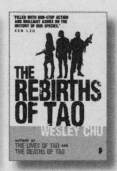

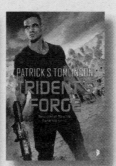

JOIN US
angryrobotbooks.com
twitter.com/angryrobotbooks